Dear Reader:

All I can say is fasten your seatbelt because you are about to go on a breathtaking ride. Allison Hobbs is an author whose time has come. It is time for her to garner the attention that she deserves with this, her fourth novel. If you have not read *Pandora's Box, Insatiable* or *Dangerously in Love,* you have been sleeping on one of the best novelists on the scene. It amazes me when so many authors or their publishers put them out there to be "hotter than Zane" or "in the tradition of Zane" and they write nothing like me, nor do they understand my market. I can honestly say that if there is any author in existence today who writes similar to me, but yet has her own controversial and erotic style, it would be Allison Hobbs.

I met Allison at the Baltimore Book Festival several years ago. She had self-published *Pandora's Box* and I approached her and asked her a ton of questions; all of which she answered with much enthusiasm and excitement. I purchased her book and was convinced it was going to be awesome before I cracked it open. Why? Because Allison was an author writing for all the right reasons. She was bubbling with creativity and believed in her product; much like myself from the onset of my writing career. I was right because the book was off the chain. I did not believe she could top *Pandora's Box* because it was so realistic, so sexy, and so engaging that I was ready to go hang out in a brothel. I was wrong because *Insatiable* and *Dangerously in Love* were equally amazing. Now with *Double Dippin'* Allison has yet again outdone herself as she journeys into the psyche of twin brothers who leave disparate lives.

I want to thank you in advance for reading this book. I guarantee you will love it. I guarantee you will love all of Allison's novels. If you have enjoyed my books, then you will go crazy over hers. The characters are conversation pieces all by themselves. The amazing storyline is the icing on the cake. This is an ideal book club selection because it can be discussed for hours among members. Some books are good for fifteen minutes of discussion and then it is time to eat and mingle. With Allison's books, you could talk and debate into the wee hours of the night. She keeps it real and serious readers cannot help but appreciate her dedication to her craft.

I want to thank those of you who have been gracious enough to support the dozens of authors I publish under Strebor Books International, a division of ATRIA/Simon and Schuster. While writing serves as a catalyst for me to release my personal creativity, publishing allows me the opportunity to share the talent of so many others. If you are interested in being an independent sales representative for Strebor Books International, please send a blank email to info@streborbooks.com

Peace and Blessings,

Zane

Publisher
Strebor Books International
www.streborbooks.com

ZANE PRESENTS

DOUBLE DIPPIN'

A NOVEL

ALLISON HOBBS

SBI

STREBOR BOOKS

NEW YORK LONDON TORONTO SYDNEY

Strebor Books
P.O. Box 6505
Largo, MD 20792

Cover design: www.mariondesigns.com

ISBN-13 978-0-7394-7230-9

Manufactured in the United States of America

For Shari Reason
My Second Daughter

ACKNOWLEDGMENTS

My dearest friend Karen Dempsey Hammond and her daughter, Dolly. You are both truly angels and a blessing in my life; I can't thank you enough for coming to my rescue while I was desperately trying to put together my first book launch party.

I've made many new friends and I'm so pleased that I can sprinkle some love in print. A heartfelt thank you goes out to: Venetta Larry and the Philly Unplugged crew, Timmy Wayne Gethers, Rashedah Lewis, and my Sagittarius Sister, Yvonne Marie Bay/aka Vonnie B, The Philly Diva!

A special thanks to Rosa Hamlet and Sharon Garrett, co-founders of Minds in Motion Book Club of Baltimore, Maryland; Michele Claybrook-Lucas and the members of the Beautiful Bodacious Bibliophiles Book Club of Philadelphia, PA; LisaMarie Heyward and the Philly African American Book Club.

Charmaine Parker, I appreciate and admire your intellect, elegance, tact, and of course, your editing skills!

Thank you, Zane, for this wondrous journey and for making my literary dreams come true.

CHAPTER 1
1990

Marguerite Batista burst into her twin sons' bedroom. She crouched down beside the lower bunk bed, and her slender but strong hand yanked the blanket off the younger twin.

"Wake up!" Her fear-filled voice broke into the peaceful slumber of four-year-old Tariq Batista.

Drowsily, cherub-faced Tariq blinked at his mother and then massaged his eyelids with his knuckles until he had rubbed away the sleepy haze that clouded his vision. One clear look at his mother's contorted features and fear-filled eyes caused Tariq to bolt upright.

"They're back," she whispered in anguish.

Tariq started to cry. "Shh!" Marguerite pressed a finger to her lips and shook her head. Danger lurked down the hall in her bedroom. They had to get out of the house—they had to escape.

Now obediently quiet but trembling, Tariq groped desperately for his blue teddy bear that had rolled out of the crook of his arm at some point during the night.

With a brisk tug, Marguerite pulled Tariq out of bed and then looked up toward the upper bunk. No longer concerned about fleeing quietly, she called the older twin. In a tone tinged with impatience, she shouted, "Shane! Wake up." Unlike his twin brother, Shane came to awareness slowly. Lazily, he uncurled his wiry body, stretched, and yawned but kept his eyes tightly closed.

She ripped the teddy bear from Tariq's arms and hurled it upward. There was a clunking sound as the plastic nose of the stuffed animal made contact with Shane's head.

"Get the hell up, Shane. The demons are back," she yelled in terror.

The ladder that came with the bed set had been broken in half during a bout of horseplay between the brothers and now stood uselessly in a corner of the room. Though the nose of the stuffed bear didn't injure him, Shane reflexively rubbed his head before he shimmied down the side of the bunk bed as far as he could and then jumped the rest of the way to the floor.

Marguerite pushed back coils of unruly hair that fell into her face. She wiped nervous perspiration from her forehead and looked warily over her shoulder in the direction of the darkened hallway that led to her bedroom. She sighed, momentarily relieved that her bedroom door was still closed; she and her children were safe for the moment.

Propped against the bed railing, the groggy twins stood in their underwear, waiting for the verdict—could they get back into their beds or did they all have to run out into the night?

With her eyes wide and fearful, Marguerite stared at the boys. "What's wrong with you two? Didn't you hear me? The demons are coming," she shrieked. "Hurry up! Get dressed—right now!" She clapped her hands to speed her sons along.

Shane jumped into action. Quickly sticking a skinny leg into a pair of jeans, he lost his balance and toppled over. While on the floor he stuck in the other leg and wiggled into the pants.

Tariq stood in stunned stillness. "Get dressed, Tariq!" Marguerite hissed through clenched teeth.

"I need Teddy," Tariq whined and pointed upward where his teddy bear lay abandoned.

"Fuck Teddy; get dressed. Let's go!"

Marguerite did not have the same concern for her own appearance. Partially dressed, she wore a white T-shirt, white panties, and black sneakers, which were covered by a blue flannel robe. The boys could not keep up with their mother's pace and though she held Tariq's hand, her stride was so quick that she practically dragged the young child through the streets of North Philly.

Frightened that the demons that tormented his mother would sneak up behind him and snatch him away from his family, Shane trotted behind his mother, trying to match her pace. After ten exhausting blocks, his legs gave out. He fell to the concrete and scraped both knees.

"Damn demons," his mother mumbled as she darted through traffic, ignoring traffic lights. She paid no attention to the sounds of screeching tires and honking horns coming from the cars that had come to an abrupt halt as she crossed Cecil B. Moore Avenue.

Her concern was not with living beings. The fear of being followed by demons had Marguerite looking nervously over her shoulder every few seconds. Thinking she spotted one, she quickly swooped up Tariq in her arms and picked up speed. "We're never going back to that house," she told Tariq. "Never!" She continued a brisk and agitated pace, never bothering to check to see if Shane was keeping up.

Although he was only five minutes older than Tariq, Shane was the big brother and was expected to behave as such. Marguerite didn't have time to coddle two boys. Besides, there was something about Shane that irked her. He reminded her of one of the guards at Byberry. Or was it a fellow patient? Marguerite couldn't remember. At any rate, Shane reminded her of someone she'd had a violent encounter with inside that horrific mental hospital. Shane was not round and cuddly like Tariq. He was wiry; his angular face reminded her of the nameless man with the dimple in his chin who'd covered her mouth with a large calloused hand and left her pregnant with twins. Like the violent stranger, her son Shane had the same indentation on the tip of his chin. Thus, on more occasions than she could count, Marguerite had left angry hand-prints on Shane's face, buttocks, thighs…wherever.

While Shane was a beautiful child, the color of red clay with an abundance of jet-black, tightly curled hair, Tariq looked more like her. He was fair-skinned, with sandy-colored soft, bouncy curls and, had no dimpled chin.

From the ground, Shane watched with growing horror as the distance between himself and his mother widened. Forgetting the stinging pain in his knees and swallowing his fear, the little boy jumped up and ran as fast as he could. Tires squealed, horns blared as the small child frantically chased after his family.

Marguerite dropped Tariq to the ground and began to drag him unmercifully. "Mommy, I'm so tired," Tariq cried, looking up at his mother with tears dripping from his thick lashes. Fleeing as if the hounds from hell were on her heels, Marguerite did not slow down or offer a word of comfort to her child.

Shane finally caught up. Sensing that his twin was in distress, he grabbed Tariq's free hand and squeezed it reassuringly.

Bending his head, Tariq blotted one teary eye and then the other with his forearm. Putting up a brave front, he looked at Shane and gave his brother a weak smile.

It was a ninety-minute walk on foot. By the time Marguerite reached the safety of her father's house on Preston Street in West Philadelphia, both boys were crying from fear and exhaustion.

Marguerite pounded on the door. Curtains at the upstairs bedroom window parted, but no one responded. She pounded for a full ten minutes before her stepmother finally opened the door.

Her stepmother stood in the doorway. She looked Marguerite up and down and frowned at her appearance and then her gaze traveled to the forlorn little children, but there was no sympathy in her eyes. "What are you doing out this time of the night? What's wrong with you, Marguerite?" Her face contorted in disgust.

"It's the demons, Miss Janie. They came back," Marguerite said in a choked voice and inched forward as if expecting her stepmother to step aside. Janie remained firmly rooted in the doorway, defiantly blocking the path to Marguerite's safety.

"Can we stay here until I can find us another place? Please!" She pulled the boys close to her as if appealing on their behalf.

Janie put her hand on her hip and reared back, waving a finger for emphasis. "Girl, you done lost the little bit of sense you had left. You know I ain't got no room for all y'all to stay here."

"What about the spare bedroom? The three of us could fit in there."

"Hmph. I just put fresh wallpaper on those walls. I'd be crazier than you if I let y'all come in here and tear up my guestroom." Janie propped both hands on her ample hips. "That room's for guests—not pests."

Marguerite let out a sigh of despair. "Is my father home?" She nervously tied and untied the sash of her blue robe. The loose knot came undone and the robe fell open.

Janie sucked her teeth when she saw what Marguerite was wearing beneath the robe. "No he ain't," Janie snarled, tilting her head from side to side. "Probably sitting up in some speakeasy drunk as a damn skunk. And even if he was home, he sure ain't got no say in this. This here is my house, left to me by my first husband." Fueled by righteous indignation, Miss Janie took a deep breath before continuing her rant. "Your daddy's here on a wing and prayer his damn self and if he don't catch up on some of these bills, his ass is gonna be takin' up residence at that speakeasy he likes so much. Shit, that's where all his money goes; he might as well rent a cot there."

"Miss Janie, please let us in." Marguerite's voice became shrill and desperate. "There was a whole lot of them demons this time. They were all up under the covers—pinching and scratching at me while I was trying to sleep. Some was trying to pull up my nightgown while the rest of 'em held me down." Marguerite hung her head in despair. "They were trying to rape me," she said in a whisper, looking down at her sneakers. "For real," Marguerite added in a voice that cracked.

Wearing a smug smile, Miss Janie reached in the pocket of her bathrobe and pulled out a pack of cigarettes. "Was they the same demons that got you pregnant with these two while you was in that place?" Janie twisted her lips and sucked her teeth loudly before lighting a cigarette. "Ain't no damn demons messing with you, girl," she said accusingly, her words rushing out with a thick stream of smoke. "Hmph. If you took your medication like you was supposed to, you could get a decent night's sleep."

Miss Janie pointed at the twins, smoke curling from the fingers that clipped the cigarette. "Get these kids out of this night air and carry your black ass home," Janie said and started to shut the door.

Marguerite pushed the door open. "Please, Miss Janie," she pleaded. "It's too many of 'em in my house. We can't go back there; I can't fight off all those demons by myself."

"Looka here, Marguerite…I'm not putting up with your shit tonight. Do you realize what time it is?" Janie asked, puffing on the cigarette impatiently.

"It's after midnight and I gotta get up and go to work in the morning. Now get off my porch, go home, and take your damn medication!"

Standing on opposite sides of their mother, the exhausted twins rested against Marguerite. Tariq wrapped an arm around his mother's left leg; Shane pressed into her right. They burrowed their teary faces into the warmth of her soft thighs, and despite Miss Janie's loud bickering and their mother's urgent pleas, the boys dozed off.

They were jarred awake by the sound of the slamming door followed by locks turning and creaky sliding bolts.

Hugging herself, Marguerite hung her head and let the tears flow. *Lord help me, what am I gonna do now?* She bit her bottom lip hard to stifle the screams that wanted to escape. Panting, she lifted her head. Just as she turned to descend the steps and head into the night, Marguerite heard the sound of the door being unlocked. Miss Janie had a change of heart. *Thank God!*

"One more thing…" Janie said with her head cocked and wearing a sour expression, "The front of your robe is soaking wet, so I guess you're still breastfeeding them boys. They four years old and you got them sucking off your nasty tits. Now, that's a goddamn disgrace. If you don't give them kids some regular milk, I'm gonna call them people at Children and Youth and make sure they take these children away from you."

The door slammed in her face before Marguerite could open her mouth to explain that she had to breastfeed her boys because she was certain that store-bought milk was poisoned by the CIA.

CHAPTER 2

An hour later Marguerite and the twins trudged into Washington Square Park and curled up together on a bench. The boys were tired and hungry. She pulled Tariq onto her lap, opened her robe, and pulled up her top. Too tired to nurse the twins separately as she normally did, she slid Tariq over to her left thigh and then yanked Shane up by his arm and roughly plopped him onto her right thigh. Leaning against the park bench; Marguerite closed her eyes and relaxed while her twins breastfed.

They were lucky to find an empty bench, for during the late-night hours the park was inhabited by homeless people who used the Seventh and Walnut Street location as a communal bedroom; the benches serving as beds. Old newspapers or rags blanketed the weary bodies of the displaced persons.

Since the recent closing of Byberry State Mental Hospital, the homeless and mentally ill had invaded downtown Philadelphia. Their presence was usually preceded by a stench so strong it parted crowds of center-city wage earners who ambled along Market, Chestnut, or Walnut Street during their lunch hour. If not hit by the odor, workers were often assaulted by the shopping carts (filled with cans, rags, and all manner of trash) that the homeless often wielded like weapons as they zigzagged through the throng of working people.

Marguerite recognized her own kind; she spoke the language also. The verbal communication of the insane was often angry utterances or frightful gibberish that would keep a sane person at a distance.

A slovenly dressed man with a dark-brown complexion, high cheekbones, and prominent nose marched as straight as a soldier down the paved path that led inside the park. Instead of wearing shoes, his feet were wrapped with rags.

Tall, lean, and naturally muscular, the man had probably been considered handsome once upon a time. If cleaned up and on medication, he could most likely still turn a few heads. But at this moment, he looked like a dangerous madman—a scary figure. His hair was long, dusty, and matted together, giving the appearance of a crown of angry spikes.

With crazed, recessed eyes, he assessed the bench situation. Finding nothing to rest upon, he saluted the fortunate bench occupants, clicked together his shoeless heels, and let out a litany of coherent cuss words before rapidly switching to the other language—a low-toned gibberish. The language of the insane.

Marguerite gazed at the deranged man with great interest and felt a profound letdown when he clicked his heels again, gestured a farewell salute, and marched out of the park.

However, when he returned a few minutes later, lugging a huge cardboard box, her spirits were lifted. How he'd acquired the portable house so quickly was anyone's guess.

As if beckoned, Marguerite removed her sons' sucking lips from her breasts, pulled her top down, and rose from the bench and glided toward the box. She didn't need an invitation to join the stranger and her children didn't need to be told to stay put.

Wiping their mouths, Shane and Tariq watched their mother slowly disappear as she crawled inside the box with the scary man. Cuddled together, and comforted by the sight of their mother's black sneakers sticking out of the box, the boys drifted off to sleep.

The twins were fast asleep by the time Marguerite's sneakers began to writhe beneath the madman's cloth-covered feet. There were the sounds of rustling and muted moaning as the two tormented souls engaged in a macabre horizontal dance inside the cardboard box.

❦❦❦

With the rising sun, the city came to life. One early riser, a woman out walking her dog at dawn, spotted the sleeping children. Assuming they'd been abandoned, she called the authorities. The boys were roused by the crisp voice of a social worker. "Wake up, boys," she said, her tone infused with cheer.

Startled, Shane and Tariq rubbed their eyes. "My name is Mrs. Fluellen and this is Officer Falcone," she said, smiling as she pointed to a police officer. "Oh, look at you two little angels; you're such *pretty* boys," she said, awed by the physical attractiveness of the twins. "Can you tell me your names? Don't worry; we're taking you to a very nice place," the social worker assured the frightened children before they could respond.

The twins looked at the woman suspiciously, and then jerked their heads in the direction of the cardboard box. "Mommeee," Shane and Tariq wailed in unison.

Marguerite scrambled out of the box. With her teeth bared and screaming like a banshee, she rushed toward her children. Her companion instantly popped out of the box behind her. Armed with a broken bottle, he advanced toward the child-snatchers. He made a hissing sound as he waved the bottle around like a swashbuckler wielding a sword.

Officer Falcone drew his weapon and without the slightest hesitation, opened fire on the homeless man. The force of the gunfire lifted the man's body. A split second later, the man came crashing to the ground. The glass bottle shattered against the concrete.

The social worker gasped and clamped a shaky hand over her mouth to stifle a scream. She then collected herself and turned toward her two charges. She used her body to block their view—to protect them. But she was too late; they'd seen it all. Terrified, both boys cried out, "Mommee! Mommee!"

Ms. Fluellen tried to pull Shane and Tariq out of the park to the waiting police car, but the boys resisted. They screamed hysterically as they battled for freedom, kicking, clawing, and biting her. Unable to handle the twins, the social worker yelled for Officer Falcone to assist her.

Momentarily stunned, Marguerite gave her fallen comrade a quick, curious glance and then dropped to her knees and fell forward. Lying on her belly, she gave an anguished cry as she beat the bloody ground beside the man. Then her body became rigid as she stretched out her arms, fingers splayed. Nonsensically, her hands opened and closed as she gripped and released dirt and pebbles.

Cautiously, his gun still drawn, Falcone crept forward.

Marguerite sprang up; somehow, she'd gotten hold of a rock, a dangerous-looking rock with several jagged edges. She curled her lips angrily and took off, whizzing past Falcone with unusual speed. Frantic to retrieve her stolen babies, Marguerite drew back her arm and hurled the rock at the social worker. The rock missed the woman and struck a tree instead.

A series of bullets fired from Officer Falcone's weapon.

The sudden blast of gunfire stilled the thrashing twins—silenced them as they witnessed their mother, back arched oddly, but still sprinting toward them.

Hope lit their tear-stained faces.

That hope faded at the sound of more gunfire. Marguerite stumbled, her body lifted slightly, twisting at an impossible angle. And then she fell face down. The red stain that spread on the back of the blue flannel robe she wore over her white top seemed to take the form of a bird with its wings spread. In flight.

CHAPTER 3

Pretty boys. Those words were frequently uttered as Shane and Tariq drew stares of admiration from just about everyone who encountered them. Their great-aunt Mazie usually puffed up with pride and would cast an appreciative smile at the person who'd bestowed the compliment.

But not today. Fuming mad, Mazie ignored the whispered compliments from passersby. Holding the hands of the six-year-old twins, she walked as fast as her swollen feet would allow.

Great-aunt Mazie, their reluctant guardian considered Shane's and Tariq's physical attractiveness one of the few perks in raising them—the other being the monthly check the state paid her for giving the two orphans a home. Otherwise, raising the two little rascals was a pain in the neck she could have lived without. She blamed her gutless brother for putting her in her present condition. That damn alcoholic didn't have the guts to stand up to his wife and put a roof over his own grandchildren's heads.

No, he'd left the burden on Mazie. And being a good Christian woman, she couldn't turn her back on two motherless children

You gonna be blessed, Sister Matthews. That's what the members of her congregation always said when she complained about being saddled with the boys for the past two years.

"Whoever heard of a first-grader getting suspended from school?" she wondered aloud and then yanked Shane's hand to emphasize her displeasure.

"They're so cuuute," cooed a teenage girl who exited the pizza parlor on the corner of Forty-sixth and Spruce Streets. With long, multi-colored braids, a short leather jacket, and skin-tight jeans, she looked like a fast number to

Mazie. Mazie acknowledged the compliment with narrowed eyes, which she hoped conveyed her disapproval of the little trollop. Then she turned her attention back to Shane.

Shane, however, had eased his hand out of his aunt's grasp and started to walk backward. Looking the young lady up and down suggestively, he then gestured holding a phone to his ear, indicating he wanted to get the teenager's phone number.

"Ooo! You better watch that big one," the young girl called out with a giggle. "He's fresh!"

Mazie grabbed Shane's hand and pulled him close. She didn't know exactly what he'd done; but she knew it was something he shouldn't have been doing.

"Now what did you do?" she asked, her voice a coarse whisper.

"I ain't do nothing. That girl's trippin'."

"She's what?" Mazie popped him upside the head. She hated making a spectacle of herself out in public, but Shane was enough to drive her to drinking. "Boy, don't use that gutter language. I don't know where you're picking it up from, but you better keep it out of your mouth. How come you don't act more like Tariq?" She gave Tariq a quick smile but then drew her lips into a tight knot and rolled her eyes at Shane.

With his shoulders slouched, Shane dragged his feet defiantly.

Mazie latched on to his arm and yanked him forward. "Pick up your feet! I guess that principal didn't have much choice but to suspend you since you're so bad; always fighting with the kids." She let out a long, exasperated breath and fixed her gaze on Tariq once again. "Honey, don't follow in your brother's footsteps. Do you hear me?"

"Yes," Tariq said, meekly.

"Shane's headed for reform school and I don't want you to end up in there with him."

"Dag, I ain't even do nothing 'til Devon lied on me. I punched him because he said I stole his money."

"Well…did you?"

"No! That big-headed dummy is always telling lies," Shane said angrily.

Tariq snickered but quickly covered his mouth when Mazie gave him a stern look. "He probably lost his money on the playground or somewhere," Shane added.

"So why'd you cuss out the teacher when she tried to break up the fight?"

"I ain't cuss out no teacher," Shane protested loudly, his face contorted.

"Stop tellin' tales." Mazie reached out to pop Shane upside his head again, but the agile and spiteful child jerked from her grasp and veered away from harm.

"Get your butt over here," Mazie hissed at Shane, who was now obstinately walking behind her with his lips poked out. She walked a few steps back and yanked Shane by the collar, pulled him forward, and then put a stronghold on his arm. "That principal don't have no reason to lie on you. Now you look here…" Mazie paused. She wanted to pinch Shane's arm to prove she meant business, but his winter coat prevented her from doing much harm, so she settled for giving his arm another hard shake. "I let you get away with a lot of mess when you was in kindergarten, but I'm not gonna be running back and forth to that school this year. Do you hear me?"

Shane mumbled, twisted his lips in bold scorn, and once again stubbornly slowed his stride.

"Boy, didn't I tell you to stop draggin' your feet? You ain't got nothing but the devil in you," she scolded him. "But I'm not gonna let the devil win. No sir-ee," she continued and shook her head determinedly. Her blood pressure was up and she sure wasn't in the mood for exerting herself physically, but she was a good Christian and would not ignore the Word. *Spare the rod, spoil the child.* Uh huh. She was going to give that boy a whoopin' he wouldn't forget. A good whoopin' was a surefire way to put a stop to all his devilment.

Since Tariq hardly ever got into trouble, Mazie regretted having to take him out of school when he hadn't done anything wrong. But she wasn't about to trudge back to that school at three o'clock to pick the boy up. No sir-ee. She couldn't do all that walking in one day. By now her blood pressure was probably sky high; she had to get home and get off her feet.

Shane's mother had been crazy, but there wasn't a thing wrong with Shane that a good old fashioned whoopin' wouldn't cure. *Cussin' at the teacher!* She looked down at Shane, rolled her eyes hard and shook her head. Shane scowled up at her.

"Ornery as the dickens," she said in disgust and had to restrain herself from dispensing some sort of punishment right then and there, but she didn't want people staring at her. Nowadays they called everything child abuse, so she'd just have to wait until they got home behind closed doors.

Mazie's shoulders slumped when they reached the front door. Taking a strap to Shane would make her miss the beginning of her favorite soap opera.

"Go upstairs and get my belt," she ordered Shane as she struggled out of her coat. "Damn arthritis is starting to kick up, too," she muttered under her breath.

Shane smirked as he climbed the stairs. He returned in a flash, calmly handed Aunt Mazie the leather belt, and gave her an amused look.

"Boy, don't be sassing me with your eyes."

"Hurry up, Aunt Mazie. You know you don't wanna miss your story," Shane brazenly advised.

"Oh, you think my arthritis is gonna stop me from putting a good whooping on your behind? I got something for you that's gonna wipe that smirk right off your face." She doubled the belt and shook it back and forth threateningly.

Tariq chewed his lip as he looked nervously between his great-aunt and his brother. Tears were beginning to well in the younger twin's eyes. "Go on upstairs, Tariq," Aunt Mazie instructed. "Go in your room and look at one of your picture books." Mazie considered Tariq tenderhearted; she knew it upset him to see his brother being disciplined.

"Please don't give Shane a whoopin'," Tariq begged, tears spilling down his cheeks. "He'll be good."

Tariq's plea on his brother's behalf was starting to get on Mazie's nerves. "Do as I say." She shook the belt at Tariq. "Get your butt up those stairs before you get a whoopin', too." Tariq bolted for the stairs.

"Now drop your pants, bend over, and grip that table." Mazie pointed to the dining room table. Shane obeyed, and then looked over his shoulder and gave his great-aunt a cocky grin.

Incensed by his impudence, she applied two strong lashes. She quickly worked up a sweat and became winded, but determined to finish the task, Mazie forged ahead. "You better mind your teacher and stop picking fights with the kids in your class." Each word was followed by a thwack of the strap. Shane refused to cry. By the time Mazie realized she was wasting her time on the bedeviled child, her heart was pumping so fast she thought she was going to have a heart attack.

"Go on upstairs with your brother," she said, gasping for breath as she reached for the remote and settled into her favorite chair. "And y'all better not make no noise while I'm watching my story," she added in a barely audible voice. Fooling with Shane had sapped all her strength. She was sixty-one years old and should have been cooling her heels instead of chasing after two rambunctious boys. She sure wished she could cash in on her blessings now instead of having to wait until the twins drove her to an early grave.

"Did it hurt?" Tariq inquired.

"Hell no. That old bitch can't hurt me."

"Ooo, you better stop cussin'. You'll get another whoopin' if Aunt Mazie hears you."

"How she gonna hear me way up here?" Shane untied his left shoe and pulled it off. "Look!" He handed the shoe to Tariq.

Tariq looked inside the shoe. His mouth dropped open when he saw the neatly folded ten-dollar bill. "Where'd you get that?" Tariq's eyes were wide with wonder.

"Where you think? I took it off Devon. That sucker's always flashing money, so I clipped him." Shane imitated the gestures of older boys—the kind who hung on street corners; the kind he looked back at longingly when Aunt Mazie picked him and Tariq up from school.

"You better not let Aunt Mazie find it," Tariq warned.

"Man, Aunt Mazie better suck this!" He squeezed his private area.

Shane's lewd gesture and blatant disrespect for their aunt caused Tariq to cover his mouth in shock.

"So whatchu gonna buy with your half?" Shane asked.

Tariq uncovered his mouth. "I can have half of that money?"

"Uh huh."

"Oh boy!" Tariq's face broke into a big grin. Then he scrunched up his face in confusion. "How much is half?"

"Five dollars, dummy! When you gonna learn how to count?" Shane threw a pillow at Tariq and then playfully tackled him onto the bed.

Mazie heard the children laughing. She shrugged, pointed the remote at the TV, and turned up the volume. She'd watch one more story—uninterrupted, if she was lucky—and then she'd start fixing dinner for the boys.

CHAPTER 4

Three years later, Mazie Matthews had a massive stroke.

Some blessings! she thought to herself as she was being carted off to the County Nursing Home. Her mind was intact, but she was unable to retrieve words to convey her thoughts. Mazie looked around and surveyed her new surroundings. In her mind, she bitterly drifted back to the circumstances that had led to her current miserable situation.

A woman her age, she scolded herself, had no business trying to keep up with two growing boys. Had she been left alone and allowed to tend to her rose bushes, go to church, and watch her soap operas in peace, she would have been able to keep her blood pressure down. She could have lived out the rest of her life in her own home taking care of herself.

Shane was a wild little hellion who was constantly involved in some sort of wrongdoing. By the time he'd reached his ninth birthday he'd caused more trouble in Mazie's life than all her former no-good boyfriends put together.

Trifling menfolk were the reason she'd found religion in the first place. With all her good deeds and perfect attendance at church she wondered why the Lord had cursed her instead of bestowing blessings upon her.

Wallowing in self-pity, she needed to point the finger of blame at someone. Shane was an easy target since her last conscious memory was of getting ready to lay a strap to his backside. The devilish rascal had taken off on his bicycle at ten in the morning and didn't come home until nine o'clock that night. After walking all over the neighborhood with her swollen feet and Tariq by her side, Mazie had finally given up and was prepared to call the police.

No sooner had she picked up the phone when Shane rang the doorbell. He walked in the house looking unfazed as if it were twelve in the afternoon. Fit to be tied, Mazie hauled off and slapped one side of Shane's sullen face and then the other. When she sent Tariq upstairs to get the strap so she could light some fire to Shane's backside, the boy took off running toward the front door. Fueled by indignation, she wrestled with him as he tried to unlock the front door.

"Hurry up, Tariq. Bring me that strap," Mazie remembered calling out as she tussled with Shane. She intended to whip him until she drew blood. Raw welts on his bare behind would be a reminder that he was just a child and had to respect her and to bring his tail home at a reasonable hour.

That was the last thing she remembered; she had no recollection of having a stroke.

If she'd have known that things would turn out the way they had, she would have never accepted those bicycles that the good people at her church had donated to Shane and Tariq. To be honest, she shouldn't have allowed Satan into her home! No sir-ee. She should have followed her instincts and taken in Tariq but locked her heart as well as her door against that bad Shane. Shane was the devil incarnate and no one could make her believe otherwise.

Mazie said a quick prayer for Tariq. He was a sweet child, but Shane was a bad influence on him. No telling how Tariq would end up if he didn't get away from his wicked brother.

Right after the stroke, before being admitted to the nursing home, Mazie was unaware that her speech was completely unintelligible. She thought she was talking sensibly to the social worker who'd come to her hospital bedside, telling the woman that it would be best to split the boys up since Shane was such a bad influence on Tariq. But in reality, all Mazie could manage was a loud gurgle and an enormous amount of drooling.

Looking frightened and repelled, the young social worker abruptly ended the hospital visit. "I promise, I won't split up the twins. I'll make sure to find a home for both your great-nephews," the young woman assured Mazie.

What's wrong with that simple woman? Didn't she hear a word I said? I told that so-called educated heifer to split the boys up, so why she just keep smiling and telling me she's gonna try to keep the boys together?

Mazie slumped onto her pillow in defeat. She supposed they handed out college degrees to just about anybody nowadays.

❧❧❧

Shane and Tariq were in a temporary youth center waiting for permanent placement. They were watching cartoons in the playroom when their social worker, a young woman named Miss Patrick, came to visit.

"Hi, boys. Remember me? I'm Miss Patrick." Kneeling down to their seated level, the young woman gave the nine-year-old boys a sympathetic smile, giving the impression that she was trustworthy, harmless.

Tariq blinked nervously. Shane's eyes narrowed into slits.

Miss Patrick cleared her throat and tossed her long glossy hair. "So, how's it going?"

Shane glared at her; Tariq shrugged.

"That bad, huh?" she said with a forced chuckle. When the twins didn't return the laughter, she assumed a serious expression. "I want to be straight with you two. I've really tried to find placement for both of you, but foster care housing is limited and at this point, I can only find a home for one of you…" Her voice trailed off. She looked from one twin to the other, as if expecting one of the two to pipe in with a resolution to the dilemma.

Shane's face did not betray any emotion. He sat still and stoic. Tariq, on the other hand, began to tremble. His eyes watered; tears erupted like a faucet turned on full force. He grabbed Shane's arm and clung to his twin brother as he began to wail.

The social worker stared at Tariq and cringed. "Shane, I think I'll try to place you first. Your brother's obviously very sensitive about being placed without you and the foster family I've contacted may not be prepared to deal with someone…well, someone so emotionally fragile. So, I'm going to place you first and who knows, the family might change their mind and take your brother as well. At any rate, we have to get going. Come on, I'll help you pack."

"I'm not leaving my brother," Shane said, looking at the woman with undisguised disdain. His tone and demeanor indicated that his decision was nonnegotiable.

"It won't be for long," the young woman cajoled. "I'll definitely find a home for both of you. I just need a little more time."

"No!" Shane clenched his fists and stood up. "I ain't going nowhere without my brother. Tariq can't make it in here by hisself." Shane's facial expression and body language threatened bodily harm. "Go 'head, take one of these other kids; they look like they need a home worse than we do. Leave us alone; we aiight." He placed a protective arm around Tariq.

Rattled, the social worker retreated. "I guess I'll have to speak with my supervisor. I honestly don't know how to handle this…this unique situation. Look, don't worry, boys, I'll be in touch," she said and scurried away.

"Shane?" Tariq whispered through sniffles after the social worker had fled the vicinity.

"What?"

"Do you remember Mommy?"

Shane, visibly startled by the question, stiffened and then dropped his head and nodded.

"Me, too," Tariq added as he wiped his nose with the back of his hand.

Shane looked up. His eyes were misty. "You know why that cop shot her, don'tchu?"

Tariq's face scrunched up in confusion. "Mommy got shot?"

"Yeah, dummy. You were there. A cop shot her."

"Aunt Mazie said she died because she went crazy."

"Fuck Aunt Mazie," Shane shouted ferociously. "That old bitch don't know what she's talking about. Mommy got shot trying to save us!" He clenched his fists, still furious with his ailing Aunt Mazie. "A white lady who looked something like Miss Patrick was trying to steal us while Mommy was sleep."

Tariq's eyes were wide in amazement. "For real?"

"Man, you were there. How come you can't remember nothin'?"

Tariq shrugged sadly and then brightened. "I remember my teddy bear. Mommy put him in the bed with me at night."

Shane sucked his teeth and poked Tariq in the shoulder. "Man, that baby stuff ain't nothing to be remembering."

Tariq smiled sheepishly.

"Mommy died…" Shane's voice cracked. "Mommy died because some white lady was trying to kidnap us. She said we were pretty boys and then she tried to drag us to her car. Me and you started screaming and crying so loud Mommy woke up and started chasing after us. She was running fast, but there was this white cop trying to help the white lady. He shot Mommy and let the lady take us."

"How come you never told me about that?"

"I thought you knew."

Tariq looked off in thought. "Well, how did Aunt Mazie get us?"

"After I kicked that white lady's ass, they had to let us go. They had to turn us over to a relative," Shane explained. Satisfied with his account of the event that had transpired five years ago and was now disjointed and vaporous like a dream, Shane resumed watching the cartoons. He hadn't actually lied to his brother. In his foggy memory he alone had tried to save their mother. In reality, he had fought the social worker with all his might, but so had Tariq. But Shane had forgotten Tariq's role in their fierce battle to break free from the social worker who had separated them from their mother.

"Do you think Miss Patrick is gonna come back and try to take you away?"

"Naw. That lady ain't coming back here no more. She'll probably give that home to one of those losers," Shane declared, pointing at the other discarded children who were watching cartoons, their sad eyes fixed on the television screen. Satisfied that his brother had saved the day, Tariq turned his attention back to the TV.

Shane, however, had mentally traveled back in time. He was four years old again in Washington Square Park witnessing his mother sprinting toward them and then leaping into a pirouette before smashing to the ground. He grimaced as he recalled the red wings that spread on her back. A bloody farewell from a mother to her sons.

Shane wiped the unexpected moistness from his eyes. "I'll be right back, Tariq. I gotta go pee. Don't let nobody take my seat," he cautioned, keeping his voice steady.

Inside the community restroom, unable to contain the sudden and overwhelming grief any longer, Shane cried out, "Mommy!" He quickly moved to the sink and twisted both handles of the faucet, allowing the loud gush of running water to drown out his mournful sobs.

CHAPTER 5

"**D**on't it bother you that you ain't got your dick wet yet?" Fourteen-year-old Shane whispered as he and Tariq sat at the dining room table of their most recent foster home.

Since the age of nine, they'd been placed in six different homes. Their current abode, under the supervision of Ms. Dolores Holmes, was back in the neighborhood where they'd once lived with Aunt Mazie who was now deceased. They'd been living with Ms. Holmes for two weeks and so far things had been going smoothly. Ms. Holmes, a stout woman who'd never married and never had children, was easy to get along with.

Shane was tired of moving around and liked the familiarity of his old neighborhood, so his behavior had improved drastically. He'd discovered that acting well mannered and appreciative got him and Tariq lots of benefits such as extra pocket money and stylish clothes instead of the typical hand-me-downs they'd previously been forced to wear.

Shane could have kicked himself for not figuring out a long time ago that he had skills when it came to manipulating women. From the moment the social worker introduced them to Ms. Holmes and she'd let out a delighted squeal—*Ooo wee, look at you two pretty boys*—Shane knew that living with her would be a piece of cake. A few compliments, a ready smile and she'd be putty in his hands. And he used that nice-guy routine on the young girls who swooned over him as well.

Pretending to be nice worked like a charm. Girls paid his way into the movies, bought him loose cigarettes, gave him lunch money and, best of all, they gave him sex.

Life was good. It was his world and his only burden was making sure Tariq enjoyed life, too.

"I ain't no virgin," Tariq whispered defensively.

"Man, dry-humpin' don't do nothing but give you blue balls."

"Blue balls?" Tariq whispered. His eyes darted to the crotch area of his jeans and then shot anxiously to the kitchen where Ms. Holmes was fixing their breakfast. Preoccupied with flipping pancakes, their foster mother wasn't listening to their conversation.

"Yeah, blue balls hurt; it's hard to get rid of, too. But you young and dumb—"

"I'm not young. We're the same age." Tariq's voice rose.

"Are you boys arguing?" Ms. Holmes called from the kitchen.

"No ma'am," they sang out in unison, their voices as high-pitched and angelic as if they were singing in a boys' choir.

"We might be the same age in numbers, but not up here." Shane's voice shifted to it's normal low register as he tapped the side of his head with his index finger. "Like I said…" Shane paused and then added with a chuckle, "you young and dumb and fulla cum." He burst out laughing, got out of his seat, and playfully put Tariq in a headlock.

"No horse playing in the house," Ms. Holmes reminded the twins in a melodic tone. Not taking her seriously, the boys continued tussling.

"Lemme go, Shane. You play too much." Tariq wriggled and squirmed, but Shane didn't release him until he was good and ready.

"Man, you gotta get your dipstick wet. If you don't hurry up and dip your stick into some hot pussy, you gon' get blue balls. A case of blue balls will mess you up for life, man." Shane gave Tariq a light shove. "Old as you is, you probably already got blue balls."

"I ain't got no blue balls," Tariq griped.

"Yes, you do. Don't your balls start hurting when you're grinding up on girls?"

"Sometimes," Tariq replied meekly.

"Well, every time you do that without hittin' that thang, you making it worse for yourself."

"How?"

"How?" Shane repeated incredulously. "By the time you're fifteen or sixteen, your dick ain't gon' be able to get hard. Girls gon' be calling you Limp Dick Louie."

Tariq looked worried. "So what I gotta do?"

"You gotta get some pussy!"

"How?"

"Stop acting like a baby." Shane gave Tariq a disgusted look. "What about Shiree? You done wasted about a month on her. It's time for her to give it up."

"She won't. I already asked."

"Then fuck it; tell her to kiss your ass."

Tariq looked distraught. "I can't tell her that. I like her. She's nice."

"If she's so nice, how come she's trying to mess up your life by giving you a bad case of blue balls? Ain't no cure for that shit, man. You gotta get rid of Shiree."

At fourteen, Shane Batista was already five feet eleven. He was thin but muscular and had already started sprouting hair on his chin and chest, but his real source of pride was the silky dark hair that covered his upper lip. His moustache was a public announcement of his manhood—a delicious indication that the real treat was concealed by a pair of jeans and colorful briefs.

Ms. Holmes set a plate of pancakes, turkey bacon, and scrambled eggs before the twins. "Eat up, you two, don't waste my food," she said cheerfully as she ruffled Tariq's curls. She stood back with her arms folded and watched with a look of pride and contentment as the boys tore into their breakfast. Then she went back to the kitchen and started running water.

"You don't have to wash the dishes, Miz Holmes. Me and Tariq can wash 'em after we finish eating. Right, Tariq?"

"Uh huh."

"Oh, Shane, you're just the sweetest angel. No, baby, that's all right. This is woman's work. You and Tariq help out enough around here. I'm pleased as punch that I don't have to remind you two to pull the trash cans out to the curb on trash day." Ms. Holmes beamed at the twins. "Somebody sure did a fine job of raising y'all. Quiet as kept," she said in a lowered voice, "that social worker warned me that I'd have my hands full with you twins. But she had y'all pegged all wrong. White folks always labeling our boys as bad. If it was left up to them, they'd have all our boys locked up in prison before they turned ten years old. Well, I can say one thing for myself. I don't allow nobody to make my mind up for me. I can see with my own eyes that you two are as sweet and kind-hearted as you are handsome. You just need a little mothering and that's what I intend to do. Now stop playing with your food, Shane, you're practically skin and bones. You could use some fattening up."

"I ain't skinny," Shane denied with mock displeasure.

"Well, you could use a few pounds here and there," Ms. Holmes said with a wink.

"You skinny as a beanpole, man," Tariq teased.

"Bet you can't beat this beanpole," Shane challenged.

"That's enough. I don't want to hear you two talking about fighting. You're brothers. You have to look out for each other."

"We were just playing, Miz Holmes," said Shane, looking contrite. "I always look out for my brother."

Tariq agreed with a head nod as he and Shane resumed eating.

CHAPTER 6

A few hours later, on their way to the public swimming pool on Kingsessing Avenue, Shane and Tariq ambled along Forty-Ninth Street, their necks draped with brightly colored towels.

"We have to make a quick stop before we go to the pool," Shane announced.

"What for?"

"We gonna see LaDonna. I told her about your situation and she's gon' hook you up with some poon tang."

"You told LaDonna that I'm a virgin!" Tariq looked horrified. "Man, why you do that? Now it's gon' be all over the neighborhood. I can't believe…" Tariq's angry words faded into a defeated sigh.

"Man, it's cool. LaDonna is cool people. She's doing it for me. She ain't gon' tell nobody about it. Man, you should be thanking me instead of cussing me out."

"I ain't cuss you out," Tariq mumbled, looking unhappy. "You sure she's gonna do it?" Tariq asked as he and Shane crossed Chester Avenue and rapidly approached Regent Street, where LaDonna Fulton lived.

"Yeah! I said she was, didn't I?"

"It just don't make sense that your girlfriend would be willing to give me some."

"She's *one* of my girlfriends. I keep a couple chicks. When one starts acting funny, I make sure I have some backup pussy waiting in the wings," Shane said, smiling. He looked pleased with himself. "And that's your problem, man. You waste all your time on that stuck-up Shiree and she don't do nothing for you."

"Shiree is all right; we only been going together for a few weeks."

"Man, you crazy! It shouldn't take more than a day or two at the most to get inside a pair of panties. You too soft, Tariq," Shane scolded. He gave his brother a playful shove as they reached LaDonna's apartment building.

"Hi Shane," fifteen-year-old LaDonna said, using a sexy voice, when she opened the door.

LaDonna was as well-endowed physically and as sexually experienced as a grown woman. By day, she was Shane's girlfriend, but after eleven at night, when her mother worked the third shift, LaDonna spent her time and shared her bed with a twenty-two-year old named Easy Money.

Today her mother was working a double shift, and LaDonna would have the apartment to herself all day and throughout the night.

"You got any smokes?" Shane asked.

"Uh huh. Easy left me a whole pack." She took the pack out of a plastic purse and shook out two cigarettes.

"Good ol' Easy Money," Shane said sarcastically.

"Don't be actin' jealous, Shane. I told you how it is."

"I'm not jealous."

"You smoke, Tariq?" LaDonna inquired.

Tariq frowned and shook his head emphatically.

"We'll be right back, man. I gotta ask LaDonna something in private."

When LaDonna and Shane went into her bedroom, Tariq felt tremendous relief. Maybe he was off the hook. He didn't want to have sex with Shane's girl. LaDonna made him nervous because she didn't act like the girls his age; she acted too grown-up—too womanly. Besides, he really didn't want to cheat on Shiree.

He could hear his brother and LaDonna arguing, but he couldn't make out what they were saying. Then their voices became whispered murmurs. The creak of the bedsprings came next, followed by the violent banging of the head-board against the wall.

Certain that he was off the hook, Tariq smiled and settled back into the soft cushions of the sofa. He clicked on the television and channel-surfed. Looney Tunes. Hot damn! Yeah, he wasn't ashamed to admit it; he still liked cartoons. Maybe if Shane and LaDonna didn't take too long, he could still meet

Shiree at the pool. He'd told her he'd be there; she'd probably stop speaking to him if he didn't keep his word.

Tariq had become so caught up in the cartoons that he hadn't noticed that the bedroom had gone silent. The bedroom door opened and LaDonna stomped to the bathroom.

Zipping his pants, Shane emerged wearing a big grin. "It's your turn, man."

Looking panicked, Tariq exclaimed, "What? I don't want none of that; you already did it to her."

"So what! I just loosened her up for you. I know you don't think I'm gonna take sloppy seconds with my own girl. Now, go 'head, man. You should be glad LaDonna loves me enough to hook you up, too."

Tariq felt frozen in place. "I don't know…"

Tariq clearly didn't want to have a sexual encounter with LaDonna, but Shane wouldn't relent. "Man, if you don't go in there and get some of that…" Shane shook his head in disgust. "All this trouble I went through for you, and you acting like you scared or something."

"I'm not scared!"

"Well, act like it. Look, we're brothers. We share and share alike. Right?"

"Yeah, but—"

"Yeah, nothing. You'd do it for me, wouldn't you?"

Tariq nodded and gazed nervously at LaDonna, who stood in the doorframe of the bedroom chewing gum and looking bored.

"Then go 'head in there and get that cherry popped." Shane flopped down on the sofa, picked up the remote, and stretched his long legs out on the coffee table.

Looking as if he'd prefer to stand before a firing squad, Tariq entered LaDonna's bedroom and slowly closed the door.

❧❧❧

Shane went to shoot craps with some old heads outside the neighborhood deli. Rushing, Tariq made it to the pool just before it closed.

Shiree gave him a wide grin.

"Oh, now you're smiling," chided Shiree's girlfriend, Tasha. "She thought you stood her up," Tasha confided to Tariq. "She was crying and everything,"

"I was not," Shiree protested and elbowed her friend.

With his arm draped across her shoulders, Tariq walked Shiree home.

"Are you all right?" Shiree asked when Tariq seemed satisfied with just tongue-kissing.

"Yeah, why?"

"Any other time, I'd have to spend half the night trying to make you keep your hands to yourself."

He went over his sordid sex act with LaDonna in his mind and cringed. He felt dirty and guilty as sin. Clearing his throat, Tariq said, "I'm a gentleman and I respect you too much to try to get you to do something you're not ready for."

"Aw, Tariq!" Shiree pressed into Tariq, then opened her mouth and kissed him. She stuck her tongue so far down his throat she nearly strangled him. Instead of having his hands smacked away by Shiree, as he usually did when he got too frisky, he had to restrain *her* from squeezing and caressing his genitals.

He wasn't suffering from a case of blue balls anymore, but LaDonna had worked him over with her mouth, sucking him until he felt drained and chafed. Now, the only thing he wanted from Shiree was pleasant conversation and a light kiss or two.

At quarter to nine that night Tariq left Shiree's house and walked to the deli where Shane was standing on the sidelines watching a crap game.

"Give me a few more minutes, man. You got any money left? I wanna get back in the game."

Tariq stuck a hand in his pocket and then checked his Timex watch. They had a nine o'clock curfew. It was important to stay in Ms. Holmes's good graces so they wouldn't have to move again. "We gotta go, man," Tariq said, hoping Shane wouldn't give him a hard time. To his surprise, Shane left the crap game without putting up a fight.

❀❀❀

They made it home on time and sat in the living room watching TV with Ms. Holmes. Later that night, Ms. Holmes went upstairs, put on her night clothes and terrycloth bathrobe, and returned to the living room to watch the eleven o'clock news.

Tariq yawned and rubbed his eyes.

"You act like you had a rough day, bro'," Shane teased.

Tariq's broad grin progressed into another wide-mouthed yawn. "I'm tired. I'm going to bed. Good night, Miz Holmes."

"Good night, sweetheart. Pleasant dreams." Ms. Holmes switched her gaze to Shane. "It's getting late, honey pie. Aren't you ready for bed?"

"I'm not sleepy. Can I watch TV with you?"

She considered his request and shrugged. "I don't see why not. It's summer time now and you don't have to get up early for school. Sure, you can stay up for a little while."

Shane settled into the cushion next to Ms. Holmes. Watching the evening news, however, was boring and before long, Shane was snoring. Ms. Holmes was too involved with the latest government scandal to give Shane a strong shake and send him up to bed. When his head lolled to the side and slumped down to her shoulder, she just smiled and patted the side of his head.

The anchorman switched to the next news report, the successful armed robbery of a Brinks truck, which had taken place at a strip mall not too far from her house. Bristling with excitement and trying to get a closer view of the scene, Dolores Holmes leaned forward. Her sudden change in position caused Shane's head to slip from her shoulder to her ample bosom.

Her heart went out to the poor motherless child. The urge to nurture was innate and overpowering and since Shane was sound asleep, what harm would it do to treat him as if she were his natural mother?

She patted his head and pulled him in closer, cradled him with one arm, and rocked him gently as if he were a young child.

Shane nuzzled against her bosom, moaning softly as his lips brushed her terrycloth-covered breasts. Alarmed, Ms. Holmes shook Shane's shoulder. He didn't awaken. In his sleeping state, Shane was like a baby whose mouth sought the comfort of his mother's nipple.

Panic ran through Ms. Holmes, who stood up so abruptly, Shane toppled onto the floor. Startled and confused, Shane rose clumsily. His bloodshot eyes locked onto his foster mother's eyes and requested an explanation.

"You were having some kind of a dream," she explained, feeling embarrassed. "Now, go on upstairs, honey, and get yourself some rest."

She watched Shane climb the stairs. He looked as if he were sleepwalking.

An uncomfortable feeling washed over Ms. Holmes. There was no denying it, her nerves were badly rattled. Times like this, she could sure use a shot of liquor, but instead she reached for the Bible she kept on an endtable next to the sofa. Hopefully, she'd find some scripture that would settle her uneasy soul.

CHAPTER 7

Shane was up early the next morning. Before either Tariq or Ms. Holmes had awakened, he'd scrubbed down the front porch, swept the sidewalk in front of the house, and had started trimming the hedges in the backyard.

Startled from sleep by the loud buzz of the power hedge trimmer, both Tariq and Ms. Holmes wore curious expressions as they ambled sleepily to the back door and gawked at Shane as he struggled with the power tool. Shane's face glistened with perspiration and his T-shirt was soaked.

"What on earth? Boy, cut that thing off and put it down. You're liable to cut off your fingers!" Ms. Holmes fussed, but the pride was evident in her tone.

"I can do it," he insisted, sounding winded. "I'm almost finished; I just need Tariq to get me some trash bags and a broom. He can sweep up the mess I'm making," Shane said with laughter.

"It seems like my handyman, Mr. Watkins, just trimmed those blasted hedges for me. Mr. Watkins must not be cutting them down low enough; those dang things grow fast as weeds." She turned to Tariq, who was still rubbing sleep from his eyes. "Go get your brother a glass of ice water and then run upstairs and put something on so you can help him. I'll get the trash bags ready."

"Miz Holmes," Shane called and then cracked an impish smile. "Go check out the front of the house."

Garbed in a cotton nightgown, robe, and bedroom slippers, Ms. Holmes happily indulged Shane and waddled to the living room. Her slippers flapped loudly as she rushed to see what other surprise Shane had in store for her. She tightened the sash of her robe and opened the front door. Ms. Holmes shook her head in amazement. The porch and sidewalk, spotlessly clean, gleamed in the early morning sun. "Shane! Boy, you're something else. The front of this house hasn't looked this good since the day I bought this place."

Ms. Holmes hustled to the kitchen cabinet and pulled out several plastic trash bags. Her heart was warmed by Shane's initiative. It saddened her, however, that she hadn't gotten the boys when they were little. Oh, the years she'd wasted trying to help out the parade of unappreciative, fast-behind girls when she could have devoted herself to these two well-behaved and beautiful twin boys who were a pleasure to behold.

Had she gotten hold of them while they were still young, who knows... maybe they'd think of her as their real mother.

Oh well, no use crying over spilled milk. She was their foster mother and she'd fight those city people tooth and nail if they ever tried to uproot and remove the boys from her loving Christian home.

While Shane and Tariq finished up in the backyard, Ms. Holmes went to her bedroom to get dressed. There was a tap on her bedroom door. "Miz Holmes?" Shane called on the other side of the door.

"What is it, baby?"

"Do we have any Band-aids?"

The bedroom door swung open. "What's wrong? Did you hurt yourself?" Her eyes were big; her voice filled with concern.

"Just a little nick." Shane was squeezing his middle finger, trying to keep the blood from spurting.

"Oh my Lord!" Ms. Holmes rushed Shane into the bathroom and ran cold water over the wound. "It's not too deep, thank goodness. Well, young man... No more hedge-trimming for you. Sit down." She nodded toward the side of the bathtub. Shane sat down and Ms. Holmes applied an ointment and carefully covered the cut with three Band-aids.

Shane watched her work on his finger and then looked up with tear-glistened eyes. "Miz Holmes?"

"Yes, honey pie?"

"Can I..." His voice cracked. "Never mind." He shook his head and then lowered his head self-consciously.

"What's wrong, Shane? You can talk to me about anything." Ms. Holmes lifted Shane's chin, forcing him to meet her eyes. "I want you to talk to me about whatever is on your mind."

"I wanna call you Mom," Shane blurted and then burst into tears.

Ms. Holmes instantly sat beside Shane and gathered the crying teenager in her arms. "Of course you can call me Mom. There's no reason to feel ashamed about needing some motherly love."

It felt natural to comfort a distressed child. However, she didn't realize that her slightly opened robe, partially revealed her triple D-sized bra and exposed talcum-dusted cleavage.

With his face pressed into his foster mother's bosom, his tears mingled with talcum powder, the distraught boy was slowly soothed by her womanly softness. When his wandering hand desperately sought and rested upon her enormous cups, Ms. Holmes's first impulse was to swat his hand away.

But while her confused mind struggled to accept the gesture as being as innocent as an infant's flailing arms or a groping two-year-old, Shane stuck his hands beneath her robe and deftly unhooked the back closure of her bra.

She knew she should push him away, but the boy was in such a peculiar state, Ms. Holmes didn't think he fully realized what he was doing. Perched on the side of the bathtub, Ms. Holmes sat trance-like while Shane, whimpering and crying, tentatively touched and then began to squeeze her breasts. In a matter of seconds, Shane's lips attached to her nipple. Helplessly, she allowed him to suckle one breast and then the other as if he were a newborn babe.

When Dolores Holmes finally came to her senses, she gently pulled her nipple from Shane's mouth. Her heart was thumping hard against her chest as she shook her head and wagged a finger. "Boy, I can't let you do that anymore. That's what babies do to their mommas—not big boys like you. Do you understand?"

"I'm sorry, Mom," Shane muttered. He looked perplexed.

She patted his arm. "You didn't mean nothing by it, I know that. But other people wouldn't see it that way. Now you can't speak a word of this to a soul. Do you hear me?" Fear of unimaginable consequences caused Dolores Holmes's voice to rise.

"Yes," he said and nodded his head.

Ms. Holmes managed to avoid Shane for the rest of the morning, but by late afternoon when it was time to shop for groceries, she called Shane and Tariq, who were playing with their Super Soakers in the backyard.

"Did you call us Mom?" Shane asked in a normal voice as if he'd been calling her *Mom* all of his life.

Tariq did a double-take. He looked at Ms. Holmes to see if she'd heard Shane and then he shifted his gaze to his brother. "What did you call Miz Holmes?"

"I called her Mom; it's cool. She wants us to call her Mom."

Embarrassed, Ms. Holmes glanced away. She nervously adjusted the hem of her dress, covering her knees—unconsciously trying to cover her sins. Some kind of mother she was turning out to be. She'd have to sit down and have a nice long talk with Shane. What he'd done—what she'd allowed him to do— was unnatural and it could never happen again.

In the Acme Supermarket later that day, Ms. Holmes steered the cart and absently perused her shopping list. Tormented by thoughts of hell and damnation, she couldn't concentrate on the scrawled list of household items.

"Mom?"

It wasn't a term she was accustomed to, so she continued to ponder the shopping list.

"Mom!" Shane persisted. Both Ms. Holmes and Tariq shot confused glances at Shane. A muscle twitched in Ms. Holmes's face.

"Start calling her Mom. She's our mother now," Shane told Tariq. "She's gonna be our mother forever; we ain't moving nowhere else. Ain't that right, Mom?"

Ms. Holmes nodded dully. What had she done? How had she allowed something innocent and good to turn to devil's work? Shane hadn't realized that what he'd done was wrong; he was just starved for love. He wasn't responsible for his actions; that ol' Satan was always busy. She'd have to try to explain to Shane that she was willing to be his mother but she just couldn't give him what he'd missed out on as a baby. He was a big boy and he'd have to behave like one.

With the shopping completed, Tariq steered the cart up to the cashier. The bill came to seventy-eight dollars and thirty-nine cents. Ms. Holmes opened her wallet expecting to find five crisp twenties, but instead there were only four. She gave the cashier the bills and looked off in thought. *Hmm.* She shrugged off her doubt as she accepted her change and decided she'd probably miscounted the money.

"Come on, boys; let's load these groceries in the car," she said cheerfully. But her forced cheerfulness flew out the window, the moment Shane called her Mom.

"Yes, honey?" she nervously responded.

"Can me and Tariq have twenty dollars?"

Ms. Holmes almost choked. "Twenty dollars apiece?"

"Yes, ma'am," Shane answered respectfully.

At first, Tariq looked as surprised as his foster mother, then he scowled at his brother as if appalled that Shane would request such a large sum on his behalf.

"What do you two boys need all that money for?" She gave Shane and then Tariq a disapproving look, although she was already envisioning herself pulling up to the ATM machine. "Huh, what do you two need all that money for?" she repeated, attempting to delay the inevitable transaction and desperately needing to make sense of the strange events that had transpired that day.

"Pretty please, Mom," Shane cajoled. "We just wanna go out and have some fun. Me and Tariq don't never hardly have no spending money."

Too weary and guilt-ridden to disagree, Ms. Holmes double-parked and withdrew the money from the closest ATM.

❈❈❈

Instead of riding the bus, Shane and Tariq saved money by walking to the movie complex on Fortieth and Walnut Streets. The movie Shane wanted to see didn't start for another hour, so the boys walked to the arcade on Spruce Street. Inside, Shane sauntered over to the arcade attendant. "I need change for a twenty."

The attendant counted out twenty dollars in quarters.

"You're gonna spend all your money in here?" Tariq asked in amazement. "I thought we were gonna catch a movie later."

"Don't worry; there's more where that came from." Shane pulled out another twenty and gave Tariq a wink.

"Wow! Where'd you get that?"

"Shootin' craps," he lied. Shane had actually lifted the twenty out of Ms. Holmes's wallet. It wasn't the first time he'd taken money from her and it wouldn't be the last.

CHAPTER 8

Shane sat at the kitchen table looking sullen and mean. While Tariq devoured the ham and eggs and guzzled down orange juice, Shane sat slouching and defiantly refused to touch his food.

"You ain't eating, man?" Tariq asked. Ms. Holmes, busy straightening up in the kitchen, cut a worried eye at Shane. His mood changed like the weather, she now realized.

"What's the matter, honey pie? Don't you have an appetite?"

Shane shook his head solemnly.

Ms. Holmes's instincts told her not to pry. Just leave the boy alone until he got in a better mood. "Tariq, are you going to the swimming pool today?" She tried to sound upbeat but was terribly disturbed.

Before responding, Tariq gave Shane a questioning gaze. Shane refused to meet his eyes, so Tariq turned to his foster mother and gave her a shrug.

"Well, you boys go on outside and get some fresh air, I got a lot of house work to do and I know you two don't want to be cooped up in here doing chores," she said with false gaiety. Shane's mood was working hard on her nerves; she could use some breathing room.

"It's burning up out here, Shane. Let's go to the pool. We'll have fun. Come on, man," Tariq prodded. Shane finally nodded. Tariq slapped his brother's palm, obviously delighted that Shane had given his stamp of approval. "I'll get your swimming trunks," Tariq yelled as he bounded the stairs.

The air between her and Shane was thick. Trying to block out the bad vibes the boy was sending in her direction, Ms. Holmes hummed a spiritual as she wiped down counters that were already sparkling clean.

Tariq came down with their swimming gear packed in a book bag. As they headed for the door, Shane said, "Hold up; I gotta pee. I'll be right back." He turned around and slowly took the stairs. A few minutes later, he reappeared, his expression more pleasant; his mood seemed lighter.

"See you later, Miz Holmes," Tariq yelled.

"Okay, baby. Y'all be safe and don't go anywhere near those street corner hoodlums. They're up to no good at all times."

"We won't," Tariq hollered as the screen door banged closed.

Just as she was expelling a sigh of relief, Shane came back inside, walked to the kitchen, and bent low enough to give her a hug. "I'm sorry, Mom. Okay? Sometimes I just get sad; I don't know why." He rubbed her back as he spoke and then lowered his hands to her broad behind.

"Shane!"

He jerked upright. "What?"

"You know what you're doing isn't right. Now where's your brother? Hurry up and catch up with him before one of those hoodlums tries to lead him astray."

"Tariq's all right. He's probably already at the pool. I told him I'd meet him in a little while."

"Well, go ahead and meet him."

"But I gotta talk to you." He looked and sounded deeply distressed.

"What's wrong?" Ms. Holmes asked in a frightened whisper, she really didn't want to hear the answer.

"It's my mind. I be thinking all kinds of things. I might need to see a psychiatrist or something."

"Why do you think something crazy like that?"

"My real mother was crazy; I heard it can be passed on." He looked tormented.

"There's not a crazy bone in your body. You're all right. Don't think about her anymore."

"Why not? You won't act like a mother."

"I'm doing the best I can. Now Shane, this conversation is getting out of hand. You go on over to the pool and look after Tariq."

"Tariq's gonna be all right," he yelled at the top of his lungs. "But what about me?" A deep rumbling moan started deep in Shane's throat. It escalated to a pitiful sound that shocked Ms. Holmes into taking a seat on the sofa.

"I want my Mommy. I want my Mommy. I want my Mommy," he chanted over and over, tears running down his face. Ms. Holmes did the natural thing that any woman in her place would do—she sat down to console the distraught child. Shane, with his brooding sensitivity, sometimes had to be handled with kid gloves.

"It's gonna be all right," she said in a comforting voice. But his lament went into another gear. "I want my Mommy." Desperate to comfort him, she pulled him to her chest, hugging and rocking him like a caring mother.

She continued cooing and uttering comforting sounds while Shane unbuttoned her blouse, unhooked her bra, and desperately licked and sucked her breasts.

She quoted scripture in her head. Said a quick prayer about the Lord giving her guidance to help such a poor motherless child. And by the time Shane had wormed a hand beneath her skirt, her rational mind was useless and she was powerless to fight off the hand that had worked itself inside her balloon-like panties and begun stroking her fleshy mound. Her mind screamed for her to put a stop to Shane's probing long thick finger that made sloshing sounds as it went in and out of her syrupy private part. Her yearning body, however, betrayed her. Celibate for the past five years, her orgasm came sudden and strong, causing her to tighten her fleshy thighs around Shane's hand, trapping his finger as she shouted out loud, "Oh Jesus, oh Jesus, oh sweet Lord Jesus."

And when she finally stopped shaking, when her heart rate calmed down, she dropped her head in shame. She was now being comforted by Shane, who hugged her and told her, "Don't cry, Mom. It's gonna be all right."

She couldn't look at him. She was too ashamed. She ran jittery fingers through her salt-and-pepper hair. Without looking up, she muttered for him to go get ten dollars out of her pocketbook. "Buy you and your brother some sodas and whatnot. It's ninety-five degrees, y'all gonna get hot sitting around that swimming pool."

Shane vaulted up the stairs. Her pocketbook hung on a hook in the bedroom closet. He quickly scrounged around for her wallet, retrieved it and parted the section where the folding money was stashed. There was a ten and a twenty-dollar bill tucked inside. He took both bills.

Ms. Holmes still sat with her head hung low. Shane gave the tortured woman a quick kiss on the top of her head, tossed her a big smile and hurried out the door.

❀❀❀

"Tariq! Tariq!" Shane stood outside the high green fence that separated the squealing, happy swimmers from the perspiration-soaked outside world.

Tariq was chasing Shiree around the pool, playfully threatening to throw her in the deep end. When he finally heard his brother calling his name, he immediately stopped joking around, assumed a serious expression, and trotted to the gate.

"What's up, man? Ain't you getting in the pool?"

"Naw, I'm gonna go see LaDonna." He gave his brother a wink.

At the mention of the hot-to-trot LaDonna, Tariq lowered his gaze and then looked back at Shiree, who sent him a patient smile as she waited for him to come back and continue their game.

"I just stopped by to bring you some ends." He stuck a ten though an opening in the gate. "Mom…um…Miz Holmes said to get yourself something to drink and whatever."

Shane felt bad. Ordinarily, he'd give his brother half of any money that crossed his palm. He felt like he was cheating the only person in the world to whom he'd give the shirt off his back. He'd fight anybody over Tariq. Fuck it—for real, for real—he'd probably even die for Tariq. That's how much he loved his brother. So he felt like shit, giving him ten dollars instead of fifteen. But he didn't have time to go to the store and break the twenty. LaDonna had said she was expecting her man Easy to drop by, so Shane had to hurry up and Tariq had to settle for just ten.

Tariq wasn't expecting anything, so he was thrilled with the opportunity to buy Shiree a couple of hot dogs, a Honey Bun, and a soda. "Thanks, man," Tariq said with an earnest grin.

Shane stuck his hand through the hole in the gate that was too small for them to slap palms. Their hands met, their curled fingers briefly interlocked. It was a gesture of affection that meant *I'll see you later, bro.*

LaDonna better not be messing around. That girl always kept him waiting while she talked on the phone, or messed with her hair, or ironed her clothes. That shit burned him up. He wasn't in the waiting kind of mood today.

After playing around in all that fat wet pussy at home, Shane was seriously ready to stick his dick into something. Yeah, he was ready to get his fuck on.

❦❦❦

LaDonna didn't disappoint. She greeted him wearing a see-through negligee that belonged to her mother and led him to her bedroom. Shane gawked at her junky bedroom and her clothes-strewn twin bed. "What the fuck happened in here? I thought we was pressed for time—it's gonna take an hour just to clear some space to get in the bed."

LaDonna gave a sigh that implied that Shane was being unreasonably fastidious. "We can use my mother's bedroom," she said, aggravated.

They went to the master bedroom, which was uncluttered and contained a queen-sized bed. During intercourse, LaDonna moaned loudly and scratched Shane's back as if he were driving her wild. She offered him her legs to hold high in the air, allowing even deeper penetration.

Later, spent and thoroughly satisfied, she lit cigarettes for herself and Shane. "I'm finished with Easy," she announced in a matter-of-fact voice.

"Oh yeah?" Shane said, taking a puff. He really didn't give a damn. "What happened?" he asked, hoping she wouldn't go into too much detail. He was ready to go shoot craps and wasn't planning on sticking around.

LaDonna huffed in indignation. "That punk ass had the nerve to slap me in my face."

"Damn," Shane said, sounding disinterested as he stepped into his pants.

"That's all you can say? I just said Easy slapped me in my face. You ain't mad or nothing?"

"That's between you and your man. I ain't trying to get in between no domestic violence bullshit."

"So what are you saying? It's just sex between us?"

Shane groaned in exasperation. "Yeah! You told me you already had a man and you're the one who told me not to catch no feelings for you. So I didn't. Now you all upset, trying to make me out to be the bad guy. I ain't the one who slapped you, so don't be going off on me."

Shane was tying his shoelaces when LaDonna scooted over to him and started rubbing on his crotch. "You right, I did tell you not to catch no feelings for me, but that was in the past. Things are different now. I really dig you."

Sighing, Shane stood up. "You better get back with Easy, because I'm not trying to be your man."

"Why not?" she demanded, wrapping her arms around his neck as tears burned her eyes.

"I like having my freedom. I don't want to be tied down to one girl." He wiggled out of her grasp. "Chill, LaDonna. You need to get back with Easy. Damn, that brother was hooking us up with smokes, weed, liquor and shit. Why you gonna fuck that up?"

"So what you sayin' now? You was just using me for the shit Easy be bringing around?"

"Look, I don't feel like listening to a lot of bullshit; I got shit to do. I'll see you later." Shane sauntered to the front door.

Before he put his hand on the doorknob, a sneaker hit the door. "Fuck you, Shane," she screamed. Her hair was tousled, her lipstick was smeared. Yelling and screaming, with her eyes bugged out, she looked kind of crazy. She reminded him of his mother. His expression softened.

But then she said, "I'm gonna tell Easy everything about us and you better believe Easy don't play that shit. He's gonna fuck you up so you better watch your back!"

Being threatened made him furious. Shane picked up the sneaker she'd thrown at him and winged it toward her. The loud *thwack* of the sneaker meeting her forehead gave him immense satisfaction as he left her apartment, slamming the door.

CHAPTER 9

"Shane!" Ms. Holmes said sharply. Shane and Tariq had just gotten in; it was an hour past their curfew. Tariq paused, prepared to share the blame, but Shane motioned for him to go upstairs.

"I know, Mom. I know we're late. It won't happen again." Shane gave her a charming smile, which Ms. Holmes chose to ignore.

"This is not about your curfew and you know it," she said harshly.

A shadow fell over Shane's face. "What's it about?"

"I told you to take ten dollars out of my wallet. Only ten!"

Shane's face broke into a hateful scowl as he reared back in indignation. "Yeah?"

"So why did you take all the money I had?"

"You trippin'," he said, his lips spread in a disrespectful smirk.

"Boy, don't you use that tone of voice with me."

"Why not? You trippin', ol' lady."

Dolores Holmes flinched, but didn't utter a word. Shane was obviously challenging her authority and she didn't know what to say. What could she say?

"I ain't steal nothin' from you. You must be getting forgetful, like the way you can't never find any of them reading glasses you got all over the house."

Ms. Holmes's lips began to tremble. There was a huge lump of fear in her throat. What sort of child was she dealing with? What had she let herself in for?

Shane stomped into the kitchen. Ms. Holmes couldn't imagine what he was going to do next. To her surprise, he yanked the calendar off the nail that secured it to the wall. It was the calendar she'd gotten from church. Shane seemed unusually preoccupied with the calendar, turning pages and running his hands over the blocked dates. There was an important Bible passage on every month and Ms. Holmes wondered if Shane was about to quote some scripture about what they had done.

But he had an even bigger surprise in store. "The eighteenth?" he asked, his thick brows curved into an arch.

"What?" The question took her by surprise. Ms. Holmes didn't have the slightest idea what he was referring to.

"It says here the social worker's s'posed to visit." He cut an eye at his foster mother. "You know, she's s'posed to talk to me and Tariq on the eighteenth?"

Hot flames of fear flicked around her collar and moved up to her face. "I guess that's the right date," Her voice quavered.

Shane marched back into the living room. "So how do you think she's gonna feel about what me and you been doin'? Ain't that child abuse?"

Ms. Holmes picked up the *Daily News*, which was sitting on top of the coffee table. Breathing hard, she fanned her face fast and furiously with the newspaper.

"Nervous?" he taunted. "I know I would be nervous if I was you!" He turned and stomped up the stairs.

Rocking and moaning and crying for Jesus, Ms. Holmes raised her hands to her mouth, muffling her woeful cries.

"What's wrong with Miz Holmes?" Tariq wanted to know. "What did she want to talk to you about?"

"You know how holy and sanctified she can get. She said she was scared I was heading for trouble. She thinks I'm hanging with the wrong crowd."

"She's right!" Tariq said with a snicker.

"Anyway, man. She started reading me the Bible and started getting all worked up when she got to the part about the blood of Jesus. I think she got the Holy Ghost or something. I don't know what's wrong with her. She's trippin'," Shane explained with devilish laughter.

"Aw, don't say that. Miz Holmes is nice. You're the one who wants to call her Mom, so why you making fun of her?"

Shane shrugged. "I don't know, I'm tired. And you know I don't like nobody trying to force all that Bible stuff down my throat."

❀❀❀

By the next morning, fifty-seven-year-old Dolores Holmes looked like she'd aged twenty years. Her eyes were red and puffy from crying throughout the night. The worrying about being accused of child abuse had her heart racing out of control.

What would her pastor think? What would the members think? They'd call her a sinner and sinners such as herself had no business sitting with the saints. She swallowed hard and rose as she envisioned being escorted out of the Holy House. Joining the church after years of sinning and drinking had been her salvation. She shook her head bitterly. Lord, she was sorry she had ever taken in these two boys.

"'Morning, Mom," Shane said and bent down and kissed her on the cheek.

Ms. Holmes's body stiffened like a rail. "Where's Tariq?" she asked nervously.

"Still 'sleep," Shane responded. His voice was normal and no longer held the threatening tone of the night before.

Ms. Holmes turned her back to Shane and started pouring water in the coffee-pot. "What do you want for breakfast?" she asked in a dull voice, her shoulders slumped from the strain of her transgressions.

Shane crept up behind her. He wrapped both arms around her thick waist. "I'm sorry, Mom," he whispered in her ear. "I'm so sorry. Somebody spiked the punch at the party me and Tariq was at. He didn't drink none but I think I had the rams."

Ms. Holmes spun around. She knew firsthand what alcohol could do to a person. It could make you happy one minute and mean as a snake the next.

"You were drinking last night?"

"Not on purpose. Somebody put something in the punch," he lied.

A terrible weight was instantly lifted. She hoped Shane didn't remember much of what he'd said. "Baby, you gotta be careful out there in them streets. The devil's always busy."

"I know," he replied apologetically again and hugged her tight.

"Shane, you listen to me. All I want to do is be a good foster mother to you and Tariq. All that ol' other mess we been accidentally doing has to stop right here and now. Do you understand me?"

Shane nodded his head in contrition. He looked up with pain in his eyes. "Do you love me, Mom?"

An uneasy feeling tiptoed across her mind. "I love both of you," she said cautiously.

Wearing a satisfied smile, Shane rattled off what seemed like a dozen different items he wanted to have for breakfast. She started peeking in cabinets, moving things around in the refrigerator, but in truth, she didn't have all the ingredients and would most likely have to make a run to the grocery store to fulfill Shane's requests.

❈❈❈

On the eighteenth, the social worker arrived at three o'clock. The visit was scheduled to last an hour. It was a common practice of the Youth Services agency to require private visits with minor children who were wards of the court. Ms. Holmes greeted the young woman, cutting a nervous eye at Shane.

"I have some grocery shopping to do, so I guess I'd better get going," Ms. Holmes said. With thoughts of the horror stories that Shane might tell the social worker flitting through her mind, Ms. Holmes gave him another nervous glance before ambling toward the front door.

Exactly an hour later, Ms. Holmes returned home. She was relieved to see that the social worker's car was no longer parked outside her house. Carrying a single bag of unnecessary items purchased from the neighborhood dollar store, Ms. Holmes hurried up the steps and swung open the front door.

The boys were watching television. "How'd the visit go?" she asked in a false nonchalant tone.

"Fine," Tariq said without taking his eyes away from the TV screen.

Shane looked at her and then dropped his gaze.

"Shane?" she inquired.

"What?" he responded in a rude tone, his eyes also glued to the screen.

The boy was so moody it wasn't even funny. She took a deep breath. "How do you think the visit with the social worker went?"

"Same ol'; same ol'," was his ornery response.

Despite the nervous feeling in the pit of her stomach, Ms. Holmes maintained a passive expression. "Well, did you talk about anything in particular?" she pressed.

"I said we talked about the same ol' shit!" Shane's voice was bitter.

Tariq and Ms. Holmes gasped. "Don't use that language; this is a Christian home and you know it."

"Whatever." Shane rose and stormed outside.

Tariq looked at Ms. Holmes and then at the door his brother had just slammed. Confusion was written on his face and she knew Tariq expected her to give him an explanation. He wanted to know why she'd allowed his brother to get away with disrespecting her so badly.

"I'm going outside, Miz Holmes. Is that okay?" Tariq asked.

She nodded and hung her head in defeat.

When Tariq went outside, he caught a glimpse of Shane walking fast as he turned the corner at the end of their block. "Shane!" Tariq yelled, with both hands cupped at the sides of his mouth. Tariq ran to catch up. "What's wrong with you, man?" Tariq asked, slightly out of breath, trying to keep up with Shane's long, angry stride.

"She gets on my nerves, man. Always asking all those dumb-ass questions."

"She was just being nice, Shane. What's wrong with you? You're the one who said we should treat her nice so we don't have to move around no more. So why you starting all this trouble all of a sudden?"

As they neared Clark Park where a basketball game was in session, Shane stopped walking. "You right, man. Look, I'm gonna shoot some hoops. You wanna hang around or what?"

Tariq wasn't good at basketball. "No, I'm gonna go see Shiree. Later, man." The brothers slapped hands.

CHAPTER 10

LaDonna just happened to be walking through the park when she spotted Shane on the basketball court.

"Hey, Shane," she said, smiling and waving as if they hadn't recently been involved in a sneaker-throwing fracas.

Shane nodded and gave her a wink, which meant all was forgiven.

"How long you gonna be out here?" She hollered as Shane thundered down the court bouncing the basketball.

Shane shot the ball into the basket, slapped a few hands, turned in LaDonna's direction, and yelled, "Hold up; I won't be long."

LaDonna, dressed in tight jeans, pranced happily over to a park bench and lit a cigarette.

When Shane finished playing, he approached LaDonna. His sweat-soaked T-shirt was draped around his neck. He sat down next to her; she kissed him softly and then placed her lipstick-stained cigarette between his lips. He pulled on the cigarette and blew out smoke. "How's Easy? Y'all get back together yet?"

"Yeah, we back. Satisfied?"

"What kind of goodies does he have stashed up in the crib?"

"Weed, some bagged-up product, and a couple bottles of Henney. You know how we do. Me and my man like the good stuff," LaDonna bragged.

"All right, let's go to your place. Kick back, get high…you know how *we* do," he said, mimicking her.

She laughed. "That would be cool, but my mom's home."

"Dag, I thought your mother worked three or four jobs."

"Shifts," she corrected. "My mother works double shifts. She likes that overtime but a bitch gotta rest sometimes." LaDonna fell out laughing.

Shane didn't see the humor in her mother's blocking his free get-high.

"Well, do think she'd mind if you have some company?"

"Yeah, she'd mind. My mom ain't all old like your foster mother. She ain't but thirty-five. She's home chillin' with her new man—well, I should say her newest man. Anyway, my mom needs her privacy just like we do."

"So what we gon' do?"

LaDonna shrugged, then brightened when an idea crossed her mind. "I know! Walk me home, I'll sneak into Easy's stash and get some weed, a bottle of Henney, and some cups. We can get high right here in the park."

Shane put a sweaty arm around LaDonna as they cut through Clark Park and walked along Woodland Avenue. They turned on Fifty-Third Street and stopped in front of the library at the corner of Fifty-Third and Regent Streets.

"Wait for me here," LaDonna said, ducking out from under Shane's sweaty arm. "Be right back." She ran down the short block lined with identical apartment buildings.

Five minutes later, she came out of her building and beckoned Shane. "Hurry up," she yelled excitedly. But Shane was too cool to run down the street. He maintained an unhurried glide. When he got to LaDonna's building, her lips were screwed up in disapproval.

"What's your problem?"

"Dag, Shane. You too smooth to rush?"

"You know it," he responded with a cocky grin.

"My mother's sleep. Her company must have been slinging some mean dick 'cause that bitch is out for the count. Come on in."

Shane cautiously crossed the threshold into LaDonna's apartment. He'd never met LaDonna's mother and hoped he didn't have to meet her while he was in her home on the creep. He didn't want any trouble out nobody's irate mother; he just wanted to get high, get laid, and be on his way.

They mixed the Hennessy with Coca-Cola. Shane licked the outer layer of the dutch when LaDonna finished breaking up the buds. She played a Toni Braxton CD to set the tone.

Shane had to admit, LaDonna was a sexy chick, but he just wasn't ready to settle down. Besides, if he made her his girl, they'd lose all the benefits that came from her man, Easy. Therefore, deciding to thoroughly enjoy the moment, Shane puffed the blunt and drank the liquor and listened to Toni blow.

Feeling amorous after he'd finished smoking, Shane turned over and started kissing LaDonna and sucking on her neck. He planned to leave a passion mark just so Easy would know he had some competition. It seemed that the moment his dick started getting hard, LaDonna broke the mood.

"I know you ain't gonna try to fuck me all sweaty and shit."

"I ain't home; what am I s'posed to do?"

"We got runnin' water. You better go wash your ass." She gave him a big sexy grin. "Plus, I'm feeling so good I think we should get into something real freaky. So, go take a shower."

"Are you talking about what I think you're talking about?"

LaDonna licked her lips teasingly.

Shane hopped in the shower. He was so happy he felt like singing. He washed every crack and crevice, making sure there were no odors when Little Miss Sexy wrapped her luscious lips around his dick. In all his fourteen years, he was ashamed to admit that he'd only had his dick sucked once. And the girl who'd done the sucking had been a skuzzy-looking, ugly girl—a crazy pimply-faced, certified nut who sucked every boy's dick at the Children's Home where he and Tariq lived before they were placed with Ms. Holmes. She was known as Kelly the Dick Sucker and the schizoid had even tried to suck Tariq's dick. But Tariq had balked and adamantly declined her favors, complaining that Kelly was too dirty and disgusting.

Shane had tried to encourage the encounter by lying to Tariq. He told his brother that his dick would grow bigger if he let Kelly suck it. But Tariq was unbending. "No!" he yelled at the top of his lungs and covered his ears to make Shane shut up. There were times when Tariq could be as stubborn as hell. Shane was fondly amused by the memory.

The bathroom door opened. He'd forgotten to lock it. He hoped LaDonna wasn't planning on joining him in the shower because he was finished and ready to get some head.

Someone sat down on the toilet and started peeing. "LaDonna, I thought I heard you blasting music in the bedroom. I must be losing my mind."

Oh shit, that's her mom! Shane became as still as a mouse.

The toilet flushed and the water turned hot as fire, scalding him. He couldn't help it; he screamed and leaped out of the shower stall.

LaDonna's mother screamed, too. "Who the hell are you?"

"Um," Shane tried to cover his private parts with his hands.

"Um! Is that your name? Um, where's LaDonna?" her mother asked sarcastically and then stormed toward LaDonna's bedroom.

"She's in her room," he said to LaDonna's mother's retreating back. *Damn! No head tonight.* Shane dressed quickly.

He could hear LaDonna's mother screaming at her, calling her all kinds of bitches and whores. He sensed something that seemed like a little more than the normal tension between a parent and a teenage child. LaDonna and her mother argued more like arch enemies who'd been rivaling for years.

Shane didn't want to go anywhere near LaDonna's bedroom, but he had to. His sneakers were in there. He slipped in like a thief, hoping to make himself as small as possible. He located one sneaker, picked it up, and scanned the junky room for the other. It landed upside his head, hurled by LaDonna's incensed mother. *Damn, this family got a thing with throwing sneakers,* he thought as he picked up his sneaker and slunk out the door.

The walk home was slow and sad. His dick was still hard. And it wasn't because of LaDonna's promise. He was feenin' something terrible for LaDonna's feisty, sexy-ass mom.

CHAPTER 11

"Where's Mom?" Shane asked as he drank fruit punch from the container.

"Man, you're such a fake. Do you know how phony you sound calling Miz Holmes, Mom?"

"Phony? She said we could call her Mom, so how you figure I'm being a fake?"

"Look how you treat her. Would you treat our real mother like that?"

Shane thought about it. "How the hell should I know? Depends on how she treated me." His thoughts turned to the numerous spankings he'd gotten from his real mother. He swallowed more fruit punch. He'd never understood why she was always so mad at him. Just him. Never Tariq. He still loved her, though. Sometimes she treated him good. She was nice when her hair was combed and when she smelled good. The nice mother took him and Tariq to the playground and pushed them as high as they wanted on the swings.

That's the mother he loved. And her breasts. They were big and full. He missed sucking her breasts. It made him feel safe and loved. Even when there wasn't enough milk left for him, he sucked anyway, just to be close to her.

Then there was the mother who terrified him. The one who had wild hair and crazy darting eyes. But as scared as he was of that mother, he loved her, too.

"Man, stop drinking out of the container. Don't nobody know where your lips been," Tariq teased.

Standing with the refrigerator open, Shane continued to gulp the cool sweet liquid, his thoughts a million miles away. He couldn't get rid of the mental pictures or horrible sounds. He heard the gunshots and saw his mother still running. He remembered being so happy that the cop had missed. Then she started running strangely, the sight of her oddly twisted torso telling him that something was terribly wrong. When her body hit the concrete, he tried to go to her, to help her, but that lady held him firmly; she wouldn't let him go.

Mommy, Shane whispered, still holding the container of fruit punch. *Mommy!*

No one would ever understand his pain and how guilty he felt that he wasn't able to bring her back to life. If only he'd been able to break away from that social worker's grasp. He would have saved his mother. He would have shielded her with his body. Or maybe he should have head-butted the police-man, grabbed his weapon, and hauled ass with his mother and Tariq safely at his side. Shane shut his eyes and shook his throbbing head. It gave him a headache to think about the things he should have done.

"Whatchu say? I hate it when you start talking to yourself," Tariq announced.

But Shane was preoccupied with thoughts of how he should have saved his mother; maybe if he'd broken free and just picked her up—perhaps that would have helped. "*Mommeee*," he uttered in the voice of little boy.

The container slipped from his hand and splattered across the kitchen floor. The color reminded him of the red bird that flew away with his mother. His mother, who never had a funeral or a memorial service. He wondered if she even had a grave. The last time he saw her she was lying in the park—never to be seen by her children again.

Shane didn't bother to clean up the spilled fruit punch; he couldn't. Fighting to hold back tears, he tried to rush past Tariq.

"What's wrong?" Tariq asked, perplexed, reaching out to console his brother, but Shane jerked away and ran toward the stairway. The tears began to flood down his face the moment his feet hit the stairs.

Resignedly, Tariq cleaned up the mess, cocking his head in bewilderment toward the sound of his brother's muffled sobs. He clambered up the stairs and knocked on the closed bedroom door. "You okay, Shane?"

"Go away!" Shane cried. Words of consolation only made Shane angry; he didn't like being reminded of his weakness. The weakness he had for their mother.

She was a saint, he'd whispered countless times to Tariq. *The cops killed her. She died for us, man. She was like an angel flying away to heaven.*

He knew Tariq had only a foggy memory of their mother. But Shane remembered everything about her and his memory of the day she'd gotten killed was particularly vivid. It angered him to no end that Tariq could barely recall the most important day of their lives.

❧❧❧

Dolores Holmes stood in her second-row position with the choir's alto section, but she kept hitting the wrong notes. Necks craned in disapproval. "What's wrong, Sister Holmes?"

"I'm having a bad night; I just can't sing on key. I think I'm gonna sit this rehearsal out."

No one in the choir disagreed. The women's choir was serious about their singing and Sister Holmes was making them sound bad.

She patted her feet and bobbed her head as the choir praised the Lord with song. She pretended to be absorbed in the spirituals, but Ms. Holmes was actually ruminating on the terrible turn her life had taken. Feeling too sinful to sit in a house of worship, she gave a sigh, slid out of the wooden pew, and lumbered toward the restroom. She peeked around to see if any of the choir members were watching. Satisfied that no one seemed to notice her, Dolores Holmes eased out of the church and got in her car.

She sat in her old Ford for a minute before turning on the motor. *I'm in a heap of trouble*, she thought and shook her head. *After all these years of living sin-free, that no-good, rotten Satan has finally had his way. It's not Shane's fault. Satan has him in a tight grip. I have to figure out a way to put things back like they're supposed to be or else I'm gonna have to let those two pretty boys go.*

The thought saddened her, but she was rushing fast toward ruination. It was just a matter of time. She turned on the ignition and with a heavy heart, Dolores Holmes headed home.

The house was quiet. Tariq was conked out on the sofa. Shane was probably out running the streets, hanging with riffraff. She sighed. *I can't even raise the boy right with Satan determined to make me weak.* She dragged her tired body over to Tariq, shook him, and sent him up to bed. Tariq was so easy. Woke up easy, always did as he was told. He was sweet as pie, but that Shane...she shook her head.

As if he'd been summoned by the devil himself, Shane came home, glared at her, and then clumped up the stairs. Greatly relieved that Shane was safely at home, Dolores Holmes dozed off. An hour later, she was startled awake when Shane stumbled down the stairs, half asleep. He looked like he was sleepwalking when he came heading straight toward her.

Dolores Holmes cringed. "Go on now, boy. You're dreaming. Go on back upstairs now. Go get yourself some good sleep," she said, backing away from Shane's begging, outstretched arm.

He backed her into an endtable and nearly toppled over a lamp, but she caught it in the nick of time.

She didn't want to alert Tariq. She didn't want him to ever find out about the pitiful mess she'd gotten herself in. "Shane!" she whispered sternly. "Go back upstairs; go to bed."

But Shane pulled on her wrist, silently urging her to sit down. She flopped down on the sofa, trying to figure out how to get him up the stairs.

Shane didn't say a word, he just started groping her, moaning softly and squeezing her breasts. She sat still, accommodating him while her mind raced. Not knowing what else to do, Dolores Holmes grabbed Shane's hands. She'd have to wrestle with him quietly; she couldn't risk disturbing Tariq and exposing her shameful predicament.

Shane pulled his hand free. He gave her an evil look, which made her simmer down. Breathing hard from all the tussling, Dolores Holmes passively allowed Shane to unbutton her blouse.

She prayed for forgiveness while Shane's mouth went hungrily from breast to breast, sucking so hard, she flinched. Martyr-like, she quietly endured the pain. There was nothing she could do but let him get satisfied until he was tired enough to leave her alone.

As Shane's hand snaked up her dress, she prayed for salvation. And as if answering her prayers, Shane suddenly withdrew his hand.

Dolores Holmes's relief, however, was short-lived for Shane apparently had another idea. He grabbed her hand and guided it to his crotch. He squirmed restlessly. She knew what he wanted—he wanted to make sure she had a one-way ticket to hell.

Accepting her fate, she stroked his hard lengthening private part until it grew so large, she withdrew her hand in alarm. Being that he was so young and all, she was shocked by the enormous size. It had been such a long time since she'd been with a man like this...a man! Shane was just a teenager, she reminded herself. He was just a misguided youth, she thought with pity for herself as well as the boy.

Shane began to make hissing sounds, words she couldn't decipher. Then she heard him say, "Suck it!" in a voice that was crystal clear.

"No, Shane. Now, that's a terrible thing to want. Suppose your brother wakes up. You know what you're asking for just isn't right."

He nudged her head toward his crotch. "Suck it." His voice was demanding and loud enough to wake up Tariq.

Resolutely, she pointed to the dining room, where a wall would block Tariq's view if he suddenly awakened and came downstairs.

In a corner, beside the china closet, the overweight Dolores Holmes struggled to get down on her knees. It occurred to her that never in her life, not even during her most despicable drinking days, had she ever committed such an outrageous act as what she was doing now.

Before she had even gotten into a reasonably comfortable position, Shane said in a hoarse voice, "Open your mouth." She did as she was told and drew his private into her mouth.

She sucked it, swearing to Jesus that the disgraceful deed was Satan in action and was entirely against her will. She was not a sinner; she'd make that claim with her hand placed upon a stack of Bibles.

Shane started making a lot of noise. Moaning, grunting, growling, and calling out, "Mommee," in a strange voice that was entirely too loud. And so Ms. Holmes sucked harder and faster, trying to hurry him along, trying to finish him off, so there could be peace and quiet in the house.

"Do you love me, Mommy?" he asked when it was over. She nodded her head. She couldn't respond verbally; her mouth was filled with semen.

CHAPTER 12
1999

On their fifteenth birthday, Dolores Holmes bought the boys a Super Nintendo and all the gadgets that went with the console, but Shane still wasn't satisfied. He wanted a new game to play every week as well as those expensive Jordan sneakers. Not just for him. Tariq, he insisted, had to have a new pair as well.

Ms. Holmes didn't have the kind of money required to buy Shane's silence. And she didn't have the willpower to make him leave her alone.

Their relationship included intercourse now. *Fornication!* She and Shane indulged the devil any time of the day or night. She sorrowfully shook her head. Now that the devil had possession of the boy, it no longer seemed to matter to Shane whether Tariq was at home or not—he had his way with her whenever he felt good and ready.

She could only pray that the sweet little lamb, Tariq, was innocently unaware that their home was no longer sacred; it was a sinful, immoral place.

Ms. Holmes could be down in the basement washing a load of laundry early in the morning and Shane would creep up behind her, lift up her dress, and snatch down her panties. Or he'd sneak up on her the minute she came out of the bathroom, quietly forcing her back inside the small room, coercing her to bend over the sink, the toilet, or the tub while he penetrated from behind.

Her knees were covered with rug burns, hidden with flesh-colored Band-aids.

If he came home late and caught her in bed, he'd crawl in there with her, too. Scared to death that Tariq would hear them, she usually waited up late for Shane, dozing off as she tried to watch TV in the living room. Sometimes he came home and didn't bother her; he'd look at her and just go straight up to bed. But most times he joined her on the sofa.

There was no hope for her. Satan had sent that boy to test her faith and she'd failed. She was a sinner—a wanton and wicked woman. She was going straight to hell in a hand basket, so why put up a fight when she'd already lost the battle?

Therefore, most nights she made it easy for Shane. She'd sit on the couch, fat and naked under her nightgown as she waited for him to come home and start messing with her. And when he did, Ms. Holmes submissively spread her massive thighs without prompting, allowing the teenager to stick his finger deep inside her, letting him work on her until her body started acting up. Twisting and turning, she'd arch her back like a nasty ol' alley cat. No decency, no self-respect left. Acting right whorish, she'd shock herself as she pushed down on Shane's finger, wiggling around, hot and bothered and anxious for the real thing.

The other downside of Satan's stronghold on Dolores Holmes's life was her money situation. She'd started ducking bill collectors because she could no longer pay anything on time. Her car needed a tune-up and had started rattling real loud. All four tires were bald. The house needed repairs but she was flat broke most of the time because she was spending and giving so much to Shane and Tariq, there wasn't hardly anything left to run the household. Shane could finagle her out of her last dime. It was a sin and a shame, but she couldn't tell that boy no.

The little bit of money she managed to hold onto was spent at the liquor store. Yes, indeed, the devil was busy. So busy he'd escorted her right back into the fire of hell, which was found in the bottom of a bottle of gin.

She needed help from the Lord but was too embarrassed to go to church. *Sinners shouldn't be sitting up in the Lord's house.* And she didn't want the pastor to know that Satan had gotten a hold on her again. She'd taken a mighty bad fall. Hard times were upon her but she didn't want any of the good church folks to know. Feeling like Satan's sister, she turned up the bottle and took a gulp of gin.

Shane knew LaDonna was on Baltimore Avenue, working at her new job at Easy's ice cream parlor, but that didn't stop him from going to her house.

"She ain't home," her mother said through the intercom.

"I know, Miss Goldie. LaDonna told me to check on you."

"Check on me? For what?" Her voice crackled over the intercom.

"To see if you needed anything done around the house or something from the store."

"Since when did that trifling girl get so considerate? All right, come on in. Let's see if I can find something for you to do." The buzzer sounded and Shane eagerly pushed the door open.

Miss Goldie was looking too damn good in a long cotton dress that hugged her body in all the right places. Big dangling gold earrings with her name set in the middle bobbed back and forth as she walked back into the living room after opening the door. She had about six or seven gold chains of various lengths hanging from her neck. Gold bracelets dangled from both wrists, and gold and diamond rings decorated her fingers. Her hair was medium length and streaked blonde. Actually, it was more gold in color than blonde.

Miss Goldie took her name seriously, Shane decided. But it was cool. She was cool. And she had a helluva body as well as a pretty face.

LaDonna looked a lot like her mother, but LaDonna was nothing more than a replica. Shane found the original version to be more mature, more confident, and much sexier. LaDonna now seemed like a little girl with no sex appeal at all. She was cute and everything, but her mom had it going on.

Miss Goldie had a round, swollen ass and big bouncy tits. Shane would have been happy to just sit and stare at the good-looking woman for hours on end.

"So whatchu want me to do?"

"Do you know where LaDonna keeps that drug dealer's stash?"

"Um...what?"

"Don't play dumb. Where's the reefer at?"

"Oh! *That* stash."

"Yeah, I know damn well you don't think I'd be messing around with no crack." Goldie curled her upper lip in disgust. Shane was transfixed. Even with her mouth held in a lopsided position, he had to admit...Miss Goldie had sexy lips. She shook a cigarette out of a pack. Just watching her put that cigarette in her mouth was fascinating. And stimulating.

With the quick flick of a lighter, she took a puff, making her lips a round and inviting circle as she blew out puffs of smoke.

"LaDonna better not touch no crack either. I let her keep small amounts of his product here because that drug dealer pays real well. He gets her hair and nails done and buys her designer clothes, which make it easy on my pocketbook." Goldie narrowed her eyes in thought. "But I'm not too sure I like her working for him at his ice cream parlor. Hmph. That place ain't nothing but a front. I told her, if she gets caught up in a drug bust, don't call me."

"She keeps the reefer in an empty box of tampons," Shane interjected.

Goldie broke out in a grin. "Damn, that's a smart little bitch. I must have taught her well." Goldie went in LaDonna's room and came back with what looked to be damn near a half-ounce of weed.

Shane's eyes widened at the large amount she'd stolen. He and LaDonna were very cautious about the amounts they pinched off, always careful not to take enough for Easy to notice.

"Yeah and…" she challenged, rotating her pretty neck. Shit, everything about the woman was beautiful, Shane decided with a lustful sigh.

"Nothing; it ain't my stuff." Shane held up both hands in surrender. The gesture also implied that he wasn't involved if the shit hit the fan.

"This ain't LaDonna's house," Goldie said, pursing her full and luscious lips. "Let that drug-dealin' nigga come see me if he got a problem with anything."

Miss Goldie talked a lot of trash; Shane liked that. He liked everything about her. Using Top paper, she rolled an old-fashioned joint, puffed twice, and passed. Shane was honored but wished she were passing him a blunt.

"You drink beer?"

"Yes, ma'am."

"But I guess they won't serve you at the deli, huh?"

"Uh huh," he said in protest. "They serve me. You know I don't look my age," he said as he smoothed the silky hair on his upper lip.

"All right," she said, smiling. "Go get us a six-pack of Bud." She went toward her pocketbook.

"I got it! Shane said, refusing to take her money.

"Aw shit. Check out the young buck. Don't tell me Easy got you working for him?"

"No. I don't even know Easy. I get money from the state."

"Whatchu mean?"

"Well, I'm in foster care, so the state has to give me money every month," he said, lying again.

"I thought they paid the people that took care of you. I didn't know they gave the kids money, too. Hey, that's a sweet deal."

"Yeah, they give you money after you turn thirteen."

"How old are you now?"

"Sixteen." He was lying so much, he'd be in deep shit if his name was Pinocchio.

"Hmph. I need to think about getting me a foster child. Maybe I wouldn't have to work so many shifts." Goldie went into deep thought, and then reminded Shane to go get the beer.

When he came back they smoked four joints and drank all six cans of beer. Everything he said was hilarious and everything she said made him laugh so hard it hurt his sides. He had more fun with Miss Goldie than he'd ever had with her daughter. She was just the type of woman he needed.

Feeling the effects of the weed, Goldie curled up on the sofa and dreamily closed her eyes.

Shane stared at her, totally captivated. She was beautiful in every way. The way she was curled up exaggerated the roundness of her ass. He couldn't resist touching it. He scooted closer. What the hell—all she could do was cuss at him and tell him to get the fuck out.

So he took a chance and softly caressed her round ass, making circular motions that he discovered turned Miss Goldie on. He knew she liked it because she started smiling with her eyes closed.

Growing a little bolder, he tugged on the long dress. Inch by inch he pulled it up until he was looking at her bare ass. No panties. Just a pretty brown-skinned ass. Round like a basketball. Something strange came over him. Miss Goldie didn't budge when he dropped to his knees and started placing kisses everywhere, even the crack of her ass. She moaned and turned over, smiled with her eyes still closed, and said, "That's enough for now." She rose up and looked at the clock. "It's time for you to go home."

"Why?" Shane felt desperate. His desire for her consumed him.

Her eyes showed amusement. "You need to go because I might be too much for you."

"I can handle it. I'm a big boy with lots of experience. Why don't you give me a chance, Miss Goldie. Please?" Shane didn't mind begging.

"Say pretty please."

"Pretty please," he gladly repeated.

"Do you eat pussy?" she asked nonchalantly.

He didn't. Hadn't planned on it, but today was a good time to start.

"If you ain't planning on going down south," she continued, "there ain't no point in wasting my time."

"Yeah, I eat it," he quickly assured her.

"Aw, you're a liar. Tell the truth. You know your young ass ain't never been down south."

"I said I did." He looked down uncomfortably.

"Whose pussy you eat? I hope it wasn't LaDonna's little stinkin' twat."

"Hell no!" He grimaced, feeling genuine disgust.

"Okay, well, show me how you do it." Goldie wiggled to the edge of the couch, pulled up her dress, and opened her legs.

Shane got down on his knees and pressed his face between her legs. She promptly clamped his head with her knees. He was locked in. A command performance was expected.

His strong desire to please her turned him into a skilled master. Without a bit of practice or any kind of experience giving oral sex, Shane's tongue found its way inside and began to slowly, lovingly suck on the dark forbidden flesh. He licked and sucked as if he'd been tonguing twat for years.

He'd stop every few moments and talk to her using a husky voice, hitting her with a long stream of sex talk that had her humming in sexual excitement. "I'm loving this sweet pussy...damn, you taste good...you done turned me out and I might not want to fuck no more. I might be satisfied just sucking your pussy all day...all night long."

Extremely aroused, Goldie said, "Take off your pants and sit over there." She pointed to a dining room chair.

Reluctantly, he stopped licking and did as he was told. She was right behind him and straddled him the moment he sat down. Taking the role of aggressor, she fucked him like she was the man. With their bodies still attached, Shane suddenly stood up. Goldie wrapped her legs around his waist while her torso and head hung low to the floor.

In that strange position, Shane's long penis found its way to her secret place—a hidden place that Goldie didn't even know existed. In her thirty-five years, she must have had thousands of orgasms, but never, ever had a dick touch that particular spot. Shane could feel it, too. The area was soft and delicate; it felt like his dick might break through. So instead of banging it hard like he wanted to, he took it slow. Pushing against the soft spot gently. His dick didn't travel to other areas; he kept it pressed against her spot. Goldie didn't thrust or buck either. She must have felt the same way because, although she remained upside-down, her pelvis didn't rotate. Tightening her legs around his waist was the only movement she made.

But the lack of frantic movement didn't stop either from howling like wolves.

Finally ready to bust a nut, Shane walked her back over to the couch. He pulled out, she tried to pull him back in, but he insisted on doing it his way—doggy-style. He wanted to see that big ass bounce. Bad mistake; it was too much for him. "Hurry up, baby," he pleaded. "Get yours, because I'm about to bust."

Goldie tightened her vaginal muscles and pushed back, enabling her clit to rub against the base of his dick. She came with a piercing scream. He groaned when he shot his load.

"Did you like it?" she asked, using a brand-new tone. A tone that sounded demure and sweet. The tone of a satisfied woman. A woman who definitely was going to want some more. If not today, then sometime soon. Shane could feel it; and he wanted her, too. But she told him he had to leave; LaDonna would be coming home soon.

LaDonna was turning into Regent Street when she saw Shane exit her block and make a left on Fifty-Third. "Shane!" She called his name, but he didn't hear her.

It was amazing what a little competition could do. Now that she was busy working at the ice cream parlor, LaDonna thought, Shane must have realized how much he missed her. She missed him, too! She called him in a stronger voice, running as she yelled his name. But by the time she got to the corner, Shane was long gone—out of sight.

Her shoulders heaved in disappointment and frustration. Oh well, she'd try to catch up with him tomorrow. Easy had let her get off early so she could bag up some product. He'd be coming to pick it up in a couple hours.

CHAPTER 13

The smell of alcohol was not only on Ms. Holmes's breath, the strong scent reeked throughout the entire house.

The odor irritated Tariq; it made him feel sick to his stomach. But the queasy feeling was not caused by the stench of alcohol alone. Tariq was also heartsick. His girlfriend, Shiree, had gone to Wildwood, New Jersey, with her parents on a two-week vacation. Tariq had yet to receive a letter or even a postcard. It seemed Shane had abandoned Tariq as well. He was never home; sometimes he stayed out all night.

Ms. Holmes just wasn't herself anymore. She didn't cook or clean like she used to. The only thing that hadn't changed was her daily Bible reading. Sipping a glass of gin while reading the Good Book, Ms. Holmes, drunk as a skunk, would mutter curse words directed at Satan as she angrily turned each page. With the Bible in her hands she would stagger around the home, bumping into the TV, tables, and chairs.

Watching her stumble around, Tariq shook his head. It was as if the town drunk had gotten hold of the key to his foster mother's once lovely home, moved in, and tore up the place.

On the social worker's next scheduled visit, Shane wasn't home, and his whereabouts were unknown. The house was a wreck and Ms. Holmes, unfortunately, was too pissy drunk to give the woman a coherent explanation. Her words were jumbled and she kept repeating a Bible passage.

The social worker scowled at Ms. Holmes. Her expression clearly indicated that she felt the Batista brothers were living in an unfit home.

"We're going to have to remove the boys from your residence, Ms. Holmes, and place them in emergency care. Where can we find Shane?" the social worker inquired, her lips pursed, her eyebrows knitted together.

Ms. Holmes was too drunk to comprehend the situation and Tariq was too petrified to speak. He couldn't go anywhere without Shane. But he didn't know where his brother was. Shane gave vague and mysterious responses regarding his social life.

Tariq feared his brother was selling drugs, but he would die before he'd give the social worker even a hint as to the places where Shane liked to hang. Feeling like he was being arrested, Tariq accompanied the social worker to her car.

"We'll send a county employee to collect your personal items," she assured Tariq.

Too traumatized to care about his belongings, Tariq nodded absently.

Half a block away from home, Shane saw his brother being carted off. Feeling like a coward, he skulked into the shadows, unwilling to expose his presence and have to endure the Children's Home or most likely, another foster home.

He'd figure out a way to get Tariq after he'd gotten his bearings. *At least one of us is still free.*

He'd known that drunken bitch would mess things up. Unwilling to risk letting nosey neighbors see him entering the house through the front door, Shane ran around the back, creeping through an alley that led to an unlocked kitchen window. Filled with rage, he climbed up the drain pipe, pushed the window open, and shimmied inside. He entered the house with a great crash. Ms. Holmes had sobered up enough to rush toward the commotion.

"Why'd you let them take my brother?" Shane spoke between gritted teeth.

She shrugged helplessly. "That social worker took him away. I couldn't stop her."

"Where'd she take him?" he demanded. When Ms. Holmes shrugged, he lost all semblance of self-control and slapped her hard across the face. Ms. Holmes started to dart toward the stairs and just as her hand grabbed onto the railing,

Shane caught her by the back of her collar. He pounded her head against the wooden railing until she lost consciousness and slid to the floor.

Shane glanced down at Ms. Holmes's mountainous body and began pacing. Imagining his frightened brother, he gripped his head in frustration. He had to locate Tariq, but he didn't know what to do or where to begin. He picked up the phone and then smashed it back into its cradle. He was just a minor; no one would give him any answers regarding Tariq's whereabouts.

Ms. Holmes was regaining consciousness. With a painful groan, she struggled to lift her head.

Shane regarded her with a sneer. "You better stay right where you at because if you get up, I swear I'm gonna knock your ass back down and stomp your stupid brains right outta your head." There was froth at the corners of Shane's mouth. His voice was a growl.

He felt like he was going insane and judging by the way his foster mother recoiled when he glared at her, he figured he looked the part as well. The hatred he felt for her was intense. He despised her for neglecting his brother— for letting those people take him.

Rubbing her head and moaning, Ms. Holmes heeded Shane's warning and remained on the floor.

"Shut up! I'm trying to think." Shane bellowed as he stepped around her body. Ms. Holmes curled into a ball on the floor. The moaning ceased.

Exasperated, Shane flopped down on the couch and massaged his head. A helpless whimper escaped his lips as he tried to come up with a resolution to the terrible predicament. "This is fucked up; my brother ain't deserve this shit," Shane lamented.

Unable to come up with a way to remedy the tragic situation, a lump began to form in his throat. Then he thought about Miss Goldie. Feeling hopeful, he took in a deep breath.

He knew LaDonna was due to get off work soon, but taking a chance that Miss Goldie would answer the phone, Shane dialed the number.

"Hello." Miss Goldie's voice sounded like music. Shane smiled. His luck had just changed for the better.

"Is LaDonna home yet?"

"Why?" Goldie asked, sounding like a jealous woman.

"I need you to do me a favor."

"Oh! No, she's not here. She came home and ran back out. For all I know she's probably gonna lay up with that drug dealer all night. You should have stuck around a little longer," Miss Goldie said with a sigh. "So what's up, you wanna come back over?"

"Yeah, but um—I need you to do me a favor. Those foster care people came and took my brother away. They're probably out looking for me. I need somewhere to hide out and I need you to make some calls. Can you find out what you gotta do to become a foster parent? I was thinking maybe you can help me find out where they took my brother." Shane held his breath as he waited for Miss Goldie's response.

She was silent for a long time. "I don't know about all that, Shane. I'm not trying to get all caught up in the system, you know what I mean?"

"No, I don't know what you mean. You talked a lot of shit when we was goin' at it, but now that I need you, you mean to tell me you can't come through?"

"Shane," she said softly. "You're asking a lot. If those foster care people are looking for you, that means the police are involved. That's putting me all up in the middle of some bullshit I don't need to be involved in."

"Oh, it's like that?" Shane sucked his teeth, shook his head, and quietly hung up the phone. Miss Goldie, along with his drunken foster mother, was officially on his shit list. Frustrated and mad at the world, he gave up and allowed the tears to fall.

Shane needed a drink to calm him down. Miss Goldie had him feeling worse than before. He felt helpless and used. Tariq couldn't make it in no foster home without him. He had to do something. If he could just find out where Tariq was, he'd get a gun and break his brother out.

"Where's your liquor at, Mom?" he asked, sniffling as he spoke.

"You want me to go get it for you?" she asked, sounding eager to assist Shane.

"Yeah, go get it. I need a drink."

When she came hobbling back with the bottle, Shane was whimpering again. "Damn, I hate that you let them bastards take my brother. Wasn't there something your drunk ass could do?"

Giving Shane a guarded look, Ms. Holmes shook her head sadly.

Shane turned the bottle up to his lips and passed it to Ms. Holmes. She chugged down two big gulps and handed the bottle back to Shane.

The alcohol didn't have the calming effect he expected. He was still mad as hell at Miss Goldie. All the dick he'd given that bitch and she had the nerve to do him like this. His rage started building. His breathing increased, his hands began to tremble, and his lips started moving as he mumbled furiously.

Ms. Holmes was too busy getting intoxicated to notice Shane working himself up.

He was unable to wrap his hands around Miss Goldie's no good, selfish-ass neck, so his foster mother was the closest target. The whole mess was all her fault anyway. With narrowed eyes, he watched her guzzle gin. He crept up on her and slapped the bottle out of her hand. It shattered when it slammed against the coffee table. Ms. Holmes yelped.

Enraged, Shane yanked the petrified woman off the sofa.

She looked around helplessly, then came to the realization that there was no one who could help her. She suffered in silence as Shane dragged her massive body down to the floor. He quickly pulled up her housedress and roughly tugged at the elastic waistband of her big baggy panties.

Lying on her back, Ms. Holmes parted her fleshy thighs. Shane poked her in the shoulder. "Turn over," he demanded in a gruff voice. He slapped her rear end. "Get on your knees."

He hadn't bothered her in such a long time, he noticed her old rug burns had healed. *Tough!* he thought bitterly. The skin was about to be rubbed off the old bag's knees again.

"Why'd you let them take my brother?" Tears streamed down Shane's face as he mounted his foster mother. "Your drunken ass could've done something to help him," he said, choking and sobbing.

"I tried..." she wailed, but Shane punched her in the back of the head. He covered her mouth to muffle her screams as he roughly penetrated her from behind. Shane raped Ms. Holmes with such force and savagery the poor woman dropped her head and cried.

Shane could feel her hot breath against his palm as she pleaded and moaned, but he was relentless in his quest to cause her pain. Her knees gave out at the moment he climaxed.

The pounding on the door caused both Shane and Ms. Holmes to jump in alarm.

"Oh Lord, please help me cover my sins," Ms. Holmes wailed as she grappled to pull up her panties.

But it was too late. The front door, kicked off its hinges, was flung to the middle of the living room floor.

"Police!" Two men and one woman from the Philadelphia Police force stood in the living room, guns drawn. An hour earlier, a neighbor had reported seeing a burglar climb through the kitchen window. In the city of Philadelphia, handcuffing a young street hustler over a ten-dollar drug deal had priority over a ghetto home invasion. Thus the police arrived an hour after the call was made and caught the teenager and his guardian with their pants down.

❀❀❀

Before Shane was allowed to see his brother, he had to have a psychiatric evaluation. During his interview with the psychiatrist, Shane spoke about his relationship with Dolores Holmes. He appeared fidgety and anxious, and spoke in a soft embarrassed whisper as he recounted the unrelenting sexual molestation he suffered at the hands of Dolores Holmes, his foster mother. He began to bite his nails; his knees knocked visibly when he spoke of his forced sexual encounter with Goldie Randolph, the parent of his girlfriend. "I trusted both of them—Miz Holmes and Miz Goldie," Shane said, wiping away a tear.

Sobbing, he told the psychiatrist that Miss Goldie had sodomized him numerous times and threatened to have a drug dealer kill him if he ever told a living soul. Ms. Holmes had ordered him into her bed soon after he'd moved in, forcing her breasts into his mouth and smacking his head until he sucked them. Forced breast-feeding and a long list of other depraved sexual acts had been going on since the day he arrived in what he thought to be a Christian home, Shane confessed, weeping.

The psychiatrist, unable to maintain a professional demeanor and unwilling to contain his abhorrence, grunted, twisted in his seat; and at one point banged his fist down on his desk. Looking heavenward, the psychiatrist said, "What's this world coming to? Our children are being handed over to predators, and society wonders why they become criminals and sexual deviants. You poor children don't stand a prayer," the doctor said to Shane.

Sniffling and wiping away crocodile tears, Shane looked sadly at the psychiatrist and nodded a silent agreement.

Later, the social worker drove Shane to the youth center where Tariq had been placed. She assured him that both women who'd abused him had been arrested. "If I had it my way those two child molesters would remain behind bars for the rest of their deviant lives."

Shane had to bite down hard on his inner lip to keep himself from breaking into an enormous grin,.

Tariq was in the TV room. Shane snuck up behind him and placed his hand over Tariq's eyes. "Guess who, my nigga," he said and then gave his brother a big bear hug.

Shane and Tariq were right back where they'd started, but they were together and that was all that mattered.

CHAPTER 14

Shane and Tariq finally got a day pass from the Children's Home.

Tariq spent his four-hour pass visiting Shiree, and Shane went looking for the closest crap game. He found one on the corner in front of a deli on Chester Avenue. When the police swooped down, everyone was caught unaware. There was a chorus of cuss words as the young men were ordered to lie on the ground with their hands behind their heads.

The police, frustrated with breaking up never-ending crap games at the same location and seemingly with the same players, lawlessly filled the participants' pockets with enough crack vials to get them locked up and off the streets for at least six months to a year.

"Man, I'm a juvenile. You can't take me to the Round House," Shane grumbled as he was being driven toward Eighth and Arch Streets.

Being almost six feet tall, and lanky, which made him appear even taller, Shane didn't look like a juvenile. Treating him like an adult, the police filled his pockets with enough of the illegal substance to ensure that Shane served some hard time.

"Show me some ID," the cop shot back.

"I ain't got no ID, I'm a juvenile. What kind of ID am I supposed to have?"

"Man, talk to the judge in the morning," the police officer said as he shoved Shane in the police van with the others.

"I can't sit in no jail overnight. My little brother is waiting for me." Shane sounded distraught. He knew Tariq would be wondering where he was and would soon start to trip. "Well, can I make a phone call when I get to the Round House?"

"Yeah, tomorrow," the cop added, laughing uproariously at his own remark.

"I can't wait until tomorrow. I'm a juvenile and you have to let my people know where I'm being detained."

"All right, who's your people?" one of the cops asked, amusement in his voice.

Shane didn't have any people and he didn't know Shiree's phone number, but he knew the number of the Children's Home.

He rattled off the number. "Ask the lady at the front desk if Shane Batista lives there."

"Front desk? What kind of place is that?"

"It's the Children's Home."

"Man, you saying your tall ass lives in that orphanage up in Germantown?"

"Yeah," Shane said, now embarrassed.

"Oh, so you ain't nothing but an orphan?"

Shane silently seethed.

"I don't believe you," the driver said. "Any of y'all know any orphans?" he asked the group.

There was a chorus of "Naw…nope…I don't think so…I know some foster kids…?"

"But don't none of y'all know no orphans, right?"

"Right," the group chorused.

"Well, let me introduce you to the first orphan any of us ever met. What's up, Orphan?" the cop said to Shane and for the rest of the ride Shane was referred to as "Orphan."

"I said my name is Shane."

"Man, fuck you and your orphan ass. You should have been at the orphanage with all them other little homeless kids instead of hanging on the corner rolling dice, now you're going to jail. Bet you gonna wish you was in that damn orphanage when Bubba gets through with you." The cops and Shane's fellow crap shooters were falling out laughing about his orphan status and the possibility of him being molested by an anonymous prisoner named Bubba.

The group of crap shooters was marched into the Round House and detained overnight. The next day they sat in front of a video judge who informed them that there was enough evidence to send them all up to State Road.

Everyone except Shane. By now, it was discovered that he was truly only fifteen, and resided at the City Home for Children.

Possession of drugs with the intent to sell is a crime that is taken seriously, therefore Shane was sent to Barney Hills Reform School for Boys, an institution in the country for boys ages fifteen to eighteen who have run afoul of the law.

"Hopefully," the judge told him, "you'll be reformed and emerge a productive member of society."

"Man, suck my dick," Shane mumbled.

The ride to Barney Hills was torturous. He didn't fear the boy's reform school, but he didn't know if Tariq could survive without him. He'd fucked up real bad. His little brother relied on him to have his back and now they were miles apart with a mountain of red tape that would make it difficult to even visit.

Shane got off the bus and took a look at the beautiful surroundings—sprawling acres of lush green, elegant stone buildings. The place was designed to look like a college campus. It was a wonderful place that offered a myriad of educational and vocational opportunities, but Shane knew it was really just a prison in disguise.

CHAPTER 15

Every week Tariq wrote Shane a lengthy, upbeat letter. He knew Shane felt guilty enough, so he never told him the real story. Truth was, Tariq was so depressed he'd been placed in group therapy. The psychiatrist at the Children's Home had strongly suggested to the Home's clinical team that Tariq be put on an anti-depressant.

Tariq wouldn't dream of confessing to his brother that he cried himself to sleep every night and woke up feeling unable to face another day. The void created when he'd lost Shane was unbearable and life without his twin felt hopeless and without joy. The only reason he hadn't considered suicide was because he couldn't do such a terrible thing to Shane. So he endured the pain.

The social worker had informed Tariq upon admission that it was highly unlikely that he'd be placed in another foster home. Foster parents tended to prefer younger children; children whom they could mold and in whose lives they could perhaps make a positive difference. Older children were considered lost causes—already scarred beyond redemption.

"You're a nice kid, Tariq. I'm going to keep pushing for you. I know there's a soft heart out there somewhere—somebody who'll see the good in you." She patted his back encouragingly.

Tariq didn't care. In fact, he preferred the Children's Home. He knew the routine and he kept to himself, the way Shane had instructed him to.

Tariq was always ecstatic whenever he received a letter from his brother. But his heart sank upon opening Shane's brief letters comprising no more than one to two sentences. The last sentence was always the same, *Stay strong, man, I'll see you soon.*

When was soon? Tariq had questioned his social worker about arranging a visit to see Shane, but he might as well have asked for an all-expenses paid trip to Disneyland, or for a visit to the moon.

"If Shane were in the Philadelphia area, in a private home, it would be easier to make arrangements. I mean, jeez, he's over a hundred miles away and he's in a facility run by the state. There's so much red tape involved. You're a ward of the city, but let's say that you happened to be in a state facility. In a case scenario such as that, the visit could probably be arranged. But the communication between city and state is hopeless; it's practically nonexistent."

Blah, blah, blah was how her words sounded to Tariq. She was just too lazy to weed through the red tape. The social worker, did, however, allow Tariq to make one phone call per month to talk with his brother.

"If he were in the city, you could get a weekly call," she said apologetically. "But Barney Hills is a long distance call, and…" *Blah, blah, blah*.

Shane was hardly ever available to receive the monthly call. "Shane Batista is in building five or building ten," a disinterested voice would inform Tariq, who waited so anxiously to hear his brother's voice that during the wait, he'd bite his nails until his cuticles bled.

On the rare occasions when Tariq's call had successfully reached the building where Shane was supposed to be, he was usually told, "Oh! You want Shane Batista? He was just here but he went to the lunch room."

Tariq's bad timing always left him hearing that he'd missed Shane by seconds, that his brother had just gone to the pool, the print shop, or the computer room. The disappointment always left Tariq in a blue funk for the rest of the month, which was why the psychiatrist was pushing the anti-depressants.

Tariq, however, had a distant memory of numerous bottles of pills that his mother refused. *Poison*, she'd scream, knocking the array of medicine bottles off the counter top. *Damn doctors trying to poison me!* Yes, he recalled vividly now how he and Shane would gather the poisonous bottles and help their mother throw them away.

The bottles couldn't go into the trash can in the house. *Oh no*, his mother would say. *The government's spying on me.* Therefore, the bottles had to be dispensed in various trash bins around the city. The Batista family would trudge for hours, scouring the city looking for trash bins that Marguerite inspected, pulling out trash and other people's waste, searching for a hidden camera before deeming the trash can a safe container for her poisonous pills.

Tariq's face grew dark at the memory of Shane getting slapped for dropping pills in a trash can that their mother said he should have known had a hidden camera. Instead of a green plastic liner that Marguerite Batista deemed safe, the can Shane had dumped the pill bottles into had been lined with white plastic. Their mother had lifted Shane and held him over the can while he waded through trash and garbage and finally retrieved the pill bottles that had to be secretly disposed into a *safe* trash bin.

Not wanting to be poisoned, Tariq began pretending to be in a perpetual good mood and presented himself as upbeat and optimistic during group therapy as well as when meeting with his psychiatrist. His sorrow and his broken heart were well hidden behind a bright smile and hearty laughter. His pleasant disposition and good manners made it easy for the staff at the Children's Home to think of Tariq as one of their success stories. Tariq was now perceived as a physically attractive, well-mannered, well-adjusted, happy young man.

❦❦❦

Even the social worker was fooled by Tariq's sunny disposition. She was so impressed that she worked overtime until she found a good home for Tariq, who was now sixteen years old.

Living in a real home was bittersweet. Mrs. Inez Packard, his most recent foster parent, was a tall, beanpole of a woman with broomsticks for legs. She wore glasses that hung from a chain around her neck when not sitting on the tip of her nose. She reminded Tariq of a strict schoolteacher or a librarian. Her medium-brown face was plain; her lips were a severe unsmiling straight line. She had short curly hair, with a touch of gray at the temples.

She ran her spotlessly clean home in a militaristic fashion. The clutter-free environment was more regimented than the routine at the Children's Home. Her husband, Mr. Packard, was a barrel-shaped short man who didn't say much but he also adhered to his wife's strict household rules.

But there were perks. Tariq had a bedroom of his own replete with a television and a Playstation, to be enjoyed only at the mandated hours. Daily chores garnered him a weekly allowance, and Mrs. Packard, though strict, was a very good cook. The food enjoyed in the Packard home was a far cry from the institutional packaged meals he ate at the Children's Home.

"I don't allow phone calls longer than fifteen minutes. And absolutely no long-distance calls!" Mrs. Packard informed him the day he moved in. His heart clenched, but when she said he'd be getting an allowance of thirty dollars every two weeks, he brightened. He could afford to call Shane from a public pay phone.

The downside of life in the Packard home was that he'd acquired two foster brothers. Twelve-year-old Keon and eleven-year-old Eddie came with the deal. They were all unrelated, yet the two boys insisted upon referring to Tariq as their other brother. Their big brother. Ugh! That irked him. He had one brother, and his name was Shane.

CHAPTER 16

The day of his first allowance was the best day Tariq had had in a long, long time. After depositing an endless stream of quarters into the pay phone, he was connected to Barney Hills without a glitch. And wonder upon wonders, Shane was on the other end of the phone in less than five minutes. They were both whooping and hollering so loud, Tariq was too excited to listen to the mechanical voice that broke into the line requesting an additional seventy-five cents.

"Man, put the money in the phone," Shane had to remind his brother, who was chattering a mile a minute. "So where you staying now?"

"I'm in Mount Airy. It's real nice. I live on Boyer Street. It's nice up here."

"That's cool. So...um...You getting your dick wet?"

"Man, come on..." Tariq responded, giggling in embarrassment. Shane would never change. "I'm going to call you every two weeks at the same time, all right, Shane?"

"Cool, man. I'll be here sitting next to the horn."

"They treat you all right in that place?" Tariq asked worriedly.

"Man, I run this place," Shane said with much bravado. "These punks up in here better be worrying about whether I'm treatin' them aiight," he said, laughing. "That goes for the teachers, the case workers, the cooks, the cleaning crew, my homies, too. Everybody up in this dip knows I'm the muthafuckin' man."

Tariq made noncommittal sounds that he hoped came out sounding like approval. He was actually stunned. Shane had always been tough, but his brother now sounded tougher than tough. His voice was deeper with a real rough edge; he sounded like someone Tariq hardly knew. And that made Tariq uneasy. He didn't want time and distance to cause his twin brother—his only family in the world—to become a stranger.

"Well, we only got two more years and we'll be living together," Tariq said, using an upbeat tone. "I'm already looking out for an apartment for us. Can you imagine the two us living together in our own place?"

"Naw, I can't even picture that shit, but yeah, you do that little brother. Keep on scopin' out a crib for us—something's bound to turn up. In the meantime, keep it tight, aiight?"

Tariq nodded and the brothers were disconnected. Yes, Shane had changed drastically, but that didn't diminish the joy and love in Tariq's heart. He felt happy enough to fly. Suddenly hungry, he decided to treat himself to some fast food. Long happy strides led him straight to the McDonald's on Stenton Avenue.

"Can I help you?" The girl was chewing gum, making popping sounds that Tariq found appealing. He never understood how girls knew how to do that. His mother could do it; he remembered fondly. In an instant, Tariq had a flash of his mother ripping a stick of Doublemint gum in half. The memory of her face was shadowy and vague, but he could hear her saying, *"One for you and one for you,"* with a smile, as she placed half pieces of gum in his and Shane's anxious, open palms. His mother would push an entire stick in her mouth and within seconds, the popping would begin. It was music. A melody of love. The memory had caught him off guard and since the cashier was responsible for bringing such a wonderful memory to his subconscious mind, he gave her a gleaming smile and placed his order.

Carrying a red tray, he found a seat near the window, looking out while munching on a burger and chomping on fries. When he picked up his soda, he was surprised to discover, a ripped off portion of the famous McDonald's French fries container on his tray. He picked it up, turned it over. Scrawled in blue ink was the name Janelle, a phone number, and the words: *Call me.*

He jerked his head in the direction of the counter, but Janelle was busy filling orders; she didn't bother to look in his direction. He tried to catch her eye, to let her know that he'd gotten the message and would definitely give her a call, but Janelle continued to take and place orders as if Tariq didn't even exist.

Trying to prolong his stay until he could catch her attention, Tariq chewed slowly, took small sips of soda, arranged and rearranged the ketchup packets on his tray. But it was to no avail, because Janelle refused to look his way.

After numerous stolen glances in her direction, Tariq had to accept that Janelle wasn't particularly pretty. She was brown-skinned with a greenish-colored birthmark splashed across her right cheek. Her short permed hair lacked luster and style. It looked as if she'd run a comb through her hair without fussing over it the way most girls did.

But there was something about Janelle that made her attractive without being pretty. She had an attitude that defied anyone to mess with her. She was a brittle young woman—no soft edges. Besides his old girlfriend Shiree, who was light complexioned, Tariq had a fierce attraction for brown-skinned girls.

The work uniform—formless slacks and the unattractive boyish shirt hid the figure of most girls, but Janelle had a body that the shapeless McDonald's uniform couldn't conceal. And she popped gum so loud and with such rapid-fire precision, it was turning him on. It sounded like she was speaking to him through Morse code.

Tariq interpreted her message with a smile. She was saying: *I love you, Tariq. Look no further, I'm all the woman you need.*

❀❀❀

He didn't wait a day or two like some boys would do when given a number. Unsophisticated in playing love games, Tariq called Janelle the evening of the same day he'd met her. Janelle could talk up a storm and Tariq liked listening to her, but the fifteen minutes' phone time he was allotted wasn't enough.

"Um…I have to go, but would it be okay if I called you around this time tomorrow night?"

"Why are you rushing off the phone? You bored?"

"No! Not at all. It's a long story, but I only get fifteen minutes on the phone."

"Dag. Well, are you allowed out of the house for more than fifteen minutes? If so, why don't you come over?"

Feeling embarrassed, Tariq chuckled uncomfortably. Janelle didn't beat around the bush. "Yeah, I can come over. What's your address?"

"I live on a little street near Wadsworth Avenue, but you're new around here. You'll never find it. Tell you what…meet me in front of the Cheltenham Mall in ten minutes."

"Okay," Tariq said enthusiastically. "See you in ten minutes."

Janelle didn't respond; she just hung up.

Tariq was intrigued. He liked the way she took charge; he liked the way she got straight to the point. So far he liked everything about her. Even the odd birth mark on her face .

He could see Janelle as he waited for the traffic light to change. She was leaning against an ATM machine outside the mall wearing a short denim skirt and a white tank top.

"Hey," she said, giving only a hint of a smile.

"Hi." Tariq felt dumb because he couldn't think of anything to say. He was shy and that was a major problem when it came to girls.

"My house is around the corner." She started walking toward Wadsworth Avenue and Tariq followed her. "I meant to tell you…" she paused.

"Tell me what?"

"I like your name."

He blushed. "Thanks."

"And I think you're fine…"

Tariq started grinning and turning red.

"Yeah, you're real nice lookin', but don't let that go to your head. Are you conceited?"

Tariq looked at her indignantly. "No, I'm not conceited."

"Good. I didn't think so."

As they continued walking, a tense silence hung in the air. Tariq wasn't good at setting the mood, so he hoped Janelle would start another conversation. Or an interrogation. He didn't mind answering her questions. He didn't mind at all.

"I live here," she said, stopping in front of the shabbiest house on the block. She stuck a key in the lock. "My parents aren't home, so we have the entire house to ourselves." She gave Tariq a sly grin.

Should he return the sly grin? He didn't know what reaction would please Janelle, so he simply shrugged and stuck his hands in his pockets uncomfortably.

"Have a seat." She pointed to a rather old sofa that was covered with a gold cloth. "I didn't get a chance to ask you your age while we were on the phone," Janelle said casually as she clicked on the TV.

"Uh, sixteen."

"I'm nineteen. Do you like older women?"

Before Tariq could respond Janelle was on his lap kissing him, with one hand under his shirt massaging his neck and his back. It felt good. So good he put more tongue into the kiss, trying to show her that he really liked her a lot.

Her hand moved around to his chest, rubbing softly, making him utter soft groans. Shiree had never touched him like that; she always monitored and controlled his groping hands. Although he was nervous as hell, this was a new and exciting experience.

Janelle didn't fumble around when she undid his belt and unzipped his pants. Experienced hands eased gently inside his boxers and began to caress his stiff member. Closing her palm around it and holding it in a loose fist, she stroked him until pre-cum moistened her palm. Tariq pushed in and out, fucking her hand as if he were inside a moist vagina. It felt good, real good, just like in his dreams. The kind that caused him to cum all over his sheets.

Tariq was sweating and breathing hard when Janelle halted his movement by withdrawing her hand. "Let's go upstairs."

As she sat down on the bed, she asked, "Are you a virgin, Tariq?"

"Um…" Technically, he wasn't a virgin, but aside from the bad sexual experience he'd had with Shane's girl, LaDonna, Tariq's penis had never been anywhere except inside his own hand.

"Yeah, you are," she said knowingly. "But not for long." Her lips twisted into an amused curl. "Come here."

Tariq stood in front of Janelle. She reached out and worked his jeans down to his thighs. "Take 'em off."

He did.

"Take those off." She nodded toward his boxers.

Tariq's eyes darted to the lamp; he wanted to tell her to turn off the light.

As if reading his mind, she shook her head. "Let's keep it on, I want to see the dick I'm sucking, and I want to see your face when you cum."

Tariq didn't think his dick could get much harder, but her sexy and extremely bold words had him throbbing in sexual pain. He quickly took off his boxers and closed his eyes. The touch of her hands on his buttocks as she pulled him to her lips gave him an internal tremor.

The smoothness of her lips, her warm tongue put shivers up his spine. The inside of Janelle's mouth felt like paradise. When the head of his dick accidentally pushed into the moist inside of her cheek, Janelle deftly used her tongue to guide it back to the center of her mouth. It wasn't his first time experiencing oral sex, but was nothing like the terrible time with LaDonna. This was beyond his expectations.

She sucked softly at first and then with great urgency, which had Tariq pumping into her mouth fast and hard as if the orifice were a vagina. He made guttural gasping sounds and, feeling on the brink of insanity, he began to pull her hair, cried out her name and told her he loved her. In fact, he told her he loved her repeatedly.

"I love you, Janelle," he shouted as he exploded, feeling deeply that his admission was true. It didn't matter that he'd just met her that very day. The intense emotions were like nothing he'd ever felt before. He loved her and would do everything he could to prove it.

Janelle's smug smile of satisfaction went unnoticed as he covered her mouth with a passionate kiss. Her mouth tasted salty but he didn't mind; she'd done something for him that diminished some of his emotional pain. For the first time in months, his thoughts weren't focused on missing Shane.

"I really love you." This time he whispered the words in her ear.

When his heart rate returned to normal, Tariq checked the time; it was past his curfew. Embarrassed that he had to tolerate such a strict and old-fashioned rule, Tariq lowered his head and confessed, "I have a ten o'clock curfew; I'm sorry but I have to go." He felt humiliated and couldn't control the pained expression that took over his face.

"For real? You have a curfew?" Janelle asked and sucked her teeth. "I wasn't finished, but it's cool," she said with a shrug. "We'll just have to finish what we started the next time we get together."

Tariq's heart soared; he couldn't believe his good fortune. Despite all the corny restrictions his foster parents forced on him, Janelle was actually willing to see him again. She hinted that they were going to have intercourse the next time. Now that would be a real first, but he hoped with all his heart that she'd also give up some more head.

CHAPTER 17

Tariq's arm was wrapped lovingly around Janelle as they stood in a long line at the movie theater inside the Cheltenham Mall, waiting to purchase tickets. Murmurs from the teenage girls around them that fluctuated between amusement and discontent did not immediately register in Tariq's mind. The malicious titters of laughter from lips drawn in indignation went unheard.

Tariq was so in love, it seemed he and Janelle were the only people in line. Janelle had control of all his senses: He only heard her voice, felt her touch, tasted her kiss, and smelled the fragrance of her personal scent. No one else existed.

A group of girls in line ahead of Tariq and Janelle kept turning around and giving Tariq flirty glances. One of the bold girls licked her lips; another puckered up and mimicked a kiss; the third girl smiled and winked. And all of this was done right in Janelle's face. The girls expected a favorable response from Tariq.

"Now, that's a shame. She know she ain't got no business being all up under that cute boy with that green shit all on her face," one of the girls complained loudly, which made everyone in earshot turn around to see the ill-matched couple.

"Who are they talking about?" Tariq asked Janelle.

"They're talking about us, but don't pay 'em any mind," Janelle told Tariq. "They're stupid little girls; trying to work my nerves."

"Why? Do you know them?"

"No. But it happens all the time. Whenever we're out together, little young skanks are always trying to hit on you."

"For real?"

"You don't notice, Tariq, but a lot of people think you're too handsome to be with me. I like the fact that you don't pay those little skanks no attention. And that's how I want it to stay. Understand?" Janelle said with a threatening edge to her tone.

"You know I don't mess around with no other girls." Tariq pulled Janelle closer and kissed her on the cheek.

"Eeow!" The three girls emitted in disgust. "She must be paying him to be with her because I know he ain't really feelin' her with that ugly scarred-up mug."

This time Tariq clearly heard the malicious words. Anger flashed across his face. Before he could defend her honor, Janelle yanked his arm.

"Don't start anything. They're just jealous because you're with me. Now show them hoes how much you love me," Janelle demanded.

Tariq had no problem following Janelle's order; he immediately cupped her face and looked lovingly into her eyes. "I love you, baby."

There were more utterances of disgust from the hostile teenage trio.

"Who do you belong to?" Janelle asked in a pitch that all could hear.

"I belong to you," Tariq responded, taking Janelle's lead and speaking loud enough to be heard by the crowd.

"Now, make those skanks jealous; kiss me!"

Tariq didn't hesitate. Tariq kissed Janelle as passionately as he would if they were alone in her bedroom.

Janelle threw the trio a look of triumph.

The girls sucked their teeth, offended by the sight. However, they didn't harass the couple again.

❄❄❄

Janelle had made her point without uttering a word of reproach to any of the silly girls. She'd also come to the conclusion that if she expected to keep the swarms of hot-ass hoochies away from Tariq, she would have to exercise complete dominion over him.

When Janelle was promoted to manager of the McDonald's, she hired Tariq and put him on her shift where she could monitor his every move. She was jealous of practically every young woman on the premises, employees and customers alike. She openly admonished Tariq whenever she felt he was giving too much attention to a female co-worker or even patrons of the fast food eatery.

Although she behaved like a tyrant most of the time, she was also compassionate. For Tariq's seventeenth birthday, they both took the day off to go visit his brother at Barney Hills. She'd made the appointment and paid for the travel expenses as a birthday present. Tariq let out a yelp of joy when she told him that they were going to see Shane.

The numerous buses and the train ride took forever and when at last they arrived at the reform school for boys, Tariq had tears of joy in his eyes.

"Yo, man. You almost as tall as me," Shane shouted when he walked into the visitor's lounge. Taken by surprise, Tariq jerked around. When he saw his brother his face broke into a huge grin. The brothers rushed toward each other.

Janelle watched the twins with great interest. Though they were both handsome, they looked nothing alike. They didn't even look like brothers, let alone twins. There was nothing similar in their behavior, either. While Tariq was a shy and basically wholesome individual, she noticed Shane walked with the swagger of the antisocial and had facial features that were hardened by fast living. The hard edge, however, didn't detract from his good looks, and the dimple in his chin, she noted, was sexy as hell.

She also was keenly aware of Shane's sexual magnetism as her eyes roved to his crotch area. Seeing the bulge, she quickly fantasized about engaging in a ménage-a-tois with the twins.

The brothers embraced. "Whassup, bro," Shane said as he gave his brother another hug.

"I missed you, man. Damn, it's good to see you," Tariq said happily. They hadn't seen each other in almost two years. After a few moments, Tariq beckoned Janelle, who'd been observing from the background. "This is my girl, Janelle," he said, his voice filled with pride. "Janelle, this is my twin brother, Shane."

"Nice to meet you, Shane. Tariq talks about you all the time." She offered a coy smile. It was subtle, but flirtatious nevertheless.

Shane gave an abrupt head nod and said, "Hey, whassup." His voice was without warmth, which Janelle interpreted as his disapproval of her physical appearance. She felt instantly offended, never considering that she had insulted Shane by disrespecting his brother with her flirtatiousness.

Shane's slight apparently didn't escape Tariq, who immediately walked Shane to the other side of the visitor's lounge. "Man, that's all you gotta say to my future wife?"

"Your future wife? Man, you must be buggin'. I know you ain't tryin' to wife *her!*" Shane frowned and looked back at Janelle in disapproval. "Man, what's wrong with you? All the pretty girls in Philly and you come up here on your first visit with that ugly chick? What's that green shit on the side of her face?" Shane asked, contorting his face in disgust. "Damn, Tariq…you making me look bad."

From across the room, Janelle could hear the hostile-sounding whispers and she figured Tariq's brother was informing him that he could do much better. She was used to it. Everyone seemed to feel that way. Everyone except Tariq.

Tariq was sweet and usually tried to keep the peace, but whenever someone made a negative comment about her looks, he became livid. Janelle sat back, unfazed that his brother didn't find her worthy of Tariq. Shane was very sexy and had far more confidence than Tariq, which had initially caused moisture between her legs. However, his rejection of her made her furious and now she despised Shane with all her heart. So why was her pussy still pulsating? Confused by the odd combination of lust and hatred, she turned her attention away from her raging libido. Curiously, she watched the two brothers' interaction, interested to see if Tariq would take her side against the brother he seemed to worship.

Tariq gave Shane a fiery gaze. "Janelle went to a lot of trouble to get us together on our birthday. None of my social workers could make this happen. This is supposed to be a happy occasion and you flippin' out because you don't think my girl looks good enough. Man, you the one buggin." Tariq's voice rose.

At first Shane glared at Tariq, and then he took a deep breath and said, "You're right, man. I'm acting like a dickhead." He went to hug Tariq, but Tariq pulled away.

"It took me and my baby almost three hours to get up here, but we can turn around and leave right now. If you can't accept her, then you can't accept me." Tariq spoke loud enough for her to hear. She knew he wanted her to hear; that's the way it was between her and Tariq. She knew Tariq loved her dirty drawers. And now his smart-mouthed brother knew it too.

"Man, I said I'm sorry. You want me to apologize to your girl?"

"What do you think? You owe her one, don't you?" Tariq said, holding his ground.

Checkmate, Janelle said to herself and smiled. She disliked Shane intensely and couldn't wait to make her feelings known.

From across the room, she watched Tariq and Shane coming toward her.

"I came at you all wrong," Shane said sheepishly. "My bad. I'm sorry. We cool?"

Janelle could have been gracious, but she didn't think Shane deserved it, so she looked him up and down and turned up one side of her lip.

"Fuck you," she said with a sneer. "I don't need your apology; I don't need shit from you." Her voice was ice.

Shane flinched. Looking shocked, Tariq's head swiveled from Shane to Janelle.

Steaming with fury, Shane's mouth fell open. He was speechless as he looked to Tariq for support. But Tariq didn't utter a word of reproach to Janelle.

Janelle glanced at her watch. "It's time to leave, Tariq. We're outta here."

"Come on, Janelle, don't be like that," Tariq finally said. He used a pleading tone. "My brother said he was sorry."

"Man, if you don't tell that ugly bitch to kiss your ass," Shane heatedly interjected. "What's wrong, man, she got you pussy-whipped or somethin'?"

"Tariq!" Janelle's voice was trill as she cut Shane off before he could get deeper into his tirade. "Let's go!"

"Look, I gotta go, man. I'll see you later," Tariq said sadly. He turned to hug his brother, but Shane backed up, refusing his brother's hug.

On the train ride back to Philly, Janelle and Tariq sat next to each other without saying a word. Tariq finally broke the silence. "How come you couldn't accept my brother's apology?"

She didn't respond, instead she turned her head and looked out the window.

"Can you answer my question?"

"I'm going to say this one time and one time only. I don't allow anyone to disrespect me. Your brother can kiss my ass and so can you if you ever bring his name up again. Shane Batista does not exist. Is that clear, Tariq?"

Tariq gulped. "He's my brother. My twin. What do you mean he doesn't exist?"

Janelle shrugged. "All right. Then you and me don't exist. Feel better?" she asked sarcastically and then turned her head and looked out the window once again.

Tears formed in Tariq's eyes. He timidly touched Janelle's shoulder. "Janelle," he said in a hoarse whisper. "I don't want to cut my ties with my brother, but Shane was wrong. Dead wrong. It's you and me, Janelle." Tariq gulped. "Shane doesn't exist. Okay, baby? Shane doesn't exist," he repeated with finality in his tone.

Janelle put her pocketbook in his lap and slipped her hand beneath it, caressing his dick and squeezing his balls for the entire train ride. Her caress was a statement that Tariq was forgiven. "I'm gonna give you your real birthday present when we get back home."

Both Janelle's parents were home when they arrived at her house at five o'clock. They liked Tariq and with Janelle now a twenty-year-old woman, her parents didn't have a problem with her keeping company in her bedroom.

Since he'd started working, Tariq's curfew had been extended to midnight. For his loyalty and devotion, Janelle planned to give him seven hours of uninterrupted sex.

CHAPTER 18

Summer was over and school was back in session. Tariq's work hours at the restaurant would probably have to be changed to accommodate his school schedule. He hung his book bag on a hook in the back room, winked at Janelle, and went up front to work the cash register. He looked back and said, "My roster's in my book bag in the blue folder."

Tariq wasn't supposed to keep any secrets from Janelle. She liked knowing what he was doing every hour of the day. It was fine by Tariq because he had no reason to keep secrets from her. He didn't cheat, wouldn't dream of it. The girls at school and at work didn't stand a chance. For Tariq, there was only Janelle. She controlled his life; she told him what he could and could not do, and where he could and could not go. With the exception of school, there weren't too many places Janelle allowed Tariq to go without her at his side. On their days off from work, it was understood that she would meet him outside his high school. Tariq didn't mind being kept on a short leash; it assured him that he was loved.

Janelle told another worker to replace Tariq at the cash register. With a crook of her finger, she indicated he should follow her into the office.

He joined her eagerly, thinking she wanted to give him a blow job or sneak in some quick sex, something they frequently did in the office.

But when he arrived, his open book bag was on the desk. Janelle was shaking as if she'd found an incriminating condom, a pair of panties, or a thong in his book bag.

"What's wrong, Janelle?"

"This!" She threw the letter across the desk.

Tariq turned red. It was a letter from Shane.

"I didn't write him back," he said in his defense.

"I read his letter, Tariq. So don't lie to me."

Tariq swallowed hard. He was beginning to perspire. He didn't like upsetting Janelle. "I'm sorry, Janelle. He wrote me a few weeks ago and I wrote him back. But I wasn't going to answer that letter. I'm through with Shane. I told you that."

"It's too late. I told you not to keep secrets from me. I feel betrayed like I can't trust anything you say. So forget it, Tariq. Be with your brother. It's over. We're through."

Tariq heard an explosion in his head as if his world was literally crumbling around him. He reached for her hand. "Please, Janelle. Please. I'm sorry."

She jerked her hand away. "Get back to your cash register. I don't have anything else to say."

Tariq returned to the cash register like a man in a trance. But he couldn't concentrate. He messed up so many orders, Janelle had to take him off the register and put him in the kitchen. But he didn't do much better working with the food.

When the shift was over, he hung around waiting for Janelle. She usually walked him home after work. Janelle had started that practice after finding out that Tariq and one of the female workers, a cute girl named Kapri who lived on Tariq's block, had walked home together one evening after work.

"We're just friends," he'd explained. "All we did was talk. Kapri's a nice girl. She goes to church, has a curfew. And after graduation, she's planning on going to school to become a court stenographer."

"How do you know all that about her?" Janelle inquired suspiciously.

"We talk while we're walking home. That's all we do—talk!"

"I'm not a fool, Tariq. All that talking can lead to other things."

"Kapri's not even looking for a boyfriend. She's focusing on her future right now."

"Let me get something straight." Janelle waved a threatening finger in his face. "Girls will play all kinds of games to try to break us up. Nobody wants to see us together and Kapri ain't no different than any other girl. She may look all sweet and innocent but she's really just trying to get inside your pants."

Tariq opened his mouth to disagree, but closed it when Janelle held up her hand.

"Now, the way I see it, innocent little Kapri is coming at you from a different angle. Those church-going girls are the worst ones. They always turn up pregnant before anybody else. I don't trust Kapri. And I don't want you around her. Understand?"

Reluctantly, Tariq nodded.

"From now on, I'll be walking you home because you can't be trusted. Do you hear me?"

"Yes, Janelle."

At the end of his shift, Tariq obediently hung around McDonald's waiting for Janelle to finish up and escort him to his door.

When she noticed him waiting, Janelle said in a cheerful voice, "Oh, you don't have to wait for me, Tariq, I'm busy. Walk home with Kapri. I'll see you tomorrow. Good-night."

Tariq felt a surge of panic. Janelle had instructed him to wait for her. Why was she now suggesting that he leave with Kapri, one of the prettiest girls on their shift and the girl she was fiercely jealous of? Janelle's easy dismissal could only mean that she was through with him—she didn't want him anymore.

Kapri had left fifteen minutes earlier and Tariq was relieved. He was too down in the dumps to be around the ever perky Kapri. Looking back at a stone-faced Janelle, Tariq retrieved his book bag and slunk away.

That night, when the Packards went to bed, Tariq called Janelle repeatedly. She hung up on him each time. After fifteen attempts to smooth things over, Tariq finally gave up. He cried himself to sleep.

The next morning, he awoke hoping it had all been a dream, but when he called Janelle before he left for school, he got a recorded message: *Janelle is not taking calls from Tariq.*

It was cruel. Torture. He couldn't endure this kind of pain and he'd do anything to make it stop. Janelle treated him as if he didn't exist. She wouldn't accept his phone calls; she only spoke to him at work if she absolutely had to.

There was a permanent knot in the pit of his stomach. His head throbbed all day long. Feeling as if he was losing his mind, he decided it was time to beg. He timidly knocked on Janelle's office door. "Come in," she called out cheerily.

When she saw him, her expression hardened.

"What is it, Tariq?"

"Janelle, just tell me what I have to do. I'll do anything you tell me to do. Anything!"

"Tariq," she said calmly. "Please leave my office. That's what I want you to do."

But instead of leaving he marched over to the desk and fell down on his knees. "I'm begging you, Janelle. I swear to God, if you give me another chance, I'll do anything for you." He noticed a glimmer of interest in Janelle's eyes, though her face remained hard and stern. The gleam in her eyes gave him hope, so he took the begging to a higher level. "Baby please; I worship and adore you." He kissed the toe of her black Reebok.

"Get up, Tariq. I'll forgive you this time, but our relationship is definitely going to change. You're going to have to make some serious adjustments."

He got up. "Okay, whatever you say…you know I'll do it."

"Come here," she said and whispered in his ear. Shocked by the words she whispered in his ear, bug-eyed, he nodded his head in agreement.

"So, you'll take care of that tomorrow, right?"

He nodded solemnly. "I'll do it. But I don't know where to get that stuff."

"In the women's lingerie department of any department store."

"Should I go to the mall?"

"I don't care where you go; just make sure you get it. Oh yeah, and until you do what I asked, don't expect me to walk you home."

Tariq bit his lip and nodded. "Can I call you tonight?"

"No!"

Paling and looking distraught, he said bravely, "Okay, I'll see you tomorrow." Tariq took slow steps toward the door, hoping Janelle would call him back, show him some affection, something, anything that would relieve some of the emotional pain, the feeling of abandonment that was strangling him.

❋❋❋❋

The next day at work, Tariq was filled with shame. He lowered his eyes in embarrassment when anyone—co-workers or customers—looked at him for longer than a few seconds. He felt like everyone knew his secret. His terrible shame. But he had to do it. He loved Janelle and needed her. She'd told him this was the only way he could prove his love and get her back.

After two hours of being ignored by her, she finally called him into her office.

"Take off your shirt and drop your pants."

His face turned crimson as he pulled his shirt up, revealing a red lacy bra.

Janelle leaped out of her seat and helped him to unbuckle his pants. His pants fell and gathered on the floor. He had on a pair of shimmering red panties.

"Damn, Tariq! You look so good in women's underwear; I'm ready to suck your dick right now. I love you, boy, and I forgive you for everything. Now I truly believe that you love me. You really love me, don't you, baby?"

"Love you? I worship the ground you walk on. I told you I'd do anything for you," Tariq told her, his eyes misted with emotion.

His growing erection slipped through the side of the red panties. Janelle's eyes slid over to his exposed member. Overcome with lust, Janelle hastily dropped to her knees and gave Tariq some well-deserved head.

Despite the tight and uncomfortable fit of the lingerie, Tariq whistled merrily for the remaining hours of his shift. He was thrilled that his compliance had given Janelle so much pleasure, but he was also relieved that he didn't have to wear the confining female undergarments ever again.

After work, during their walk to his house, Janelle announced, "Tariq, I want us to pick out your lingerie together. Okay? You're off punishment and you don't have to make any more choices on your own."

Tariq looked stunned. "I thought you said I only had to wear this stuff one time—today!"

"No, Tariq," she said, shaking her head adamantly. "I want you to wear the lingerie a couple days a week."

"But…" Tariq weakly objected.

"Tariq!" Janelle's tone was harsh. Tariq fell silent. "Do you know how hot my pussy feels right now?" she asked in a soft sultry voice. "I'm furious that we can't fuck right now. But you and that damn curfew…" Janelle stopped walking. "I have an idea. We could do it over there." She pointed to a desolate playground. "Behind the bushes."

In the playground, Tariq and Janelle lowered themselves on the ground behind the bushes. "Take off your shirt," Janelle demanded, holding out her hand.

Tariq unbuttoned and took off his shirt. Janelle licked her lips at the sight of the frilly red bra he wore. She spread his shirt on the ground and kneeled upon it on all fours. "Do you want to fuck me right here—outside?"

"Uh huh." Tariq's tongue hung from his mouth lustfully. He panted like a dog.

"You like wearing panties for me, baby?" Janelle asked, her breathing quickened.

"Yeah." Tariq gave a throaty groan as he mounted Janelle and slipped inside her from behind.

Janelle murmured and moaned. "Oh damn, you feel so good tonight. Fuck me like you mean it. Harder, Tariq. That's right, fuck me harder. Damn, we're outside, baby—fucking like animals. Let's pretend like we're dogs," she shouted in wanton abandon.

All the pent-up passion, the pain and fear of abandonment from everyone he'd ever loved came out in a growl very similar to the sound of a dog. He pushed in hard.

"Bark, Tariq. Bark for me, baby. Bark just like a dog."

Tariq barked for Janelle.

"Louder, baby," she insisted. "Bark like you mean it."

With every thrust, he barked, he growled, he snarled. When he reached a howling climax, Tariq collapsed on the ground. With his hands wrapped tightly around Janelle's waist, Tariq broke down and sobbed.

CHAPTER 19

"I'm pregnant," Janelle said, nonchalantly.

"What!" A big grin covered Tariq's face. Then he noticed Janelle looking pensive. "This is a happy occasion, right? Because I'm ready to start handing out cigars to everybody here," he said, waving his hands at the patrons and staff at McDonald's. "I wanna load up on cigars and pass them out to my classmates at school—to strangers on the street. How come you don't look happy?"

"I'm happy; I'm just a little worried about how we're going to support a child."

"I can work overtime," Tariq suggested.

"How? You have to go to school."

"Sundays; I'll work on my day off and a couple extra hours during the week."

Janelle added Tariq's name to the Sunday schedule and also gave him additional hours during the week.

Tariq was more than happy to work the extra hours. With a baby on the way, he and Janelle could use all the money they could get. Tariq was so happy and so proud, he wished he could share the news with Shane. But Janelle hadn't forgiven Shane, therefore, Tariq was forbidden to speak to his brother.

The pain of losing his brother had dulled over time. Janelle had miraculously filled a void that he didn't think possible to fill. She'd rescued him from the loneliness that was a sad echo of his past. Janelle provided everything he needed, he convinced himself, as he mentally pushed away the pain of losing his twin brother.

"No one needs to know about this, especially not your foster parents," she'd said, referring to the pregnancy. "You're still underage. We'll wait until you turn eighteen."

On countless occasions, Janelle had proven that she knew what was best for him and he would not second-guess her decision now. If she thought it best to keep the pregnancy a secret, he had to trust her judgment.

"Nine months from now…when the baby is born, you'll be eighteen and you can get out from under your foster parents' thumb."

"Can I get out from under your thumb?" he asked playfully.

Janelle gave a mirthless chuckle. "Now you know that's never going to happen. Tariq," she said, looking serious, "you're under my thumb for life."

"Sounds good to me; I don't have a problem with it, baby. You know you're the boss." Tariq was proud to be under Janelle's control. He lived to please her. After the experience of being banished from her life, he tried to anticipate her every need and continued, at her insistence, to wear female lingerie several times a week. The bra, however, was so uncomfortable, she no longer forced him to wear it in public.

"Keeping you in women's panties or glittery female thongs is my assurance that you'll keep your dick where it belongs—in your pants. I know you're not gonna be cheating on me when you got a pair of red panties on," she'd told him.

"I don't care what I'm wearing; I'll never cheat on you," Tariq told her.

And now that she was carrying his child, he cherished Janelle even more. Cheating on her was unimaginable. No other woman attracted him. He was devoted to Janelle. For Tariq, his relationship with Janelle was perfectly normal and heavenly bliss.

He'd been trained to rely on her good judgment in every way. He didn't object to signing his paycheck over to her. It seemed perfectly within the boundaries of normalcy to go to Janelle for everything from money for school tokens to school supplies. The pocket money she allotted him had to be accounted for down to the dime.

She told him he didn't need any friends; all he needed was her. He believed her because friends don't provide the type of sex that Janelle lavished upon him. Freaky sex that he'd never would have thought of in his wildest dreams.

Her imagination was unlimited. Without her good sex, Tariq thought he would die.

On occasion, she still doled out punishment, but it was minor compared to the pain he'd felt when he'd almost lost her. He could accept any punishment she dispensed as long as she didn't turn her back on him and send him away.

The baby was his insurance that Janelle would never reject him again.

"We're going to get married on your eighteenth birthday; nothing elaborate. They do ceremonies down at city hall."

"Did you say we're getting married?" he asked in awe.

"Uh huh. Gotta problem with that," she asked, smiling.

Ecstatic, Tariq picked her up and swung her around.

"Put me down, boy," she said, laughing. "You might hurt the baby."

❀❀❀

In her fourth month of pregnancy, Janelle, feeling feverish, her fingers and ankles swollen, had to leave work early to go home and lie down. Tariq wanted to leave with her, but she told him he had to stay. They couldn't afford to have both their paychecks docked.

Immediately after work, Tariq hurried to Janelle's house.

"She's upstairs 'sleep," her mother told him. "Go on up."

Tariq bounded the stairs and found his angel sound asleep. Defiantly refusing to adhere to his curfew, he called his foster mother.

"Mrs. Packard, Janelle is sick and I'm staying with her tonight." He wasn't asking permission, therefore being told no wasn't an option. Mrs. Packard mumbled a few discontented words and then said, "Okay, well, make sure you get to school on time."

He took off his clothes and hung them in the closet. It was Tuesday, one of the days he was allowed to wear boxers. He folded them neatly, and then crawled into bed with Janelle, rubbing her cute round stomach until he too fell asleep.

In the morning, Janelle was running a temperature. Her feet and fingers were grotesquely swollen. "My head hurts," she cried. Tariq was flabbergasted;

he'd never seen Janelle cry. She moaned and rolled back in forth in pain. "My head is killing me, Tariq."

He massaged her temples. Her face was burning hot. Something had to be done but he didn't know what to do. Janelle's mother had already left for work, so it was up to Tariq to figure out something. "Should we call your doctor?"

"Oh God, my head. Oh God." Janelle grabbed her head and balled into a knot.

"What's your doctor's number, Janelle?" He was panicked and had never assumed any responsibility.

She pointed to a phone book. "It's under V—Doctor Vaughn. Hurry up, I'm dying, Tariq."

He tried to squeeze her fingers soothingly while he fumbled with the pages in her phone book. Her fingers felt fat and hot—like sausages about to pop.

When he got the receptionist on the line, he gave Janelle a reassuring glance. "My girl is having a baby; she's hot and everything is swelling up. Her head hurts, too," he babbled.

The receptionist asked for Janelle's information, beginning with her name.

"Oh, her name? It's Janelle Dennis. How many months? Um…four. Do we have a thermometer? No, we don't have one, but I'm feeling her head and her temperature's gotta be sky high."

Janelle cried and panted as if in labor during the exchange between Tariq and the receptionist at the doctor's office, causing Tariq to have to walk away from Janelle in order to hear the instructions clearly.

"So, you saying I should take her to the hospital? Okay. . .all right."

Tariq hung up. "Janelle, you gotta get dressed, baby; the nurse said you gotta go to the hospital. She said we can call an ambulance but it's gonna cost about three hundred dollars and your insurance don't cover it. Or we can take a cab to Einstein. What do you want to do, baby? Take a cab or call nine-one-one?"

Money conscious even while in pain, Janelle whispered, "Call a cab, Tariq. And then help me get some clothes on."

Tariq and Janelle took a cab to Einstein Medical Center. Janelle was kept overnight for observation and because Tariq was underage, he couldn't stay with her.

Scared out of his wits and with no one to turn to, he did the unthinkable and called his brother, Shane.

"I shouldn't even be speaking to you, man, after the way you let your girl shine on me."

"Can we get past that, man? Janelle's pregnant, but something's wrong. She's in the hospital.." Tariq swallowed. "I think she's gonna die."

"Listen to me, man. That bitch ain't gonna die."

Tariq bristled at Janelle being referred to as a bitch, but he was too weak to verbally reprimand Shane.

"I don't know much about female issues but she probably just got heartburn. I hear females talkin' about heartburn a lot when they're pregnant."

"You got somebody pregnant?"

"None that I'm claiming. But you know, they call me with that ying yang shit and I let em rap, but I ain't claiming no babies. No…not the kid. But anyway, that's how I know about that heartburn shit."

"How did you get off the premises of that reform school to even possibly get somebody pregnant?"

"Man, we go out on field trips. I'm still smooth enough to have my pussy lined up in advance. Sometimes I knock off two or three broads on one trip," Shane boasted. "Like the time we went to the Smithsonian Institute. Man… I ain't seen none of that scientific memorabilia bullshit. I was too busy in the restroom, getting my dick wet."

"Thanks for taking my call, Shane. I apologize for everything. But you gotta understand, when you insulted Janelle like that…man, I had to stick up for my girl."

"I can dig it. I know what's up. You ain't have nobody after I took this fall. I can dig how you let that ug—" Shane caught the insult before it completely passed his lips. "I understand how she got her hooks in you. She used pussy didn't she?"

"No! I love Janelle, but I didn't call you for this. I feel a lot better knowing she has some common pregnancy disease. Heartburn is curable, right?"

"Yeah, man. Like I said. She's gonna live. Congratulations, big poppa," Shane said. "You bringing your seed into the world. You better have some strong-ass sperm 'cause the first one is supposed to be a boy."

"I don't know; she didn't take the ultrasound test yet, but I'll let you know as soon as I find out."

"Aiight, man. I want you to know that I didn't give up on you. Ain't shit I can do for you being locked up in here. But as soon as I get out, we gon' be rollin' again. Me and you. Man, you know Mommy wouldn't have wanted no girl to come between us. She died for us, man, now act like you got sense and honor her memory. She'd be turning in her grave if she knew we weren't speaking all this time. Now, when I get out in a few months, you gonna have to put a bug in that girl's ear or else you gonna have to let her go. Don't even worry about nothin'; I got your back."

Thinking about their mother filled Tariq with an overwhelming sorrow. Letting Janelle go was unthinkable. But Shane had a point; they'd been through too much together to let the riff continue any longer. "You right, man. I'm gonna talk to her; she'll come around. Everything will be straightened out by the time you get out."

Feeling jubilant, Tariq hung up. He wanted to get on his knees and thank God. His girl was gonna survive and his relationship with his brother was healed.

Janelle was going to have to understand; he'd do anything in the world for her. She was his heart; his whole life. But Shane. Shane meant the world to him also and just talking to him made Tariq feel stronger—more like a man.

CHAPTER 20

Toxemia was the name of Janelle's condition and her doctor advised her to cut back on salt and to stay off her feet. He strongly advised complete bed rest, but Janelle wouldn't hear of it and continued to work at the fast food restaurant.

One day her face swelled to what seemed the size of a balloon. She complained of severe abdominal pain and seeing flashing lights in front of her eyes. Again, she was admitted to the hospital and when she returned home she could no longer ignore the doctor's orders for she was so swollen, she was literally unable to get out of bed.

Tariq helped her to the bathroom, bathed her, and changed her clothes. He performed the tasks with the care and the same sense of duty he'd demonstrated throughout their relationship.

Their sex life, however, was nonexistent, so young and horny Tariq was not a very happy young man. Ever since Janelle had become bedridden and unable to endure intercourse, her bedroom, formerly a place of great passion and pleasure, had begun to feel as confining as a prison cell.

"I'll see you tomorrow, baby." Tariq stood up, eager to leave.

Janelle looked crestfallen. "Aw, baby. Why you gotta leave? It's only nine o'clock," Janelle complained, trying to lift her heavy body into an upright position.

"Homework. I have a test tomorrow."

"Can't you study here?"

"I left my notes home." He walked around the bed and kissed her on the cheek.

"Is that all I get?" Janelle puckered her lips and Tariq had to avert his gaze. With her balloon-sized face, it wasn't a pleasant sight.

He quickly kissed her on the lips and then he kissed her stomach and told the baby, "See you later, lil' man."

"Keep callin' him that. You gonna get your feelings hurt when it turns out to be a girl."

"I can adapt." He kissed her stomach again, "See you later, lil' lady." He flashed Janelle a big smile and she returned it, watching him leave with adoring eyes.

How had the tables turned, Tariq wondered? He believed he still loved Janelle, but the passion was no longer there. He recalled the first time he defied her and wore boxers on a designated panty day. She did the panty check from bed, but was feeling too sick to muster up any rage.

In a weak voice, she'd said, "Just because I'm lying up in this bed doesn't mean you can disobey my rules." But she knew as well as Tariq that things were not the same.

❦❦❦

The one secret that Tariq kept from Janelle was that he and Kapri were good friends. Platonic friends. But he'd led Janelle to believe that his only words to Kapri were *hi* and *'bye*. They still communicated at work and now that Janelle was laid up, they talked at length after work and even studied together at Kapri's home.

One day at work he'd confided to Kapri about Janelle's pregnancy and that his relationship with his brother had become strained. He didn't tell Kapri the full extent of his relationship with Janelle, yet he could tell that she didn't approve of the iron-clad grip Janelle had on him. No one understood.

"I don't know, Tariq," Kapri said, pausing to choose her words. "Your relationship with Janelle seems somewhat—abusive."

"Abusive!" Tariq fell out laughing. "Abused people are sad and depressed. I'm walking on cloud nine—so how can you even think I'm abused?"

Now, after leaving Janelle home in bed, Tariq bounded up the steps to Kapri's house. Kapri answered his knock on the door.

"I was gonna study without you if you didn't hurry up," she informed him, rolling her eyes and pretending she had an attitude.

Kapri made popcorn and poured two tall glasses of iced tea. Tariq felt at peace in the comfortable kitchen as he and Kapri quietly studied their Black History notes.

"Okay, ready?" Kapri asked, closing her folder.

"Not yet."

"Too bad, you were supposed to get here at seven and nobody told you to come dragging in at nine-fifteen. I'm getting tired."

"All right, Kapri. I was late; I was wrong. Now can we get started?"

Kapri smiled and cleared her throat. I'll ask you a question first and then you ask me. We'll rotate. Okay?"

"Cool."

"Okay. Who is the first African-American world renowned opera singer who performed at the White House?"

Tariq searched the ceiling for the answer.

"Here's a clue…she's from Philly."

He gave her a blank stare.

"Tariq, you should know this."

Shrugging his shoulders, he speculated, "Um…Mahalia Jackson?"

Kapri threw a kernel of popcorn at Tariq. "I didn't say anything about a gospel singer. You're obviously not ready for the test. The first black opera singer who performed at the White House is Marian Anderson, born and bred right here. Another reason for Philadelphia pride."

"All right. I blew that one. Okay, let's see how much you know. What famous world leader spent twenty-seven years in prison?"

"Nelson Mandela."

"You're sharp, girl. I need to study with you all the time."

"And you're obviously not prepared for this test," she admonished.

"I'll study some more at home."

"Tariq. If you don't start applying yourself, you're gonna be working at Mickey D's for the rest of your life."

"Yes, teacher," Tariq said jokingly as he started stuffing his notebooks and folders into his book bag.

"I'm serious. You're going to be a father soon and that's more reason to start looking toward the future. Have you thought about college or even a trade school? High school doesn't prepare you for any job that would support a family, I hope you realize that. Another thing, Tariq," Kapri said, her tone softer as she eased up on the subject. "I know you think Janelle is looking out for you, but sometimes I wonder if she's deliberately trying to keep you down."

Tariq yanked the zipper on his book bag. With a confrontational arched brow, he asked, "Why would she try to keep me down? Before I had Janelle I didn't have anything."

"And what do you have now?"

"A family," he said with finality as he zipped his book bag. "See you tomorrow at school."

As he walked home, snowflakes began to fall. The sky was very dark and he felt very alone. What would his life have been like if his mother had lived? Kapri had given him something to think about. What did the future hold for him, he wondered? It wasn't a good time to ponder the issue; it was all about Janelle right now. She needed him and it would infuriate her if he started talking about bettering himself at a time like this. If he mentioned going to trade school, he knew she'd flip and probably start to cry. *What about me and the baby; you can't change your routine at a time like this.* Lately, she'd become very moody and everything made her cry. No, he couldn't change the game plan. At least not right now.

His feelings for Janelle were confusing enough. His dick was constantly erect. He seemed to be in a constant state of arousal, except when he was around Janelle.

She'd told him that just because her pussy was out of commission didn't mean she couldn't give him head. "Come here, Tariq. Let me suck it so you won't think you have to go out there and get it somewhere else." But one look at her swollen face, fingers, feet, and toes and his dick went soft. He really didn't want any head. Not from her.

He found himself looking at the girls at school, the video dancers on BET and MTV. He'd started checking out Kapri's cute little butt, which was sick considering Kapri was his one and only friend.

Admittedly, Tariq was in bad shape. He probably had a serious case of blue balls, but he'd just have to ride it out until after the baby was born.

Hopefully, after giving birth, Janelle would return to her normal strong self. He wasn't accustomed to whiny, helpless Janelle. As it stood right now, he didn't feel any passion for her, which both scared him and filled him with shame.

CHAPTER 21

Restless and bored with being cooped up in Janelle's bedroom, Tariq spent most of his time at work or hanging out with Kapri. Their relationship, though merely platonic, was still conducted behind Janelle's back.

One of their coworkers at McDonald's had thought it her civic duty to call Janelle and inform her that something was "going on" between Tariq and Kapri.

"So it's you and Kapri now? Is that why you never want to be here anymore?" Janelle accused, her voice a scratchy whine.

"Me and Kapri are just friends," Tariq was weary of Janelle's insecurities, but he managed to inject patience into his tone.

"But I told you I didn't want you hanging around with her; she's just trying to get inside your pants."

Tariq sighed. Audibly. Perhaps it was because he was getting older. Maybe it was because he knew Shane would be home soon, or maybe it was simply human nature that he would choose a time when Janelle was in a weakened condition to begin to express irritation.

Their relationship was based on Janelle being a dominant woman who expected Tariq to submit to rigid rules of behavior. But now his oppressor was emotionally fragile and physically weak. The power in the relationship had inadvertently shifted to Tariq.

"I told you me and Kapri are just friends!" he shouted this time. "Stop acting all jealous over nothing. You can't tell me who to be with no more."

At first, Janelle stared at him in startled bewilderment. But when Tariq stood up as if he were about to leave, Janelle narrowed her eyes. "And where do you think you're going?"

"To work!" he said tersely.

"Oh, no, you're not." Using her palm for leverage, Janelle lifted herself off the bed, but too weak to stand, she flopped back down. Frustrated, she gave in to tears. "Please, Tariq. Don't leave me," she pleaded, surrendering her power to Tariq.

Tariq ignored her sobs and pleas for him to stay. She was being ridiculous; she knew he had to go to work. Tariq stormed out the bedroom, his angry footsteps pounded down the stairs. Finally, there was the sound of the slamming front door.

In a bout of crying that lasted hours, Janelle, only seven months pregnant, worked herself into contractions.

❦❦❦

"Did I tell you I'm turning in my resignation next week?" Kapri asked Tariq as they worked side-by-side at the cash registers.

"No, you didn't mention it. Why are you quitting?" He took Kapri's announcement personally; it felt like he was being rejected.

"It's time to move on. My dad got me a summer job as receptionist at an architecture firm downtown on John F. Kennedy Boulevard. One of his friends works in construction at one of the sites. My dad said working at a prestigious firm will look good on my resume."

Tariq didn't have a resume and saw no need to have one. He wasn't ambitious and was content working at McDonald's. "When are you leaving?"

"I'm supposed to give two weeks' notice, but I'm quitting tomorrow after I pick up my check. I mean, think about it. What can they take from me? I'm just a part-time worker so they can't take away any benefits. At my new job, starting next month, I'll be working full time and I'll get full benefits."

Tariq was ashamed that he didn't know what Kapri was talking about. "What kind of benefits?" he asked.

"Vacation, sick days, paid holidays, I'll be in their credit union."

"What's a credit union?"

"Let's say I wanted to buy a car."

"Uh huh," Tariq said with great interest. He'd never even imagined owning a car.

"Well, the credit union would pay for the car and take a portion of my paycheck. I wouldn't even have to worry about paying the bill, the payment would come right off the top."

"Dag, Kapri. You're the bomb!" Tariq said in admiration. "Do you think you can get me in there?"

"I'll be on probation for the first three months, so I won't be able to help you out. But as soon as my probationary period is over, I'll be keeping an eye out. When a job opens up, I'll be sure to let you know."

Tariq looked wistful. "I wonder what kind of job I could do?"

"You could be an engineer. I don't think I want to be a court stenographer anymore. I may go to college to become an engineer. We could go to college together," Kapri suggested, brightly.

"Naw, after graduation I'm through with school. I never liked it and I'm not smart like you."

"Don't say that, Tariq; all you have to do is apply yourself. You let Janelle take up all…"

Tariq gave her a look, which caused Kapri's voice to trail off. The subject of Janelle was off limits. She was going to be the mother of his child and his wife, and despite their current problems, his loyalty remained.

The call came while Tariq was taking his first fifteen-minute-break. He rushed past Kapri with his book bag slung over his shoulder. "Tell Ms. Turner I had to go; Janelle had the baby. It's a boy!"

He was moving so fast, he didn't even hear Kapri yell, "Congratulations!"

Waiting for the bus that would take him to the hospital to see his baby son was excruciating torture. He thought about Kapri's new job and wished he had a job that offered credit to purchase a car. Kapri really had him thinking and now that he was a father, he was going to have to try to better himself.

Tariq Batista, Jr. was a beautiful child. He only weighed three and a half pounds, but he was perfectly healthy with everything intact and possessed all his fingers and toes. Janelle came home two days later, but the baby had to stay until he gained more weight.

Tariq stopped going to class and set up camp in the hospital. Janelle was still sickly and was at home confined to the bed.

In the hospital Tariq bonded with his son, held him, changed his diaper, and fed him a bottle filled with Janelle's breast milk. He tried to keep his son in the room with him for as long as the nurses allowed.

"I love you, Lil' Man. I'm gonna make sure you have something I never had. A real family. A mother and a father you can call your own. Me and your mommy…well, we're going through something right now, but we're gonna have to work it out for you. I love her, man, but she can be a trip." Tariq laughed. "You'll see."

He kissed his son's nose and grinned at the miniature version of himself. "I'm giving you my word of honor, Lil' Man. I ain't never gonna leave you."

❀❀❀

The money Janelle had been saving enabled them to move into their own apartment when the baby came home two months later. The apartment was on Rittenhouse Street in Mount Airy and the rent wasn't cheap.

Janelle had dual reasons for refusing to return to work. She didn't trust leaving the baby with strangers in a day care center; and she was breastfeeding with no idea when she'd be willing to wean the baby. So she remained at home, uncertain if she'd ever be willing to place her precious infant in, as far as she was concerned, incompetent and uncaring hands. Then there was their money situation. They still had some savings, but the money was dwindling fast. If she didn't contribute to the household funds soon, they'd be saddled with debt and on the brink of collapse. It gave her a headache to think about not being able to meet their financial commitments.

Tariq had started working double shifts at McDonald's, trying to help pay the rent and other bills. He often complained that he needed a third job just to pay for the baby's disposable diapers. Janelle wouldn't buy the cheap generic brand; the cheap diapers gave the baby a rash.

Their life together had become bittersweet. They had serious money troubles, but were blessed with a healthy child they both adored.

Janelle had already been given the green light by her doctor when she went for her six-week examination, but for some reason their sex life still wasn't up to par. Tariq was so tired from working around the clock, he didn't seem to mind the absence of sex During her difficult pregnancy, she knew that Tariq had discovered that masturbating in the shower provided quick relief.

One day Janelle was feeding the baby when the phone rang. "Hello."

"Yo, where's my little brother at?"

"Who's this?" She knew it was Shane, but was stalling while she gathered her thoughts, figuring out how to prevent him from speaking to Tariq.

"Who you think it is? How many brothers does Tariq have?"

"How'd you get the number? We've only been here a few weeks?"

"I called your mom's crib; she gave me the number. Yo, Janelle…me and Tariq are twins. Jail was the only thing that could keep us apart. You would have never got your hooks into him if I had his back like I was supposed to. Yo, I don't like you and you don't like me—that's a fact. But we gonna have to fake it for Tariq's sake. Feel me?"

Janelle sighed. She absolutely despised Shane, but was in no shape to try to battle with him. Untreated and undetected postpartum blues had her off balance, depressed, and too weak to put up a vigorous fight.

"Now where's my little brother?"

"He's at work." She paused for a second. "Aren't you going to ask how your nephew's doing? Oh, that's right, I forgot…you're just totally rude," she added sarcastically. She couldn't conceal her distaste for Shane.

"Yo, I ain't gotta ask you shit," Shane snarled. "I'll check on my nephew when I speak to Tariq." Shane hung up.

Pacing briskly with the baby in her arms, Janelle sensed trouble hovering over her home. The baby began to fret; she rocked him anxiously, wanting him to settle down so she could concentrate on the massive task of figuring out how to prevent Shane from connecting with Tariq. She had to prevent Shane from destroying their lives.

CHAPTER 22

As Tariq ate dinner, Janelle gently rocked the baby. The mood was tranquil. Then the sudden ring of the telephone broke the serenity. Sensing bad news on the other end of the phone, Janelle cradled the baby tightly and shot Tariq a look of alarm. She hadn't told him that his brother had gotten released from Barney Hills and was back in town. Agitated, Janelle started rocking the baby fast.

Tariq strode from the kitchen to the living room and picked up the phone. "Yeah," he said, still chewing a piece of baked chicken.

"This is the front desk, you have a visitor—Shane Batista. Should I send him up?"

Tariq almost choked on the chicken. "Yeah, send him up," Tariq said, grinning from ear to ear. "Shane is home!" he said to Janelle and then ran out of the apartment and down the hall to the elevator.

A few minutes later, Janelle heard the whooping and hollering though their apartment was quite a distance from the elevator. As the voices grew closer, she also heard the distinct voice of a female.

Tariq, Shane, and two other shady characters, a thug and a hot-to-trot ride–or-die-chick, entered the apartment. Janelle bristled.

"Janelle, you already met Shane. This is Shane's friend Brick and his girl, Misty."

"Hi, have a seat," Janelle mumbled in a defeated tone.

"Ooo. Can I hold the baby?" the young woman named Misty asked. Janelle noted that Misty, unreasonably pretty, was dressed in designer everything from her Von Dutch cap down to her Von Dutch sneakers. Long, dark-brown hair trailed down her back. She had a cute little body and was far too attractive to be in Tariq's presence while Janelle was in her current incapacitated condition.

The petite little nymphet looked like she wore a size zero. She wore a short tank top that exposed a flat tummy and a navel from which a diamond heart-shaped earring dangled.

The heart shimmered as Misty slithered over to Janelle. She was an unkind reminder of Janelle's recently acquired stretch marks and sagging tits. Having the baby had taken away something vital to her womanhood. She knew she'd never been a beauty queen, but her body had always been a source of pride. Breastfeeding was wreaking havoc on her once uplifted bosom. Her body was a mess now, too; there was nothing that made her special.

She thought about her situation and had to admit that her thoughts weren't entirely true. She had a beautiful baby and a gorgeous man. In a warped way, Janelle was grateful to Misty. Seeing Misty made her remember that nasty skanks were still out there waiting to pounce on Tariq. She made a mental note to tighten her reign on Tariq. Janelle didn't care how many raving beauties pranced around her; she'd make sure his level of commitment to her and Lil' Man never changed. There was no way she'd ever find herself in the position of clinging to their relationship more tightly than he. Tariq had to be kept in his place at all times.

Reluctantly, Janelle handed the baby over to Misty. She had one eye on Misty to make sure she held the baby right; the other eye was on Tariq to make sure he wasn't eyeballing Misty.

In an instant, Janelle determined it was time to return to the work force. Her precious son would have to be placed in day care. Looking and feeling good about herself required more money than Tariq was bringing in. In addition to going back to work, Janelle decided in that moment to make use of the apartment complex's fitness center.

Carrying the baby, Misty sashayed her little butt over to the men and offered Shane and Brick a peek at the sleeping child. "He looks just like you, Tariq," Misty said, and then looked back at Janelle. "No offense, but I don't see you in him at all."

"Well, he's mine," Janelle said testily. She'd already received enough sidelong glances from people at the pediatrician's office and other places. People looked suspiciously from her to her baby as if she'd stolen someone's child. Being insulted in her own home was an unexpected blow.

"So, how does it feel being a father, man?" Shane's friend Brick asked. Brick was tall and thick. He was a mountain of a man with a nasty scar running down his forehead. He and Misty looked like Beauty and the Beast. Misty was too pretty to be with him. They looked ill-matched just like she and Tariq, Janelle thought to herself. She would have felt more secure if Misty had been introduced as Shane's girl. Shane was good-looking and confident enough to keep Misty from wandering. She wasn't sure if that ugly Brick character could control the little ho and keep her away from Tariq.

Despite her ill feelings toward Shane, there was no denying that he was handsome. Disturbingly handsome. And sexy as hell. And he knew it, which made Janelle livid. It also infuriated her that he treated her like something he'd scrape off the bottom of his shoe.

"Being a father feels good. Real good," Tariq admitted, beaming at Shane. The look he gave his brother was one of near worship. Janelle felt disgusted.

"We should celebrate. I missed the wedding…"

"Oh we didn't really have a wedding, we just went to city hall," Tariq explained.

"That's still important. It was your big day; I'm sorry I missed it. But now that I'm out, I won't be missing any more important events. And that's real rap," Shane said with a head nod.

"Is it time to give him his present?" Misty asked excitedly.

Brick gave her a look. "Why you spoil the surprise?"

She covered her mouth and widened her eyes in an affected way that made her look childlike and adorable—as if her good looks pardoned her social blunders. "My bad. Forgive me. Now, give him his present," the doll-like young woman said bossily.

Janelle could have slapped the look of pride off Tariq's face. He hadn't had so much attention bestowed upon him since the baby was born. The nurses at the hospital had doted on him; some even flirted right in Janelle's face.

Shane nodded to Misty who looked like she was ready to jump up and down with joy. She flipped open her Prada bag and took out a card and gave it to Tariq.

Tariq respectfully presented the card to Janelle. It was a congratulatory card, addressed to Tariq only. The word *Fatherhood* was embossed in bold letters on the front of the card. Inside, there were five one-hundred-dollar bills. The card was signed by Shane, Brick, and Misty.

Janelle sucked her teeth as Tariq was pulled away from her and gripped in a group hug. Ignored and apparently undeserving of any congratulatory wishes, Janelle glared at Shane. She held him responsible for the blatant disrespect. She caught a fleeting glimpse of triumph on Shane's face. Her hatred for Tariq's brother was palpable. Someday, she vowed silently, Shane Batista was going to pay for treating her like a social outcast in her own home.

"So where you staying, man?" Tariq asked Shane.

"I'm in between places right now. Brick and Misty stay over in West with Misty's mom. I crash on the couch and, you know…" His voice trailed off as he assumed a cocky stance and expression. "I have a couple of female friends that I crash with from time to time," Shane said with much bravado.

Worry lines formed on Tariq's forehead. "Man, if you need a place to stay, you can always stay here." He peered anxiously over at Janelle. He nodded at her, as if to prompt her to pipe in with an endorsement.

Ignoring Tariq, Janelle kept her focus on her son and fiddled with the pacifier that had slipped from the sleeping child's lips.

"Don't worry about me, big poppa, I'm straight," Shane said, affectionately ruffling his brother's curly hair. "We want you to come out with us and celebrate, but since you're the one with all the money, you have to buy the drinks."

Shane and his partners in crime waited in the lobby while Tariq tried to placate Janelle.

"Tariq, how you gonna let your brother and his friends disrespect me like that? And now you want to leave me here all by myself? That's not right, Tariq, and you know it." She got up and started pacing with the baby in her arms.

"I just want to spend some time with my brother. I won't be out long." Tariq peeled off one of the bills. "Here, hold the rest of the money, so I don't go buck wild."

Janelle snatched the money from Tariq and rolled her eyes at him.

"Baby, stop acting like this. I have to get up early for work, so you know I won't be out too late. Chill, all right?"

"Chill!" Janelle reared back, offended. "Now you starting to talk like your brother. Please don't start bringing your brother's ways into our home."

The veins in Tariq's neck stood out. "Stop talking about my brother like he's some kind of monster." Tariq's words came out in a violent rush that made Janelle pause. She folded the four hundred dollars and turned her back to Tariq.

❈❈❈

Reeking of alcohol, Tariq stumbled into the apartment at three o'clock in the morning. Tariq had never had a drink in his life. Too drunk to take off his clothes, he laid across the bed. He passed out the moment his head hit the pillow.

Janelle pulled off his shoes and then his pants. She scowled at his boxers. They were twisted in an odd way and there was something else about them that looked strange. She worked the boxers over his hips, down his legs, and snatched them off his feet.

Hardened stains were on the inside at the slit; yellowish-colored stains were also smeared on the inside of both legs.

"Tariq!" She shook him roughly. "Tariq! What the hell is this?" She held up the incriminating drawers, pinched between her fingers.

Tariq opened one eye and mumbled, "I must have cum on myself."

"What? You were out there fucking some skank?"

"No," he said sleepily. "We went out to a strip club to celebrate. I wasn't doing nothing but getting lap dances. That's all," he said, and fell asleep.

Janelle sat on the side of the bed and held her head in her hands. That fucking Shane had her husband out in a titty bar with nasty whores rubbing their funky asses on his dick.

This is it; I have to get back my control. I don't know how I let the tables turn. I gave this ungrateful bastard a baby and now he thinks he can treat me like shit.

She didn't know how she was going to do it, but somehow she'd find a way to get Tariq back under her thumb—back like he used to be. And then she'd figure out a way to hurt him—to hurt both him and his shady brother for treating her so unkind.

She trembled with excitement at the thought of revenge.

CHAPTER 23

Along with an exotic dancer named Star, Brick, Misty, Shane, and Tariq had all piled into Brick's borrowed car. After dropping Tariq off, Brick weaved wildly through traffic, swerving like a drunk. He struggled to steer the car toward Star's apartment on Pulaski Avenue.

"Do you mind if my friends crash at your place? My man's too messed up to drive." Shane asked the dancer, with a worried gaze fixed on Brick.

"Sure, if they don't mind sleeping in the living room. I only have one bedroom."

"That's cool," he responded and then scowled at his friend. "Yo, Brick. You want me to drive, man?" Shane shouted.

"Naw, I'm straight, man. I got this." Brick's words came out slurred.

"He ain't got shit," Misty interjected. "Pull over, Brick; let Shane drive."

Jumping the curb when he pulled over, Brick hit the brakes. "Damn, that was fucked up," he said, cussing as if the car was at fault.

Shane took the driver's seat. Misty got in the back with Star while Brick slid drunkenly into the passenger seat.

"You dance real good." Misty sidled next to Star. "I wish I could dance like that."

"It ain't even about dancing; it's working your body like you getting some good dick. Anybody can do it."

"Yeah, but I'd be so scared to take off my clothes like that." Misty made her voice sound small, like the voice of a little girl.

"Girl, as pretty and young as you are…" Star paused and shook her head as if Misty had no idea of the untapped goldmine she possessed. "Girl, you wouldn't even have to work up a sweat. The only thing you'd have to do is come up on stage, swivel your little hips, and rub your crotch. If you showed those perverts just a little bit of tits, they'd break their necks to stuff your thong with cash."

"For real!"

Star nodded with a smile.

"But is it worth it? You know…do you make enough to really get up there and take off your clothes?"

"If you get some lap dances in to supplement what you get on stage, you can make out pretty good. Like tonight. Here it is a Monday night. Most people don't think of Monday as a money night. But I made out pretty good."

Misty's dark, round eyes grew large; her heavy silky lashes fluttered with interest. "So you're saying this is a career I could think about getting into and I could make enough green to survive?"

"Survive! Girl, stop playin'. I made three hundred in lap dances and a buck twenty on stage. On a Monday night! That ought to tell you that you can make some nice change."

"Do you think you could get me in there?" Misty asked, her voice filled with hope.

"Um. I can put in a good word, but you're still gonna have to audition for the manager. I'll give Shane my number; give me a call tomorrow and I'll try to set something up."

"Oh, that's so nice. Thank you," Misty gushed.

Star was tall and slender. She looked to be in her mid to late twenties. She wore a curly ponytail and had a nice-looking face. Her body wasn't spectacular but she worked it so well, the men forgot that they'd been initially disappointed when she turned around and revealed an ass so flat it looked like someone had beaten it with a board.

"Right there," Star said, pointing. "Pull up behind that white van."

Misty and Star walked together like two best girlfriends while Shane held up Brick, who was so drunk he could hardly stand up.

Star waved to her leather sofa, indicating that Brick could lie down there.

"Oh, hell no," Misty said. "I'm sleeping on the couch; let his drunk ass sleep on the floor." Everyone laughed at Brick's expense.

Shane tried to ease the big man down to the floor, but unable to hold the dead weight any longer, Shane dropped his friend. Brick's body hit the floor with a great thump. Brick lay sprawled, but didn't awaken, which caused more titters of laugher.

"I'm sorry I don't have an extra blanket, but I have plenty of clean sheets," Star said, her faced fixed in an apologetic expression.

"That'll work. Girl, I'm so tired I'm gonna pass out in about five minutes," Misty informed Star as she pulled off her sneakers and make herself comfortable on the leather sofa.

She threw a sneaker at Brick when he began to snore. They all erupted into more laughter when, after getting clunked in the head with Misty's sneaker, Brick's snoring grew even louder.

Shane and the willowy exotic dancer went into her bedroom and in a matter of minutes, Shane had Star hitting high notes, chanting, praying, and begging for more. Her cries of passion continued until the sun lit up the bedroom. Satisfied, Star fell asleep in Shane's arms, wearing a contented smile that looked as if it were permanently in place.

Shane woke her up around nine in the morning, "Baby, I gotta go. Can I get your number? You know I want to see you again." He was holding a cell phone.

"Why you gotta leave?" she asked, lifting her head slightly.

"I'll be back tonight if I can borrow my man's car."

"Okay." Star gave Shane her number, reciting each number slowly and deliberately. Shane pressed the numbers, each button making a different musical sound. "All right, baby. I got you on lock."

Shane kissed her and hugged her tight. Contentedly, Star turned over and snuggled into her pillow. "Damn, I hate to leave you," he said, patting her flat buttocks. "You better have that ass ready for me tonight."

She smiled dreamily and went back to sleep.

In the car, Misty counted the money that Shane had lifted from Star's purse.

"That bitch can lie," Misty accused and sucked her teeth. "This is only three hundred and fifty dollars; she said she made four twenty."

"It's cool, though," Brick said, grinning. "I gripped her jewelry box." Brick displayed a blue wooden musical box.

"Now, that's what I'm talkin' about. You go, boy!" Misty squealed with glee. She sat in the backseat, but stretched her arm across the front seat to investigate the pieces inside the jewelry box.

"Yo, stop grabbing everything," Shane said, giving Misty an evil look.

"Y'all dumb asses don't know fake stuff from real, so hand me the muthafuckin' jewelry box," Misty replied, snatching the jewelry box from Brick.

"And your violent ass better not hit me with your stinkin' sneaker no more," Brick said, laughing. "Won't even let a black man get his snore on."

They all let out big guffaws. "Damn, you was convincin' like a muthafucker when you be playin' your drunk role," Misty complimented him.

"That's how niggas get robbed. They be thinkin' I'm twisted, but I be all up in they shit, taking everything," Brick bragged.

More laughter followed and then Misty took out a sparkly tennis bracelet and solemnly handed it to Shane.

"Aw shit. This jawn is worth some money. That bling is about three or four carats, right, Misty?"

"Look at it real good, Shane. You know that dancin' bitch can't afford no real bling. Chips maybe, but not three or four carats. "

Shane held it in his palm as if weighing the bracelet. "It's heavy; it's blinging like crazy. It looks real to me."

"Turn it over."

Shane turned it over and shrugged.

"That shit is set in silver." Misty sucked her teeth in disgust. "Real diamonds are not set in no damn silver. Fucking fake-ass bitch!"

"Well maybe we can sell it to some knucklehead who don't know no better. How much you think we can get?" Brick asked.

"I don't know. Let's see what else is in here." Misty rifled through the seemingly worthless pieces of jewelry. She held up a pair of diamond earrings. "These look real?" she asked, contemptuously.

"Damn, I don't know. Just hand me the fuckin' jewelry box," Shane suggested.

Misty sucked her teeth and shoved the box toward Shane. He looked through it and then, shaking his head in disgust, he gave the jewelry box back to Misty.

"So what did you get, Miss Know It All?" Brick asked.

"Man, I clipped that bitch in the backseat of the car last night." Misty proudly held up a wallet and extracted two credit cards. "Now let's go spend some money before that lap dancin' ho wakes up and starts canceling these credit cards. Yeah, she's gonna be madder than a muthafucker when she finds out how much Shane's dick cost her."

Headed for the Gallery Mall, Brick sped out of Germantown, Misty threw the jewelry box out the window.

"Whatchu do that for?" Brick asked, astonished.

"There wasn't nothing but a bunch of worthless costume jewelry in there. The box was wooden; that should have told you something."

"She ain't have no gold chains or nothing in there?" Brick asked, obviously disappointed.

"She ain't have nothin' but a bunch of bullshit in there. But don't worry, baby. We gon' see how much she got on these cards. I hope she got enough for a shopping spree for all of us."

Twenty minutes later, Shane and Brick hung out in the food court while Misty tested one of the cards at a woman's boutique. She met up with them swinging two bags.

"Look at this greedy bitch, she done bought up the whole store." Brick's gruff voice carried, causing diners to turn their heads toward Misty.

"Okay, genius. Go ahead and bring a lot of attention to us." Misty sat down and took a bite of Brick's sandwich.

"So how much is on the cards?" Shane inquired.

Misty shrugged. "No way to tell unless I have her PIN number. But here's how we can work it. Y'all can't use a female's credit card, so go look around and see what you like. Go in separate stores. Then come tell me and I'll go make the purchases."

Shane nodded.

"Sounds like a plan," Brick agreed, bobbing his head up and down as he gobbled down his food.

The two men got up to do some window shopping. Misty stuck out her hand.

"Split the cash, Shane. I know you don't think you're keeping that hooker's money all to yourself."

"I did the work, didn't I?"

"Oh, that's how we're playin' now? Okay, I didn't know the rules. But I'll remember the next time y'all want me to lure some nut to a hotel or some dark alley somewhere. Uh huh. I'm sure gonna remember this shit." There was no mistaking the threat behind Misty's words.

Slowly, Shane pulled out the knot and gave Misty and Brick one hundred dollars apiece. "Y'all know I was just playin'." He laughed sheepishly.

"I don't know. You can be real shiesty when you wanna be." Misty gave him a smile and hopped up from her seat. With her two bags hanging from the crook of her arm, she went to investigate the myriad of choices in the mall's food court.

During the drive back to West Philly, the trio was exhausted. "Y'all feel like stopping for a minute so we can hollah at Wayne Gee?" Shane asked. Wayne Gee was a friend as well as their weed connection.

"We'll have to hollah at the Gee man later," Misty said, shaking her head. "I'm too tired to stop anywhere."

There wasn't much conversation until they got close to the house where Shane had been staying off and on.

The red pickup truck parked in the middle of the block indicated that Paula, Shane's latest benefactor, wouldn't be able to admit him into the premises. Unfortunately, her husband was home.

Misty sucked her teeth. "What's that muthafucker doin' home?" She sighed deeply. "Oh well, I guess you'll have to come to our place. My mom's at work. You can get some sleep until she gets off and then call that bitch Paula and see what's up with her husband. Ain't he supposed to be on the road driving an eighteen-wheeler?" Misty questioned Shane.

"That's what I thought. Fuck it. I'll call her later."

Shane, Misty, and Brick piled their packages in Misty's bedroom. Her mother didn't like Brick staying there, and she'd made it abundantly clear that putting a roof over the heads of two male slackers was absolutely out of the question.

Misty locked her bedroom door. "Can't have my nosey mother all up in our business."

The three friends, too exhausted to undress, fell asleep in Misty's queen-sized bed.

❋❋❋

"Misty!" her mother yelled as she banged on her daughter's bedroom door.

"What?" Misty sat up, cracked open an eye, and looked at the clock. The red digital numbers announced that it was 8:30 and the darkened bedroom was evidence that the day had turned to evening. "Damn," Misty said, shocked that they'd slept so long.

"I know you and that Brick ain't still laying up in that bed 'sleep. Get the hell up, Misty. Brick, you, too. Both of y'all get out that bed right the hell now."

"Okay, Mom. But damn, you ain't gotta be all loud and bangin' on my door."

"Who pays the bills around here?"

Misty sighed and rolled her eyes. "All right, Mom. We're getting up now."

"I'm getting ready to go get a drink around the corner at the bar. When I get back, I want y'all up, dressed, and out!"

Brick slept through the bickering and continued to sleep.

Shane woke up instantly, stretched his sinewy body, and cut his eye at the clock. He sat up and massaged his head. "Who got the weed?" Shane sat on the edge of the bed. "Damn, my whole body hurts; cramped up in this bed with you and Brick ain't no joke."

"Me? How much room did I take up?"

"I know you tiny and all, but you sleep wild and crazy. You be moving all over the place. And that big ox," he said, pointing to Brick. "My arm is numb; feels like him and all his ten tons was laying on my shit all night." Shane grimaced as he rubbed his arm. "I need some weed."

"We didn't stop and get none, remember?" Misty reminded him. "We'll have to hollah at Wayne Gee later on."

"Damn, I don't like waking up with no weed," Shane grumbled as he worked his hands upward and began to massage the top of his head.

Shane took out his cell phone and called Paula. When she picked up, he said, "Is your old man still at the crib? No? Well next time the plans change, hit me up on my cell; give me some kind of warning. That shit was fucked up.

Yeah, aiight. I'll be over soon." He paused. "Oh, now you trying to rush me? I'll get there when I get there. Damn."

"What did she say?" Misty asked when Shane hung up.

"Said her husband's trip got delayed. But it's cool, the muthafucker's on the road now."

"For how long?"

"I don't know. Probably three or four days. I gotta take a shower. Did your mom leave yet?"

"I don't know; let me check." Misty unlocked the bedroom door. "Mom! Mom, are you still here?" She closed the door. "She must have left."

"Aiight; I'm gonna take a quick shower." They both cast a curious gaze at Brick, who had rolled over on his side.

Misty pulled open one of Brick's eyes. It was unfocused as if he were dead.

"Come on; he's out for the count. He took a couple Xanies on the way home. He ain't waking up no time soon."

Misty and Shane got in the shower together. "You know you gotta tighten me up before you go fuck that bitch." She closed the shower curtain and turned on the water.

Brick startled them when he stumbled into the bathroom. With his eyes closed, he lifted the toilet seat and began to urinate. When he finished, he didn't flush the toilet and he didn't wash his hands. Like a zombie, he went back to the bedroom.

Misty and Shane, crouched in a corner as they hid from Brick, doubled over in laughter when he left. Misty's drenched hair was plastered to her face.

"You look so beautiful right now," Shane said in a tender voice. "I really don't want to go over Paula's."

"I know you don't, Shane, but we spent all the money. You gotta go get some more." Misty washed Shane's well-developed-shoulders and back. She handed him the washcloth, which he soaped up and gently washed her small breasts, and stomach, He stopped when he got to her groin. He placed the soap and washcloth on the plastic shower rack.

Misty put a foot up on the side of the tub as Shane delicately separated the folds of her vagina, got down on his knees, and licked it clean.

CHAPTER 24

Shane walked to a Chinese take-out restaurant located in a strip mall on the corner of Fifty-Eighth Street and Baltimore Avenue. He bought a ten-dollar bag of weed from one of the young hustlers standing outside the store, then went inside the take-out spot and slid a dollar into the opening of the bullet-proof partition. Pulling open the plastic bag, he inhaled the weed, smiled, and said to the weary-eyed Chinese merchant, "Gimme a green Dutch."

Paula lived nearby on Ellsworth Street. Shane, on high alert, looked up and down the street for Paula's husband's truck before he approached the door.

Paula had on a short black, sheer mesh babydoll set with a sequined hem, cut high on the side to show off the matching thong. Ostrich feather-topped heels completed the sexy look. At thirty-eight, Paula's body looked pretty good. Thick and womanly and soft in all the right places. Shane knew Paula dug having an eighteen-year-old in her bed. She couldn't get enough of him.

The way she was all over him as soon as he crossed the threshold caused Shane to wonder if her forty-four-year-old husband probably needed a refill on his Viagra prescription.

"Damn, I missed you, baby," Paula said, pressing against Shane. She craned her neck and kissed him hungrily. "Mmm, you smell good, too," she murmured. "What's that you're wearing?"

"Mania by Armani," Shane told her and smiled proudly. The cologne he wore was one of the purchases made using the exotic dancer's credit card.

"I love a man who smells good." Standing on her toes, Paula inhaled the fragrance. Her lips brushed Shane's neck. She lifted her chin in expectation of another kiss, but instead of kissing her, Shane cupped her face and looked into her eyes intensely. "You fucked up my schedule this morning. Don't do that shit no more," he chastised irrationally.

"I'm sorry, my husband had a change of plans." She caressed Shane's arm. "You want a drink?" she asked brightly.

"You got any St. Ides?"

"No," she said with laughter. "I have vodka and rum. Do you want me to mix up something special for you?"

"Aiight. Go ahead. Hook me up. But I gotta keep my eyes on what you putting in it; can't let you slip no Mickey in my drink."

"The only Mickey I'd slip in your drink would be Spanish Fly."

"What's that?" Shane frowned. "It sounds nasty as shit."

"Oh, something they used to put in girls' drinks back in the day. Nowadays, they use Ecstasy."

"Oh, what you know about E?" Shane asked, smiling. He liked that Paula was hip to the modern-day aphrodisiac.

"I'm only thirty-eight; I still keep up with what's going on. You act like I'm seventy-eight." She didn't realize that Shane considered her ancient. Good looking or not, as far as Shane was concerned, Paula was an old-ass-broad.

While Paula mixed a concoction of vodka, rum, and pineapple juice, Shane got busy rolling a blunt.

"You gonna smoke with me?"

She wrinkled her nose up. "I would if you rolled it with regular rolling paper. I don't think I'd like smoking a cigar."

"You ain't gonna hit this with big daddy?" he inquired, cocking his head to the side.

"Big daddy! Boy, you better stop talking like that if you want me to finish mixing this drink. You're getting me so hot, my crotch is already wet," she admitted with a coy smile. "And if you don't stop giving me those sexy looks, I'm gonna be so weak, I'll probably smoke ten blunts with you if it'll make you happy."

"Just being with you makes me happy," Shane said, flashing a dazzling smile.

Blushing like an adolescent, Paula handed Shane a tall glass filled with the alcoholic mixture, took him by the hand, and led him upstairs to the bedroom she shared with her husband.

Shane sat on the side of the bed and lit the blunt. Paula sat on his lap and ran her fingers through his dark curly hair. She scratched his scalp lightly while kissing his cheek, but Shane didn't return the affection. His lips were already occupied. Inhaling deeply, he puffed the blunt.

"Is something wrong, baby?" Paula asked as she stroked the hairs on Shane's chin.

Shane blew out a cloud of aromatic smoke and shook his head.

"Yes, it is. Tell me what's the matter? Did I do or say something? Because if I did I wasn't trying to hurt your feelings or make you mad or anything."

"You ain't done nothing," he said, passing her the blunt.

She readily accepted the blunt. Being inexperienced, she inhaled too much smoke and started choking.

Shane patted her back. "You okay?"

Tears trickled down her cheeks. She held up a hand as she tried to catch her breath. "I'll be okay in a minute," she said in a raspy voice and then darted into the bathroom where she hacked, gagged, and coughed for about five minutes. Afterward, she wiped her eyes, touched up her make-up and returned to the bedroom where she attempted to resume her sexy demeanor.

Shane leaned against the headboard. Paula eyed him quizzically. "Why you staring at me?" he asked.

"It could be that I'm extremely high, but I swear—your body looks so long. it seems you're longer than the bed. Is it my imagination or are your Nikes hanging off the foot of the bed?"

Shane found her question hilarious. He erupted into a bout of laughter. It was contagious and soon Paula was giggling too.

"You high, baby. You feelin' good?" he asked, pulling her close. She smiled and nodded as she snuggled up next to him. With the TV on and the remote in his hand, Shane flicked through channels while Paula caressed his arm, rubbed his face. Her eyes adored him. Shane, however, didn't return any of Paula's intimate gestures. He averted his gaze; her look of sheer worship was comical and he didn't want to break out into another fit of laughter. So to keep himself composed, he kept his hands to himself and assumed a somber mood.

"Are you hungry? Do you want something else to drink?" Paula encouraged, her forehead wrinkled in thought.

"I'm straight," Shane responded with a slight frown and a one-shoulder shrug.

"You're awfully quiet—you're so aloof all of a sudden." Her voice trembled with anxiety. Desperate for Shane's affection, Paula ran her hand up and down his denim- covered thigh.

"I'm just chillin'," he explained calmly. Shane was well aware that Paula was ready to get busy in bed. Feigning affection in the strained atmosphere, he began to caress her shoulders.

When the first moan escaped Paula's lips, Shane withdrew his hands from her shoulders and folded them in his lap.

"What is it?" Paula asked.

"Nothing," Shane mumbled and shifted his position, which caused Paula's hand to slide off his leg. "Look, I know I'm not being good company. I got a problem—a situation I gotta deal with." Shane shook his head woefully. "I shoulda stayed home."

"What problem? What happened? Is there something I can do?"

"I don't know," he said with a heavy sigh. "See, I bought this car from a friend of mine. It ain't nothin' but a squatter, but you know, if I had my own wheel, I wouldn't have to rely on my man for a ride when I'm tryin' to get over here to see you. I could see you on the regular."

Shane paused to observe Paula. He could tell by her expression that she was flattered. "My buddy said the car needed a transmission, so I put the jawn in the shop where another friend works. My man, the mechanic, said he could fix it; he said he was only gon' charge me a buck fifty." Shane leaned forward and let out a heavy sigh. "But when I went to pick it up today, he started talking this ying yang shit about the owner being on the premises. He said with the owner hangin' around, he'd have to charge me the full price." Shane shook his head and grimaced. "I told him, I know you ain't trying to beat me, you s'posed to be my man!" Shane held out a long arm demonstratively.

Paula rubbed his arm soothingly. "So how much does he want?"

"He said he gotta charge me three hundred and sixty-five dollars." He flopped down on the bed, pretending to be frustrated. He allowed his head to bang against the headboard.

Paula tilted her head slightly, staring at Shane as she tried to absorb the situation. She continued rubbing and squeezing Shane's arm. "So you still owe him—what? Two hundred and fifteen?"

Shane looked startled by the total Paula had deducted. "No, I owe him the whole amount."

"I thought you gave him a hundred and fifty dollars."

"Yeah, but when I couldn't get the car, I got mad and went to the mall. I spent the money trying to look nice for you. See…" Shane pointed to his feet. "I caught a deal and bought these new sneakers and I bought the cologne. And…" he looked up in thought. " Oh, yeah and I bought this bag of weed for us."

Paula shook her head and smiled indulgently. *What am I going to do with you?* her loving eyes seemed to ask.

"Stop worrying; I'll give you the money." She patted Shane's knee and then reached up and hugged him, pressing into him, her body urging him to reciprocate the affection. He didn't. Trying to arouse him, she ran her fingers over the six-pack that Shane had done nothing to acquire. No sit-ups, no leg lifts. Nothing. His toned abs were just some of the many physical benefits of being young. He knew Paula was getting off on just touching him.

"Well—can you get it?" he asked, pulling away and putting a halt to her foreplay.

"Get what?" Paula tilted her head to the side.

"The money! I'm gonna call my man and tell him to meet me at the Chinese store. That way, he can start working on the car first thing in the morning."

"Didn't you say the car was ready?"

Shane didn't miss a beat. "No! I wish it was ready; I'm tired of waiting on my wheel. He said he couldn't get started until I give him the money. You know how the white man is. He always think a black man gon' try to get over." As if suddenly hit by a bright idea, Shane silenced Paula with an upward-turned index finger. "Hold up!" He pulled out his cell phone. "Let me hollah at my man." He pushed some numbers, pretending to call the fictitious mechanic, but he actually called Misty's cell phone. "Can I speak to Brick?"

"You got skills," Misty said, giving Shane his props. "Hold on a second."

"Yo, whassup," Brick greeted him.

"Yo, can you meet me at the Chinese store on Fifty-Eighth and Baltimore?" Shane made eye contact with Paula. She looked comfortable so he proceeded. "I got the money for my wheel. So what time you gon' have my shit ready?" Shane gave Paula a wink as he held the cell to his ear. "Tomorrow?" he said excitedly. "Oh, aiight!" Shane started grinning. "Okay, see you in a short."

By the time Shane hung up, Paula was out of bed and taking money out of her pocketbook. She counted out exactly three hundred and sixty-five dollars. She handed it to Shane. "Here, baby, hurry up. How long you think you're gonna be?"

"I'll be back before you can get that black negligee off. You look sexy, baby, but I wanna see that pretty body." He gave her a quick kiss, ran down the stairs and was out the door.

Brick and Misty were waiting outside the Chinese store. Shane pulled the wad of money out of his jeans pocket. "Here, Misty," he said, handing her the money. "Y'all can buy some weed, but hold about three hundred for me." Shane grinned. "Yo, that bitch was trying to get her freak on and she wasn't trying to give up no green. Talkin' some wait 'til mornin' bullshit. But you know the kid…I'm about my business. I wasn't tryin' to hear that shit."

"You going back?" Misty asked, pouting.

"Yeah, I gotta tap that ass real quick, but soon as she starts to nod, I'm gon' hit her up for whatever dough she got stashed in the crib."

Shane and Brick pounded each other's fists. Shane playfully tugged on Misty's long hair. "Ow!" Laughing, Misty bent over and picked up a small stone; she threw it at Shane. "Ooo. I'ma get you!" He picked up a discarded beer bottle and chased Misty. Careful not to aim at Misty, he hurled the bottle over her head. It hit the hood of a passing car. The car screeched to an angry stop. Howling with laughter, the three friends ran from the scene of the crime and scattered in different directions.

A few minutes later, as promised, Shane returned to Paula's house. She opened the door, still wearing the black mesh set. Kissing her, Shane picked her up and carried her up the stairs. Paula was impressed. She weighed one hundred and sixty-five pounds but in Shane's arms she felt demure and petite as if she weighed about one hundred and five.

He placed her on the bed. His mouth began on Paula's lips and then traveled down to her chest. His tongue wet the mesh fabric as he licked her C-cup breasts, arousing her until her nipples became so hard they seemed close to poking a hole through the mesh material.

Paula panted as if she hadn't had any dick in a long time, which bolstered Shane's ego and encouraged him to give one hundred percent.

He laid her down flat, and sucked and bit her nipples until she started making crazy mewing sounds. Next, he kissed her navel and abruptly stopped. "Didn't I tell you to take this shit off?"

Apparently incapable of responding verbally, Paula moaned incoherently. Shane softly bit her inner thighs and then her vagina without removing her thong. Paula tried to move the fabric to the side, but Shane pulled her hand away and began to lick the thin mesh fabric between her legs. Ever so often his tongue would touch upon skin. Her body quivered and shook with each touch of his tongue.

Shane raised his head. "Tell me what you want me to kiss."

Paula gasped and pointed to the hot spot between her legs.

"Tell me," Shane insisted. "Tell me what you want me to kiss. Talk to me, baby. Talk to big daddy. Where do you want me to put these chocolate lips?"

"All over me, I want to feel them all over me," she said, panting for breath.

Shane shook his head. "Aiight. Dig…you can only get these lips on one place. Do you want me to choose what I wanna suck?"

Paula nodded her head, happy that she didn't have to tell him what she wanted.

Shane's voice was low. He brought his lips close to her ear. "So if I choose to suck your elbow, you gonna be okay with that?"

"No," she whimpered.

"So whatchu want me to suck?"

"My pussy," she finally admitted, her voice an urgent whisper, her face flushed in embarrassment.

"You gon' let me lick your cat after I suck it?"

"Oh yes, baby. Please." Paula's breathing deepened; her body twisted in agony.

"What about your pussy hole? You want some tongue deep down in that hole?"

All Paula could do was moan and nod her head, *yes!*

And Shane did more than lick and suck. He nibbled on her outer lips, he softly bit the inner lips, he sucked her clit and rubbed his tongue across the sensitive flesh inside her vagina.

Then he started coming out of his clothes and it was a truly magnificent sight.

Having caught her breath, Paula asked, "Can I film us making love?"

"I ain't never made no porn video—but aiight, I'm with it. I don't mind steamin' up the screen." Shane shed his clothes and walked over to the mirror. With his fingers interlocked behind his head, he turned his torso from side to side and appraised his image. He could see Paula, standing behind him. Judging by the grin on her face, she liked Shane's image also.

CHAPTER 25

For the benefit of the camera, Shane and Paula made phony exaggerated sounds of ecstasy. Their movements were stiff and awkward. "I'm not feelin' this shit. Come on, baby, forget about the camera—fuck me like you mean it," Shane told Paula, cupping her face and staring into her eyes.

Paula began to relax after Shane kissed her. He kissed her tenderly, raking his fingers through her hair, murmuring, "I dig the shit outta you; you got me strung, Paula." He scowled. His tone was gruff and accusing, intimating that his inability to control his emotions was upsetting. "I ain't mean to catch no feelings—not like this," Shane said breathing hard as he caressed her body.

"What kind of feelings?"

Shane's face crumpled; he shrugged helplessly. "This shit is deep; it might be love. I don't know...I ain't never felt like this before," he admitted reluctantly and then gave Paula a tortured look. Shane prided himself on his acting ability so he grimaced again to convey his severe discomfort with his inconveniently timed but overpowering emotion.

"I love you, girl," he muttered and dropped his head sorrowfully.

"Oh, baby; it's okay," Paula cooed. "It's okay to feel love." She stroked the side of Shane's face; her index finger traveled down to the dimple in Shane's chin. "I love you, too; I fell hard the first time we made love," she admitted, smiling as if revealing something Shane didn't already know.

"Come 'ere, lil' girl," he mumbled, wrapping Paula tightly in his arms. He could just imagine the giant grin on her face. Paula got all giggly whenever he called her, *lil' girl*. Made her feel young, Shane presumed.

"Dayum!" Shane exclaimed when he slipped a finger in Paula's pussy. "You leaking like crazy; you want big daddy right now?"

Paula moaned a response and climbed on top of Shane; she urgently guided him inside her. Shane appreciated that she'd cut to the chase, relieving him of the burden of tedious foreplay.

Paula rode Shane's dick. Holding her around her waist, Shane suddenly sat up. He slid off the bed with Paula still attached. Standing next to the bed, Shane started doing squats—taking a loudly moaning Paula along for the ride.

She gave a tiny cry and held on to Shane's shoulders. "Baby, nobody can do me like this. You have the best dick in the world. I love you!" she proclaimed as she clawed his back."

Shane was quiet. He had to concentrate on holding on to all one hundred and sixty-five pounds of Paula while he continued to fuck her and do squats simultaneously. He offered only grunts in response to her passionate outbursts.

Paula bit Shane's shoulder while emitting tiny murmurs that escalated to loud shouting. Shane felt Paula's inner muscles contracting; she gave a shudder and a long moan. He stood up and walked her over to the bed. He gently placed her onto the bed. Tears rose in Paula's eyes but Shane didn't have time for that sensitive shit; it was time for him to bust a nut and be out! He plunged inside hard and fast and in less than a minute his face crinkled; he groaned violently. "Dayum, girl. Whatchu doin' to me?" Once again he implied that Paula was so special, she'd forced him to surrender to love.

They lay together for a while, breathing hard and smiling at each other. Giving Shane a look of pure adoration, Paula wiped the perspiration from his brow.

"Damn, baby. Whassup? You tryin' to turn me out or something?" Shane asked, with his lips poked out, and furrowed brow.

"Turn you out? What about poor me?" she asked with a chuckle. "I'm beyond turned out; I'm a lost cause. I'm done. You got me, Shane; you own this pussy. It's going to be real hard to get rid of me."

Shane smiled knowingly. The night had turned out just as he'd wanted. "I should turn off the recorder and put it away; we don't want to leave that around. Where should I put it?"

"You're so thoughtful…so considerate. So sweet." She sat up and hugged him tight and gave him another passionate kiss. "Put it in the closet in the basement," she said, and then collapsed happily onto the pillow. There was a smile plastered on her face. She looked like she had died and gone to heaven.

When Shane returned to the bedroom, Paula was asleep, which was his queue to start pillaging. He rifled through her purse and bureau drawers, then snooped inside the bedroom closet. He poked around the top of the shelf, searching for valuables that might be secreted inside or behind several hat boxes.

He pocketed three gold and diamond bracelets. Inside the bureau drawers were so many glimmering items, Shane considering going downstairs to look for a shopping bag. He went downstairs to her kitchen and came back with a large department store bag with handles. Shane emptied out Paula's husband's jewelry drawer, which contained two diamond rings and several expensive-looking watches, and a thick wad of cash was stashed inside a tin can. Shane stuffed the money into his pocket without counting it. Next, he added Paula's jewelry to the shopping bag. He gazed at her, wondering if he could work her wedding rings off her fingers without waking her up.

He screwed up his lips in thought, but decided against that idea. Instead he ransacked another pocketbook, which was dangling on the handle of the closet door. The pocketbook was empty. Shane felt along the pocketbook's satin lining and found several secret places with green folding money inside. He promptly tucked the cash inside his other pants pocket.

Shane tiptoed down the stairs and picked up the camcorder he'd hidden behind a flower pot. Like the thief that he was, Shane exited quietly into the night.

There was a little over five hundred dollars in cash extracted from Paula's two pocketbooks; seven hundred was taken from her husband's bureau drawer.

Shane bought a half-ounce of weed and a couple bags of blow from a street-corner hustler. He bought ten blunts from an A Plus mini market and took a cab to a motel near the airport on Island Avenue.

Once settled inside the motel, he turned off his cell phone so he could party alone; he wanted peace and quiet for the remainder of the night. Misty and Brick would be aiight, they could get through one night without his company.

The next day, instead of getting in touch with Misty and Brick, Shane had his twin on his mind. He turned on his cell and punched in Tariq's number. He twisted his lips in annoyance when Janelle answered the phone.

"Can I speak to Tariq?" he said, his voice low and sullen.

"He's at work," she said, speaking in a hostile tone.

"What's the number at his job?"

Janelle sighed loudly, but gave Shane the number.

Shane called Tariq at McDonald's and arranged to meet him on his break.

"Whassup, man. What brings you out in the daylight hours? You know you're like a vampire; you don't usually come out until it's dark," Tariq said, grinning broadly when Shane arrived.

"You was on my mind, man. Pressing hard. Strong. Whassup witchu? You aiight?"

"Yeah, I'm good. I'm straight," Tariq said, nodding his head reassuringly. "Been thinking about you, too."

"Yeah? I'm not surprised…you know how we do." Shane chuckled. "Yo, I been meaning to ask you something."

"Whassup?" Tariq tilted his head.

"Whatever happened to Miz Holmes?"

"You didn't hear about what happened?"

"No, what happened to her?"

"Shane," Tariq said softly. "They said she was molesting you." Tariq lowered his head.

Shane let out a loud guffaw; he stomped his feet as his body rocked with laughter. "Who said that shit? How the fuck that old drunk gon' molest me? Eeow, now that's a nasty-ass thought." Shane wrinkled his face in disgust.

"Well, why didn't you speak up? They locked Miz Holmes up. LaDonna's mom, too." A shadow fell over Tariq's face. "At least that's what Shiree said in a letter she wrote me while I was at The Children's House."

"Miz Holmes started drinkin' all the time; I don't know how she caught them charges," Shane said, pleading innocent. "She probably said something dumb while she was drunk. You know she stopped making sense long before you got sent to the Children's Home. But I think LaDonna's boyfriend, Easy, set up her mom. He probably blamed her for letting me come over to see LaDonna."

Tariq nodded. "Yeah, he probably found out about you and LaDonna and wanted to get some kind of revenge."

"How much time did they get; do you know?"

"Man, I really don't know. But I heard Miz Holmes is out and living in some boarding home near that church she used to drag us to. I wanted to go see her because she was so nice to us, but I was just too embarrassed after everything that happened. Shiree said LaDonna's mom only had to do a couple months. She said it seems like Miss Goldie bounced right back." A worried scowl formed on Tariq's face. "You should stay away from Southwest, man. You probably got a lot of enemies around there," he cautioned Shane.

"I ain't worried 'bout no Southwest niggas." Shane patted his side pocket, indicating he was carrying a gun. "I got my burner, man. Southwest don't want no trouble from me, I'll blast them pussies in a heartbeat," Shane said with much bravado. "By the way, did you ever fuck Shiree?" Shane asked, wearing a devilish smile.

Tariq blushed. "No, it wasn't like that with her." Tariq drifted off in thought. "Anyway," he said, changing the subject, "I asked the social worker about Miz Holmes and she said you testified against her, but they didn't call on me because I was in therapy. Plus, she said I'd been through enough and testifying in court might be too much for me. I told her I didn't have nothing to testify about because I didn't know what they were talking about." Tariq looked at Shane and sighed. "Is that true? Did you go to court and testify against Miz Holmes and LaDonna's mom?"

Shane turned up his top lip in bitter denial. "That social worker's full of shit. Yeah, I went to court but it was on some trumped-up charges against me. I told you those cops put those drugs on me." Shane frowned at the memory of being falsely accused. "So what did you say about therapy?"

"They thought I was depressed. I guess I was feelin' a little sorry for myself. You know, everything happened so fast. The social worker was at our house; me and Miz Holmes were waiting for you. That social worker could tell Miz Holmes was drunk and the next thing I know, they took me back to the Children's Home…without you. We were together again for just a hot second before you got sent away for three years." Tariq sighed.

"I knew you was goin' through it; but there wasn't nothin' I could do. I tried to call you, but I didn't even know where you was at first. Then when I found out, there was all this red tape between the city and the state."

"I know. I went through it, too. The social worker was trying to act like she was trying to help, but she really wasn't doing nothing. That had to be the worst time of my life, man."

"Mine too, man. Mine, too." Shane hugged his brother. It was a tight and emotional embrace. Shane released Tariq and did the only thing he could do to make himself feel better. "Here you go, man." Shane gave Tariq three hundred dollars.

"What's this?" Tariq asked, looking at the money with a confused expression. "You just gave me money, Shane. I can't keep taking money from you."

"I always share whatever I have with you, ain't nothin' changed. I know it's got to be hard on y'all with you being the only one workin'."

"Janelle's getting ready to come back to work," Tariq said in his wife's defense. "But man…I feel bad taking more money from you when you ain't even set up in your own place. You probably could have used that five hundred on getting yourself an apartment…"

"That wasn't just from me. That was a gift from me and my crew. I'm cool, man. I'm hooking up a crib right now. But look, dawg, I'm real proud of you," Shane said, grinning. "You're somebody's pop. Now that's whassup. You the muthafuckin' man, Tariq. That's real rap."

Feeling proud but also self-conscious, Tariq smiled and cast his eyes toward the ground.

"Look, little bro, what's mine is yours and I know what's yours is mine. That little rough patch we went through wasn't about shit. I knew I was gonna make that shit right, but I couldn't do nothin' about it while I was locked up."

Tariq looked near tears. "I can't believe I treated you like that. My own brother; I'm so sorry, Shane."

"That's the power of the pussy, man. I knew what was up. Just don't let that broad chump you like that no more. You gotta control the pussy; you can't let it control you. Remember that, aiight?" He patted Tariq's back. "I gotchu, man. I got your back."

With those words ringing in his ears and an extra three hundred dollars in his pocket, Tariq returned to work feeling loved and secure. It was good to not feel afraid, which was how he'd felt ever since his son had been born. Afraid that he'd fail as a provider, as a father, as a husband, afraid he'd fail as a man.

With his true other half back in his life, he felt like a total person instead of like half a man.

CHAPTER 26
2002

The exchange between him and his brother had Shane feeling emotional and in need of something that was hard to find. Getting high and raising hell with Brick and Misty would not soothe him tonight.

Shane thought about a girl he'd met a few days before, a pretty Puerto Rican named Valencia. Valencia was hot and he had every intention of getting with her…but not tonight.

He couldn't define what he was feeling; it was a carnal urge—a yearning that he couldn't begin to analyze, but recognized as being absurd. Without allowing himself to be motivated by conscious thoughts that would deter him, Shane simply hailed a cab and hopped in. Seated comfortably in the back, he told the driver where he wanted to go. "Forty-Second and Wyalusing," Shane said, knowing there was no turning back.

"Forty-Second and Wyalusing," the driver confirmed.

"Yeah." Shane kept his eyes closed throughout the cab ride. When they reached his destination, Shane got out of the cab, paid the driver and looked over at the church. His lips curved into a satisfied smile. There was no church activity going on and therefore no prying eyes that might recognize him.

He trotted up the stairs to the boarding home and rang the bell. An old woman peeked through the peephole. "Whatchu want?" the woman yelled.

"I came to see my mother."

"Who's your mother?" the old woman wanted to know.

"Miz Holmes, but don't tell her. It's a surprise. I've been over in Iraq; I just got home."

The elderly woman smiled and nodded in approval as she started unlocking the multiple locks on the door.

The boarding home held a musky odor that Shane associated with old people, but he wouldn't be deterred by an unpleasant scent. "Which room?" he asked in an excited whisper.

"Upstairs. First room on the left," the woman also spoke in a conspiratorial whisper.

Shane climbed the stairs. He knocked on the door softly. "Who is it?" asked a familiar female voice.

"It's me, Mom. Open the door."

The door opened instantly. His foster mother, Dolores Holmes, stood wearing a printed housedress, eyes widened. Blinking back tears, she opened her arms to Shane. "My boy," she cried. "My boy."

Shane fell into her embrace. "I'm sorry, Mom," he said, his voice pained. "I didn't know it would end up like that."

"I know, honey pie," she said, patting him. "I prayed for you every day." She let him go and wobbled over to the sofa. The years had not been kind and she had gained a tremendous amount of weight.

Exhausted from the walk to the sofa, Ms. Holmes gasped for breath. Shane sat next to her and tenderly rubbed her back while she tried to catch her breath.

"You had a nice house, Mom. This ain't right. I'm gonna get you out of here." He set his chin firmly, impressing the sincerity of his words upon her.

"It's all right. I'm grateful for what the church does for me. They never believed that I was a fallen woman; they blamed everything on you. But I told them the real culprit was Satan. He had a hold on me and you."

"I never thought about it like that. You think it was the devil?"

"Oh yes. He's always busy."

"And you never blamed me?"

"Never. We were both under his power. I tried to fight it but it wasn't nothing I could do. But he done loosened his grip off me now. I don't drink no more of them evil spirits. I'm back in good standing with the church."

"But what about me, Mom? I need you. You gon' turn your back on me?"

Ms. Holmes closed her eyes and mumbled a prayer. "You almost grown.

You don't need me no more." Ms. Holmes shut her eyes again and shook her head determinedly. "No, you don't need me no more."

"Yes I do," he shouted. "You the only mother I ever had."

She rested her head on the back of the sofa and pondered his words.

"I guess some things are just unexplainable. And when I meet my Maker, He can tell me if I did wrong. But I don't think so. I never had no kids and you lost your mother. The good Lord put us together but it was Satan that got everything all confused."

"What's done is done, Mom. We can't change it. You say I'm almost grown and that might be true but I still need you to be my mom." He started crying, mournful sobs that would not stop.

Ms. Holmes sighed in resignation and pulled Shane's head to her bosom and began to smooth the back of his curly hair. Still weeping, Shane began unbuttoning her blouse. With her chest exposed, he opened his mouth wide as his lips went from one huge breast to the other, licking and slobbering as he desperately sought solace, satisfaction. Redemption.

Panting hard, Shane pulled up her skirt and tugged on her enormous panties. Tears of release fell from his eyes as he mounted her and eased his penis inside. With every stroke, he promised her complete devotion. "I swear. I love you, Mom. I'm gonna treat you right; I'm gonna be a good son."

❈❈❈

He easily acquired the money he needed. He gave the pretty Puerto Rican a sob story before he served her some dick. He got some additional cash by serving as lookout while Brick stepped out of the shadows and surprised a couple of suckers who were withdrawing money from an ATM, situated in a desolate location.

He also had his secret place. Not one soul—not Tariq, Misty, Brick, or any of his many female benefactors knew that Shane had taken up residence in a cozy little apartment. No one would ever dream that Shane was now leading a double life.

It was a very small furnished apartment with just one bedroom. The wide-screen TV was the only thing Shane purchased. It took up most of the space in the living room. Ms. Holmes loved it. The surround sound was an extra perk as she had become somewhat hard of hearing. When she wasn't watching TV she was reading the Bible or cooking. There was lots of food that had to be stored in the freezer when Shane didn't come home, which was often.

Shane still crashed with Misty and Brick and the ever-growing list of female conquests. But he believed in taking care of home; the refrigerator and cabinets in the apartment were well stocked and there was plenty of extra cash left in the bureau drawers.

The new neighbors thought Shane was Ms. Holmes's grandson. "How you doing, young man?" asked one nosey neighbor. "And how's your grandmother?"

"That ain't my grandmother; that's my mother," Shane corrected the man with a scowl.

He could stay away for days at a time. When he returned there were no questions asked and no attitude problem, just an abundance of love and affection. When he crawled into bed and lay beside the only woman who was capable of giving him the thing he really needed, Shane was truly at peace.

The thing that Dolores Holmes gave that every other woman in his life was incapable of giving him was motherly love.

CHAPTER 27

The video camera Shane had stolen from Paula would be a good gift for Tariq. He could film the baby's progress. Keep a record that would last a lifetime. Shane and Tariq didn't even have any photographs of themselves as babies or small children. Any school photos taken during their early years in Children's Home had gotten lost in the shuffle of moving here and there.

But before he passed the camera on to Tariq, he wanted to show Misty and Brick his porno debut.

"Check this out, y'all," he said, handing Misty the camera. "I don't have the instructions so I don't know how to put it on DVD; you have to check it out on the camera."

With one eye closed, Misty peered into the lens. "Ooo, Shane!"

"What?" Brick asked.

"Shane filmed him and that lady fucking. Hmph! Her body ain't bad for an old jawn, but she don't look as good as I do," Misty remarked with a pout.

"Let me see!" Brick asked, reaching for the camera.

"Wait your turn." Misty plopped down on the sofa and got comfortable. Shane was watching her, checking out her reaction. She seemed mesmerized. "Brick, I don't know if you want to see this," she said with a sly grin.

"Why not?"

"Because Shane is hung like a damn horse." She patted Brick's arm. "You might get jealous, baby."

"His dick ain't bigger than mine!" Brick proclaimed. "Trust me," he said, laughing. "I done took many a shower with this nigga up at Barney Hills and he's kind of lacking in the dick department."

"Yo, dawg. You can't measure the size of a man's pipe when it's all shriveled up in the shower."

"I'm just saying," Brick said. "Ain't no way yours is bigger than mine because I'm laying down pipe with ten thick inches."

Shane looked at Misty.

"Don't look at me."

"Why not? You the only one that can verify what kind of dick this lying nigga is really slinging."

Misty handed the camera to Brick. "He ain't lying. He might even be eleven inches. I ain't measured him in a while." She gave Shane a catty smile. "You looked like you were having a good time with Miss Paula. That shit didn't look like work at all."

"It's not supposed to look like work," he said sullenly, perturbed over her insinuating that Brick had a bigger dick.

"I got an idea." Misty announced. "We need to do something useful with that video."

"Like what?" Suddenly more interested in what Misty had to say than watching another man fuck, Brick laid the camera down.

"After the way Shane robbed his girlfriend, it's not like he can go back for seconds. So we could keep a steady cash flow by telling her we're gonna give the tape to her husband."

"Aw shit, yeah!" Brick jumped up, excited.

"We could make her pay once a week or every two weeks, depending on how her husband gets paid."

"Blackmail ain't no joke, Misty. We could all do some serious time."

"That bitch ain't gonna call no cops. And anyway, how she gonna prove who's blackmailing her?"

"When Shane picks up the money," Brick said.

"Wrong answer. Shane ain't picking up no money. I'm gonna use my phony ID and get a post office box. Then I'm gonna call Miss Paula and accuse her of fucking with my man. After I tell her about the proof I have, that bitch will be ready to give me the shirt off her back."

Brick and Shane smiled in agreement. There was no denying it, Misty was devious and smart. No one would expect that a sweet-faced little child/woman like her could be so gansta.

"I'm gonna call her first and feel her out. Then I'll set up the post office box tomorrow. Shit, depending on what she's working with, this could be a regular source of income."

"Aiight. You got it, Misty. Me and Brick gon' let you handle this one."

"Give me her number, Shane. But I need privacy to really put my thing down. I'll call her when y'all go cop some weed." Misty looked at the clock. "Y'all should go now, my mom will be home in a couple hours."

Shane gave Misty the number, which she wrote down. They all left the house together because Misty didn't want to use her house phone to engage in blackmail.

Using a pay phone inside a Laundromat on Baltimore Avenue, Misty called Paula.

"Hey whassup, Paula. How you doin,' girl?"

"I'm fine. Who's this?"

"This is Shane's wife."

The line went silent. "Are you still there, Paula?"

Paula cleared her throat. "Um, I didn't know Shane had a wife."

"Oh no? Not only does he have a wife, he has a very angry wife. A wife that just got finished looking at a video of you fucking him and sucking his dick. Now how do you think seeing that shit made me feel?"

There was silence.

"Oh, you ain't got shit to say? Well, let me tell you something, Paula. I'm a jealous bitch and right now I'm fired up and ready to kick some ass." Misty let out a deep breath. "But I'm too cute for all that, so you can calm the fuck down. Damn, I can hear your heart pounding all the way over here. Don't worry, I'm not gonna drive over to Ellsworth Street. Not yet," Misty said threateningly.

Paula gasped.

"Yeah, bitch. I know where you live," Misty taunted. "You better hope I don't come over there and blow up your crib."

"How do you know where I live?"

"My husband tells me everything! He told me he only fucked you so you would give him the money to get *my* transmission fixed. Oops! Did he tell you he needed the money for *his* car? Yeah, well that was just game. When he left you, he came straight to me and gave me the money. I let him go back to your crib because he lied and told me y'all was just going to talk." Misty paused. "I know…I know. I should have known better because I'm just as good looking as my husband and dudes be trying to pay to fuck me, too. Old dudes and young ones be all up in my grille trying to pay me the same way you like paying to be with my fine-ass husband." Misty paused and let her words sink in.

"I really didn't know Shane was married," Paula said apologetically.

"Yeah, well now you know. So I figured…you being all old and washed up…I figured you just wanted some eye candy. Can't say I blame you, with Mr.…um…what's your husband's name? You know, the ugly dude who drives the red truck. Mr. What's His Name ain't too easy on the eyes, is he? With an ugly-ass man like that coming home trying to hit it, I can't say I blame you for trying to steal yourself some pretty dick. But you know what, Paula? There's a penalty for accepting stolen goods."

"What do you want?" Paula's voice sounded anguished.

"I've already made three copies of the tape. One for your husband, one for your next-door neighbor, and one for your son. Your son's away at college, isn't he?"

Paula started crying. "Don't do this to me. What do you want?" she screamed.

"Let's put it this way…how much can you afford to pay—by the week?"

"You want me to give you money every week?"

"I didn't stutter."

"I'm not sure. This is such a surprise. I. . ."

"All right, " Misty said abruptly. "You figure it out; I'll be calling you back in three days. Don't disappoint me. Okay, sweetie?" Misty said with mocking laughter. "Oh, and by the way, I dug that black babydoll shit you had on. Shane liked it, too. He told me to find out where you bought it." Misty paused, waiting for Paula to respond. Paula said nothing; she sniffled and made annoying whining sounds.

Pissed off by Paula's sniveling, Misty went for the jugular. "You should be ashamed of yourself for messing with my husband. Bitch, you're old enough to be his mother!" Misty scolded. "Anyway," she said in a softer tone, "Shane said that baby doll shit will look way better on me than it did on your big ass." She laughed. "Now where the fuck did you get it?"

Still sniffling, Paula said, "I don't remember where I bought it."

"Yeah, well, think real hard and come up with an answer when I hit you up in three days. Smooches." Misty made a kissing sound and hung up.

Misty began to jump up and down like an excited child when she saw Shane and Brick approaching. "I did it. That bitch is scared as shit."

"What she say?" Brick asked.

"She said she gonna come up with the money. I'm gonna call her back in three days. In the meantime, I gotta fill out the paperwork for the post office box. I sure hope it don't take a long time to get that shit hooked up."

As the trio stood on the corner, laughing it up, a car filled with Hispanics of all ages—grandparents, teenagers, little kids, and a very pretty Hispanic woman—pulled up to the curb.

"Is that him, Valencia?" asked a mean-looking teen who jumped out of the car wielding a lead pipe.

"Yeah, that's the muthafucker," yelled Valencia, her eyes blazing as she climbed out of the backseat. She stood on the pavement with her arms folded. Her face was so contorted with rage, her beauty was completely disguised.

Shane stepped forward. "Yeah, whassup?"

"You know what you did, man. You borrowed money from my sister and didn't pay it back." There was a chorus of angry murmurs inside the car.

"So! Whatchu gonna do about it?" Misty asked brazenly. Pointing the index finger of both hands, she gestured confrontationally.

"Yo, Mami. This ain't about you," the teen said, giving Misty the brush-off.

"Why ain't it?" Misty snarled. "You don't roll up on my crew with a car fulla Ricans and expect us to back down. Fuck that." She shot a hateful look toward Valencia. "Bitch, you got played, now be a big girl—suck it up," Misty said with a smirk.

Valencia winced.

"Move it, bitch," Misty hissed. She reached up and gripped the taller woman's shoulder and gave her a shove. Taken off guard, Valencia stumbled and swayed to the side. She glowered at Shane.

Shane sucked his teeth. "Yo, if I was you, I'd get back in that car," he advised Valencia and then burst out in scornful laughter.

"You better hurry up; Misty has a short fuse," Brick taunted. "Don't let her size fool you. She'll whip every ass inside that car if any one of y'all even looks at her the wrong way."

Looking defeated and suddenly haggard, Valencia slid inside the car. An older Hispanic woman, probably her mother, patted Valencia comfortingly.

Sensing that Misty was unreasonable, Valencia's brother directed an appeal to Shane. "Man, I just want to know if you're going to pay my sister back; she got a little kid," Valencia's brother said. The teen's voice had softened considerably. The metal pipe, which now seemed more like a prop than a weapon, hung limply at his side.

Brick suddenly snatched the pipe from the youth's hand, collared him, and knocked him up against the car. "Man, don't be comin' at my man with no pipe. I'll bash your muthafuckin head in." The Hispanic family inside the car started yelling and screaming for Brick to leave the boy alone. "Oh Jesus, he's going to kill Julio," said the old woman who sat in the front passenger seat.

Valencia jumped out of the car. "Get the fuck off my brotha." Brick pushed her aside like she was a rag doll.

Then Misty hit her. Right in the face. The punch from Misty's small but powerful fist knocked Valencia on her behind.

"You ain't shit, Shane," Valencia yelled, rubbing her face. "You're a dirty bastard," she cried.

Shane just smiled and stuck out his hand to help pull her up.

"Damn, whatchu helping the bitch for?" Misty asked, furious. "Don't make me knock her on her ass again."

Shane let Valencia's hand go. "I tried to be a gentleman, but she won't let me," he laughingly explained to Valencia as she picked herself up and limped back to the car.

"Why you so mean?" Shane asked as he gave Misty a quick kiss on the lips and then whispered in her ear. "You know my jawn gets hard when you bring out your can of whoop ass."

"And you know my pussy gets wet when I get a chance to smack one of your bitches around."

Busy manhandling and threatening bodily harm to Valencia's brother, Brick didn't notice the intimate interaction between Misty and Shane.

CHAPTER 28

Janelle returned to her management position at McDonald's. She barked out orders to Tariq and the other fast food employees all day. At home, she continued to boss Tariq around.

"Tariq! Don't you hear the baby crying!" Janelle yelled. Tariq, engrossed in a TV program, was oblivious to his son's cries. Janelle's loud voice snapped him into awareness. Tariq jumped up immediately and retrieved the baby. He brought his son into the living room, rocking him as his eyes returned to the TV screen, but the baby continued to cry.

"Tariq!" she yelled again. "He's probably wet. I can't do everything, you know," she said, sucking her teeth. "I'm trying to fix dinner. Can you please make yourself useful?"

Tariq stuck his hand inside the baby's diaper. "Yup, you're soaked," he said, smiling at his son and then proceeding to change the diaper.

"After you change him, give him a bottle of water. I know he's starving; I'll feed him in a few minutes."

Living with his bossy, hard-to-please wife was a lot better than living with the whining, wimpy woman she'd become during her pregnancy. Things were slowly getting back to normal.

Quite a few changes had taken place in their relationship while Janelle was on her emotional hiatus. For one thing, Tariq didn't wear women's undergarments anymore, and he no longer gave his wife a detailed account of his every move.

Their sex life had resumed, but something was missing. Sex with Janelle had become mechanical and mundane as if her heart wasn't in it. Tariq missed the freaky things they used to get into.

Once, when he'd tried to get her in the mood by caressing her hips and gently running his fingers down her thighs, she'd snapped at him, saying, "Don't you ever try to initiate sex with me. I call the shots around here. I'll let you know when I'm in the mood."

He masturbated regularly, hoping for the day when Janelle resumed the aggressive role in bed that she used to enjoy. He yearned to cry out in ecstasy the way he always did whenever Janelle took control in the bedroom. He hoped he didn't have to wait too much longer.

As Tariq finished changing the baby's diaper, the phone rang. Janelle answered it. "It's for you," she said, her lips twisted in a sneer. It had to be Shane. Of course it was Shane, Tariq concluded. No one else called him and no one else had that effect on Janelle.

"Whassup, bro," Tariq said while trying to give the baby a bottle of water. The baby squirmed and pushed the nipple out of his mouth, fretting and whimpering. Tariq rocked him faster, cutting an eye at Janelle to see if she was ready to nurse their son. Her rigid back turned in his direction answered his question.

"I got something for you and Janelle," Shane told Tariq. "A video camera. A Sony—top of the line."

"For real? A Sony?"

"I'll stop by with it in a short."

"Thanks. Okay, see you soon," Tariq said cheerfully.

Janelle glared at Tariq when he hung up the phone. "See you soon?" she repeated sarcastically. "I'm not fixing an extra plate for your brother," she snarled, placing a hand on her hip.

"Yo, chill," Tariq said in a raised voice.

Janelle lifted an eyebrow in surprise. "Oh, I forgot—whenever you talk to your brother, you start acting like you have an extra set of balls."

Tariq ignored her comment about his balls. "Shane's not trying to hustle us for no meal. He's coming over to give us a camera so we can start filming the baby."

Janelle softened perceptibly. "Oh! That's thoughtful of your brother," she said, unable to suppress a smile.

"Yes it is, so try to treat him nice."

Wearing a bright smile, she nodded. "I can't wait to start filming Lil' Man."

The desk clerk called and announced Shane's arrival fifteen minutes later.

Shane entered his brother's apartment proudly carrying the video camera. "I don't have the booklet that goes with it, so you'll have to take it to one of those camera shops in the mall. Maybe they can sell y'all the booklet that goes with this. Check it out," he beckoned Tariq. "I can show you the basics."

Janelle and Tariq hovered nearby as Shane filmed the baby as he played with a rattle. He turned the camera toward Tariq and Janelle. "Stand close, love-birds." Shane smiled when Tariq pulled Janelle close to him. "Now, give me some action," he said teasingly. Surprisingly, Janelle smiled broadly and then turned around and gave Tariq a passionate kiss—tongue and all. Tariq thought her behavior was a little over the top considering she'd been rather cold for months, but he'd take affection and the promise of sex however he could get it. He assumed that being filmed was a turn-on for his wife.

"Here, Janelle, get some footage of me and my brother," Shane said, handing her the camera. He took the baby out of his baby seat. "We can't leave out the little playa." He looked approvingly at his nephew. "Damn, Tariq. You put your back all up in Lil' Man. He ain't nothing but *you*, man. Straight-up Batista!"

Tariq smiled proudly.

Janelle's smile dimmed. "Damn, everybody acts like all I did was carry Lil' Man. I know Tariq's fine and everything, but he didn't make this baby by himself," she said, pouting.

Shane ignored her outburst and directed his attention to his nephew.

Tariq could tell by the glimmer of pain reflected in his wife's eyes that he was going to pay dearly for her hurt feelings. Any hopes he'd had that his wife would be in a an amorous mood later on that night had instantly gone out the window.

After Shane left, Janelle ignored Tariq completely.

Surprisingly, later that evening, when Janelle got out of the shower, she came in the bedroom wearing a hot pink satin-and-lace gown—no panties underneath. She got in the bed and smacked Tariq on the ass. "Turn over."

Tariq turned on his stomach. Janelle climbed on top of him and slipped her hands beneath his chest. Pinching his nipples while she rotated her hips, she thrust her pelvic area against his ass. Following her lead, Tariq fell easily into his role.

"You're a pretty bitch, Tariq, you know that?"

Tariq was silent, not knowing how to respond.

"Did you hear me? I said you're a pretty bitch. My pretty bitch!"

Tariq loved it when Janelle started talking crazy shit. It got him hot and horny.

Janelle thrust hard against his ass, pushing against him as if she had a dick. "What are you, Tariq?"

"I'm your pretty bitch," Tariq exclaimed, excitedly.

Janelle rolled off Tariq. "Take your drawers off and give me some pussy."

Tariq got up and kicked off his boxers. He returned to the bed and lay on his back, with his arms to his sides, unmoving. Submissive.

Janelle straddled him quickly. She was dripping and hot. As she slid down on him, the pleasure caused her to cry out. Then, pulling herself together she regained control. As Janelle rode him hard and rough, she asked him in a throaty whisper, "Who runs things in this house, Tariq?"

"You do, Janelle," he gasped, feeling himself quickly rising to a crescendo of passion he hadn't felt in a long time.

"Tell me why I run things around here."

He knew what she wanted to hear and felt no inhibitions. However, fighting an unwelcome orgasm, Tariq could not speak. His face at the moment was contorted in sweet pain; the only sound emerging from his lips was an outcry of pleasure.

"What do I have that you need, Tariq?" She rephrased her question, strangling his penis with tightened inner muscles, making it nearly impossible for him to speak.

"A big dick," he uttered in a voice that sounded anguished. The force of her violent lovemaking was delicious torture.

"That's right," she said humping fast, "and if I have the dick in this house, what do you have? Tell me, Tariq—what do you have?"

Afraid he'd lose control if he spoke the words audibly, he mumbled with his lips pressed against his wife's chest, "A pussy."

"What else? Who am I and what do I do?" she prompted.

Tariq trembled. "You're my wife and you fuck me with your big dick." His words caused them both to lose control. Tariq and Janelle came together, shuddered together; the release was long overdue.

Janelle was back in control and Tariq couldn't help but wonder if Shane's visit had provoked her aggressive behavior. It didn't matter; he couldn't have been happier. She could treat him any way she wanted—she could call him every name in the book. He had no problem submitting to his wife. What went on behind closed doors was their business alone.

CHAPTER 29

Obtaining a post office box was easy. As promised, Misty called Paula three days later.

"You got my dough?" Misty asked, her face bright with anticipation.

"Yes." There was a tremble in Paula's voice.

"Drop some numbers on me."

Paula was silent for a moment and then inhaled deeply. "I'm not rich, you know. I don't work. My husband—"

"Kill that noise! Whatchu workin' with, bitch?" Misty spit out the last word venomously.

Paula gasped. "Well, I can give you…um, about fifty a week."

"Fifty dollars a week?" Misty repeated for Shane's and Brick's benefit. Brick's face broke up in disgust, making the scar on his forehead seem more pronounced. Shane's expression was impassive. He knew Misty would handle the situation.

"Make it seventy-five," Misty said. "Cash money, baby, and make sure it's on time. Late money carries a stiff penalty. And you don't wanna know about that so don't fuck with my money."

Misty gave Paula her alias as well as the number to the post office box. Before hanging up, she poured salt in the woman's wound. "I know you ain't no spring chicken or nothing, but damn, I ain't think my man would fuck around with a bitch old enough to be having memory problems."

"What are you talking about?" Paula said, now weeping audibly.

"I asked you where you bought that black baby doll shit and you said you didn't remember. Duh…figure it out, bitch," Misty said. Turning up the corner of her top lip, she gave Shane and Brick a look.

"Stupid bitch," Brick spat, disgustedly referring to Paula. Misty broke up laughing, her eyes fixed on Shane, encouraging him to join in. Shane simply smiled and shook his head as if Misty was just the cutest thing.

Showing off for Shane's benefit, Misty continued, "Send me a set just like it, but don't go to the big girls' shop," she warned, and then doubled over in malicious laughter. "I don't shop in the plus-size stores, I wear a size three. Now, make sure I get my package in two days." Misty hung up the pay phone and took a theatrical bow. Shane and Brick clapped their hands and then the trio quickly departed the vicinity of the pay phone.

"So what y'all wanna get into today?" Misty wanted to know.

"Depends on how much money we got," Brick said.

"Misty opened her purse and counted their money and then screwed up her lips. "We only got fifty-two dollars."

"Where'd all the money go?" Shane asked. He was glad he kept a separate stash at his secret home.

"Me and Brick bought some clothes and *you* know how you do. You spent a lot on coke."

"I only spent sixty dollars on blow."

Misty shrugged. "So what we gon' do—stand around out here arguing over who spent what, or are we gonna go get some more money?" Wearing a pouty expression, she gazed at Brick.

"It's daytime. I ain't steppin' up on no suckas at the ATM machine with the sun shining on my ass."

"Daytime is probably the best time to pull the shit off. Suckers who withdraw money this time of the day are bound to have their guard down."

"She got a point," Shane said.

Brick squinted in thought. "I don't know. I work best at night. And I follow my instincts. I ain't trying to do no time over no dumb shit. We just gotta come up with a plan—something safe."

They murmured in agreement.

"Whassup. You got any new bitches?" Misty asked Shane.

"I'm tapped out," Shane admitted.

"What!" Misty and Brick said in unison. "All those bitches looking for dick—boy, you must be slippin'" Brick said. They all knew that despite Brick's big dick, he could never pimp women. He was big, unattractive, and had that hideous scar. No woman would ever pay to fuck him.

Shane, however, wasn't at a loss for female clientele; he was putting in more time at home. When the weight of the world came crashing down, he'd buy some blow, some weed, and head on home where he could rely on finding peace and serenity. And love. Real love.

He loved Misty in an odd way, but being that Brick was his dawg and she was Brick's girl, he wouldn't allow himself to fall deeply in love with her. Shane had a feeling Brick knew what was going on. Brick had to know they were sharing Misty. It was an unspoken agreement. Too touchy a subject to admit with words. Yeah, Misty had to be kept at arm's length.

Misty was extra special—a pretty, sexy little thing who was as criminal-minded and fearless as the most treacherous man. There were so many fine bitches out there who gave him a sexual rush. But neither Misty nor anybody else could compete with the woman he had at home.

Shane and Dolores Holmes had an understanding. He didn't expect society to approve of their relationship, but as he matured, he came to an acceptance within. He no longer felt guilt about what they were doing. It wasn't wrong. It was just different.

Maturity had taught him to appreciate what she did for him. He was addicted and needed her like a drug. Her soft flabby body was a comfort to lie close to. And when he needed to release his emotions with tears, she was there to wipe his eyes and rock him until he calmed down. And like any mother, she figured out ways to keep him pacified.

The last time he'd come home agitated and became inconsolable and caught up in a crying jag, she promptly got up, went into the kitchen, and came back with a cup of evaporated milk. She stuck a finger in the milk and gave him a taste before dousing herself with the liquid and holding him close while he licked and sucked it from her heavy tits.

Heaven. It was heaven. Sucking and tasting something so familiar and sweet brought back memories. With her he felt as sheltered and protected as a newborn.

He was deeply ashamed of the way he'd treated her when he was young, He hadn't known any better when he'd taken something from her she'd been so willing to give. When he needed comforting like a baby, she allowed him to feel reborn, and when he had manly urges, without question, she parted her legs.

No, there wasn't another soul in the world that could do what she did for him.

"So what we gonna do?" Misty asked impatiently.

"I don't know. But I feel like I gotta check on my twin."

"What? You feel like something's wrong?" Brick asked.

"Yeah, but I'm not sure what it is."

"Well, call 'em and find out if he's all right. Why would you go all the way to Mount Airy for nothing?" Misty asked, peeved.

"Naw, I gotta go up there," Shane said adamantly.

"It's that twin shit," Brick explained. "He used to go through this all the time when we was up in Barney Hills."

"Whatever!" She was pissed off that Shane wanted to leave. Then she brightened. "I know!" She looked at Brick with mischief in her eyes. "Want to get into some freak shit? We don't need no money for that."

"I'm down."

Misty smiled and pulled out her cell phone.

Shane gave his buddies a hug. "Y'all have fun." When he was sure he was out of their eyesight, he flipped open his cell and called home. "I don't feel good, Mommy," he said in a choked little boy's voice.

"Don't start crying, Shane. Not out in public, you hear me?" As if she could see him, he nodded his head.

"Pull yourself together and come on home."

"Okay," he said and hailed a cab.

❦❦❦

Blindfolded and with his hands tied together with Misty's bra, Brick waited. He heard Misty speaking softly, then a baritone voice responded. When their footsteps and voices drew closer, Brick took a deep shuddering breath.

He felt the mattress sink from the weight of the man's body. Brick tried to imagine what the anonymous man looked like, but couldn't come up with an image. It didn't matter. He was a faceless man whose forbidden intentions caused Brick to tremble with expectancy. He wore a blindfold because he didn't want to see or be seen. His secret passion for homosexual activities was something he'd rather feel than see.

He felt Misty's soft, small hand. "See," she said, lifting Brick's stiffened dick for the man to appraise. "Ten inches. I didn't lie, did I?"

The man emitted a guttural sound that vibrated against Brick's scrotum, giving Brick the impression that his face and his lips were near.

"Mmm," Brick groaned in a tone that sounded like a low rumble and bordered on being a growl.

"Not so fast," Misty said, interrupting the encounter. "That's ten inches and I'm charging twenty dollars for every inch."

At that moment, Brick felt like punching Misty in the head for breaking the mood with her greedy money transactions. Couldn't she take care of that later? Jutting his groin in desperation, Brick cried out, "Stop wasting time, baby, get the money later. Let dude get on my jawn right now."

Misty kissed the head of Brick's penis. "Be cool; let me take care of the business end. He gon' take care of you in a minute."

The bed creaked, which meant the man had stood up. Brick heard the rustle of money being counted, followed by the snap of Misty's purse.

Trying to control his sense of sexual urgency, he refocused his mind. He conjured an image of a tool kit filled with a grimy set of tools. In his mind's eye, he examined screwdrivers, wrenches, pliers. Masculine items that would remind him of who he really was before he gave in to the all-consuming and unnatural desire to have his dick sucked by a man.

CHAPTER 30

"The job pays sixteen dollars an hour and that's a lot more than I make now," Tariq explained to Janelle. "After I get my driver's license, my pay rate increases to eighteen dollars an hour. Plus, I get tips."

Unwilling to find anything good about Tariq's decision to work for a moving company, Janelle rolled her eyes in disgust. "I don't like it, Tariq. You said you'll be away for a couple of days, sometimes. Suppose something happens to the baby…then what? What am I supposed to do? You can't take that job; me and Lil' Man need you here," Janelle said firmly.

"Baby, I already quit McDonald's; it's a done deal. If there's an emergency and I'm out of town, you gotta call Shane."

Incensed, Janelle threw a plastic baby bottle. Tariq ducked. "Fuck Shane. You know I can't stand your brother and he can't stand me either. Tariq, why would you go behind my back and make a major decision when you know you're supposed to ask for my permission?" She sighed heavily. "How'd you find out about this job, anyway?"

Tariq swallowed. "Kapri told me about it. Her brother works for the company and she recently got hired as the office manager."

"Kapri! You still talk to Kapri?"

"No, I just happened to bump into her."

"Oh yeah? Where?"

"In the supermarket. I was in Pathmark picking up a box of Pampers for Lil' Man. I just asked her if she ever went to that court stenographer school she had planned to attend."

"You ain't supposed to be talking to no skanks and you know it." Janelle's angry tone shifted to an insecure whine.

"I don't talk to no skanks. Kapri's not a skank. She's an old friend. I couldn't see myself ignoring her—treating her like she's a stranger. Baby, why you worried about Kapri; she ain't got nothing on you."

"I'm not worried about Kapri," Janelle snapped. "I don't like it when you break my rules."

"Okay. I'm sorry I didn't discuss it with you, but I knew you wouldn't like it, so I went behind your back. But it's not like I'm cheating on you. I'm trying to look out for us as a family. Look, with the baby's day care bill and the high rent we pay to live here, one of us has to bring in more money. I promise you, I won't look at no other women when I'm on the job. After I finish working I'm coming home to you. When I get paid, I'm giving it all to you. Now, do you trust me?"

"I thought I could trust you; but I don't know…"

Tariq sat on the sofa and pulled Janelle on his lap. He could feel her weakening as he spoke to her softly. "Can't no other woman come between us, baby. Can't nobody do what you do and you know it."

Janelle and Tariq held each other. She unzipped his pants, slipped her hand inside his crotch—a panty check. Feeling reassured, she smiled as she caressed the soft red satin panties that concealed Tariq's manhood.

❧❧❧

Brick was blissfully asleep and Shane was with his brother. Or so he'd claimed. Shane had been pulling quite a few disappearing acts lately. Misty hoped he didn't have another woman hidden away in the cut somewhere. Shane couldn't possibly think she would sit back and let some other chick have him. Sex for play-and-pay was one thing, but catching feelings for a bitch was an entirely different matter.

Something was up; her feminine intuition was telling her that Shane had another bitch on his mind.

She shook Brick. "Baby, wake up."

"What?"

"Have you noticed anything different about Shane?"

"You woke me up to ask me that?"

"It's important, Brick. Wake up."

Brick rubbed his eyes and slowly sat up.

"I think Shane is doing something behind our backs."

"Like what? He checks on his brother. They twins. You know how that twin shit goes. They be feeling each other's emotions and shit."

"I know Shane well enough to know when he's lying and you should know him better than I do."

"So why he gotta lie to us?" Brick asked.

"Stop playing dumb. I think he's cheating on us."

"Whoa, Misty. I'm not the one fucking Shane. He's my man and everything but that emotional stuff is between you and him."

"Well, you're part of a threesome, so you should care, too."

"I ain't part of no damn threesome. You and me been dealing with each other since…for how long, Misty?"

"I don't know. Since the first or second grade."

"Right. We don't have no secrets. I got mad love for you and that's why I don't trip. But in my opinion, you and Shane let y'all selves get out of control. Both of y'all is wrong as hell. Y'all shouldn'a caught no feelings for each other. It was supposed to be just a sex thing."

"I know," she said, looking down. "But baby, I love the shit outta that pretty nigga. Shane's sneaky ass is driving me the fuck crazy!" Misty stamped her foot to make her point. "Whatchu think we should do?"

"I don't know, Misty. Don't drag me into this. If you let Shane know I'm down with what y'all been doing, then you gonna have to tell him that I don't mind. And he's gonna wonder why. Then you gonna have to admit that I share you with him because you share me with other men." Brick shook his head. "Everything ain't for everybody. That's our secret, baby. I can't let my man know about that part of my life. He'd hate me and think I'm a fag if he found out I like getting my jawn sucked by men. "

Misty sighed. "You're probably right. Shane wouldn't understand. But baby, he's breaking my heart. Don't you care?"

"Yeah, I care. But it ain't nothing I can do about it."

"Yes, you can. You can call his brother's house and see if he's there. If he's there tell him to get his ass back to West Philly. Tell him you need his help on an ATM job."

"Calm your little ass down, Misty. You can wait 'til tomorrow. When he comes through you can take him aside and ask him if he's cheating on you."

"Right! You think he's gonna tell me the truth?" She sat and briefly pondered the situation. "I know what we're gonna do! The next time Shane says he has to leave all of a sudden, we're gonna follow his ass. I wanna see with my own eyes who this bitch is."

"All right. We can do that. Now come on and lay down and get some sleep."

"I can't sleep. I wanna fuck. You done let dude suck you off about three or four times, so what can you do for me? Not a damn thing!"

"You right. I ain't gon' front, but I *can* do that other thing you like." Brick paused. "And I know *how* you like it."

Misty smiled. "Well, stop talking about it and do it! I'm miserable. Make me happy, Brick," she whined.

She quickly pulled off her jeans and panties and put one foot up on the bed. Brick got off the bed and walked around to the side of the bed where she was sitting. He got down on his knees submissively and started kissing her feet. Then he worked his way upward. When he got to her crotch, he steadied himself by gripping the edge of the bed.

Just before his tongue touched her vagina, she pushed his head away. "Brick!"

"What!"

"Pretend like you're Shane. Suck on it like he does."

"I gotchu, baby," Brick said soothingly.

"And baby…"

"What?"

"Can I call you Shane?"

"Uh huh," he grunted as he began to circle her clit with the tip of his tongue.

Misty imagined Shane's lips—his beautiful full lips. His lips looked naturally outlined and were darker than his reddish-brown skin. They were smooth and perfect as if he were wearing a muted shade of dark lipstick. When he parted his pretty lips, giving just a hint of a smile, the glimmer of perfect white teeth dazzled Misty to the point of making her knees go weak. Damn, she loved that pretty muthafucker.

"Oh, that feels so good," Misty moaned. "Goddamn, Shane. I love you, boy. Do you hear me?"

"I hear you, baby; I love you, too," Brick said, speaking in a tone similar to Shane's.

CHAPTER 31

Shane was a blessing in her life but Dolores Holmes sorely regretted having to give up her church. The members from her old congregation would never forgive her for taking up with the boy whose lies—as far the church members were concerned—had landed her in jail.

But it didn't feel right just reading the Bible at home. She had to find herself a new church and church members with whom she could fellowship.

If Shane loved her like he said he did, he'd accompany her into the Lord's house every now and then. A little bit of holiness would do the boy some good. Maybe he'd stop all that crying if he turned himself over to the Lord. Wasn't nothing but Satan working on his spirit and causing him all that inner torment and misery.

She poured a quarter cup of evaporated milk into a saucepan and added a little sugar to sweeten it up. With the burner turned low, she went in the bathroom to freshen up. No sooner had she put on her robe and brassiere when she heard her boy's key in the door. He came in looking agitated and near tears, pulling on her robe and tugging on her bra.

"Go sit on the couch, honey pie. Give me a second. I'll be right there." She poured the warm milk in a cup and lifted up her bra and dipped her nipple into the cup. She repeated the procedure with her other breast.

With the cup set on the end table, she pulled Shane over to her, cradled him in her arms, and nursed him until he was soothed and satisfied. With his face resting peacefully against her breasts, she stroked his hair and hummed a Christian hymn.

"Shane."

"Hmm."

"You know what I miss?"

"What?"

"Church, baby. I miss going to church."

"But you can't go back to that church."

"I know but there's nothing stopping me joining another one."

Shane was silent for a moment. "Can you find a church in the phone book?"

"Yes, but I saw one right around the corner."

Shane lifted his head. "What were you doing going around the corner? You know I don't want you walking nowhere."

"Boy, when you call me on the phone crying and carrying on, what am I supposed to do if we don't have that milk you like in the house? You sounded so upset, I got up and walked around the corner to the store."

"Mom, you gotta tell me when we need stuff around here."

"I know, but we ran out of that evaporated milk real quick and you're to the point where you won't take my tit without the milk."

"Okay, so now that I know how fast it runs out, I'll start buying it by the case. Next time we run out, just tell me when I get home, I'll go get it. You too heavy to be walking around outside. You start breathing hard just trying to make it from the living room to the kitchen. And you're startin' to scare me," he added, looking nervous.

"Oh, I'm all right. I just gotta lose some of this weight." She patted a meaty hip.

Shane rubbed her big belly and then laid his head in her lap. "I love all this fat."

Ms. Holmes bent over and kissed his forehead. They'd never kissed passionately on the lips. Their relationship didn't require that.

"Well, baby, how am I going to get to the church if you don't want me to walk?"

"Take a cab."

"Around the corner?"

"Why not?"

She inhaled. "Well, I was wondering about something."

"What's that?"

"I feel kind of shy joining a new church. Do you think you could make some time out for me and take me to church?"

His face was turned away from her, therefore, she didn't see him frown. She heard him say, "Okay, Mom. I'll go with you."

"Oh Hallelujah! You're finally going to have a relationship with your Lord and Master, sweet baby Jesus! Shane, I'm so proud of you. I never cared what other people said about you, I knew ol' Satan couldn't keep his evil grip on my boy."

❊❊❊

It was times like this, when she got all religious on him and started talking like a religious fanatic, that Shane wished he were somewhere else. His peace was broken, but it was too late to go out looking for a quick fix. Besides, he was too tired to go back out.

"You gonna stay up and watch TV?" he asked.

"No, I'm gonna sit out here and read my Bible."

"Okay, I'm going to bed."

"Okay, honey pie," she said, smiling and reaching for the Bible.

Shane went in the bedroom, closed the door, and rolled a blunt. He needed to get high after hearing all those hallelujahs.

An hour or so later, Ms. Holmes got in bed beside him wearing a cotton night-gown. He was asleep but sensed she was near. Snuggling up next, he rubbed on her back and then groaned. Even in his sleep, he didn't like fabric between them. He needed to feel her flesh with its many folds and cushiony flab.

❊❊❊

Shane didn't own a suit, but he looked well groomed and handsome enough in a white shirt and dark blue slacks to turn heads when he and Ms. Holmes entered the church the following Sunday.

During the middle of the service, the visiting pastor, Reverend Daniels, asked the parishioners to bow their heads in prayer for Reverend Bradley, who was recovering from a long illness. After the prayer, he called for all guests to rise and come to the front of the church and introduce themselves. As Shane and Ms. Holmes walked down the aisle toward the short line of guests, a sea of ornate and intricately designed hats all turned at the same time, curiously observing the mother and scrutinizing the son with keen interest.

Later, downstairs in the church's basement, where lunch was being served, Ms. Holmes was treated like a queen. Smiling women offered to make her and her son plates with choices of homemade fried chicken, roast beef, macaroni and cheese, collards, yams, green beans, potato salad, cornbread, rolls, and a host of desserts.

"You see," Ms. Holmes said before biting into a piece of cornbread, "coming to God's house is like coming home."

Shane shook his head in solemn agreement. He was suffering in the religious atmosphere, but it was a small price to pay to please the woman he loved.

"Here you are, Ms. Holmes," said an attractive, statuesque woman. The woman was stunningly well dressed in a tailored suit. She looked to be in her early forties, but it was hard to put an age on a woman that well put together. As she bent to hand Ms. Holmes a cup of fruit juice, she turned her face toward Shane and winked.

"My name is Felicia Bradley. I'm the pastor's wife as well as president of the Women's Auxiliary," she said with a confident smile.

"I'm Dolores Holmes and this is my son, Shane."

"Ms. Holmes," Felicia Bradley replied seriously, "we'd be honored if you and your son would consider joining our church. My husband has been the pastor of this church for fifteen years. I'm sorry you're not able to meet him at this time. He's a wonderful pastor. Since he's been on board, we've added a day care center, a literacy program, a Meals on Wheels program for the shut-ins. I could go on and on about the wonderful things my husband has done for Bright Hope Memorial." Mrs. Bradley spoke in glowing tones about her husband, but then her smile dimmed. "My husband is in poor health right now, but we haven't missed a beat here at Bright Hope Memorial. I offer my assistance to our visiting pastor and I make sure the church still functions in a manner in which my husband would approve. "

"It does seem like a lovely church," Ms. Holmes said, looking around approvingly. "The people are very nice. Me and my boy will think about it and let you know." She peered at Shane, her eyes beseeching him to consent to joining the church, but Shane's eyes wandered, refusing to meet his foster mother's gaze.

Felicia Bradley forged ahead. "While you're making a decision, perhaps you'd be interested in participating in some of our committees—you know, to get a feel of the spirit of Bright Hope Memorial." She flashed another dazzling smile. "We're involved in community service work and we—"

"It sounds wonderful, but my health isn't so good…"

"Oh, I certainly understand." The woman turned to Shane. "You know, we like to keep our young people busy and some of our activities include young men." On the sly, she gave Shane a seductive smile.

With a quick wink and a head nod, Shane assured Felicia Bradley that he was willing to accommodate her in whatever she wanted to get into—within reason. He was certain she knew not to come at him with any further talk of community service. Giving the pretty preacher's wife a tune-up was the only kind of service he was interested in performing.

Felicia Bradley gave Shane her card and told him to give her a call at his earliest convenience. She was the kind of woman who went after what she wanted without hesitation. She was about her business and played no games; he could dig it.

Next, she dug into her purse and pulled out a Blackberry and turned to Dolores Holmes. "Ms. Holmes, may I have your telephone number? I'd like to stay in touch with you. Bright Hope has a meal delivery service and being that you're a senior in failing health, I'm sure you fit the criteria." She bent over, speaking to Ms. Holmes directly. "Now, this service is limited to members only, but I can pull a few strings." She gave Ms. Holmes a conspiratorial wink this time.

After getting Ms. Holmes's information and welcoming them once more, Felicia Bradley walked away. The faint smile she wore conveyed she was satisfied with the connection she'd made.

Ms. Holmes was gushing from all that attention from the preacher's wife. "Now see that, Shane. You've just been invited to fellowship by the reverend's wife and she's going to get me placed on a meal service. Now isn't that something." Ms. Holmes patted Shane's hand and looked up at him, smiling with pride and joy.

"She's a real important woman and I want you to show off your good home training. Make sure you give that lady a call." Ms. Holmes, overcome with pride, began to fan herself. "Lord, my boy's going to be fellowshipping with the saints." Ms. Holmes shook her head in pleasant amazement.

No matter which direction Shane turned his eyes, there were females, varying in age from sixteen to sixty, giving him suggestive looks. All trying to make his acquaintance.

Shane never dreamed that going to church could present so many possibilities.

CHAPTER 32

Wheeling a new BMW M5, Felicia Bradley rolled into the lot of their designated meeting spot, an Exxon service station on Sixty-Third Street.

Shane flashed a grin when he saw the expensive car. He had to restrain himself from whistling at Felicia's top-of-the-line set of wheels. The sleek, sexy car was giving him a powerful erection. He felt a rush of anticipation and instantly began plotting on how to finagle his very affluent female admirer into letting him borrow the car at a later date.

He slid inside. "You look beautiful," he told Felicia, but his eyes were focused on the vehicle's plush interior. Shane shifted his gaze to Felicia and attentively leaned over to kiss her cheek, but Felicia grimaced. She dodged Shane's kiss as if his lips carried an incurable communicable disease.

Shane flinched. Having a woman shun his advances was an unfamiliar and unpleasant experience.

"Please! Not here. One never knows who's watching," she explained in an admonishing tone. With her lips pursed tightly, Felicia's eyes darted about as she suspiciously investigated the service station lot for prying eyes.

He wanted to say, *Kiss my ass, you fuckin bitch!* But he held his tongue. He dug her car too much to piss her off. So, pretending to feel remorse, Shane lowered his eyes in contrition. "My bad," he muttered. "But you gotta understand…" He shook his head.

"Understand what?" Felicia asked, her face twisted in annoyance.

Had Shane acted on his impulses, his fist would have been inside Felicia's smart-assed mouth, but he wanted to drive her car so badly, he chose not to offend her. "You look good, Ma. It's hard to keep my hands off you." He folded his hands and dramatically placed them in his lap. "But I'm gon' try, aiight?" He flashed her a disarming grin.

Shane expected Felicia to accept his flattery and return his smile, but instead, the preacher's wife gave a heavy sigh. "I'm not going to waste your time, Shane; I'm a very busy woman," she said. "My husband is ill and as I would expect you to know…" —she paused and checked the rearview mirror, then backed up and made a sharp turn out of the lot— "A woman has her needs," she continued. "You're a handsome young man and if you can take my mind off my current problems…" She became silent. "Well, let's put it this way. If you make me happy, you'll be very handsomely compensated." She smiled coyly.

Shane didn't particularly like Felicia, but he had to respect her. She didn't bullshit; she got right down to business. Felicia wasn't trying to catch no feelings or fall in love; she just wanted some good dick.

"Cool," he responded. "So, where we goin'?"

"I can't risk being recognized, so I figured we'd go to a motel in Jersey. I'm taking a huge chance meeting you in a public place like this," she said with an extravagant wave of her hand as she pulled out of the parking lot.

"I can dig it. Jersey sounds good." Shane reclined his seat, prepared to enjoy the ride. Felicia was quiet also. They were on the same page, silently agreeing that there was no need for meaningless chitchat.

It was just an ordinary motel, but Felicia didn't have an ordinary body. She was a female bodybuilder. Her clothing hid her muscles. As far as Shane was concerned, she looked better with her clothes on. Naked, she looked like an Amazon, more muscular than the average man. Her breasts were practically nonexistent and what she did have looked like hard little rocks. Her small tight ass looked hard as a rock also. Every part of Felicia's body was tight and toned. Hard. Masculine.

Shane shook his head. He liked to see shit jiggle when he hit it. Felicia's body looked like it was made of cement. Fucking the preacher's wife wasn't going to be very much fun.

"As you can see, I work out," she boasted.

Shane grunted an unimpressed response. He couldn't fake it; all those muscles looked nasty.

"Don't tell me you're intimidated by muscular women?" she asked as she pranced around, striking poses to show off her muscles

His dick was limp and Shane worried that he might not be able to get an erection. He wanted to give it to her the way she wanted it, since Felicia Bradley was the type of woman he'd like to keep around. But he was finding it increasingly difficult to become aroused by the muscle-bound woman.

He thought of his pretty little petite Misty. Admittedly, Misty had small boobs and a tiny ass, but Misty wasn't sporting a six-pack and a bulging set of biceps bigger than his. Naw, this shit wasn't going to work.

As if reading Shane's mind, Felicia pulled him onto the bed and on top of her. In the missionary position, Shane noticed she felt like an ordinary woman. She felt feminine. Damn shame her chest was so flat, though.

Shane and Felicia shared a kiss. A bland kiss. There was no sexual chemistry between them. Something was missing. Or maybe there was too much of something. Yeah, too many muscles. Shane closed his eyes and imagined Felicia was Valencia, the Spanish spitfire he'd fucked over. He was sorry he'd ruined that relationship so early in the game. Valencia was a hot Puerto Rican mami with a round bubble butt; he should have hung with her a little while longer.

Felicia kissed Shane again. It was a lingering kiss, intended to be passionate. But Shane simply wasn't feeling her. Trying hard to get into the mood, he gave her tongue; he made all the sounds and movements of an aroused man. But his dick was soft. He blamed Felicia. There was something cold and asexual about the preacher's wife.

Imagining Valencia wasn't working, in an act of desperation, Shane switched the mental image to the singer Beyonce Knowles. He imagined Beyonce giving him a lap dance. In fact, in his imagination, Beyonce and her crew were doling out exclusive lap dances—dancing exactly the way they did on the BET Awards show—just for him.

The provocative images of the sexy singing trio had Shane's dick standing at attention. A few seconds later, Shane was serving up pipe. Using well-aimed strokes to hit it hard and fast, Shane had Felicia purring like a kitten and promising him the clothes off her back, which was music to his ears.

Afterward, Felicia checked her watch, washed up and dressed quickly. "I have to be at choir rehearsal in an hour." She spoke in a crisp, formal tone.

Shane wasn't offended. He wished all his women could separate business from pleasure as smoothly as Felicia could.

Shane went into the bathroom behind her. There were four fifty-dollar bills on the toilet top. It was an odd place to leave the money. It felt insulting, actually. But what the fuck did he care? Felicia obviously had a problem putting money in his hands. Fuck it; he'd take it any way he could get it.

During the ride home, Shane schemed on how to break down Felicia's hard exterior. He needed her soft and pliant if he expected to get the keys to the BMW. In fact, he'd like to borrow it that very night. She didn't need the car while she was at choir rehearsal. But not wanting to turn her off by rushing things, Shane decided he'd bide his time and after he'd uncovered her weaknesses, he was certain she'd give him his own set of car keys. If the shit went as planned, Felicia would be asking him permission to drive *her* car.

❊❊❊

"Where you been, man?" Brick bear-hugged Shane when he joined Brick and Misty in a corner bar on Cobbs Creek Parkway.

Misty, playing a poker game at the bar, pointedly ignored Shane.

"What's her problem?" Shane asked Brick.

"You ain't call or nothin', man. You know how we do. That shit ain't cool."

"Yo, Misty," Shane said, pulling her long ponytail.

"Yo, my ass," she snarled and yanked her head away without looking at him.

"Oh! You don't want me to fuck with you? Aiight, ain't no thing," Shane said and turned toward Brick. "So, what's been up, dawg? Y'all get any dough from Paula yet?"

"Yeah, man, she paid two weeks in advance." Brick turned and nudged Misty. "Give Shane his cut," Brick said delicately.

"I ain't giving him shit," Misty said huffily. Her eyes and fingers remained focused on the tabletop video poker game.

"It's cool, Misty. Keep that chump change. I'm straight," Shane told her.

"I bet you are," Misty replied sarcastically. Her eyes drifted to Shane's hardened face.

Ignoring Misty's remark, Shane scanned the dimly lit room. He spotted two women sitting together at the bar. One of the two women was heavily made up with eye shadow, lipstick…the works. The other had a pecan tan complexion. No makeup—a natural beauty with a clean-scrubbed look. Shane caught the eye of the natural beauty. She giggled appreciatively.

Shane gave Misty a sidelong glance and then dismissed her with a flip of his hand. With his lips curved into a cocky smile, Shane sauntered to the other side of the bar.

"Hey, sexy, what's your name?" Shane asked the attractive woman; who seemed too clean-cut and innocent to be sitting up in that hole-in-the wall bar. However, as Shane well knew, looks could be deceptive. Misty's girlish beauty and impression of innocence attested to that fact.

"Nina," the young woman answered. Her eyes twinkled delightedly.

"My name's Shane. How you doin', Nina? Whassup? Where you live? Can I get that number?" He asked the personal questions in rapid succession without waiting for a response. "Yo, I'm not trying to play no games," he said, explaining his aggressive approach. "You lookin' kinda good, shorty, and I'm tryin' to make you my business. Know what I'm sayin'? So whassup? Can I buy you a drink?" He cast a quick look at the woman sitting next to Nina. "Your girlfriend can get a drink, too."

Nina looked excitedly at her girlfriend as if Shane had offered to buy them each a bottle of Cristal.

"Whatchu drinkin'?" Shane inquired in a low voice as he stroked the fine hairs on his cleft chin.

"Vodka," Nina told him, gazing dreamily into his eyes.

"How you like it?" he asked, his expression neutral, his tone sexy and hypnotic.

"What?" she whispered with her eyes pinned to his face.

"How you like your drink? Mixed or straight?"

"Oh!" Nina exclaimed. "Straight…no chaser," she replied, and gave a nervous chuckle.

"Oh, yeah? Is that how you like everything?" Shane sidled closer. "You like everything straight with no chaser?" His voice was husky and sensual.

Nina cut a nervous eye at her girlfriend.

"Whew!" Nina's girlfriend exclaimed as she comically fanned her face. "He's too much for me! Go 'head, Nina, answer the man," she said teasingly. "Tell him how you like it."

Both Nina and her girlfriend appeared smitten by Shane. The delight in their eyes and their gleeful chatter confirmed their appreciation of his presence.

Shane felt like patting his own back. Real rap; he was the muthafuckin' man! He was getting his mack on—working his magic. He sized Nina up—taking a quick inventory. She was plainly dressed in jeans and a stretchy pink top. No artificial hair or fingernails. Nina looked to be in her late twenties and Shane, knowing women the way he did, figured Nina to be the dependable type, a reliable employee who brought home a steady paycheck. She probably didn't make much, but he was sure Nina would figure out a way to include him in her budget. Yeah, Nina seemed like a soft touch; he was certain he could convince her to break him off on the regular. Fifty here; a hundred there. Quick pocket money is what Shane saw in Nina. With a self-satisfied smile, Shane beckoned the bartender.

The bartender appeared, his face expectant.

"Give her whatever she's drinkin'," Shane told the man, leaning his head toward Nina's giggling friend. "And give her…" Shane paused and looked Nina up and down like she was something edible. "She's drinkin' vodka. Top shelf. She said she likes it straight. No chaser." Shane winked at Nina. Nina flushed and seemed to swoon.

Shane had one eye on Nina and the other on Misty. Misty, pretending to be immersed in the video poker game, looked up. She bristled when she saw Shane extract money from his pocket and peel off a twenty.

Before Shane could brace himself or warn Nina that trouble was brewing. Misty had slid off the bar stool. As fast as a locomotive, the petite dynamo stormed to the other side of the bar.

Seemingly from out of nowhere, a snarling Misty appeared in front of Nina and without warning, she cold-cocked the unsuspecting woman. Misty's punch sent Nina flying off the bar stool.

Nina's girlfriend screamed. The bartender came running. And Nina, her face crinkled in astonishment, lay sprawled out on the dirty bar room floor.

"Help, somebody!" her friend screamed.

In an alcohol-induced frenzy, patrons of the bar quickly converged and hovered. Taking in the scene, they murmured excitedly, but none of the bystanders offered support.

"Stomp her!" shouted a drunken woman.

"Yeah, stomp her," a male patron heartily agreed.

With a drink in hand, the inebriated woman brazenly tottered over to Nina and looked down upon the unfortunate fallen woman with angry bloodshot eyes. "Stomp the shit outta that bitch." She clumsily lifted her foot, demonstrating the movement she wanted Misty to execute.

The other bar patrons, stirred to rowdiness, fervently agreed. "Stomp her," they all chorused. Of course, the bloodthirsty mob had no quarrel with Nina; they hardly knew her. But they thrived on dissention and mayhem.

Misty, eager to oblige, raised her size-five boot over Nina's head. Nina squeezed her eyes shut and screamed.

Shane snaked an arm around Misty's waist and snatched her up before she could bring the heel of her boot crashing down upon Nina's skull.

"Lemme go, dammit," Misty exploded, swinging wildly as she twisted and struggled to tear free from Shane's tight hold. "I'm gon' bust that bitch's ass!"

Scrapping with Misty was exhausting. "Dayum, Misty—you a beast," Shane exclaimed, unable to mask the pride in his voice. Misty had just cost him some paying pussy, but he wasn't mad at her. Still, he had to control her before she killed the innocent victim who lay on the floor looking confused as she grimaced and squinted and tried to make sense of the tragic situation.

Misty, kicking and still trying to wriggle from Shane's grip, screamed for Brick. "Get this muthafucker off me, Brick!"

Shane yelled for Brick's help, too. He was breathing hard from tussling with the feisty petite woman. He knew Misty would never give up and he feared she'd break free and try to kill Nina.

Brick looked confusedly from Shane to Misty as if unable to determine whose orders to take.

"Yo, help me get her outta here, man—she gon' get us all locked up!" Shane barked at Brick.

Motivated by the words *locked up*, Brick took control of the situation and grabbed Misty's kicking feet. Together, Shane and Brick, both tall and strong, wrestled with the cussing and spitting ninety-nine-pound hothead and carried her out of the bar.

After being deposited on the pavement outside the bar, Misty started swinging on Shane, pummeling him with a rain of blows. He ducked the punches from her tiny fists and then grabbed Misty and restrained her with a tight hug.

"Why the fuck you make me go off like that Shane?" Misty demanded after Shane released her. She stood on her tiptoes, fists balled, veins popping out of the sides of her neck.

"I ain't make you do shit. Now back the fuck off," Shane advised, but Misty took another step forward.

"How you gon' be all up in some other bitch's face when I ain't seen your ass in damn near a week?" Misty said hotly.

"Yo, Brick," he said, looking at Brick for support. "Handle your business, man."

"Don't be draggin' Brick in this. This is between me and you!"

"Yo, Brick!" Shane's voice grew louder, more determined.

"Brick ain't stupid; he knows whassup with you and me."

Shocked, Shane glanced anxiously at Brick.

Wearing a blank expression, Brick didn't say a word.

"You wasn't playin' him," she shouted. "Brick knew what we were doing the whole time," Misty said with a sneer.

Shane gulped and blinked rapidly.

"That's right, nigga…blink! You the one who got played." Misty was still on her toes, trying to get in Shane's face. "You thought you was creepin' behind your best friend's back—well, you wasn't. Brick knew about everything. Ha ha ha!" Misty scoffed. "I guess the joke's on you, Shane." She shook her head and smiled sardonically. "And that's fucked up. You don't care about nobody but your damn self," she continued.

"Yo, Misty, back the fuck off. Don't be comin' at my neck like that. I wasn't tryin' to play nobody." Shane gestured threateningly. "What happened between me and you just happened. You know I wasn't trying to hurt Brick."

"So what! You didn't care if Brick got hurt. Brick knew you'd probably try to hit on me…that's why he was willing to share me."

"Hit on you!" Shane frowned in disgust. "Man, you came at me!"

"Whatever," Misty muttered. "The point is, Brick's heart was in the right place. He had your back." Misty placed a palm across her heart and began patting. "Out of the kindness of his heart, he let you fuck me. And look at how you treat him; he damn sure don't get the same type of loyalty from you. You ain't shit, Shane," Misty spat maliciously.

"Yo, Brick. I'm sorry, man. I wasn't never tryin' to play you. It's just…"

"It's cool, dawg," Brick said. "Real rap—it's cool," he insisted. "You know how we do."

Shane shook his head regretfully and gave Brick a hug.

Misty glared at the pair. "Why don't y'all tell *m*e how we do, because I'm confused," Misty said and petulantly folded her arms across her chest. "I thought the three of us had a commitment, but it looks like this muthafucker can vanish at the drop of a hat and he don't think he owes nobody no kind of explanation."

"I had personal issues with my brother," Shane explained. "Y'all can't understand me and Tariq—so don't try." His expression quickly changed from apologetic to dark and brooding.

Misty and Brick both knew better than to argue with Shane when it came to his brother. An uncomfortable silence ensued.

"Come on, y'all; fuck this shit. Let's go get high," Brick recommended. "Y'all can kiss and make up later."

"He can kiss my ass later," Misty said, rushing ahead of the two men.

"Me and Misty got a room while you was gone."

"No shit?"

"Yeah, man. We was sick of having to follow her mother's rules. Our crib's right around the corner, on Washington Avenue. It's costing us a bean a week. So, you know that money from Paula is coming in handy. The landlady tried to hook us up with a queen-sized bed, but knowing how much room your lanky ass takes up, we told her we needed a king-size."

Later, in the tidy rented room, a blunt was passed from Misty to Shane and then to Brick. The tobacco leaf-covered marijuana served as a peace pipe. With each puff all the tension washed away and Misty was soon perched contentedly on Shane's lap, kissing him and laughing at everything he and Brick said.

Then she got serious. With one hand she stroked the side of Shane's face. The other hand rubbed Brick's crotch. "Shane, we're family, right?"

"Right," he said inhaling the pungent smoke.

"I mean, I know you don't think of us as family like Tariq and all. But me and Brick love you, man. We both really love you."

"I dig the hell out of y'all, too." Shane blew out a cloud of smoke. "Y'all my niggas—real rap." He passed the blunt to Brick.

"Well, stop treating us like we don't count for shit," Misty said, sulkily.

"I feel you," Shane said. "The next time I go spend some time with my bro, I'll let y'all know how long I'll be gone. Aiight?"

Choking from inhaling too much smoke, Brick could only nod.

Misty gave a reluctant nod, and then she smiled devilishly. "So how you feel?"

Shane shrugged. "About what?"

"You know…how you feel knowing Brick knew about us all this time?"

Shane shifted uncomfortably. "Cut that shit, Misty. You fuckin' with the vibe."

"Now that everything's out in the open, it's time to get real."

"What's on your mind?" he asked her, skeptically. He really didn't want to know.

"I want both of y'all to do me."

Shane looked at her like she was crazy.

"Brick already said it was okay, didn't you, baby?"

"It's up to Shane," Brick mumbled and looked away in embarrassment.

"That ain't how you put it when I brought up the subject," Misty said, her nostrils flared in anger. "Don't be frontin' for Shane. You know you said you wanted to get into something with all three of us."

"I ain't feeling that shit, but ya'll go 'head. Knock yourselves out. I'm not into no three-way action." Shane puffed hard on the blunt, annoyed that Misty's proposition had totally blown his high. Feeling disgusted, he suddenly wanted to go home. He took another puff, passed it to Brick, and stood up. It was one thing to get with Misty on the low, but having Brick join in…well, Brick was his man and everything but that bullshit they were talking was real fucked up. What the hell was up with Brick? Letting Misty run the show was cute sometimes, but Brick was letting his girl take it to a whole other level. Oh well, Shane decided, live and let live.

"I'm out," Shane announced. He gathered his lighter and an unopened Dutch. "I'll get with y'all tomorrow."

"Why you leavin'?" Misty screeched.

"I gotta see my brother. Is that aiight with you?" Shane gave her a flaming look, daring her to make one sarcastic remark about his relationship with his twin.

Misty fidgeted in agitation but didn't open her mouth. She puffed and passed to Shane. Satisfied, Shane puffed on the blunt. He knew how to shut Misty up.

He passed the blunt to Brick and then walked toward the door. "Hollah back," Shane announced with a hint of defiance in his tone.

CHAPTER 33

Hopping in a cab, Shane was anxious to get home. He felt edgy. Misty and Brick were trying to draw him into some freak shit. He needed a break from his two friends; it was time to handle his hustle solo for a while. He'd hollah at them in a month or so—or however long it took for them to come back to their senses. Shane preferred creepin' with Misty. Brick had to be out of his mind to even think Shane would participate in a threesome with another man. Shane and Misty could pick things up where they left off when Brick decided to once again look the other way and pretend that Misty and Shane weren't knockin' boots right under his nose. Shane would be ghost until then.

"Mom!" Shane yelled when he walked into the quiet apartment. Surprisingly, the TV wasn't blaring. He figured she was probably in bed reading the Bible. He felt depressed and dispirited. He felt bad enough to let her read him a few Bible passages before he went to sleep. *Yeah, she'd like that*, Shane mused.

"Mom!" Still no answer. He stopped in the hallway and peeked in the bedroom. She was sound asleep. He stood outside the bedroom door trying to decide if he should wake her up so she could comfort him or just get in bed and try to fall asleep on his own.

He'd let her sleep, he decided, and went to the bathroom to take a shower.

After his shower, Shane made it as far as the doorway of the bedroom when he noticed the room was frigid and ominously quiet. With baited breath, Shane slid a glance at Dolores Holmes's chest, waiting to see the rise and fall of her breathing. She was still. A wave of panic thrust him inside the room.

Trembling, he knelt at the side of the bed. "Mom!" he yelled, his voice filled with terror. "Mom!"

Dolores Holmes's open eyes stared at nothing. Engulfed by fear, Shane called her again. He shook her urgently. "Please, Mom, wake up!" But Dolores Holmes didn't move. She lay stock-still.

"Wake up," he continued to plead, shaking his foster mother's lifeless body. "Please," he begged. "Wake up!" Crying bitterly, Shane collapsed upon the dead woman's chest. After nearly twenty minutes of sobbing, he finally pulled himself together enough to pick up the phone and call for an ambulance.

❀❀❀

"No point in taking your mother to the hospital, sir," said the emergency technician after examining Ms. Holmes. "We're going to take her straight to the city morgue. After you make funeral arrangements, the mortuary can pick her up from there."

Shane openly shed tears as the attendants lifted Dolores Holmes onto a stretcher. Shane touched her face tenderly before the men carried his foster mother's body to the waiting ambulance.

For over an hour, he wept bitterly. Shane saw flashing images of his birth mother as well as his foster mother as he cried out, *"Mommy"* in child-like repetition. In his mind's eye, the images of his biological mother were faded, but he recalled sharp, clearly focused images of his foster mother.

It wasn't fair. No one should lose two mothers in their lifetime. Filled with fury, Shane smashed an ashtray, flipped over the coffee table, and kicked the wide-screen TV. Drained, he picked up the phone and called Tariq.

"Put my brother on the phone," he said to Janelle in a choked voice.

"He's not here."

"Where is he?"

"Tariq's working for that moving company now. He's out of town until tomorrow."

Shane realized Janelle could hear the tears in his voice and was being uncharacteristically helpful.

"He should be calling me later on tonight. Do you want him to give you a call?"

"Yeah, tell him I need to talk to him," Shane said, his voice breaking like a child's. Shane didn't have any knowledge of how to handle funeral arrangements; he needed Tariq. He'd tell his brother as much of the truth as he felt Tariq could handle.

After a couple hours had elapsed without hearing from Tariq, Shane gave up and called Felicia Bradley's cell phone. Being a preacher's wife, he figured she'd have plenty of experience with death and funerals.

He got a recorded message; apparently Felicia's cell was turned off. Taking a chance, Shane called her home phone. Felicia answered sleepily, but became alert when Shane, still pretending that Ms. Holmes was his mother, told her what had happened.

"Who has the body?" she asked him.

"What?"

"Which mortuary?"

"I don't know; they took her to the morgue."

"Does she have an insurance policy? Did she make any burial arrangements?"

"I don't know, I doubt it," he said, frustration in his tone.

"Was she collecting social security?"

"Yeah, I think so. She got a little something from the government once a month."

"Social security will pay a portion of her funeral costs, but not much. If your mother doesn't have insurance and doesn't belong to any church that would help with the expenses, your best bet is to have her cremated. It's cheaper."

"How much is cheaper?"

"Different prices; it depends on what you want."

"My mother wouldn't like that; she'd want a decent burial and a preacher to say some words over her," Shane lamented, imagining Ms. Holmes's displeasure at her body being burned to ashes without being sanctioned by a minister.

"I can hold a small memorial service for your mother in our church," Felicia offered. "I could also get the reverend to speak at the service. Would you like me to make the arrangements for the cremation?"

"Yeah, would you, please?"

Shane hung up feeling a little better, but when he walked around the empty apartment, grief sent him out into the night. Out on the prowl.

❀❀❀

The bar he selected catered to a much older crowd, which was fine with Shane. The patrons were quiet and laid-back. The barmaid, who told him her name was Trisha, looked to be in her late forties, maybe fifty. Obviously attracted to Shane, Trisha kept up a steady flow of free drinks, which he had no problem accepting.

Despite being grief-stricken, lost, and distraught, Shane managed to hold a conversation with the mature barmaid.

Trisha's face was pleasant enough, with a wrinkle or two here and there, but that didn't bother Shane; he was used to older women. She was also rather flabby around the waist, which wasn't an issue either. It wasn't her face or her waistline that was of interest to Shane.

It was her breasts that had him transfixed, making him want to get to know her better. Her big sagging breasts influenced him to leave the bar with her at closing time.

Trisha revved up the sputtering engine of an old, cranky Chevy. She drove toward Elmwood Avenue and pulled into the Bartrum Garden apartments where she lived.

She wore a pleased expression, which seemed to imply that she had lucked up in bringing home a fine young specimen such as Shane. Nosey neighbors sitting on the stoop drinking and shooting the breeze fell silent when Trisha and Shane approached. Trisha cast them a triumphant expression as she led Shane to her apartment. They went straight into her bedroom. She dimmed the lights and took off her clothes and quickly got under the covers to hide the bodily imperfections brought on by years of eating greasy food and leading a sedentary lifestyle.

Shane undressed and joined her, instantly fondling the flabby softness of her protruding belly. He caressed the woman's saddlebag hips and the excess rolls of flesh around her midsection and up and down her back. His mouth sought the comfort of her big pendulous breasts. Her bosom was a lifeline.

Shane sucked hard and hungrily until Trisha gave subtle signals that it was time to move down further. Ignoring her signals, Shane kept a suction hold on her nipple.

"That's enough, baby," Trisha said, trying to ease Shane off her breast. "Don't you want to get busy?" She spread her legs invitingly.

Shane stuck a finger in the moist fleshy area to appease her, but he continued sucking her nipple.

"Stop!" Trisha said in a harsh tone. "You're hurting me." She tried to disengage her nipple from Shane's mouth.

"Just another minute," he pleaded. Damn, he missed his mom. He missed the warm milk. He didn't like Trisha's dry-ass titties. Not wanting to give in to more tears, Shane chose anger as an emotional release. He deliberately bit Trisha's nipple.

"Ow!" she shouted.

"Why you gotta keep complaining?"

"I know you don't think I brought you home with me so you could bite on my boobs all night!" She rolled her eyes in indignation.

And that's when Shane felt the pain of his loss—and the rage it brought on. Who would ever treat him the way his mom had? Nobody. Hot fury washed over him. He slapped Trisha across the face.

With her mouth opened in shock, Trisha turned her head in the direction of the telephone. No doubt, she was going to call the police. Shane balled his angry fists and sent a flurry of blows to her face and head.

Screaming, she protected her face with her hands. His punches now landed on her chest and arms. A powerful gut punch left Trisha breathless. As she lay gasping, Shane kicked her and then dressed hurriedly. He knew Trisha had made tips that night, so he quickly dumped out the contents of her pocketbook, seized eighty dollars in small bills, and fled the apartment.

He started running when he got outside. Running in case Trisha had called the police. Tears wet his cheeks as he recalled the violence he'd inflicted upon his foster mother years ago. Was he crazy, he wondered? His birth mother was crazy. Had she passed her insanity on to him? No, he wasn't crazy, he told himself as he continued to run like the wind. Crazy people walked around mumbling and harassing people. He just had a bad temper. That was all. A really bad temper.

Running from his demons, Shane didn't stop moving until his legs finally gave out.

CHAPTER 34

Dolores Holmes would have been proud of her memorial service. The choir sang two selections and Reverend Daniels preached a sermon with such passion, one would have assumed he was personally acquainted with the large woman who'd been reduced to ashes inside an urn. The urn, illuminated by light, was positioned prominently before the altar.

Tariq attended the service with his brother. Shane's request that he accompany him to the funeral had come from out of the blue. He had no idea Shane had renewed a relationship with their ex-foster mother. Although he was more confused than bereft, Tariq was nevertheless moved to tears by the fervent words of the minister.

Shane wept unashamedly throughout the entire ceremony. Afterward, he thanked and shook hands with the pastor. He introduced Tariq to Reverend Daniels and Felicia Bradley, whom he referred to as Mrs. Bradley in public.

"Your mother's with the Lord now, boys. She's at peace," Reverend Daniels said to Shane and Tariq.

Tariq nodded uncomfortably. His head was spinning in confusion as he shook hands with the parishioners who came up to shake his hand, wearing grave expressions as they offered their condolences for his "mother."

When Tariq had a moment alone with Shane, he said, "I can't believe you and Miz Holmes were living together. How come you never mentioned it?"

"Man, she was doing bad, living in some boarding home. I was just trying to make up for all the bad stuff that happened to her. You know…help her out and everything."

Tariq listened intently with an arched brow, his chin cradled between the V of his thumb and index finger. "Okay, but how come you got all these people believing she's our real mother?"

Shane narrowed his eyes. "She's the only mother we ever had."

"I know. But we haven't seen her in years."

"*You* ain't seen her. I been lookin' out for her for a while."

"You should have told me, Shane. You didn't have to carry the burden by yourself."

"You got your own family and everything; you didn't need no extra mouth to feed. Anyway, I wanted to do it. I was the one who got her in all that trouble."

Tariq grimaced. "You lied on Miz Holmes?"

"No, I didn't lie on her. She was so drunk when they came to the house, she wasn't making any sense. Somehow they got her words twisted and *thought* she molested me," Shane explained.

"So, how come you didn't tell the truth?"

"I was scared, man. I didn't wanna testify in no courtroom." Shane hung his head in shame. "That's why I had to help her out. I owed her that much."

"What about Miss Goldie?"

Shane shrugged. "I don't know nothin' about that. I swear, Tariq," Shane said, lying. "I don't know how Miss Goldie's name got dragged in that mess."

"You ever hear from LaDonna?"

"Naw and I ain't trying to see her either. I know she hates my guts." Shane was thoughtful for a moment. "Look, man, let's leave Miss Goldie and LaDonna in the past." He looked down in thought. "I don't know how to explain my relationship with Miz Holmes…" Shane paused. "You have Janelle and your son. You have a family. I don't have nothing. I needed her, man; she was more than a mother. And she needed me. You hear what I'm saying?"

Despair emanated from Shane; his tortured expression nearly broke Tariq's heart. Tariq realized how fortunate he was to have Janelle. Janelle was more than a wife. Like a mother, she was a strict disciplinarian. He loved her so much he was able to tolerate the cruel streak she exhibited at times when she seemed to maliciously test the boundaries of his love by making unreasonable demands of him.

Still, Tariq believed with all his heart that Janelle loved him. Maybe not as much as he loved her, but enough to keep him satisfied. Tariq didn't think he could survive without Janelle. He wasn't strong enough.

Scratching his head, he tried to make sense of the relationship between Shane and Ms. Holmes, but he couldn't figure it out. Shane had vehemently denied the rumors that Ms. Holmes had molested him. Tariq frowned at the thought. He couldn't even begin to imagine the sweet woman doing what she was accused of.

Still, there was no denying that there was something weird going on with Shane and Ms. Holmes, Tariq thought, grimly recalling how disrespectful she'd allowed Shane to treat her back when she was their foster mother.

But it was safer to let sleeping dogs lie, so he decided not to pry into Shane's business. Hell, he didn't fully comprehend his relationship with his own wife, so how could he begin to understand what Shane and Ms. Holmes were doing? The one thing he did understand was his brother's need to belong. Apparently, Ms. Holmes was a comfort to Shane.

"Why don't you stay with me and Janelle tonight?" Tariq offered. "You probably shouldn't stay in that apartment tonight. Um…too many memories in there," he stammered. "I can help you get rid of her things tomorrow if you want."

Shane shook his head. "No, I'm leaving all her stuff just like it is."

Tariq didn't argue with Shane; he didn't want to provoke him into shedding more tears. Trying to come up with a way to take his brother's mind off of his grief, Tariq said, "Yo, man. My job is hiring. You looking for a real gig?"

"Naw, I like pimpin'," Shane said, and finally submitted to laughter. "Pimpin' ain't easy, the pay ain't dependable…but I do aiight," he bragged.

Tariq shook his head. He didn't approve of the way Shane used women but he was relieved to see his brother finally smile. "Man, I'm only offering the job so you can get away from here for a while. You know…take your mind off everything. We have a job coming up in a couple of days—moving some stuff to South Carolina. My boss is looking for a few extra hands. We hardly see each other, I could use the company and you can get your rent without pimpin' innocent women," Tariq said, laughing.

Shane thought for a moment. "Do I have to fill out an application and shit?"

"No, I can get you in on this job on the strength that you're my twin brother. I'm cool with the office manager. Her name's Kapri; she can get you in."

"Aw shit," Shane teased. "Don't tell me you're creepin' on Janelle?"

"Never." Tariq said, appalled that Shane would even entertain such a thought. "No, me and Kapri are real tight. She's like the sister I never had."

"Aiight, man. I'll check out the job situation, but I'm staying at my own place tonight."

"You sure you gon' be all right?"

"Man, I ain't no baby. I'm cool," Shane said gruffly. "Let's go, I'll walk you to the bus stop."

When the bus arrived, the brothers embraced. Tariq gave Shane a cautious look. He knew Shane was in emotional turmoil but he repressed the urge to beg his brother to spend the night with him and Janelle. He hated the thought of his grief-stricken brother returning to the apartment he shared with Ms. Holmes.

"Seriously, man. I'm aiight," Shane said in response to Tariq's worried expression. He shifted awkwardly and then added, "Look, I'm gonna take that trip to South Carolina just to spend some time with you. Aiight?"

As he stepped onto the bus, Tariq leaned out the door. Cupping a hand to the side of his mouth, he yelled out to Shane, "Don't let me down, man."

Shane whirled around. "I'm there, man. I gotchu!"

❦❦❦

Unaccustomed to keeping morning hours, Shane overslept. Knowing Tariq would be disappointed if he didn't show, he called his brother immediately. "I overslept, man. I'm not gonna be able to make it to your place by seven. I guess I'll catch you on the next trip."

"You can make it, Shane. You're closer to Rose Moving Company than you are to my apartment." Tariq gave Shane the address of his employer. "Take the bus over there and wait for me in the lobby. I'll call Kapri and tell her to look out for you."

"Aiight," Shane said reluctantly. He was hoping to get out of the moving job. Moving furniture and shit sounded like something more suitable for a husky dude like Brick. Shane wasn't cut out for hard labor. Pimpin' was a pain but it bought weed and paid the rent. Damn, he was sorry he let Tariq talk him into this bullshit.

An hour later, Shane sauntered into the office of Rose Moving Company. A cute, peach-colored young woman sat behind the desk. She wore glasses, which didn't distract from her good looks. In fact, the glasses added something—made Shane think of the meek type who'd whip off the glasses in the bedroom, yank the hair pin from her modest upswept hairdo, and transform into a sexual beast. Shane smiled at his inner vision.

"Good morning," she said sweetly and smiled back. The woman's warm smile didn't surprise Shane; he was accustomed to good treatment from females. But he *was* surprised at the rate his heart was thumping.

She stood up and stuck out a dainty little French-manicured hand. "I'm Kapri. You must be Shane Batista." The scent of citrus wafted from her. Unconsciously, Shane inhaled generously.

"Whassup, Kapri," Shane said. With the sweet smell of citrus filling his nostrils, it was difficult for Shane to keep his voice steady. He felt an instant and powerful attraction to the pretty, petite young lady. He wrinkled his forehead in confusion.

"I feel like I know you," Shane added, hoping Kapri wouldn't think it was just a line. "Tariq talks about you all the time."

"Tariq and I have a very special friendship. It's so nice to finally meet you." Kapri was now beaming, which made her appear even more attractive. Her smile caused an even stronger tug at Shane's heartstrings.

"Can I get you some coffee or tea?" he heard her say.

"Naw, I'm straight."

"Orange juice…Pepsi?" she pressed with a tilt to her head.

"Yeah, some OJ might do it for me. Wake me up, know what I mean?"

Kapri stepped from behind the desk. "I'll be right back." She glanced at her watch. "Your brother should be here any minute."

The front view was tight. Shane definitely liked what he saw. Kapri had a pretty face, wide brown eyes, and a perky set of boobs. She wore her hair in a conservative style that was pinned in place with a wide, plain barrette. Shane checked out Kapri's back view as she bustled off down the hall. His eyes clung to the curves of her body; he nodded with approval. Her thick shapely legs were visible below her short pleated skirt. She had a nice ass and sexy hips. He couldn't help envisioning his hands tightly gripping her round hips as he drove some pipe up in her. A low guttural moan escaped as his manhood began to swell.

Shane wanted to get to know Kapri better. A lot better. *And Kapri can get this dick for free*. Amused by the thought, Shane gave a little chuckle.

Tariq bopped in a few moments later. He broke into an ear-to-ear grin when he saw Shane. The brothers slapped hands.

"Yo, bro. Whassup with Kapri? Shorty's got it goin' on! You didn't tell me she was all fine and shit."

"Man, Kapri has plans and stuff; she's not with all that dumb stuff you're into. She's into getting an education, working, and saving her money. Don't mess with her, Shane," Tariq cautioned. "Man, don't even go there."

"Why not? You trying to hit it?"

"Why you gotta be so crude all the time? Kapri's my friend. She was my *only* friend after I lost you."

Shane flinched.

"I love her like a sister. Man, leave her alone; I don't want Kapri getting hurt. She deserves better."

Shane's face pinched up in indignation. "What? I'm not good enough for her?"

Tariq sighed. "That's not what I'm saying and you know it."

Shane's expression softened. "I'm not trying to hurt her; I just wanna…you know…hit it a couple times," Shane said, laughing.

Tariq didn't laugh. "I said she's not like that." Tariq's face reddened; he was visibly upset.

"Man, I'm just playin'. Stop actin' all serious all the time." Shane shot Tariq a dazzling smile that persuaded Tariq to smile also.

"Good morning, Tariq!" Kapri said, carrying two containers of orange juice. She handed one to Shane, then immediately got down to business.

"Do you have identification, Shane?" she asked after she resumed her seat behind the desk. Her voice now sounded crisp and professional.

"Just Pennsylvania ID."

"That's fine. I need your Pennsylvania ID and your social security card."

Shane shot Tariq an unpleasant look. "Man, you didn't tell me I needed to bring no social security card."

"You always need to bring your social security card when you're seeking employment," Kapri said, maintaining her professional voice.

"I'm not seeking employment," Shane responded. "I'm just...you know... gonna travel with my brother. Help him out with his gig."

"No, that's not the way we do things here. I'll need to file some paperwork— an employment application, a short questionnaire, and you're going to have fill out a W-2 form."

"Man, I'm not trying to get all deep into this employment bullshit."

Tariq was appalled by his brother's crudeness, but Kapri found it hilarious. Laughing she asked, "Well, exactly how deep were you planning to get?"

Not realizing she was joking, Shane responded in a serious manner. "You know, I just wanna do this one job with my brother. I'm not trying to get hired for real. So look, just take my name and um...I don't wanna give out all my personal information. You could be a cop for all I know."

While Tariq looked mortified by his brother's bad manners; Kapri seemed to be having fun. She chuckled as she slid Shane a blank piece of paper. "Write your address and social. I'll fill out the application for you while Tariq shows you around. Do you think we have a spare uniform, Tariq? Your brother is so tall, I don't know if we have anything that'll fit him."

"A uniform? Man, I ain't wearing no monkey suit. What's wrong with the clothes I have on?" Shane shot Tariq another accusatory look, frowned, and then blew out a rush of exasperated breath.

"You're really difficult, aren't you?" Kapri said. "I'll tell you what. Can you meet me halfway on this?" she asked in a lowered tone.

"I'll try," Shane said, a smile playing at the corner of his lips.

"Just wear one of the Rose Company shirts. You can keep on the jeans you're wearing. I doubt if we have slacks long enough to fit you, anyway."

After giving Shane a quick tour and briefing him on company policy, Tariq and three other men piled into a huge moving van decorated with a Rose logo. Shane pretended that he'd left something behind and made a quick pit stop back into the office.

"Yes?" Kapri said, looking up at Shane.

Shane didn't say a word. He didn't have to. He assumed Kapri found him as desirable as most women did. Smiling, he held his thumb up to his ear and little finger pointed toward his mouth. "Can you jot that information down?"

He was right. Kapri blushed and without hesitation, she tore off a pink Post-It and wrote her full name and phone number in large script and handed it to Shane.

"I'm gonna call you while I'm on the road," he informed her.

"And I'll be waiting," she said, with her eyelids lowered. Then she looked up and boldly added, "Don't make me wait too long."

Shane gave her a broad smile and tucked the Post-It in his shirt pocket. He patted his pocket. "I'm keeping you close to my heart. You'll be hearing from me real soon."

CHAPTER 35

The heavy lifting wasn't the worst part of the trip. Realizing he'd left his phone charger at home was devastating. Shane made this discovery when his cell went dead right in the middle of a spicy conversation with Kapri while he was confined inside the moving van.

After what felt like hundreds of miles on the road, the crew selected a motel to stay the night. Shane, anxious to resume the conversation, immediately picked up the phone in his room and tried to call Kapri, but to his chagrin the phone system was outdated and the desk clerk had to place the call. When Shane asked the clerk to hit Kapri's digits, the crotchety old clerk told him she couldn't get through.

In Philly, Shane could find practically anything from socks to phone chargers at any hour of the night, but there were no late-night vendors hustling anything in the rural area where the moving crew was spending the night. Shane had no choice but to wait until morning to purchase another charger. There had to be a Verizon store somewhere in the hick Southern town.

The next morning, while Tariq and the rest of the crew were moving furniture, Shane hitched a ride to the nearest Radio Shack and bought a charger, brought it back to the home they were moving furniture into, and plugged it in.

When the charger's red light turned green, Shane started pushing numbers.

"Are you working hard?" Kapri asked softly.

"Real hard," Shane said and grunted theatrically. "This big-ass sofa is 'bout to break my back." He grunted again as he stood against the wall, chilling on his cell while his brother and the other men worked like slaves.

"You must have a strong back," Kapri said.

"I do, but um—we shouldn't get into a conversation like this right now. Not while I'm at work. But I'd be glad to show you how strong my back is when I get back in town."

She gave an embarrassed gasp. "I didn't mean it the way it sounded." Then Kapri laughed. "I meant…carrying a heavy sofa while holding and talking on your cell must require a lot of strength."

"I'm wearing a headset," he lied.

"Well, you must be extremely strong," Kapri's voice sounded whispery. "You're not breathing hard; that sofa must be as light as a feather."

Shane groaned sexily. "Did you hear that?"

"Uh huh."

"That's how I sound when I'm working hard."

The sexual innuendos weren't lost on either Shane or Kapri.

"Yo, Kapri. You gon' let me take you out when I get back in town?" *Did I really ask her that?* Shane had never asked a girl out on a date, but he had to come at Kapri from a different angle. He figured she'd bang on him if he used his normal approach and said, *Yo, Kapri. You gon' let me hit it when I get back in town?*

"Okay, that would be nice. What do you like to do for leisure, Shane?"

If he were truthful, Shane would have responded with *I like to smoke weed, snort a little blow, shoot craps, I get a rush from periodically engaging in strong-arm robbery, but I'm really into big pimpin'—on the regular.*

But Shane wasn't an honest person, so he said the things he thought Kapri would like to hear. "I love basketball," he said truthfully. Then he lied. "I like to take long walks in the park, especially when it rains."

"Really!"

"Yeah. I don't usually reveal this type of information. But, I'm really feelin' you," Shane said tenderly.

Kapri sighed as her breath caught.

"I also like to go bowling. I like all types of sports. Do you like bowling?"

"I've never gone bowling," Kapri admitted wistfully and Shane knew he had her.

"Wanna learn?"

"What?"

"How to bowl." Shane had bowled frequently during his stint at Barney Hills.

"Oh, okay," Kapri agreed.

"Aiight. When I get back, I'm gonna teach you how to bowl."

"Sounds good," she softly murmured.

"Aiight. Hey, look. The fellas are calling me. Those weaklings can't lug shit without me. I gotta get back to work." He paused. "Smooches, baby. I'll hollah the next time I get a break."

"'Bye, Shane," Kapri said dreamily.

❀❀❀

"Why haven't you been answering my calls?" Felicia Bradley shouted so loudly, Shane had to pull the cell away from his ear.

"Damn, ma. Why you acting all hot and bothered? You miss big daddy?" he asked.

"Don't disrespect me, Shane. We had an arrangement. I've been holding up my end. Didn't I do everything I agreed to do regarding your mother's memorial service?"

"Yo, I'm not trying to be disrespectful, but you didn't pay one dime toward the cremation, I had to come outta pocket and because of that, I had to go out of town to make some money."

"Doing what? Nothing illegal, I hope."

"Naw, the work I did was legal like a muthafucker," Shane said, laughing.

"Don't be crude, Shane."

"Yo, I'm being myself. Chill, ma. What's the problem? You miss big daddy or what?"

Felicia hesitated and then sighed out a reluctant, "Yes."

"That's all you had to say. When you tryin' to see me?"

"Now."

"Right now?" He looked at the clock and frowned. "I just got in from doing a moving job. I have to shower and change."

"You can do that in the motel room," Felicia insisted.

"Aiight. Well, swing by and pick me up, I'm too tired to walk to our usual meeting place."

"I'll be there in fifteen minutes sharp," she said in a formal tone.

Shane was not in the mood for tussling around with the muscle-bound woman, but he could use the extra cash. The money he'd made on the move was needed to pay his rent and other obligations. If he expected to show Kapri a good time, he was going to need some extra dough.

Fifteen minutes later, Felicia honked the horn twice.

Shane slid in the passenger seat. "Hey, whassup?" He reclined in the passenger seat and closed his eyes.

"What kind of work did you say you were you doing?" Felicia asked, attempting to engage Shane in light banter during the drive.

Shane opened his eyes. "Heavy lifting. I did some work for a moving company."

"I hope you didn't injure your back," she said with a smirk.

"I'm straight," he responded and closed his eyes. The discussion was over; Shane didn't intend to respond to any more meaningless questions. He had Kapri on his mind and wanted to get the session with Felicia over with as soon as possible.

She rolled into the parking lot of a different motel on Admiral Wilson Boulevard in New Jersey. There were a plethora of liquor stores in the vicinity and there was one right next to the motel. "Yo, let me hold something so I can pick up a bottle. You drink, don't you?"

Felicia pursed her lips disapprovingly and piously shook her head no.

"Well, I do."

Felicia huffed in annoyance before extracting two twenties from her wallet. Shane got out while she took care of the room arrangements. When he returned to the parking lot, Felicia was sitting in the car, smiling and dangling the key ring while wearing a naughty smile.

Shane struggled to suppress a yawn.

He took the bottle of Absolut into the bathroom with him, drinking as he urinated. He continued to drink from the bottle as he showered. He had to be feeling nicer-than-nice to fuck Felicia.

Nothing jiggled. Felicia's buns-of-steel ass was like a statue's. Still, hitting it from the back wasn't too bad. Shane worked up a rhythm and didn't have to rely on an imaginary lap dance from Beyonce. He thought about Kapri and started working it as if Felicia had the softest ass and the best pussy in the world.

"Smack my ass," Felicia ordered.

Shane was happy to oblige, but her hard ass hurt his hand. "Harder," she insisted.

Shane applied more pressure. "Harder!" she screamed.

"Yo, I ain't trying to break my wrist. How hard you want me to hit it?" he asked. Irritated, he dismounted her.

Looking frantic, Felicia jerked her head around. "What's wrong?"

"It's cool, ma. I ain't goin' nowhere. You can turn back around." He pulled his belt out of the loops of his pants, returned to the bed, and commenced to whipping her hard ass.

Felicia screamed and then started emitting sounds of pleasure. "Oh yes, baby. You know how I like it; beat my ass. Beat it!"

Only too happy to fuck her up, Shane swung the belt until welts covered her backside.

Breathing hard, Felicia collapsed onto her stomach and began grinding against the mattress. Shane felt repelled. Not wanting to prolong the sickening session much longer, Shane decided to help the sick bitch out. He stuck his finger beneath her and fondled her clit. She came with a loud scream that could have easily awakened the dead.

He wiped her juices from his finger on the bedspread.

While Felicia was still caught up in the throes of orgasmic pleasure, Shane asked, "How much you kickin' out, ma?"

"Look in my wallet, Shane," she said, still panting and apparently unable to move.

Four fifty-dollar bills didn't seem fair after all she'd put him through, so while she panted and sighed, he browsed through the hidden compartments of her wallet and extracted an additional two hundred dollars.

He dressed quickly, put the money in his pocket, and sat on the bed. Mimicking a voice that sounded concerned, he said, "You all right, ma?"

"Yeah, I'm fine." She winced when she positioned herself into a seating position. "That was fabulous, Shane. I really enjoyed it." She got up and examined her rear end in the mirror on the outside of the bathroom door. Smiling approvingly, she said wistfully, "It's a good thing my husband isn't in the best of health, otherwise I don't know how I'd explain these welts."

She seemed quite proud of her battle scars. Shane would be only too glad to oblige her again in the future, but at the moment he didn't feel like participating in a long discussion about the welts on her manly ass. He had his money and he was ready to roll out.

The drive over the Walt Whitman Bridge was quiet. Felicia squirmed in her seat, obviously in severe discomfort brought on by the whipping. Shane refused to offer her sympathy. She asked for it and he gave her what she wanted. He kept his eyes focused on the bridge traffic. With all her squirming and carrying on, he didn't want her to lose control of the car and send them careening over the side of the bridge.

Felicia paid the bridge toll and merged onto the Schuylkill Expressway. She cut her eyes at Shane. "I'd like another session later on tonight."

"You must be crazy!" Shane blurted.

"I'll pay you double," she said anxiously.

"Why? Ain't your ass on fire? Why you want some more?"

"I want to try something different," she confessed.

Shane, always on top of his game, wasn't about to miss out on a great opportunity. "Well, look. Check this out. I got something to do. Why don't you let me hold your wheel and then I can make it back at a decent hour."

"Hold my what?"

"Your wheel. Your ride. Your car. Damn!"

"My car! Shane, do you have a driver's license?" Felicia asked, lines of apprehension forming on her forehead.

"Forget it!" Sulking, he turned his head away from her.

"All right," Felicia said desperately. "But please be careful. Please follow all traffic laws and don't have a gang of young hoodlums in my car. That'll attract too much attention—"

"Yo! Chill. I gotchu. I ain't no chump. You ain't gotta tell me how to handle myself. I know what to do."

CHAPTER 36

"**N**ice," Kapri commented when Shane opened the car door for her. Being with Kapri made him want to behave like a gentleman, but on the real, he felt like a weirdo; he'd never opened a door for a woman in his life.

"It's not my ride; I borrowed it from a friend. I'm trying to make a good impression on you," he admitted with a bashful grin.

"That's so sweet. But you didn't have to go to all this trouble, I have a car." She pointed to a cute Mazda 3 parked at the curb. "It can't compete with this, but it'll take us wherever we want to go."

"That's you!" Shane said, referring to Kapri's car. "It's cute; just like you."

Kapri blushed. "Thank you."

"So, tell me—what's this about? You seem like a nice girl. You got it going on—decent job, your own place, a nice set of wheels...why you interested in a thug like me?" he inquired challengingly.

"You know what they say. Every lady needs a thug in her life!" Kapri chuckled. "But no...seriously. I liked you before I met you. Tariq loves you; he's told me all about you. He said you ended up in that reform school due to circumstances beyond your control. I know about..." Kapri shifted uncomfortably and looked down. "I know about your past...your mother's death, all the foster homes."

"Yo!" He held up a hand to silence her. "I'm not tryin' to go down that old road. We're goin' out to have some fun. Feel me?"

Kapri nodded. Her expression told him that she was sorry she'd touched upon a sensitive topic.

"Baby," he said, softening his tone. "Can you think of something else we can do? I have to pass on bowling. When I mentioned it, I didn't realize how sore I'd be from all that heavy lifting I do on the job."

"No, I don't mind at all," Kapri said.

"You hungry?"

"Starved."

"You like seafood?"

"Love it!"

"Me, too."

They drove to Red Lobster on Baltimore Pike in Springfield. It was pretty crowded; the smiling hostess informed them there'd be a forty-five-minute wait, so Shane escorted Kapri to the bar.

She ordered a White Russian, he had three Heinekens, and by the time their table was ready, they were both feeling slightly intoxicated. They laughed gaily as Shane escorted her to their table with his arm around her waist.

During the meal, behaving amorously and uninhibited, Kapri reached across the table to lightly stroke the fine hairs that sprouted from the top of Shane's hand and traveled up his arm.

"Watch yourself, shorty; you don't wanna play with fire," he warned.

"Why not? I don't think you'll burn me. In fact, I think you're my knight in shining armor. You're the man who's going to protect me from harm," Kapri said flirtatiously. Suddenly turning red, she covered her mouth. "This isn't me," she explained with a giggle. "It's this," she said, pointing to her drink. "It's making me act…"

"Like you got the hots for me," Shane said, teasingly finishing her sentence. "Suppose I was real honest with you and told you that I'm not trying to get serious. Suppose I told you that I'm freelancing right now and all I want to do is get you in bed, no strings attached, I'll see you when I see you. What would you say?"

"I'm up to the challenge," Kapri said boldly. "But make sure you can handle it when I'm not in the mood to see *you*." She gave Shane a wink; her tongue touched her top lip naughtily.

"It's a deal, shorty," he said, reaching for her hand, caressing it. Shane hadn't felt this good in quite a while. He was comfortable around Kapri and felt he could put his guard down—reveal his softer side.

"Shorty!" She wrinkled her nose. "Shorty sounds so impersonal. Don't you think I'm special enough to be called by my first name?"

Shane nodded, thinking that Kapri's ass looked real *special* in the tight jeans she had on. *Her ass would look even more special if those jeans were on the floor!*

They left the restaurant and went back to Kapri's place—a small, nicely furnished apartment. Shane and Kapri didn't waste time sitting and chatting in the living room. Their physical attraction for each other was so strong, the couple made a beeline straight to the bedroom.

Standing on her tiptoes, Kapri threw her arms around Shane's neck and kissed him passionately. "I feel like I've been waiting for you all my life, Shane. I fell in love with you at first sight," she confessed. "No, that's not true," she corrected, shaking her head. "I fell in love with you a long time ago—years ago."

Shane furrowed his brow.

"I know it sounds crazy. But back when Tariq and I worked at McDonald's, he talked about you constantly. He described you physically, so I already had a mental image. He spoke of your dual personality."

"My what?"

"He said you showed the world your fiery temperament, but he and possibly your former foster mother knew about your deep sensitivity. He told me you've been looking out for him for as long as he can remember. As far as Tariq is concerned, you can do no wrong. You've always been his protector. You're his hero, Shane."

Shane felt touched by her words. He wasn't big on kissing, he typically liked to get to the good part as soon as possible, but Kapri was speaking to his heart; he was really feeling her. So, he offered his lips—softly at first and then he slowly slipped his tongue inside her mouth. Her mouth tasted sweet, as if she'd been eating tangerines. Shane rubbed his tongue against hers, while his fingers unbuttoned her blouse and eased it off her shoulders and unhooked her bra.

He fondled her firm breasts, kissed them. But afraid he'd lose control, Shane forced himself to move away from dangerous territory. Laying Kapri down on her stomach, he softly brushed his lips across her back and nuzzled her thighs through the denim fabric. She moaned when he placed little bites all over her butt cheeks. Turning her over, he kissed her stomach and unsnapped and unzipped her jeans.

He helped her wiggle out of the tight jeans and then kissed and licked her crotch until the flimsy satin fabric of her underwear was soaked from the mingling of her juices and the moistness of his tongue.

Kapri pulled Shane's curly hair, which enticed him to lick with an intensity that made her shudder.

Finally putting them both out their misery, Shane pulled down Kapri's tiny thong and slipped it off her ankles. He parted her vaginal lips as if they were delicate flower petals and placed his tongue inside, stretching it as far as it would go, pushing in and out until Kapri whimpered with desire.

Shane ripped off his clothes. "Kapri," he whispered huskily. "You gon' get on the mic?"

She nodded and took in as much of his oversized dick as she could take without choking. She let it slip out of her mouth and slid the shaft across her face. Shane kept his eyes open, enjoying the erotic sight. Watching her give him oral sex sent ripples of pleasure through his body.

"Damn, baby. I didn't know you could rap like that," he said with a forceful thrust. Then he pulled out. "That's it; that's enough! You gotta stop, baby. The way you spittin' out lyrics, you 'bout to make me cum."

He rolled over and got on top of Kapri. Slipping inside her, Shane tried his best to hit every inch of her inner walls: the sides, the top, the bottom. Then, he drove in even deeper. He wanted to please this woman—this sexy little angel. It was a brand-new feeling, something totally unfamiliar. Love? He wasn't sure, but he knew what he was feeling was something much more than lust.

"Shane," she said, holding him tight and breathing hard. "You ever been in love? I mean, really, truly in love?" Kapri asked as if reading Shane's mind.

"Never." He answered breathily. He couldn't count his feelings toward his foster mother as romantic love. It was a different kind of love. He shook away an image of Dolores Holmes; he didn't want to break the mood by thinking about her.

"Do you want to be in love?" Kapri persistently inquired.

Damn, he wished she'd shut up so he could concentrate. "No, I'm not ready," he said in a pleading voice that begged her not to take him there.

"But can't you feel it?"

"Yes," he admitted in a husky whisper.

"Do you like it?"

"No."

"Why not?"

"I'm scared."

There was silence. Shane couldn't believe that he'd just confessed that he was scared. Though he wanted to retract the statement, he knew it was too late.

He pulled Kapri tightly against him. Her heart beat against his as he rocked her into his mating rhythm. Pumping, thrusting, undulating as he tried to block out all thoughts. He blocked out all the words of love that poured past Kapri's passionate lips. When she screamed his name, her cries broke through his barrier and Shane could no longer hold back the words. "I love you, too. Kapri, I need you, girl."

❋❋❋

Tariq wasn't happy with the relationship between his brother and his best friend. Kapri had no idea of the type of man she was dealing with; she hadn't a clue that nothing good could result from a relationship with Shane. Shane couldn't help himself. He had a destructive side that would eventually touch Kapri's well-planned life and throw it out of whack. Knock her off her mark.

From Tariq's point of view, it seemed Shane just didn't like women very much. His brother's only use for women was for pocket money and sex. Despite Kapri's beauty and sweetness, Tariq doubted that she could change Shane's true nature. Shane didn't mean to hurt the people who loved him, but that's what he did.

Tariq felt powerless. There was no point in trying to talk either one out of the relationship. Kapri and Shane had become inseparable, and were head over heels. She'd told Tariq she wanted Shane to move in with her, but Shane kept hedging the discussion.

Tariq was relieved that his brother and Kapri maintained separate residences. Living with Shane would bring Kapri nothing but misery. Shane would never settle into a monogamous relationship. He really wished Shane would come to his senses and leave Kapri alone. Couldn't Shane see that Kapri deserved better? Tariq did not want to witness Kapri's downfall. Shane had the power to change Kapri from the sweetest girl in the world to a bitter and disillusioned woman. No, Tariq did not want Kapri to experience the unique brand of pain that Shane could dispense without as much as a blink of an eye.

CHAPTER 37

Reverend Bradley's health was declining rapidly. Desiring to give the parishioners who visited frequently the impression that she was a long-suffering but dutiful wife, Felicia stayed close to home. The good reverend was now kept heavily drugged, thus Shane was often a late-night visitor in Felicia's bedroom while her husband convalesced in his study downstairs, which had been converted to a bedroom.

Pretending to be the delivery person from a twenty-four-hour pharmacy, Shane rang the bell at the spacious Bradley home. "Oh hi," Felicia said cheerfully. "I've been waiting for the reverend's medication. Thanks for getting it here so quickly."

"Who is it, Felicia?" her husband called out in a weak croak.

"It's the delivery person from the pharmacy. We're going to go upstairs for a while. I want to count your pills and make sure they're all here."

"That's good. Don't let those people cheat us."

"I won't. Now, you go back to sleep, darling."

A few seconds later, Shane could hear the ailing reverend's raspy snores.

Shane and Felicia had developed a very close relationship, but she maintained her position—sexual release was all she wanted from him. A type of sexual release that the average man wouldn't understand.

Shane didn't pass judgment; he had his own demons to deal with. What he liked about Felicia was that she wasn't clingy or needy; she didn't require pillow talk after having sex. She got straight to the point, got her freak on, and didn't mind when Shane hastily dressed so he could be on his way.

Now, there were times when she wanted to see him more than once a day, but that had nothing to do with an emotional attachment to him. That was just the freaky deaky coming out in her. Shane also liked the fact that Felicia never expected freebies. She paid for every session and never haggled over the price.

Felicia stripped naked within seconds. Shane had grown accustomed to her muscular body. It no longer bothered him. Besides, Felicia hardly ever wanted to fuck in the traditional manner.

She strode over to the closet and pulled out a four-inch-wide black leather belt and then sauntered over to the bed, passed the belt to Shane and lay on her back.

"Why ain't you laying on your stomach?" Shane asked.

"I'm in the mood for something different."

"Oh yeah? What?"

"My pussy needs a whipping." She spoke in a manner that was as cool and detached as if she were instructing someone to mow her lawn.

Shane's lips stretched into an uncomfortable smile of disbelief. "You're kiddin'."

"I kid you not." She propped her head up on two pillows and closed her eyes as she blissfully awaited the first blow.

Grimacing, Shane held the belt awkwardly. "Hard? You want me to hit your thing, hard?"

Felicia opened her eyes. "Shane, my husband's medication is going to wear off in a half hour, so our time together is limited. The reverend is going to be crying out in pain and calling my name. I deserve some pleasure until then; that's what I pay you for."

"I'm just saying…you throwing me off with this. I ain't never beat on no pussy before. I mean…damn. That ain't my twist."

"Shane," she said with a sigh. "Stop wasting time."

"Well, how you want me to do it?"

"You can start softly—a series of soft smacks that increase in intensity with each blow. You're not to stop until I cum. Understand?"

Damn, Felicia was more throwed off than Shane had realized. He needed to be getting some extra cheddar for this freaky shit.

Felicia settled back into her position and Shane hit her hairy vagina with the belt. The hair of her mons cushioned the blow.

"Harder," she whispered as she gyrated as if being fucked.

Wanting to get it over with quickly, Shane put a little more strength into the next blow.

Felicia cried out and then began to thrust her pelvis upward, gyrating and breathing hard as she awaited the next thrash.

Shane hit her again and this time he almost passed out from shock. All of a sudden, Felicia's clit popped out of her pussy as if awakened from the dead. Her clit looked unusually long—like a small finger, protruding from her vagina.

Shane actually wanted to drop the belt and bolt, but Felicia was panting and demanding that he now beat her clit. He hit it softly. It turned red and looked swollen and now resembled the first joint of a thumb.

"Harder!"

Repulsed to the point of anger, Shane lit up Felicia's clit with a rapid series of slaps. When she reared up and hollered, "I'm cumming!" Shane had never felt more relieved.

Felicia squeezed her legs together, her body jerked in orgasmic spasms. Her protrusive clit had increased to the size of a small penis.

Had Felicia's little dick-looking clit suddenly started shooting off and ejaculating like a man, Shane would have had no choice but to kick her ass. Damn, she was a weird bitch. He wondered if she was on steroids.

"The money's in the bathroom," she said in the throaty voice of a sexually satisfied woman.

The money—six fifty-dollar bills—was neatly placed on the toilet top. Shane hated the way she always left his money on top of the toilet. It was disrespectful. Like he was such a lowlife, she couldn't bring herself to pay him in a normal manner, such as putting the cash in his hand or even putting it on the dresser. He felt like she was calling him a ho of the worst type—like he was one of those dudes that hung out in public rest rooms trying to get laid. *Whatever. Fuck Felicia and her buffed-up masculine ass!*

Not wanting to be anywhere in the vicinity when her old man woke up yelling from pain, Shane pocketed the money and made a quick exit.

Shane spent more time at Kapri's apartment than he did at his own crib. There were too many sad reminders at his apartment—his mom's Bible was the most painful. Had he been able to give her a proper burial, he would have put her Bible in the casket with her. The way she went out wasn't right. Feeling tearful, Shane rushed to change clothes and drop off some of the money he'd gotten from Felicia.

On his way to Kapri's, he purchased a twenty-dollar bag of weed and two blunts.

Kapri had let Shane know that she didn't approve of his smoking weed. She wasn't aware that he occasionally snorted coke as well. Had she known that he dabbled, Kapri would probably start trippin' and try to get him to enter a rehab. Shane laughed to himself at the idea of being in rehab. Then his expression turned serious.

Kapri loved him. And being loved felt good. Hell, he loved her, too. He loved her enough to wife her. Shane smiled, imagining himself married to Kapri. It wasn't a bad idea. But not right now. He still had a lot of running around to do—there were too many pocketbooks still out there that he needed to get into. But he was certain he'd be ready to settle down with Kapri in another couple of years.

Driving Kapri's Mazda, Shane called her from his cell. "You want me to pick up anything from the store?"

"Haagen-Dazs ice cream," Kapri responded. "Caramel Cone."

"Aiight. You want the big one or the small size?"

"All I need is a single serving. I'm not trying to get fat!"

"Hey, what's wrong with that. If you get fat, I'll love you more."

"Yeah, right," Kapri replied, having no idea that Shane was dead serious.

Later, in bed, Kapri ate ice cream while Shane smoked a blunt and watched the lions ravage the zebras on the National Geographic channel.

"Baby," she said softly.

"Uh huh," he responded absently, eyes glued to the TV screen.

"I missed my period; I might be pregnant. I'm not sure."

Shane jerked his head away from the TV. "Pregnant? Already?"

Kapri looked afraid. "But...I'm not sure."

"When you gon' find out?"

"I took a home pregnancy test, but it could be wrong. I have a doctor's appointment. Next Monday."

Shane was quiet.

"Are you upset?"

"I don't know how I feel. I know I'm nervous. Shit, on the real…I'm scared to death," he told her with a forced smile.

Kapri held out her arms and Shane eased into her embrace. He loved her softness and her warmth.

"What are you afraid of, Shane?"

"I'm not even gonna front, Kapri. I don't know how to be a father. I don't have the slightest idea. I wasn't raised by a father; don't even know who the dude is."

"I'm scared, too. Do you think I know how to be a mother?" Kapri said with a nervous giggle. "The important thing is that we both know how to love. I love you, Shane, and I'm going to love your child with all my heart."

Shane wrapped his arms around Kapri. "I gotchu, baby girl. If you're pregnant, we're gon' do this thing together. Live together—get married, whatever. I'll even work at that back-breaking moving company. Aiight?"

Kapri nodded and snuggled up next to him. He handed her the remote. It was an act of love; he knew she didn't share his enjoyment of watching animals rip each other to shreds. Bloodshed and mayhem were definitely not Kapri's twist.

CHAPTER 38

Three months later, Shane and a pregnant Kapri got married at City Hall. For the first time since Dolores Holmes's death, Shane felt a true sense of belonging. He promised himself he'd be a good father and husband. He loved Kapri with all his heart. She made him feel whole. Normal. Being with her kept his demons at bay. He gave up all his other women, including the affluent Felicia Bradley.

Misty was long gone. Out of his life. They were too much alike. Both were big-time scam artists. But after Misty had tried to con him into a threesome with Brick, Shane had to question her sanity. He felt disgust. That shit was sick, she'd gone too far. Misty was the bomb, but she always tried to take shit to the next level, never knew when to quit.

He shook his head, reminiscing about how Misty had gone ballistic in the bar when he bought that chick Nina a drink. If Misty had the slightest notion that Shane had caught feelings for Kapri, she'd transform into a wildcat so fierce, she'd be clawing at Kapri's throat. Had Misty been aware that Shane had gone so far as to get married, there was no doubt in Shane's mind, Misty would be plotting murder. A double murder. With Brick by her side, she'd be out to kill both him and Kapri.

There was no room in his life for his former partners in crime. He was out of the game. He was now walking the straight and narrow, a working man, a married man, soon to be a father. *Now that's some deep shit.* Shane shook his head in wonder.

A few hours after the wedding, Tariq helped Shane move some of his belongings out of the furnished apartment he'd shared with their foster mother. "You want the TV, man?" Shane asked Tariq.

"You're kiddin'. You don't want your wide screen?"

Shane shook his head. "Too many memories. Besides, Kapri has two of those plasma jawns. I'm straight."

"Thanks, bro. This should put a smile on Janelle's face. We can put our TV in the baby's room. Lil' Man loves watching *Sesame Street*, *Sponge Bob*—all those kiddy shows."

"Aiight. That's whassup. My little nephew can chill with his bottle and watch his programs in private. Who knows. Lil' Man might be hitting the remote trying to check out the porno flicks," Shane said, laughing.

"Lil' Man might be chillin', but it won't be with a bottle. The only thing he drinks out of a bottle is water and he rarely wants to drink that." Tariq scowled and spoke in a whisper. "Janelle's still breastfeeding Lil' Man." Tariq shook his head. "Can you believe it? Our son is a year old and I keep telling her it's time to put him on a bottle or let him drink out of one of those baby cups, but she won't. I don't like it. What do you think I should do, man?"

Shane was uncomfortably aware that Tariq expected a response from him. He knew his brother was waiting for him to express feelings of indignation or anger. But all Shane could do was shrug.

"Don't you think that's strange?" Tariq asked his brother.

Shane frowned and shrugged, but didn't say anything.

"She pumps her milk out for him when she goes to work," Tariq said, continuing to provide Shane with the damning information. "He was a premature baby; he only weighed about four pounds and Janelle's still worried about his health. He's cool now. Healthy as a horse. But she insists on feeding him breast milk—says she doesn't want him drinking anything that doesn't come from her. Man, I can't do anything with Janelle. You know how she is—hard-headed." Tariq looked at Shane intently and repeated the question. "So, what do you think I should do, man?"

Shane squirmed. "Yo, that's between you and your wife. I don't know shit about that type of thing."

Tariq sighed. "I hope my son is drinking regular milk out of a glass by the time he's two," Tariq said with a sigh. "All this breastfeeding might turn him into a fruit," Tariq said, frowning. He gave another sigh, which Shane interpreted as the end of the excruciatingly uncomfortable breastfeeding topic.

Shane gathered and boxed their foster mother's clothing. "I'll just give Mom's stuff to Goodwill," he told Tariq. He picked up her Bible. "This goes with me," he announced, holding up the worn Bible with reverence.

Tariq scowled. "You just called Miz Holmes, *Mom*. I'm still trying to figure out when you and Miz Holmes got so close. You acted like you couldn't stand her around the time that social services got involved. And when I told you she had done time, you fell out laughing like it was a big joke. What's the story, man?"

"It's a long story, Tariq. Put it like this…I didn't appreciate all she did for us back when we were young bucks. Being older and wiser, I recognized what I put her through, so I did my best to make up for it. That's all I can say on the subject."

"You're full of surprises, man. Who would have ever thought you'd be such a softy. I mean taking in an old woman and looking out for her like she's your natural mother. Man, that's something special."

"*She* was special," Shane replied as he recalled how his foster mother had told him not to worry himself about what they were doing. She said it wasn't wrong; that it was just different. He believed her. But he knew there wasn't a living soul on earth who would understand how badly he needed her. As she did, he'd also take their secret relationship to the grave.

Carrying three large boxes from the Rose Moving Company, Shane moved his belongings into Kapri's apartment.

❀❀❀

Married life was pleasant— blissful. Shane worked as many days as he could, but often there were more men than available work. His lack of regular employment didn't affect their lifestyle since Kapri still worked full time.

Shane was fascinated by her growing belly. That his seed had caused her stomach to swell with life was amazing. He kissed her tummy, he sang to the baby, and he rubbed her feet when she was tired. Shane was every woman's dream husband. And for the first time in his life, he wasn't acting. Shane was a man in love.

One night while making love, Shane's lips traveled to Kapri's ever increasing bustline. "Baby, I love your titties." He covered her breasts with his mouth, kissing them and softly sucking her nipples. Heaven couldn't possibly feel as good as Shane felt at that moment.

"Oh baby, don't do that," Kapri said in a pained voice. Grimacing, she gently nudged Shane's head away. "My breasts are so tender, honey. It hurts when you even touch them."

Hiding his disappointment and his hurt feelings, Shane wore an impassive expression. Being denied something he craved caused a feeling of anguish that was almost palpable.

His own mother had frequently denied him her breasts, and the sensation of having a nipple withdrawn from his lips was a familiar stab in the heart. His mother had not loved her twin sons equally. She'd shown Tariq tenderness but did not hide her disdain for other son. The memory of her contempt made Shane furious.

Rationalizing the anger he now directed toward Kapri, Shane convinced himself that he deserved a reward for trying to live a normal life. For months, he'd controlled his urges—his overpowering desire to seek out women with big titties. And he'd done it for the sake of his marriage. Kapri was an ungrateful bitch and had a hell of a lot of nerve pushing him away. His resentment toward his wife distorted his facial features.

"You okay, baby?" Kapri asked when Shane ceased all foreplay, moved away from her, and sullenly sat on the edge of the bed. Picking up the remote, he clicked on the TV.

"Yeah, I'm cool," he said, but the air was tense.

Kapri inched up behind Shane. She stroked his back, rubbed his arm, and massaged his scalp, but Shane ignored her efforts to get him back in the mood.

"Since everything on you seems to hurt, why don't get on the mic?" he said crudely. He didn't move a muscle nor did he so much as give Kapri a fleeting glance. He kept his eyes focused on the TV screen.

Kapri winced. "I didn't say everything hurts, Shane. My doctor said we can still have intercourse. My breasts are sore, that's all," she said, now running her fingers through his hair. "I'm sorry if I hurt your feelings; you know I didn't mean to." Her eyes pleaded for understanding but Shane refused to look at her.

He yanked his head away from her wandering fingers. "Cut it out—that shit feels creepy." He could feel Kapri stiffen. *Good*, he thought to himself. *Now you know how it feels to get your feelings hurt.* "You gon' get on the mic or what?" His tone was gruff—impatient.

Looking close to tears, Kapri slowly got out of bed, walked around the bed, and paused in front of Shane as if waiting for him to say something. He was silent. Kapri picked up the remote and turned off the TV. Shane still refused to talk or look at her. "Shane," she whispered pathetically.

"Yo, if you ain't givin' up no head, turn the TV back on," he bellowed.

With tears streaming down her cheeks, Kapri awkwardly struggled down to her knees and orally pleased her husband.

As the pregnancy progressed and regular intercourse became uncomfortable, Kapri found herself on her knees on a regular basis.

❀❀❀

Bored with his home life and unforgiving of his wife, Shane was rarely at home. When Kapri questioned him, Shane would defiantly refuse to account for his whereabouts.

Night after night, he cruised around in his wife's Mazda. Shane became a regular at all the hottest night spots in the city. No longer faithful, he picked up a different woman every night. After sex, he always found a way to get paid, usually by requesting a loan, knowing he'd never see the woman again. And when a woman didn't willingly press money against his palm, Shane would steal it.

Shane wasn't giving out any more free dick...or love. He loved only his brother, his nephew, and his unborn child. He planned to stay with Kapri for the sake of their child, but the love he'd felt for her was gone.

One night while out on the prowl, he found himself missing his old lifestyle and decided to look up Misty and Brick. He figured they'd moved on from the house where they'd been renting a room, so he swung by Misty's mother's house in West Philly.

"They ain't here," Misty's mother said, scowling at Shane and rotating her neck. "Misty's little ass is locked up for mail fraud and I don't where that damn Brick is. He could at least help pay for some of these damn collect calls she keeps making. You best believe whatever scam Misty was involved in, Brick damn sure had something to do with it, too. If you catch up with him, tell him I said, he ain't shit!"

Shane was deflated by the news. Misty had probably gotten popped for blackmailing Paula. But as bad as he felt for Misty, he didn't want to be implicated in the scam, so he turned the car around and sped out of West Philly. The last thing he needed was a federal case involving mail fraud.

More depressed than ever, Shane drove around feeling like a lost soul. He had some extra cash in his pocket, so as a last resort, he decided to check out the broads at a downtown strip joint called Phat Philly Girlz. Upon seeing the blinking neon sign that advertised the titty bar, Shane felt somewhat uplifted. He parked the car and strolled into the club.

"My name's Aisha. You dancin,' handsome?" asked an attractive and very busty light-skinned, damn-near-white dancer. Her blonde braids trailed down to the back of her knees.

"Naw, I'm trying to get into something extra. Whatchu doin' later?"

"We can work something out. You got a place?"

"Naw, but we can get a room. How much you talkin' about?"

"Hundred fifty—plus the cost of the room."

"Ain't no thing," Shane said, giving the dancer a nonchalant shrug. "I gotchu. What time you get off?"

"Shit, it's dead tonight; ain't no money up in here. We can leave as soon as I change into my street clothes."

"Aiight, I'll be out front in the blue Mazda."

Aisha slid in beside Shane. "Try that hotel in North Philly—on Broad and Ridge. They charge by the hour."

Shane paid the money for the room and was given a key to room number six. The room was sparse, but had clean sheets, which was good enough for his lustful intentions.

Shane's hands went straight to Aisha's big boobs. But the instant he touched them, he jerked both hands away as if he'd touched burning coals. "Yo! Whassup wit them jawns? Why they all hard and shit?" Clarity hit him and his eyes went cold. "They fake, ain't they?"

"Implants," she said without shame. "And they cost a fortune," she added, sounding extremely proud.

Shane scowled.

"Suck 'em," Aisha offered. "My nipples are real sensitive." She fondled her breasts invitingly and moistened her lips with her tongue.

Shane felt disgusted. "I ain't suckin' shit. Fuck that. I'm out!"

Aisha reared back as if Shane had slapped her. "You took me off my job, so you better pay me my damn money!" Aisha jumped off the bed and took a confrontational stance. She was a tall girl; her breasts poked him in his chest.

Shane's face tightened and then contorted into an evil grimace. "Yo, if you don't wanna have to scoop that slimy silicone shit up off the floor, you better back the fuck off. Matter of fact, bitch…give me back the money I spent on this room," Shane demanded and stuck out his hand.

Aisha cupped her breasts protectively. Her eyes stretched open wide at the thought of having her implants punctured. She quickly whipped open her purse and gave Shane twenty dollars.

As he was leaving, he heard the distraught dancer asking the dude at the front desk to call her a cab. *Fuck that fake bitch!* He felt no pity for the dancer as he rapidly left the seedy hotel.

Driving past the speed limit and feeling a familiar rage, Shane headed home. He had a bag of weed and a blunt inside his pocket. He hoped Kapri would be sound asleep by the time he got home. He wasn't in the mood to hear her mouth; he just wanted to get high and go to sleep.

But Kapri was wide awake. "Shane, where have you been? It's two in the morning!" Shane gave Kapri an evil look. "Stop trippin'," he said grumpily.

"Trippin'!" Kapri yelled. "You think I'm trippin' because it bothers me that my husband stays out until all hours of the night—every night?"

"Kapri," Shane said in a controlled tone. "I was taking care of something for Tariq."

"Tariq is home in bed. I already called and woke up the entire household," Kapri snapped.

"Well, stop checking on me!" he yelled. "This is between me and Tariq. He ain't gotta tell you what I'm doing." Then softening his tone, Shane said, "Look, baby. I'm sorry I was out late and didn't call. But my brother needed me to do something. I'm not gonna let Tariq down. You know how I feel about my brother." Shane hugged his wife.

After she was sufficiently calmed, Shane didn't even ask, he just pulled her to the side of the bed. With her enormous belly, Kapri could no longer get down on her knees; she had to sit while she gave Shane oral sex.

CHAPTER 39

"What's going on with Kapri?" Tariq asked Shane a few days later while they were at work.

Shane looked bewildered. "I don't know. What did she say?"

"First of all, she called late last night and woke up Janelle and Lil' Man. Janelle was furious. Then when I called to check on her thing this morning, she growled at me like I've done something wrong. She said if I need you to do something for me, would I at least have the decency to make sure you get home before midnight." Perplexed, Tariq cocked his head to the side as he waited for an explanation.

"So, what did you say?" Shane asked in a calm tone while wearing an impassive expression.

"Man, I didn't know what to say. I didn't know what you had told her."

"I didn't tell her much of nothing. I came home a little late. She was trippin' and so in order to calm her down, I had to come up with something. I told her I was out doing a favor for you."

Disgust creased Tariq's face into a scowl. "Why you gotta put me in the middle of your domestic problems. Now Janelle thinks I'm up to something with you."

"My bad. Sorry, man. But look, next time Kapri comes at you trying to get some information, just cover for me. You know how we do. Make up some shit. As far as Kapri's concerned, your mouth is a prayer book. This pregnancy is making her crazy, man. So please, for my sake, can you cover for me sometimes?"

Tariq didn't look pleased with the position Shane was putting him in, but reluctantly agreed. "I gotchu, but man, you gotta try to do better. Kapri's six months pregnant, she shouldn't be worrying about where you are all the time. You should be spending more time at home with her, especially now. Besides, man—I hate lying to Kapri."

"I don't need no lecture, bro," Shane said as he walked away from his brother and sauntered toward the Rose moving van. The crew was preparing for a moving job in the local vicinity, but Shane wished they were going out of town. He needed some excitement. Married life was not turning out to be the safety net he'd imagined. Kapri was too clingy. He missed Misty and Brick. He missed his old life.

He felt stuck and he hated the feeling.

❦❦❦

During most moves, the same team that picked up the furniture delivered it to its final destination. But in this case, the drivers who had picked up the furniture from Arlington, Virginia, were taking on another job. Tariq was going out of town on a job while Shane and the crew he was working with for the day were assigned to the task of unpacking and hauling the furniture from Virginia into a home in Villanova, Pennsylvania.

When Shane's crew arrived in Villanova, they were greeted by a leggy brunette who introduced herself as Lisa McLaurin. "Please be careful with that," she said. Lisa wore a lime-green silk robe and was sipping something alcoholic at eight in the morning.

Since Shane carried a lightweight box that didn't test his endurance, he looked around to see who the lady was talking to.

"That has a very fragile and extremely valuable item inside," she said, pointing to the box. "Just be careful with it."

Shane felt an instant dislike for the snotty broad. "Where should I put it?"

"Oh, take it upstairs. First bedroom at the top of the stairs. There's no furniture up there, so place it—very carefully—on the top shelf in the closet. If you're a good boy, I'll make you a Mimosa when you're done."

Shane sucked his teeth and muttered under his breath, "What the fuck is a Mimosa?" Whatever it was, he damn sure didn't want it. He wanted his tip in the form of paper. Green paper. Once he was upstairs and out of view, Shane was curious about the contents in the box. Unable to resist, Shane turned the box back and forth, trying to figure out what was inside. Unable to ascertain the contents by the sound, he gave it a hard shake and heard something shatter. *Oops!*

Ever so gently, he put it on the closet shelf and trotted down the stairs, as if he didn't have a care in the world. He added a whistle to further declare his cheerful disposition and most important, he hoped his whistle as he worked would proclaim his innocence if the snotty broad decided to check the box and accuse him of breaking whatever the fuck was inside.

An hour later, when the box and its precious contents were no longer lingering in his mind, Shane and the crew heard an ear-piercing screech.

"Oh my God, I told that bastard to be careful!" Lisa screamed at the top of her lungs.

Shane, realizing the gig was up, wanted to run, but instead he climbed the stairs to face the music like a man.

Crying pathetically, Lisa shook the rattling box at him. "You broke a family heirloom. A priceless figurine; it belonged to my husband's mother. He's going to be inconsolable." She sniffed and wiped her eyes. "Your company's going to have to pay for this, you know," she said coldly as she dabbed at her eyes with the back of her hand. Then, in an instant, she turned on the tears again.

Shane didn't know how to get out of this mess. His wife was pregnant; he needed his job. "Look, I'm sorry. I didn't mean to break it. Maybe we could put it back together with some Krazy Glue?"

"Krazy Glue!" she shrieked. Lisa's face contorted horribly before she began to wail.

Trying to quiet her before she alerted the other men, Shane asked, "What can I do? Do you need some extra work, you know, so I can make up for it? Maybe I could clean up or something after we move all your furniture in the house."

She looked at him through eyes that had become angry slits. "How can extra labor make up for a priceless family heirloom? I'm afraid to even open this." She shook the box again. The broken pieces made a horrible clattering sound.

Shane shrugged helplessly. Lisa wept into her hands and then fell against Shane, shaking and crying like it was the end of the world. Not knowing what to do, he patted her back, hoping that a show of sympathy would keep her mouth shut and get him off the hook. He couldn't afford to get fired. Her shoulders heaved, he patted faster. And then she pulled away. Shane noticed that the sash of her robe had become undone. Her robe fell open, revealing an oyster-colored thong and strapless bra. Considering the mess of trouble he'd gotten himself in, it surprised him when he inexplicably found himself aroused by the tan lines on the woman's shoulders.

Lowering the distraught woman onto the plush Persian rug, Shane consoled her with his fingers, his mouth—his dick.

"Oh my God, it's true," she said, fondling his thickened manhood. "You black guys really are hung like fucking horses. This is unbelievable. I can't believe I'm making it with a black stud."

As long as she was happy and willing to keep quiet about the family heirloom, Shane didn't mind giving her what she wanted. "Oh my God!" She screamed as he thrust deeply. "I can't get enough of this. Don't stop; don't stop!"

He didn't stop, but after a while he started slowing down. "Did you cum yet?" he asked hopefully.

"No! Don't stop, dammit, make me cum."

Shane wondered how he'd gotten himself into such an awful situation. He was tired and embarrassed, thinking that by now his crew noticed his absence and were all standing outside with their ears pressed against the bedroom door. He wished she wasn't so loud. Damn, why didn't this goddamn bitch hurry up and cum? Once she reached a climax, he'd feel like his debt was paid in full, he could get back to work and then go the hell on home without the fear of employment termination hanging over his head.

After such a disastrous day, being with Kapri was going to feel like a slice of heaven and listening to his wife's whining-ass voice would be music to his ears.

"Ram it in me, stud. Ram it hard."

Shane wanted to ram his fist in her fucking mouth, but instead he complied and rammed and rammed, but no amount of ramming was hard enough. "Yo, I'm tired; I can't do no more."

"Oh no? Some stud you turned out to be…get the fuck out!"

Shane winced, but for the sake of his livelihood, he took the verbal abuse.

"Tell that short guy with the muscles to come up here. And tell him to hurry up."

Quickly getting his clothes back on, Shane was delighted to pass the torch. "Yo Mac, the lady upstairs wants to see you 'bout somethin'," Shane said to the short, muscular man named Mac.

After the Villanova job, the moving crew rode home in virtual silence. The woman of the house, Lisa McLaurin, had engaged in a sexual tryst of marathon proportions with each member of the four-man work crew. After sapping each man of his strength, she then insisted they all continue lugging and lifting heavy furniture.

Lisa McLaurin had to be a real twisted bitch. She'd run the same story to every man, giving the story different twists. She told the driver he'd been driving too fast and shattered the glass, and she accused two other men of behaving recklessly and thus being responsible for the demise of yet another priceless family heirloom.

But Shane knew the real deal. While she was getting her freak on with one of the guys, he'd gotten hold of the precious box, opened it, and discovered several old glass Christmas balls.

Lisa was a bored and stingy white bitch. She'd played them all and had received long-lasting, free black dick.

It was the first time Shane had ever gotten fucked over by a woman. He'd heard about karma and all…but damn, he hadn't realized that getting played would feel so fucked up.

CHAPTER 40

T he doctor and nurses expected Shane to remain by Kapri's side during the emergency Caesarian Section, but once she was cut open, Shane started hyperventilating. He began to back away until he had backed completely out the door. For Shane, the waiting room was a much more comfortable place.

Tariq paced the floor with him. Janelle sat quietly—expressionless. When the nurse came to deliver the good news, Tariq jumped and headed toward the delivery room with Shane. "Just the father," the nurse told Tariq.

Janelle sucked her teeth and gave Tariq a look that screamed, *you're such a moron.*

Taking the *K* from Kapri and dropping the *e* from his name, Shane chose the name, K'Shan for his son's first name. "K'Shan Batista," he said, as he held his son for the first time.

"K'Shan? I don't like made-up names," Kapri said disapprovingly, but was too exhausted to forcibly voice her opinion.

K'Shan was a healthy boy weighing eight pounds and seven ounces. The spitting image of Shane, K'Shan had his father's tight curly hair, ruddy complexion, big hands and feet. He even had Shane's cleft chin. There were no traces of Kapri's physical characteristics. Like Lil' Man, K'Shan was straight-up Batista.

Shane's face lit up when he held his son; his anger toward Kapri slowly began to dissipate. Perhaps they could work things out for the baby's sake, he thought, casting his wife a pleasant gaze.

Along with Tariq and Janelle, Kapri's parents and siblings also came to extend their good wishes to the new parents.

"You know, son…" Kapri's father said, placing a paternal arm around Shane's shoulders. He cleared his throat and continued, "Parenting never stops. Even when this boy turns forty years old—as long as you have breath in your body, you're going to always worry about him and you're going to always think you know what's best for him. Parenting isn't easy, son. Just remember, you have to put your child's needs in front of your own."

Shane's smile dimmed. He nodded respectfully, but he wasn't interested in Kapri's father's long-winded words of wisdom. Shane would learn parenting skills in his own way on his own time. So if her parents thought they were going to meddle in the way he raised his son, they'd better think again. Today, he had politely held his tongue, but there was no telling how much cussing he'd do the next time a member of Kapri's family decided to offer a word of advice.

Still, it was a happy occasion and Shane had a feeling that the birth of his son would give him a reason to turn his life around and spend more time at home. Living with a woman he no longer loved had been inconvenient and unpleasant. Shane wanted to be a good father to his son and vowed to make every effort to rekindle his feelings for Kapri.

But, two weeks later, his home life seemed worse than any of the places he'd ever been forced to live. It was worse than the Children's Home and worse than Barney Mills. Home was a living hell.

K'Shan seemed to cry nonstop. And on the rare occasions when the baby wasn't screaming at the top of his lungs, Kapri would start.

"What's wrong?" Shane asked his wife, disgusted.

"I don't know," she responded with an annoying sniffle as she wiped her nose. "Postpartum blues—I guess."

"What the hell is that?"

"Depression. After giving birth, some women…"

"Never mind!" He cut her off rudely. "I'm sorry I asked; only *you* would come up with some ying yang shit nobody ever heard of."

"It's a medical condition. I need support. Some understanding—"

"Yo!" Shane roared, silencing Kapri. "K'Shan is the only baby in this house, so cut that shit." His scalding words reduced Kapri to more tears and inconsolable wailing. Shane covered his ears with the palms of his hands, walked over to Kapri, and hollered, cruelly mocking her wailing. He yelled until her mournful sobs trailed off into a pitiful whimper.

Satisfied, he showered and changed clothes. "I'm going out," he said with a sneer and slowly put on each article of clothing without giving his wife the slightest hint of where he intended to go.

"Please don't leave me here with the baby," Kapri pleaded as she helplessly watched Shane tie his sneakers.

"I'm not sitting around here listening to your bullshit all night," he shouted as his mind searched his mental Rolodex, flipping through pages, trying to decide which female admirer could soothe his soul. "I'm out," he declared, grabbing Kapri's car keys. An anonymous encounter with a stripper might suit his mood tonight. He wasn't sure, but he'd soon find out. The moment Kapri's crying resumed, Shane slammed the front door.

A few nights later, during one of K'Shan's late-night crying bouts, Shane snapped at Kapri. "Can't you do something to keep him quiet? I have to work in the morning."

"I'm trying," she said, pacing the floor, holding the baby close to her bosom. She switched the baby's position and began pacing back and forth with him cradled in her arms. Shane noticed that the front of Kapri's pajama top was damp. It was another reminder of what a whining wimp he'd married. Claiming that breastfeeding K'Shan was too painful, she'd given up and had recently begun bottle feeding him. "You know my doctor said I shouldn't be on my feet too much. I'm still healing from the c-section. Why don't you walk the baby for a while?"

"I can't walk K'Shan all night and get to work on time in the morning." Shane gave her a look of loathing. That look brought Kapri to tears, which gave Shane another reason to get dressed and leave her alone with their son. Leaving in the middle of the night had become routine.

But Shane was sick of fleeing to titty bars; he needed to go somewhere peaceful.

Paula came to mind. Maybe Paula had gotten over her anger and was ready to kiss and make up. Shane turned the ignition of his wife's Mazda, gunned out of the parking spot, and sped to West Philly. Hoping Paula's husband was out of town, Shane mentally crossed his fingers.

When he reached Cobbs Creek Parkway, he turned slowly onto Ellsworth Street. He checked for the red truck. It wasn't there. So far, so good.

Feeling slightly nervous, Shane rang the bell. He could tell Paula was looking at him through the peephole and trying to figure out whether she should curse him out or shower him with kisses. To expedite the inevitable, Shane flashed a brilliant smile toward the peephole.

As expected, the door opened. Smiling, he turned off his cell phone before he stepped inside. He had to make sure Kapri couldn't track him down.

"Hey, gorgeous," Shane said and stepped inside Paula's home.

"I shouldn't even be speaking to you," Paula said sternly, but a hint of a smile on her lips told Shane she was happy to see him.

"I heard what happened," he said sadly. "But I ain't have nothing to do with it. I wasn't married to that chick. Misty's a nut—she's throwed off. Anyway, I heard she's doing time."

"She certainly is. When my husband found out what was going on, he called the cops. They turned it over to the feds."

"For real? It was that deep?"

"Mail fraud is a federal offense. So what was your role in the scam?"

"I told you…nothing!" Shane feigned a look of shock. "You thought I was mixed up in that foul shit?"

"What else could I think, Shane?"

Shane dropped his head. "I was over my man's house and his girl, Misty, got hold of the tape and decided to blackmail you. Now, that's what I heard. I don't know all the facts because I was between apartments at the time and was getting information in bits and pieces. I really didn't know they was into that kind of slimy shit."

"Why did you take my video camera in the first place, Shane? It wasn't your property." She chastised him, folding her arms and pursing her lips primly.

"Baby," he said, approaching her and reaching for her hand. "I wanted my own copy so I could look at you on the lonely nights when we couldn't be together. I was gonna return it. I swear to God," he said, holding up his right hand. "You know I wouldn't do you like that. But after I found out about all the drama, I was afraid to get in touch with you."

"So why are you here now?"

"Because I miss the shit outta you," he said, his dark lips pouty.

"Really, baby?" Paula purred.

Shane could see the relief in Paula's eyes. He pulled her into his arms, picked her up, and kissed her. He continued to kiss her as he carried her up the stairs. Between kisses, he promised to make up for all the misery his so-called friends had put her through.

Instead of the sexy lingerie she usually wore, Paula was clad in an oversized T-shirt. However, after being with a wife whose stomach was clamped with staples and whose leaking tits hurt too bad to be of any use to him or their baby, Paula looked like a cool drink of water to a dehydrated man. Shane was ready to give her a sexual workout that she wouldn't forget. He was depending on an open invitation to share Paula's bed whenever her husband was out of town.

With her back facing him, Shane placed Paula on his lap and fucked her until she whimpered in defeat. He sexed her in every position he could imagine until they both collapsed, exhausted. Afterward, he snuggled up and spooned with Paula. Damn, it felt good to be with a real woman and not a whining, complaining little girl.

And after a peaceful night's sleep, Shane went to work feeling invigorated and back on top of his game. The next morning, Paula had shown her appreciation by giving him two hundred dollars and the promise of more when he returned later that night.

Pretty good compensation for an impromptu visit.

When he walked in the door of Rose Moving Company, the temporary chick who'd taken over Kapri's duties, held out five pink message slips. All from Kapri. The phone started ringing. "I'm not here," he whispered to the young woman. "Tell her the truck just pulled out." To ensure his instructions would be followed, Shane gave the receptionist a lingering look that suggested he found her attractive and would like to get to know her better.

While the receptionist relayed Shane's lie to Kapri, Shane held his thumb up to his ear and his small finger to his lips, silently requesting her number in exactly the same manner in which he'd gotten Kapri's attention.

The receptionist, an eighteen-year-old recent high school grad, instantly scrawled her number, but Shane kept on walking to the rear of the building. He'd get the number later, if at all.

Kapri had held three positions at the Rose Company—administrative assistant, part-time receptionist, and office manager, and she'd been well compensated. A temporary receptionist probably didn't make enough money for him to even waste his time.

While Shane changed into his work uniform, Tariq stormed into the locker room. "Man, what is your problem? Why would you leave your wife and infant alone all night without so much as a phone call? Damn, man. I told you not to get involved with Kapri if you weren't ready to change. She just had your baby, man. Don't you care about anybody but yourself? Man, what's wrong with you?"

Shane scowled at Tariq. "Yo, dawg. What goes on between me and my wife is our business."

"Your wife is making it my business, too. Who do you think she cries to every time you pull one of your disappearing acts? Me! And how do you think that makes me feel? How long can I cover for you, man? You're acting like you don't give a fuck about Kapri or your newborn son.

"Man, you trippin'," Shane said with a smirk as he finished buttoning his shirt.

"Oh, I'm trippin'? Well for your information, your family problems are spilling into my life. Janelle is getting tired of Kapri crying on my shoulder when she has a husband of her own."

"And that's exactly what your problem is, Tariq. You too soft. Lettin' that broad run your life. It ain't healthy for a grown man to let a woman run the show."

"Me and Janelle don't come to you with our problems, so leave her out of this."

"You and Janelle didn't mind accepting cash when I was breaking y'all off with half of my dough."

"If that's what this is about, I'll pay you back. You want the TV back? How much do I owe you? Tell me. I'll work overtime to pay you back."

"Get the fuck outta my face, Tariq. You ain't got nothing for me. And tell that bitch you got at home that I ain't nevah liked her ugly ass nor do I appreciate the way she treats you. Damn man, who's wearing the pants—you or her? You tell that bitch that I said she can suck my muthafuckin' dick!" Shane's face was a mask of evil.

"Don't call her a bitch, Shane," Tariq warned. "Don't you ever even speak her name again."

"She's a bitch, man, and a ugly fuckin' bitch at that. What the hell do you see in her? You should be ashamed to even walk down the street with that dog."

Tariq, unable to bear hearing Janelle so badly maligned, swung on Shane without giving it a thought. But he missed. Shane laughed and knocked his brother into a row of lockers. The clamor caused the other workers to come running into the locker room. They all wore expressions of shock when they realized they had to break up a fight between the twin brothers who'd always shown each other the utmost respect and love.

Thankfully, the foreman separated Tariq and Shane, sending them to work on separate jobs.

❀❀❀

With the two hundred dollars Shane had gotten from Paula plus the fifty-dollar-tip he'd gotten from the family the Rose Company had moved, Shane was able to afford a dozen roses for his wife. He bought the flowers from a vendor who was peddling his wares on the concrete divide that separated traffic on Girard Avenue, near the Philadelphia zoo.

Next, Shane swung by his weed connection's crib on Parkside Avenue and bought a little something to keep him nice and mellow.

With flowers in hand, he arrived home and found Kapri sitting on the sofa rocking the baby and as usual, she was crying. Shane's disgust escalated to a feeling of rage so palpable, it was hard not to slap the shit out of his stupid, crying-ass wife.

Angry, Shane threw the flowers at her. "Goddamn! Is this what I have to look at every goddamn day? You cry in the morning, you cry at night. And if *you* ain't crying, I gotta listen to K'Shan screaming his head off. What the fuck did I get myself into?"

"I called my doctor and he confirmed my suspicions. He said I'm suffering from postpartum depression. It's common after childbirth."

"Post pardon my ass!" Shane said sarcastically. "You and your quack-ass doctor can kiss my ass. Ain't no excuse for all this fucking whining and crying. I'm sick of it!"

"Why are you being so mean? What did I do besides give you a son?" Kapri's bottom lip trembled as she tried to keep from crying. "Shane, do you realize I haven't even had my six-week check-up yet? I'm going through hell. I take care of K'Shan all day. I'm depressed, lonely. and I'm in constant pain from the c-section. And you're not helping the situation at all by staying out all night."

Shane glared at her. "You know what? Fuck this poor little Kapri bullshit. I'm out!"

Kapri was speechless and before she could utter a word, Shane had grabbed the car keys and was heading out the door.

With their newborn in her arms, Kapri ran barefoot out on the front porch. "Shane! Shane!" she screamed his name.

Ignoring his wife's call, Shane revved up the motor and gunned Kapri's car out of the parking spot. Shane pointed the car in the direction of Paula's house.

But Paula's husband's truck was parked in front of the house. Damn, the cock-blocker was back in town. *Dude musta known I been tappin' his wife's ass.* Shane gave a harsh-sounding chortle and roared off.

CHAPTER 41

While incarcerated, Misty had put on a few pounds. Now, fresh out of the slammer, with wider hips and a little more meat on her butt, she was filling out a size five nicely. Though still a tiny little thing, Misty carried herself in a manner that informed anyone in close proximity—male or female—that her tolerance for bullshit was extremely low. Doing a bid in prison had toughened her even more. Her con game had improved; Misty was hyped and ready to test her skills and raise some hell.

"So whatchu mean you don't know where he's at?" she asked Brick as they stood outside a deli sharing a forty-ounce bottle of beer. "Where could he be?" she demanded, her face a mask of fury.

"I ain't seen him. Shane went underground or something. I been asking around, but don't nobody know where he's at," Brick told her, shaking his head. He looked clearly sorry that he couldn't offer more useful information.

Brick was a giant of a man and even though Misty was just a little over five feet, he was afraid of her; had been ever since elementary school. He'd been the muscle that backed up the big mouth that always had her getting into scraps with the other kids. He couldn't count the number of heads he'd cracked on Misty's behalf. He'd always done her bidding and that would never change. Whatever Misty requested of him, he'd try his best to do.

Back when they were kids he had to play the games that Misty wanted to play. And if she wanted him to play with her dolls or dress up in her mother's clothes, that's what he did or risked her wrath.

An unhappy Misty meant there was no joy in Brick's life. Being Misty's cohort was one outrageous adventure after another. Everything bad or dishonest he'd ever done had been Misty's idea. He'd always been merely the enforcer of her devious plans.

"My mom said Shane came around her house looking for me about a month ago," Misty said, punching an open palm with a balled fist, working herself up. "The way he just left me hanging…how could he do me like that? That shit wasn't cool; it was so fucked up."

Brick nodded. "Real fucked up," he agreed. "I don't know what's wrong with Shane. He used to be aiight, like a brother; now he's acting all shady and shit. Actin' like he don't know nobody no more."

"Yeah, well, I think it's time for Shane to come out of hiding. He knows we don't roll like that. He can't just walk the fuck off with no explanation and just get ghost! I don't appreciate it. Shane is gonna be sorry for treating *me* like I'm one of his tricks. How he gon' let me do all that time and not even so much as write me a damn letter. Fuck that! Shane's gon' get his." Misty screwed up her lips and swung furiously at the air.

"Aiight, Misty. Calm down, baby. We'll get Shane, but right now we're supposed to be celebrating. You're home, baby! Let's go out and have some fun."

Misty looked up thoughtfully. "Whatchu wanna get into?"

"Don't matter…anything," Brick said with a shrug. "But we need some money. I'm fucked up; I ain't been on my hustle like I shoulda been. Couldn't jam up niggas like I wanted to. I needed you and Shane for backup," he admitted solemnly.

Misty sucked her teeth. "I bet Shane's got some dough; his trick bitches keep his pockets fat," she said resentfully. "Besides, he owes me! I took that fall and he ain't put not one dollar on my books." She lowered her head, thinking hard. Brick stood beside her, patiently waiting for her to come up with a plan.

"Brick, I don't hold you responsible; I know you were out here struggling to survive. I know it was hard on you being out here without me. But ain't no excuse for Shane." Misty gave Brick a narrow-eyed look and continued punching her palm threateningly. "Okay, listen. I got a plan…"

"What?" Brick asked suspiciously.

"You gon' have to hustle us up some cheddar."

"Me? How? I can't rob no more ATMs; they got me on tape," he said, grimacing and shifting awkwardly from foot to foot. "My muggin' game is raggedy, baby. My game is off like a muthafucker. I couldn't keep that shit up with you and Shane both out of the picture."

"Well, you're gon' have to tighten your game back up." Then she looked off in thought for a moment. "All right—this is what we're gonna do."

Brick gave Misty his undivided attention.

"I'll hustle us up a freak," she announced and then gave Brick a wicked smile. "I bet you ain't had your dick sucked the whole time I was upstate," she said teasingly.

"You must be crazy," he responded gruffly.

"Stop lying, Brick. You don't even know how to approach dudes. Yeah, you probably had a couple skanks slobbering on your jawn, but you ain't had it sucked the way you really like it."

"You right, you right," Brick finally admitted.

"Well, we gotta find a freak. That's where the real money's at. Bitches are okay, but they're stingy. Dudes don't mind kickin' out serious dough."

"It's been a long time, Misty. I might not be ready to get down with a man. I'm nervous; I'm not mentally prepared for that type of party."

Disgusted, Misty sucked her teeth.

"Why I gotta be the ho?" Brick asked. "Why can't you get down with a dude and let me watch? I ain't ready for nothing real freaky. I gotta ease back into that lifestyle."

Misty gave Brick a smoldering look. "I just did a bid for all of us. I know you don't think I'm gonna prostitute myself? I'm not the ho in this relationship; I'm the fuckin' pimp! You know damn well I'm not gon' let no freak-ass nut run his dick all up in my shit. That ain't my twist. It was bad enough in prison with all those bitches trying to suck on my clit," she ranted and then suddenly softened her tone. "This pussy belongs to you," she said, giving her crotch a couple pats. "It used to belong to you and Shane, but he got new on us." She looked off wistfully. Her eyes were sad.

"Baby, stop worrying about Shane, we gon' find him."

"Shane played us and he's the reason our money's all fucked up. We had a system; he knew we relied on his hustle to make ends meet. But he got greedy and decided to go solo; he just left our asses hangin'." Misty's eyes were dark and brooding. "That's why I always told you we had to keep our ace in the hole." She ran her hand across Brick's groin. "You got this big dong. Your big dick makes horny muthafuckers give up their rent money just to kiss it. Shane can't top what you got, baby." A morose look covered Misty's face. "But he really hurt me, Brick. And you gotta do something about that."

"Whatever you want, I'll do it. Okay, Misty?" Brick said sadly.

"Okay," Misty said brightly. "First things first. We gotta get some money, and then we'll find Shane." She rubbed Brick's groin again and laughed when it stiffened.

"Stop, Misty," he complained, squirming away. "Quit it unless you gon' do something about it."

"I'm tempted, but we gotta save your strength for the sucka we run into tonight. I'll get mine later on…that is, if you have any juice left."

"Aiight, so where we gonna find this freak?" Brick said, looking doubtful.

"Oh you don't think I can find us a freak? Brick, when you gonna get it through your head? Every black man, white man, red man, Chinese man—or whatever, every man on this planet ain't nothing but a stone cold freak. They might pretend that they ain't trying to get it on with another man, but I know how to get to the truth."

"Aiight. So where we goin'?"

"We should go to a hotel bar. Someplace where honkies hang out. We need a big payday and white men are willing to pay top dollar for big black dick." Misty paused and looked Brick up and down. "You still gotta wear that blindfold?"

"Yeah, why?"

"Because everybody ain't into your hang-ups. Wearing that blindfold is a turn-off for some men. We ain't in no position to be turning off no paying customers."

"Whassup with you, Misty? You know I don't get down like that. I don't wanna look at no strange dude sucking my dick. I ain't no damn faggot."

Misty sighed. "You think because you're not looking, that makes you normal?

You ain't normal, Brick," she yelled. "It's time to face up to the fact that you're on the down low."

Brick shook his head in denial. "I ain't no homo; I ain't on no damn down low!"

"Did I say you were a homo? No! I said the shit you do ain't natural and you're on the down low. There's a big difference. A homo switches his ass and wears wigs and makeup, trying to look like a bitch. But you're all man," she said in a seductive tone. "Your dick is too big to satisfy females only. You're blessed, baby; you should feel honored that all those men wanna suck on your jawn. Feel me?"

"Yeah." Brick smiled broadly.

"And since we're on the subject, let me ask you something."

"Whassup?"

"You know, we could make a lot more money if you started giving up some head."

"What!" Brick's voice boomed so loud it seemed to make the pavement vibrate.

"You gotta do it for me, Brick. We need the money. We could get even more cheddar if you reciprocated and gave up some brain, too."

"You know I can't do that," Brick said, angry.

"I bet you'd give Shane some head."

Brick flinched. "That's different; you was in love with Shane. If I gave that nigga some head, it woulda been on the strength of you."

"Yeah, right," she said with unmasked disdain. "If Shane would have agreed to it, you might have tried to whip *my* ass if I stood in the way of you and that nigga's dick."

Brick puffed up in denial.

"Oh, stop trying to act like I'm lying. You wanted Shane ever since y'all were in the joint together. You probably would have let Shane fuck you in the ass."

Brick took a swig from the forty and then hung his head—a silent and embarrassed admission.

"But it's a shame, though," Misty continued. "I tried to make life real sweet for Shane. I was willing to let him have both of us, but when we tried to show that nigga love, what did he do? He ran from us like we had a damn disease. Fuck Shane." Misty yanked the forty from Brick and downed the remaining contents. She wiped her mouth with the back of her dainty hand. "And fuck you, too," Misty shouted furiously. "You ain't worth a fuck, either," Misty snarled.

Brick looked near tears. Misty glared at him. "I got knocked! I spent months in jail and how many times did you and Shane visit me? Um…how 'bout… never?" She gestured with her arms spread; palms up.

Brick fiddled uncomfortably. "You know I ain't have no way to get all the way to that women's prison. They stopped the van service that takes people to the prison."

"No they didn't; that van comes to the prison every weekend. You just didn't feel like getting up at six in the morning. But you know what? Forget you, nigga. Go 'head, and do *you* because I'm damn sure gon' do *me*!" She dismissed Brick with a hand flip. "I know what I have to do." Misty turned away from Brick and started walking fast in the opposite direction.

Brick ran behind her. Caught her by the back of her jacket. Misty jerked away. "Aiight, Misty. Set it up. I'll do it," Brick said, looking miserable.

"And you're not wearing no damn blindfold," she said in a no-nonsense tone.

"No blindfold," Brick sadly conceded.

❊❊❊

After being chumped by Paula's husband, Shane turned the car around and decided to go home and patch things up with his wife. Kapri wasn't much fun anymore, she didn't look anywhere near as good as she'd looked when he met her. She didn't keep herself up, she was unkempt, and unappealing. Her brittle ponytail and sallow complexion irked him.

Her gloomy presence filled Shane with a fury that was difficult to contain. Often, he had to control himself from smacking her across her tear-stained cheek or smacking her upside her head for crying for no reason at all. Everything about Kapri pissed Shane off. But he would never put his hands on the mother of his son. It was best to just walk away until his rage subsided.

The despair in the Batista household was suffocating. Shane needed fresh air; he needed to breathe again. He yearned for his old life with Misty and Brick. But he was stuck; he couldn't abandon his wife and son. His feelings toward

Kapri confused him, but he was sure there was still love for her buried some-where in his heart. But it was buried so deeply, it was hard to find.

He loved his son, without a doubt. K'Shan was his heart. He just hated all the constant crying and couldn't wait for the little guy to start walking and talking.

When he got home, the apartment was dark and quiet. He figured Kapri was probably lying in the dark bedroom sniffling into a pillow. Shane sighed and braced himself for his wife's sad, bloodshot eyes. Shane clicked on the light switch and saw a note lying on the dining room table. Instinctively, he knew that Kapri had taken the baby and left.

I'm not a martyr and I'm not taking any more of your abuse. Leave my car in front of the apartment; my father will be picking it up first thing tomorrow.

Kapri

Dayum! He couldn't believe she'd leave like that. Shane reached for the phone in the kitchen. Hell if he was going to let her just take his son.

"Lemme speak to Kapri," he demanded when her mother answered the phone.

"The only way you're ever going to speak to or see my daughter again is in divorce court, so I suggest you get yourself a lawyer." Kapri's mother slammed down the phone.

Shane held the phone in disbelief. *Fuckin' bitch banged on me!*

He stormed into every room. And every room was empty. Kapri and her parents had cleaned out the place. There wasn't a shred of evidence that Kapri or the baby had ever lived there.

Shane sank onto the sofa and buried his head in his hands. The last time he'd felt this bad was…he didn't even want to go there. If he thought about either of the two important women in his life—his birth mother and his foster mother—he'd lose it and start smashing mirrors, dishes, anything breakable.

Though he could barely remember his birth mother, he'd always remember her scent. She smelled like milk.

And his foster mother smelled like talcum powder and had tried her best to duplicate what he needed and missed so much. He'd spent more time with Dolores Holmes and missed her the most.

"Mommy!" Shane grieved and wept openly for Dolores Holmes, the woman who'd given him unconditional love.

CHAPTER 42

He had to patch things up with his brother. What had gotten into him? He'd never laid a hand on Tariq in his life. Shane decided not to call Tariq; he'd just go to his apartment and face him like a man. Damn, he needed a brotherly hug.

Shane stopped at the front desk and the desk man called Tariq's apartment and announced that Shane was in the lobby. "Go 'head up, man," the clerk said.

In the elevator, Shane wondered what he was going to say. Knowing Tariq, he wouldn't have to say anything. Tariq would understand the meaning of the visit. His presence and a big hug would let his brother know that he was sorry.

No, fuck that! He owed Tariq an apology. He'd be a man and tell his brother face-to-face that he was wrong. Dead wrong! He was wrong for everything—the things he'd said about Janelle and the way he'd been treating Kapri.

Maybe together, he and Tariq could put their heads together and figure out a way for Shane to get Kapri and K'Shan back. Damn, he'd really fucked up his life.

With an expression of disgust, Janelle opened the door. "Tariq ain't here," she announced.

"So, why ain't you tell the dude at the desk?" Shane asked, his face contorted in annoyance. He couldn't stand Tariq's wife, there was no getting around it.

"Thought you might want to see your nephew; guess I was wrong."

Shane's face softened. "Lil' Man's still up?"

"He's about to fall asleep, but he's fighting it." Janelle drifted toward her son's bedroom. Shane followed.

"Look who's here, Lil' Man."

"Unc Shane," the toddler said, reaching for Shane.

Shane threw his nephew in the air and caught him, causing the little guy to erupt into squeals of laughter. "Man, you look so much like your pop, it's scary," Shane said, observing his nephew with wonder.

Janelle took her son from Shane's arms. "All right, tell Uncle Shane good-night. It's time to turn your light out."

Lil' Man said goodnight by opening and closing both fists. Janelle smiled; Shane laughed. He and Janelle had something in common after all. They both thought Lil' Man was adorable and they didn't compete for his affection they way they vied for Tariq's.

"So where's Tariq? What time's he coming home?"

"He's on a job out of town. You two work together, didn't you know that?"

"We had a little problem in the locker room," Shane admitted. "I came over to see if everything was cool."

"He sounded all right when I spoke to him. He didn't even mention it," she said, wearing a puzzled expression. "It's not like Tariq to keep secrets from me. What happened at work?" she asked, her brow arched.

"Something stupid."

Janelle looked at Shane with penetrating eyes. "Why don't you like me, Shane?" Her question came completely out of the blue.

Taken off guard, Shane's gaze dropped to the floor. "You aiight," he said and then looked up. "But for real though, I don't like the way you treat my brother. You treat him like he's your son—like he's Lil' Man or somebody. Tariq's a grown-ass man; he don't need you to lead him around by the nose," Shane said, relieved to release the angry words.

"And what do you really know about Tariq? I'm his wife and I know exactly what he needs and when he needs it. All you can do for Tariq is get him in trouble; break up his happy home life the way you've broken up your own. You're nothing but trouble, Shane," Janelle said with a sneer. "I saw it the first time I laid eyes on you. If I really led Tariq by the nose, as you say, he wouldn't even be in the same room with you. I wouldn't allow it. But having a relationship with you is one of the few things Tariq gets away with." Her eyes gleamed as she challenged the great Shane—Tariq's hero. "If I didn't run a tight ship, who knows…Tariq might have ended up being a no-good husband and a terrible father just like you."

"Who da fuck you think you talking to? You don't even deserve to be with Tariq and you know it. It's a miracle Lil' Man came out aiight. He coulda caught that shit you got on your face."

"A birthmark isn't contagious, you idiot," Janelle said with a sneer.

"Whatever. But you should be ashamed to be walking around in public with that green shit splattered all over the side of your mug."

Janelle glared at Shane, but didn't say a word.

"You only got your hands on Tariq because I was locked up. He must have been crazy. He couldn't have been thinking straight, fucking around with a ugly-ass bitch like you!"

Janelle didn't flinch. She smiled. She'd been working out, her body was back in shape. She stood in a sexy stance. "Oh, so you think I'm ugly, Shane?"

After an awkward silence, Shane nodded his head. He turned up the corner of his lip for emphasis.

"Tariq says I'm beautiful. And sexy…so it must be true," she taunted. She glided toward him. She smiled provocatively as she approached.

"You ain't shit," Shane said. He backed up uneasily. "Now you tryin' to fuck around on my brother."

"You're scared of me, Shane, that's the problem. That's always been the problem."

"Why the fuck would I be scared of your *scuggly* ass?" He spat out the words.

"Because I'm too much woman for you. I'm a strong woman. I'm not one of those weak chicks you can treat any way you want. You know I got something that none of your weak chicks have. But most of all, you're mad because this *ugly* chick took your brother from you."

Without realizing it, Shane backed into the sofa and fell into a seat. Janelle's words were like a windstorm, throwing him off balance, knocking him down.

Janelle sat next to him. "You can't forgive me for taking Tariq, can you?"

"Man, you ain't take Tariq from me. We're twins. Can't nobody come between us."

"I did and you know it. But that doesn't mean we can't all be a happy family." Janelle's vocal quality had turned sultry. "Kiss me and tell me if you still think I'm ugly."

"Get the fuck outta here."

"Scared?"

"I wouldn't do that to Tariq and I'm definitely not feelin' you."

"I think you are," she insisted. Janelle pressed her lips against Shane's mouth.

He felt such hatred for her, he kissed her back hard, trying to hurt her lips. He tried to strangle her with his tongue. He felt like raping her, just to hurt her.

She forced herself into his lap and wrapped her legs around his waist. She pressed her chest against his, enticing him to help himself to what he wanted.

But he didn't want her to give it to him. Shane wanted to hurt her, shame her. Show her *he* was a man and not someone to toy with the way she did Tariq.

But before he could turn the tables on her, Janelle softly cupped his face and kissed him again. Her tongue slid into his mouth in a way that aroused him against his will. Janelle took control of the situation and pulled him closer to her.

Her top was damp, which confused Shane. Then he recalled what Tariq had told him...Janelle was still breastfeeding Lil' Man.

Shane could feel the damp stickiness through his shirt. And then he caught a whiff so powerfully familiar, it sent a flood of images across his mind. He saw his birth mother breastfeeding Tariq while he waited his turn. He felt the sorrow as he tearfully waited.

He felt the disappointment when his mother roughly plopped him on her lap and impatiently stuck her breast in his mouth. He remembered the desperation with which he latched onto her nipple, how hard he had to suck to get just a few drops. There was never enough for him because Tariq had depleted the supply. Unable to draw milk from his mother's breast, Shane would frantically switch to her other breast. He'd suck hard and urgently.

"Ow!" his mother would say and smack the back of Shane's head. "Get up; you have to wait until the milk builds back up," she'd say as she pushed the young Shane off her lap.

The visit to the past sent Shane into a state of profound sorrow. Once again, he felt like a neglected child. An unloved child. Now he remembered clearly. He'd loved his mother with a passion, he'd always tried to please her, tried to make her love him. But she wouldn't. Everything about him made her mad and caused her to draw back her hand, making him cower as he dodged blows. His mother had loved Tariq but she'd hated him; Shane remembered everything now.

The sweet smell coming from Janelle reminded him of what he'd never had enough of. And like a savage, like a starving man, Shane started whimpering as he ripped the buttons off Janelle's blouse, moaning and speaking gibberish as he unhooked her bra.

❀❀❀

Janelle wore a shocked expression; she didn't understand what was happening. But when Shane clamped hungry lips onto her nipple, she felt a rush of power and felt instantly victorious. Shane sucked hard as if expecting to be disappointed, but when the sweet elixir touched his tongue and filled his mouth, he moaned in ecstasy as if he'd experienced a lifetime of thirst.

Greedily, he went from one breast to the other, sucking, swallowing, moaning, calling out Janelle's name. Shane emitted sounds of raw ecstasy that would have frightened an ordinary woman.

But Janelle was no ordinary woman. She withstood the stares of people who deemed her too unattractive and unworthy to be Tariq's wife. No, there was nothing ordinary about Janelle. And now that she knew Shane's weakness, she was ready to have something no ordinary woman had. Two men.

It wouldn't be hard to convince Tariq that the three of them should be together. After all, Tariq had always told her that he and Shane shared everything. Once Tariq was convinced, they'd all move into a larger place.

Janelle looked forward to the day when people would stare, with their big mouths wide open, when she, Tariq, and Shane went out in public. Yes, she'd be adoringly flanked by two handsome brothers. And eventually she'd give birth to a tribe of beautiful children fathered by both men. She'd show the world that she was special enough to have the love and devotion of a set of gorgeous twins.

As she smoothed Shane's curly hair and caressed his hair on his face, Janelle couldn't help imagining what a child by Shane would look like. After he finished breastfeeding, she'd consummate the union.

It would be wonderful, she thought wistfully, if she were ovulating; it would be absolutely fabulous if she and Shane were able to conceive a beautiful daughter that very night.

CHAPTER 43

Three hundred dollars richer after a sordid tryst with a Caucasian tourist they'd was picked up at a little pub in the Old City section of downtown Philly, Misty felt emboldened by the cash and decided she wanted to look for Shane.

"Let's take a cab to his brother's apartment in G-Town," she suggested.

"You wanna go all the way to Germantown! Damn. Why can't we get a hotel room on Delaware Avenue and get lit. I'm tired; I don't feel like running all over the city looking for Shane."

"I know you're tired, baby. But just do this for me. Let's just drop by Tariq's crib; he'll give us Shane's current address or phone number. Then, after we get the info, we'll go get a room. Okay?" she asked sweetly.

"Aiight," Brick reluctantly agreed.

The clerk at the front desk in the lobby of Tariq's apartment building told Misty and Brick that he hadn't seen Tariq and didn't think he was home. "But I'll check," he volunteered. He called Tariq and Janelle's apartment. Janelle answered the phone.

"Your husband has two visitors," the clerk told Janelle.

"Two visitors? Who? My husband isn't expecting any guests," she said, angrily.

"Hold up," the desk clerk said. "What's your name, Miss?"

He came back on the line. "The young lady says her name is Misty and she's with her friend…um…Brick."

"Misty and Brick!" Janelle blurted in shock.

Shane's dick slipped out of her pussy; he sat up in bed. Janelle covered the phone. "Why would your criminal friends follow you here?"

"I don't fuck with them no more." Shane was as shocked as Janelle. Misty and Brick in the building was not a good sign. "Tell 'em I'm not here."

"Put her on the phone," Janelle said.

"Hey, Janelle," Misty said, using a pleasant vocal tone. "Me and Brick was just wondering if you and Tariq have Shane's address. Or phone number. We been trying to hook up with him."

"Look, I don't give out other people's personal information. So, let's get something straight. I don't like you or your man. My advice to both of you is to fuck off and don't come around here looking for Shane anymore."

"Dayum. Why you gotta come off like that? I just asked you a simple question, bitch—"

Janelle slammed down the phone.

"That bitch banged on me; she better be glad they got guards and shit up in here or I'd be up there scratching that green birthmark off her ugly grille." Misty no longer used her childlike voice.

The desk clerk, however, seemed to like Misty's rough edges. She could see the beginning of an erection bulging in his pants.

Apparently wanting to keep her around a little longer, the clerk volunteered, "You looking for Tariq's brother? The real tall dude—curly hair?"

"Yeah," Misty and Brick said simultaneously.

"Well, if I'm not mistaken, he's up there." He pointed toward the elevator.

Misty and Brick exchanged knowing looks. She thanked the man.

"Is she your girl?" the horny clerk asked Brick.

Misty gave Brick the evil eye.

"Naw, we just friends."

The clerk practically rubbed his hands together. "Can I get your number?" he asked Misty while giving her a leering look.

Misty realized the clerk could keep her abreast of Shane's comings and goings, and therefore didn't hesitate to give him her number. "Here's the number to my cell. Call me the minute he leaves."

The clerk gave Misty a look that asked, *what's in it for me?*

"What time do you get off?" she said sexily

"Midnight," the clerk readily responded.

"Check this. The right information can get you the best sex in the world—that is, if you like your pussy tight."

"Aw, you killin' me, ma," the clerk said.

"Yeah, well, don't try to kill me. My coochie tight as a virgin's. So be gentle with me. Aiight, big boy?" she said and winked. "Hit me up the minute Shane leaves."

"I gotchu, Little Misty. Damn, you fine." The clerk looked at Brick, now curious as to what his connection was with Misty. "Y'all related, man?"

"Naw, that's my shorty, man." Brick threw up his hands in mock defeat. "Man, she runs the show. When she sees something she likes, ain't shit I can do."

"For real, man. It's like that?"

"Hey, we gotta understanding."

The clerk slapped hands with Brick. "That's whassup, man."

Brick had to laugh. He couldn't hold it in. Misty was a cold-blooded ho. She knew just what to say when she wanted something. The clerk would be giving up all the tapes on Shane.

As he and Misty were leaving the apartment building, Brick pulled her to the side. "Don't be trying to twist that shit around. That's your trick. You fuck him and don't be trying to get him to suck my dick."

"Man, your dick ain't gold. That freak wants some of my tight shit." She patted her crotch.

"Why you lie to that man. Your pussy ain't tight. You know my eleven inches got your shit stretched wide open."

"No, baby. I've been away and my pussy done tightened up."

"Whatever. Why ain't you tell dude to get us a cab; I gotta get some sleep," Brick complained.

Misty and Brick turned around and walked back to the desk clerk.

"Do you know where we can find a room somewhere nearby?" she asked.

He gave her the address of a rooming house on Chelten Avenue.

"Can you call us a cab?"

"You can walk. It's right up the hill. Walk down Rittenhouse, make a left on Wissahicon and another left on Chelten. The rooming house is on the left-hand side of the street." The clerk paused. "Can I stop by after I get off?" Then he deferred to Brick. "If it's all right with you, man."

Brick yawned and shrugged. "That's between y'all. I'ma be knocked out—sound asleep."

The clerk smiled at the notion of Brick being asleep while he and Misty knocked boots.

With the address in her purse, Misty and Brick left the apartment building.

"Can you believe Shane is getting it on with his own brother's wife?" Misty said. "What a dog; dicking down his brother's wife. Shane ain't shit. Nevah was; nevah will be."

As they neared the corner of Rittenhouse and Wissahicon, Misty and Brick stopped. Astonishment covered their faces as Tariq came out of the A Plus mini market. Striding toward Rittenhouse Street, Tariq turned a bottle of Mystic Ice Tea up to his lips.

"Aw shit. It's gonna be some drama tonight. Fuck that rooming house, we gon' follow Tariq."

"Dayum, he looks happy as hell," Misty commented.

"That sucka ain't got no idea what he's about to walk into," Brick replied, shaking his head. "Knowing Shane, he's probably charging up Janelle with his brother's hard-earned money."

"That shit ain't funny. I'm starting to hate Shane," Misty said in a soft voice.

Lurking in the shadows, Misty and Brick followed Tariq. They watched through the big picture window of the apartment building as Tariq waved to the guard. They saw the guard call him over and say something that made Tariq's face break into a wide grin.

Misty shook her head again. She knew the clerk had told Tariq that his brother was upstairs visiting. Being the stupid-ass she perceived Tariq to be, she figured the poor fool probably thought the brother he worshipped was upstairs making a social call.

"Every dog has his day," Misty said to Brick. "And Shane's about to get busted."

※※※

"Damn, I don't know what got into me. How could I do this to Tariq?" Shane asked aloud. He grabbed his head in anguish.

"Shane, don't worry. It's okay. I'll talk to Tariq. He loves you; he'll understand."

He pushed Janelle away from him as if he didn't have a clue as to how he'd ended up in her and Tariq's bed. He felt as if he'd been hypnotized. How could he ever look his brother in the eye? A lump formed in his throat. Their lives had irrevocably changed. And it was his fault. All his fault.

He didn't want Janelle; he couldn't stand her. It was the milk that had caused him to lose all self-control. "What do you mean, you'll talk to him? I'll bust you in your mouth—I'll fuckin' kill your ass if you ever mention a word of this to Tariq."

Shane would rather kill himself than hurt Tariq. He had to be crazy to stick his dick inside his brother's wife. Insanity ran in families, he'd heard. He was probably as crazy as his birth mother had been. He had a mental problem; he needed help; he realized that now. He prayed to God to spare Tariq the knowledge of his betrayal and promised he'd go to a psychiatrist and find out what was wrong with him if God would just answer his prayer.

"Shane, what are you saying? I thought we had an understanding."

Naked, Shane got out of the bed and started looking on the floor for his clothes. He had to get out of there.

At that moment, the lock to the front door clicked and turned.

Shane's and Janelle's eyes locked in terror. By the time he spotted his jeans, which were tangled in the bed linen, Tariq was walking fast down the hall that led to the bedroom.

"Janelle," he sang his wife's name. "Hey, baby! We finished the job early…"

CHAPTER 44

In a matter of seconds, Tariq was in the bedroom. His eyes took in the surreal scene. As if paralyzed by disbelief, at first he didn't react. Then, his head snapped back as if he'd been sucker punched. He shook his head and rubbed his eyes as if hoping against hope the unbelievable scene wasn't real. Tariq let out a loud gasp. Both hands cupped his gaping mouth, and then Tariq took off running. He ran blindly out the door and darted down the stairs that led to the main lobby.

Shane shot Janelle a murderous look and roughly shoved her out of his way. Cursing Janelle, he hurriedly put on his pants and shirt. He didn't have time to put on his shoes; he had to catch up with Tariq. He had to explain. He had to beg his brother for forgiveness.

Barefoot, Shane ran to the elevator. But there was no sign of Tariq. His brother must have taken the back stairs. Calling Tariq's name, Shane ran down the seven flights of stairs. When he reached the lobby, the desk clerk pointed to the front door.

Running as fast as he could, Shane zoomed out of the building, not feeling the pain as his bare feet hit the hard concrete. However, he stopped cold when he saw Misty and Brick. Their presence in the scenario seemed crazy, like a senseless, disjointed dream. With no time to figure out why they were there, Shane ignored his former friends and ran down Rittenhouse Street, yelling Tariq's name at the top of his lungs.

As Shane barreled down the street, he heard screeching tires and then a nasty thud, like the crashing sound of a car making impact with something.

The sudden and horrifying sound brought his movement to a terrifying standstill.

Shane's chest felt like it had caught on fire. He couldn't breathe, he couldn't speak. Most likely he was having a heart attack, he decided, as he found himself on the ground unable to move—gasping for air. He tried to scream his brother's name, but it came out in a hoarse whisper, *Tariq!*

Shane tried to pull himself up; he had to move; he had to get up, he had to find Tariq and make sure his brother was all right.

Shane crawled until his head stopped spinning. When he stood up, Misty and Brick vaulted past him, faces etched in morbid curiosity as they hurried to the scene Shane was too afraid to see.

Hobbling like a drunk, Shane finally made it to the corner of Rittenhouse Street and Wissahicon Avenue. He saw a man pacing frantically. "He came out of nowhere," the man shouted. "It wasn't my fault. I didn't see him until I hit him. I swear to God, he deliberately ran right into my car."

Tariq's body, twisted in an unnatural position, lay in the middle of the street. Blood poured from the back of his head, his mouth, his nose, and his ears. The blood flowing from Tariq trailed down the black asphalt until it pooled and formed into a bizarre shape. Squinting in disbelief, Shane made out the image. Just like their mother, Tariq's blood had spread into the shape of a pair of red wings.

"You no-good bastard, look what you did to your own brother," Misty spat in Shane's face. Brick shook his head in disgust. But their insults and open loathing didn't penetrate. Shane's world stood still and then went black as he collapsed to the ground beside his twin.

CHAPTER 45

"It was a beautiful funeral," Janelle reminded Shane a year later. "Tariq didn't even look dead. He was as handsome in his casket as he was in life."

"Tariq's dead?" Shane asked in an eerily vacant voice. It was his depressed voice. And although Janelle didn't enjoy hearing *that* voice, it was far better than listening to the harsh ranting tone he'd started using after Tariq's death.

Back then Shane's behavior could only be described as psychotic, but Janelle convinced herself that his angry utterances were caused by grief. She'd taken him into her home with the idea that once Shane's grief had subsided, he'd replace the father Lil' Man had lost; the husband she'd lost.

Kapri had divorced Shane, kicked him to the curb, and Janelle believed that since Shane was a free man, it was his responsibility to help her raise his brother's son. She couldn't imagine any other man raising Lil' Man. She was certain Tariq would approve of her decision.

Janelle hadn't, however, bargained on living with a man whose violent eruptions were so frequent and so severe she had to confine him with handcuffs and isolate him from the public.

Handcuffed, furious, and frothing at the mouth, Shane would shout obscenities for hours on end. He was delusional, and when he tired from shouting, he'd mumble a litany of false accusations. A frequent theme was that Tariq was still alive. At other times, he ranted that Janelle had murdered Tariq and had hidden his body in the basement or locked his body away, unclaimed, in a hospital morgue.

Desperate to escape, desperate to rescue Tariq, Shane often tried to break free of the handcuffs. "I have to go get Tariq. I gotta get him from that funeral parlor before the mortician puts that embalming fluid in him."

"Tariq's gone," Janelle would say. "He's dead."

Then Shane would drop his head, disconsolate, and mutter in anguish.

Whenever his ex-wife Kapri called, he would accuse her of starving their son, K'Shan. Shane also had a beef with his former friends, Misty and Brick. In Shane's mind, the duo had conspired with the driver of the car that had hit Tariq. He vowed to strangle them both the moment he was free of the handcuffs.

Finally worn down, Janelle had no choice but to accept that Shane's mental status was beyond grief. He was getting crazier by the minute and she wanted him back to normal. She and her son deserved an intact family, so Janelle had Shane committed to a psychiatric hospital, demanding a quick cure for his condition.

The psychiatrist diagnosed Shane as schizophrenic. His condition wavered from catatonic, where he sat in one spot for hours, to paranoia when he was terrified of demons coming to get him. And then there was rage.

"But he was perfectly normal before his brother was killed," she'd said to the doctor, bewildered by the diagnosis. "He wasn't crazy at all."

"During the course of his life, I'm sure there were some telltale signs that his mental health was abnormal. There were probably subtle indications that went undetected due to his inconsistent home life and upbringing," the doctor said. "Seeing a patient presenting symptoms seemingly for the first time between the ages of eighteen and twenty-two is not uncommon. In Shane's case, there could be a genetic factor involved. Based on the information you've provided regarding his mother's mental health, it's possible that both he and his deceased brother could have been afflicted with the disability. But today, with modern medicine, Shane should be able to function normally."

After his thirty-day stay in the psychiatric hospital, Shane returned home medicated and submissive. While he was subdued with medication, Janelle promptly marched him to the justice of the peace and became his wife.

"Tariq is dead, Shane. You were at the funeral," Janelle finally told Shane. "Don't you remember how Kapri had a fit when I told her you wouldn't be sitting with her and K'Shan...remember how she started crying and making a scene when I told her you'd be sitting up front with me and Lil' Man?"

Shane shook his head. "How long does Tariq have to stay at the funeral?"

"Forever, Shane," she said, as if talking to a child. "He's not coming home."

Janelle instantly regretted her words. Shane's expression darkened and then the tears began to fall.

She missed Tariq, too, but she had moved on. Shane had taken his place. As soon as Shane was back to normal, they'd put the past behind them and move forward as a real family. A husband and wife with kids.

And she was working hard at getting Shane back to speed. For one thing, she'd made a risky decision and had taken him off his medication. Janelle didn't like her husband moving around like a zombie. Besides, the medication had side effects that made him feel sick and had also decreased Shane's sex drive, and his inability to perform in bed was unacceptable.

Shane had been off his medication for months and his symptoms hadn't returned. He wasn't his normal self yet, but miraculously, he wasn't psychotic either.

Janelle attributed his ability to function without medication to her breast milk. Her milk was a healing elixir without troublesome side effects. It nourished and soothed her husband and also seemed to heighten his performance in bed.

"Come here, baby. I'll make you feel better." Janelle reached out to Shane. He snuggled close as she pulled up her top and unhooked her bra and then settled into a comfortable position. As she wiped Shane's tears and cooed in his ear, she noticed that Lil' Man had come into the room.

"I'm hungry, Mommy."

"Daddy's hungry, too. Be a big boy and go in the kitchen and get yourself a cup of juice."

"That's not Daddy; that's Unc Shane," Lil' Man objected as he watched his uncle slurping the milk that was supposed to be his.

"Not anymore," Janelle said firmly. "This is your daddy now and Daddy needs Mommy's milk until he gets better. Do you understand?"

Lil' Man nodded.

"Take the juice in the play room. When Daddy gets finished, there might be a little left for you. Okay, sweetheart?"

Lil' Man smiled at the prospect of there being some milk left for him. Carrying a plastic cup, he trotted to his spacious playroom to watch cartoons.

For Tariq's accidental death, Janelle had filed claims with two separate insurance companies and had acquired a small fortune. She purchased a beautiful home in a gated community in Fort Washington, Pennsylvania, where she and Shane and Lil' Man lived in seclusion.

When the phone rang one day, Janelle leaned over to observe the caller ID. She saw the name Kapri Batista and sucked her teeth. Shane and Kapri were divorced; Shane was Janelle's husband now. It didn't make sense for Kapri to continue to carry his name.

No matter how many times she explained to Kapri that Shane wasn't well enough for a visit with his son, Kapri continued to harass them. When the phone finally became silent after the fifth ring, Janelle made up her mind to get the number changed. Again.

She had worked too hard to get Shane back to his normal mental state to have his ex-wife ruin everything by trying to force him into a situation he wasn't emotionally prepared for. The only family Shane knew was Janelle and Lil' Man. He barely remembered K' Shan or Kapri. And Janelle planned to keep it just like that.

For a man that used to call her ugly, Shane sure couldn't get enough of Janelle now. Smiling proudly, she ran her fingers through her husband's curly hair. Squeezing her breast, she encouraged Shane to nurse. Janelle refused to ply him with the pills the psychiatrists wanted him to take. Her breast milk was all the healing her husband would ever need.

"Shane," she whispered in his ear. "The baby's kicking. Do you want to feel it?" She put his large hand on her belly. "Twins. Remember I told you, we're having a boy and a girl."

Shane, more focused on slurping breast milk, murmured nonsensically. Janelle didn't mind doing all the talking. "What names did we pick out for the twins?" she asked.

Shane stopped sucking and looked into her eyes intently. "We're gonna name our twins Tariq and Marguerite," he said in a voice as clear as a bell.

Janelle smiled and nodded. And while Shane was experiencing a lucid moment, Janelle took his hand and led him to their bedroom where she was guaranteed an hour or more of the best sex in the world.

CHAPTER 46

After their intense lovemaking session, Janelle ran her fingers across Shane's beautiful face. *I'm so lucky.* She smiled as she placed her pinky inside Shane's cleft chin. The dimple seemed to have deepened over time, making him more handsome, if that was possible. She would have preferred to take a long nap and cuddle with her handsome husband, but Lil' Man was alone in the playroom and needed some attention.

Reluctantly, she untangled herself from Shane's embrace. She took a quick shower, returned to the bedroom, and threw on a plain cotton dress.

Naked, Shane rested on the bed with his eyes closed. "Shane! Get up, honey. Go wash up and get dressed. I'll have your dinner ready soon."

Shane rose and walked—no—he sauntered to the master bathroom. Was it possible? Was her man finally coming back to his senses? Damn, she was good. Shane had his swagger back! Good loving and breastfeeding was all he had needed.

Carrying a change of clothes for Shane, Janelle went into the bathroom behind him. "Put these on after you wash up," she instructed as she folded a white T-shirt and a pair of jeans over the towel rack.

Shane smiled at her and then amazingly, he gave her a sexy wink.

Janelle's pussy muscles involuntarily clenched up. She'd have to quickly attend to dinner and Lil' Man's needs. She could tell that she and Shane were going be tangling up the bed sheets for hours.

❧❧❧

Alone in the bathroom, Shane's mind was crowded with jumbled thoughts. Everything was mixed up. He had faked a smile for Janelle's sake, but he was actually quite miserable. Nothing seemed quite right. Janelle made him feel better when he was sad, but he didn't belong with her. She told him he was her husband and that Lil' Man was his son, but that wasn't true. Lil' Man was Tariq's son.

Tariq! The yearning started at the pit of his stomach, moved up to his ribcage, and settled in the center of his chest—his heart. Pain. Unbearable pain.

Shane remembered that Tariq had run away from him—had run because of something terrible he and Janelle had done. And then Tariq flew away with their mother, leaving Shane alone and miserable.

I'm sorry, Tariq. I never meant to hurt you, man.

Mounting pain consumed him. Shane hugged himself to control the intensity of this overwhelming torture. An agonizing headache that began at his temples began to slowly move to the top of his head. Shane opened the medicine cabinet and searched for a bottle of Tylenol or any kind of pain reliever. His head was pounding as he frantically moved items around in search of something to relieve the headache. A green cardboard package fell out of the cabinet and onto the floor. Stooping down to pick up the fallen object caused excruciating pain, but Janelle was a neat freak and would complain if he left a mess. He picked up the box and read *single-edge razor blades*.

Feeling suddenly enlightened, Shane smiled.

Breathing hard with excitement, he sat down on the toilet seat. He shook a razor out of the pack, looked at the razor and then down at his arm. Shane was mesmerized by the thick throbbing vein in his wrist. Without hesitation, he placed the razor on the fleshy underside of his wrist and pressed, gradually increasing the pressure. He drew a deep straight line from one side of his wrist to the other. There was a rhythmic spurt of blood and he was flooded with a feeling of great relief as the headache and emotional turmoil instantly ceased.

He watched with interest as the blood flowed down to his palm. Absently, he smeared the blood across the left side of his chest.

With his wounded hand, he slit his other wrist and watched in awe as the blood pooled into his right palm. With a large sweeping motion, he smeared bright red blood on the right side of his chest.

"Shane!" Janelle called out as she approached the bathroom.

Shane stood up and turned his back to her, but his image was clearly reflected in the large bathroom mirror. Janelle gasped; her hand covered her mouth. For a few seconds she was mute and frozen in place as she gawked at Shane's reflection.

She uncovered her mouth and emitted a piercing scream. Janelle rushed over to Shane and forcibly turned him around to face her. "Oh my God! Shane! What have you done?"

Wearing a lopsided smile, Shane presented the blood-covered razor blade. The razor he held clattered to the tiled bathroom floor when Janelle knocked it out of his hand.

Blood pumped fast from both slit wrists. Shane smiled proudly and stuck out his chest. On his chest were blood smears that resembled a pair of giant red wings.

"Look! I'm ready to fly away," he said, smiling dreamily, looking toward the ceiling.

Janelle screamed, "Don't you leave me, Shane. Don't die, baby. Please!" She grabbed a towel and frantically tried to tie it around one of his wrists and then grabbed the T-shirt he'd never put on and tried to tie that to his other wrist, but blood pumped out of his veins and quickly saturated the shirt and towel.

In her frenzy to stem the flow of blood, Janelle slipped in the red puddle that was spreading around the base of the toilet. Lying in a stunned heap and covered in Shane's blood, Janelle tried to get up to make one last effort to save Shane's life.

Losing blood quickly, Shane collapsed and lay on the floor beside Janelle. She screamed and tried to get up, but kept slipping in his blood. "Lil' Man, bring me the phone. Hurry!"

Janelle continued to scream but her voice sounded distant. Shane thought he heard Lil' Man crying, but the child's cries also seemed far away and muffled.

More clearly, he heard a male voice call his name. The voice was familiar and seemed to speak directly into his ear. He tried to answer, but he was losing consciousness fast.

Finally, Shane lapsed into what he thought would be eternal sleep, but he awakened surrounded in brilliant light.

And there was an image too marvelous to believe—his brother, Tariq, standing in the light and smiling at him.

"Whassup, bro?" Tariq said, looking vibrant and alive. His tone was warm and loving. Shane wanted to tell his brother that he was sorry, but he was so stunned by Tariq's presence, he could not utter a sound.

Before Shane could respond or fully comprehend his transition, Tariq stepped forward with outstretched arms. "It's cool, man. You don't have to apologize," he said, as if he'd read Shane's mind.

In the distance, Shane could see Aunt Mazie, Ms. Holmes, and his mother. They all advanced toward him wearing smiles that conveyed love and forgiveness. In life, his mother had never looked as beautiful and serene. It all made sense now. Shane realized he'd crossed over.

Tariq embraced his brother and smiled broadly. "We've all been waiting for you, man. Welcome home, Shane."

ABOUT THE AUTHOR

Allison Hobbs was raised in suburban Philadelphia. After high school she worked for several years in the music industry as a singer, songwriter, and studio background vocalist. She eventually attended Temple University and earned a Bachelor of Science degree. She is the author of *Pandora's Box*, *Insatiable* and *Dangerously in Love*. Hobbs currently resides in Philadelphia. Visit her website at www.allisonhobbs.com or email her at pb@allisonhobbs.com.

Dangerously
In Love

ALLISON HOBBS

Chapter 2

I gnoring the 25-mile-an-hour speed limit on Lincoln Drive, Reed pushed the needle on the speedometer to seventy. Like a man possessed, he took the dangerous curves without a thought of decreasing his speed. The former Victorian hotel on the corner of Lincoln Drive and Gypsy Lane that now served as a police station became a quick blur as Reed defiantly zoomed past. Official Philadelphia police cars parked outside did not deter Reed. As far as he was concerned, the officers of the law that occupied the ancient-looking police barracks seemed more like park rangers than real cops. Fuck 'em. Those suckers were probably inside knocking off a couple boxes of Krispy Kreme donuts.

Reed gave a snort as he imagined his wife's reaction if she were sitting in the passenger's seat. He could just hear her: *Slow down, Reed,* she'd whine. *It's dangerous to speed on Lincoln Drive. You know what happened to that famous singer when we were kids—*

Then Reed would interject: *Chill out, Dayna. I can handle these curves without breaking my neck.*

He suffered a spinal cord injury, Dayna the Know-It-All would correct.

Neck, spine, whatever. Your face isn't buried in my lap, so I know I won't be going out like him.

Irked by Dayna's superior attitude, he'd feel compelled to drive even faster. Throughout her squeals of protest, her face contorted in fear, his wife would undoubtedly be holding on to the overhead handle while pressing her foot into an imaginary brake on the floor.

But thankfully, he didn't have to listen to her whine. Not tonight. Reed swerved to the left and headed for City Avenue. When he neared the Hilton Hotel, he accelerated instead of turning toward the parking lot entrance.

He checked the time. Six-thirty. Plenty of time to take care of what he had to do. Then, after a couple of hours of stress release, he'd head back to the Hilton to network for the last half-hour of the seminar. Yeah, a half-hour was all a brother needed to make some connections. Reed had little patience for sitting around listening to a bunch of speakers.

His car might as well have been on automatic pilot, for Reed had made no conscious decision to drive to Thirty-Eighth and Chestnut. He chuckled to himself and gave a shrug of indifference as he parked and then quickly ducked into the discreet entrance of Lizzard's, a strip joint in the heart of University City. The club featured a large selection of women with varying body types.

The few black chicks employed by Lizzard's were exceptionally pretty with perfect bodies. Indeed, some of the best black eye candy in the city was found swiveling down the pole at Lizzard's. Problem was, you could look but you couldn't touch unless you paid a crazy amount of money for a quick and unfulfilling couch dance. The stupid no-physical-contact rule irked the hell out of Reed. Still, just being in this tits and ass environment gave him a rush.

"Corona," he said to the bartender, knowing he'd get a scowl of incomprehension if he asked for a can of Old English, his preferred libation.

Sipping the weak beer, he winked at the dancer on stage. Heidi, a petite busty brunette, instantly sauntered over to Reed, trying to give him the impression that her performance was exclusively for him. But after licking her lips and rubbing her tits for over sixty seconds without a tip, she huffily moved on to the next lustful patron.

"Is Sensation dancing tonight?" he asked the bartender.

"Yup, she's up next," the bartender said, yawning pointedly as he looked down at his watch.

Reed gave the bartender a sneer; the guy had to be a fucking faggot to act like he was all bored and bothered by the never-ending parade of tits and ass featured at the strip club. His annoyance with the bartender, however, became a foggy memory the moment his favorite girl, Sensation, hit the stage in a flash of pink.

Coffee-colored with a drop of cream, Sensation looked good enough to eat in her glow-in-the-dark neon pink thong set. Curly blonde waist-length extensions swayed as she undulated to a slow song.

Sensation gave Reed a come-hither look, seducing him with pouting lips as she sensually rotated her hips, persuading him to dig deep into his pockets and pay for the special attention she was giving him. With a subtle pelvic thrust she urged him to be generous. *Pay me!* her body screamed.

Reed, however, interpreted her body language in an entirely different way. Her body was talking to him. Writhing with mounting desire, she was begging to get sexed up. Every gyration was a cry for release. Release that only he could provide.

Talk to me, baby! I know you want this dick. He almost shouted the words out loud, but restrained himself as he imagined himself and Sensation sweaty and naked, engaging in all the positions of the Kama Sutra.

With his eyes fixed on Sensation, his imagination running wild, Reed was at first unaware that many of the men in the club, also aroused by her display of oozing sexuality, had moved to the front of the stage and were showing their appreciation by flinging fives and tens onto the stage. These men, mostly suit-wearing Caucasians, seemed to be of one mind and had left Reed behind with their display of generosity.

Fighting for position was a wearisome reality at his place of employment. But he'd be damned if he'd allow himself to be chumped outside of the workplace and in front of a sister. Reed pulled out a neatly folded wad of one-dollar bills. He scowled at the money and stuffed it back into his pocket. Sensation deserved currency of a much higher denomination—a twenty at the least.

From his back pocket, he extracted another wad and peeled off a twenty, changed his mind, put it back in his pocket, and pulled out a ten. Ten dollars was enough for the moment. He'd give her much more when they got together later at her place or at a hotel.

Quite suddenly, Sensation dropped to all fours and went into a sexy panther-like crawl, her hair sweeping the floor. Transfixed by this carnal exhibition, Reed forgot to throw his money on stage. Moments later, his reverie was broken by rude catcalls and whistles as a slew of drunken pink-faced college students rushed the stage. They made airplanes out of five-, ten-, and even twenty-dollar bills. Airborne money crash- landed on the stage. Caught up in schoolboy-ish frivolity, the men in suits decided to join in. As drunk now as the college kids, the suits absurdly attempted to transform their bills into airplanes, but having forgotten the technique, they quickly gave up and resorted to balling up the dollars and throwing them onstage.

Seemingly unaffected by the ever-increasing mounds of cash, Sensation eased into the next song. Climbing the pole like a slithering snake, she descended upside-down with only one leg wrapped around the pole. When both feet hit the stage, she stood stock still with her back turned to the crowd. Nothing moved except her perfectly round buttocks. One cheek at a time, her ass danced. The white guys howled in drunken delight, and threw more money at Sensation. Reed, an admitted ass-man, felt tortured as he watched Sensation's cheeks clap.

She moved quickly across the stage and jumped into a handstand. Working her ass muscles to the beat of the song, Sensation drove the crowd wild.

A hot current raced through Reed's loins, causing a swelling so painful, he prayed he wouldn't explode in his pants. He couldn't think straight. His dick was too hard. His mind was muddled and the only coherent thought running across his brain was that he had to get inside that pussy.

At this point, had he dwelled in a world without social constraints, Reed would have simply snatched Sensation off the stage, thrown her luscious body over his shoulders caveman style, and whisked her off to his private cave where he'd devote hours to ravishing her ass, her pussy, her mouth. What the hell, he'd fuck her tits, too. He'd fuck them until the skin was chafed and raw.

But sadly, he didn't abide in such a world. In his world, a man had to exercise great patience to get what he wanted. He had to put in the time to flatter, court, cajole, and ultimately pay for what should rightfully be his.

Paying for pussy seemed unfair, but Reed wanted Sensation and he was willing to pay. Fuck getting her digits and bullshitting on the phone, fuck dinner and the movies. Plain and simple, he just wanted to fuck.

When the song ended, Sensation gathered and picked up the cornucopia of bills that were strewn around the stage in various shapes and denominations. She tossed the money inside a plastic bucket and sashayed off the stage. There had to be at least four hundred dollars in that bucket, Reed surmised. Not bad for fifteen minutes' worth of work.

Sensation had another set, but Reed had grown tired of this rock-hard-dick-inducing atmosphere that encouraged suckers to throw away their money, but offered no prospect of relief. He decided to go outside and chill in his whip…roll a Dutch and listen to some sounds until Sensation came out. It was now 8:03. Reed knew her four-hour shift ended at eight-thirty, so he had less than a half-hour wait. He hoped her price wasn't so steep he had to stop and tap an ATM machine.

When Sensation finally emerged from the club, Reed unconsciously began stroking himself. Looking like a chocolate milkshake poured into skin-tight jeans, Sensation slung a huge plastic Von Dutch bag over her shoulder and ambled toward the pizza parlor next door to the club.

Reed honked the horn. She stopped, turned in his direction. Recognizing him, she smiled and waved, but continued her purposeful trek.

Damn, now he had to wait for her to order a damn pizza! He leaned back in his seat and got comfortable. Though there'd been no verbal communication between him and Sensation, and though no plans had been made to spend an evening together, Reed was convinced they shared the same carnal desire. That smile and the wave she just gave him was her way of asking him to wait a minute while she bought some grub. He knew she wanted some dick, but due to her line of work, she probably would expect to be compensated.

Hey, he couldn't blame her for mixing business with pleasure.

Swinging her hips, Sensation trotted past the pizza parlor, then slowed her stride and sauntered over to a parked gray Bentley. The driver, a young black man wearing a bright-colored do-rag, rolled down his tinted window. Sensation leaned in and gave the driver a kiss, and then dreamily glided around the car to the passenger side.

It was a startling revelation; Sensation was getting it on with Stone Allen, the star of the Philadelphia Seventy-Sixers! And if that wasn't Stone Allen, then he damn sure had a twin. Stunned, Reed didn't know how to feel. Damn! Stone was the man and everything, but goddamn, he could have any female on the planet, why'd he have to roll up and grip Sensation?

Defeated, Reed watched the Bentley as it ripped down Chestnut Street.

Chapter 3

Sensation had played him. That shit she had pulled was real greasy. Quietly seething, Reed entered the Apache, a strip joint on Masters Street in West Philly. Predictably, the club was dark, crowded, and funky. The Apache was a dive and any female who walked through the door could get hired. Fat, skinny, young, old—it didn't matter as long as the woman had a pussy, a set of tits, and an ass.

He scanned the pickings. It wasn't a pretty sight. Never in his life had he seen so many trifling-looking women parading around half naked. They were all drug addicts; they had to be because any woman who put herself on display looking that damn bad in a thong had to be on drugs. And even the women who had banging bodies and nice-looking faces were crazy—certifiably! He knew this to be true because he'd been intimately involved with enough dancers to know they all had issues.

Each woman who sidled up to him quickly scurried away. His scowl of disgust dissuaded even the most ambitious dancer from soliciting him for a lap dance.

The hell with a lap dance. The only thing on Reed's mind was sex. He wanted to fuck. Straight up! No chitchat, no persuasive sweet talk, no haggling over the price. And the only girl who clearly understood his needs was Buttercup. He usually gave her forty dollars for a lap dance that quickly progressed to intercourse. So where the hell was she? Searching for Buttercup, Reed squeezed through the dark, musty, smoke-filled dive. He wished he were carrying Chuck's flashlight. Chuck managed the Apache and one of his responsibilities was to patrol the place, looking for any couple who appeared to be engaged in more than a lap dance. Chuck used his flashlight to illuminate the dirty dealings of any girl who was trickin' on the low. When caught, the girl had to give Chuck his cut. Any slick bitch with her thong pulled to the side who didn't pay up was instantly ejected and banned from the club permanently. Chuck didn't play those types of games.

"Hey, playa, you dancing?" asked a nutritionally challenged woman. Her practiced smile radiated confidence, but desperation shone in her eyes.

"You seen Buttercup?" Reed asked the woman.

The woman huffed up; her fake smile quickly twisted into a sneer. "Damn, nigga, why you gotta come off like that? I axed if you was dancing? Now, how you sound axin' me 'bout some other bitch?"

"My bad," Reed said, admitting to his bad manners. He pulled out two dollars. "I'm not dancing, sis, but here's a little something for your time." He took a deep breath to calm himself for he felt on the verge of strangling the little toothpick of a woman, an obvious smoker who was wasting his time and withholding important information.

Like a magician, the skinny dancer did a hand trick so swift, the two dollar bills went poof! The money disappeared somewhere inside her sagging costume. "My name is Flava, nigga—not *sis*," the dancer snarled once the money was safely tucked away.

"Yo, don't be comin' at me like that! I gave you a couple of dollars. Now, whassup? Is Buttercup here or not?"

"How the fuck should I know? Ax Chuck. He got the list; he oughta know whether or not she signed in tonight." Flava rolled her eyes at Reed and then weaved through the crowd, walking fast like she had just picked somebody's pocket.

Standing still, Reed scanned the dark room hoping to see the flicker of Chuck's flashlight. Or better yet, he hoped to catch a glimpse of Buttercup. He located neither. Feeling like a voyeur, he unwittingly observed couple after couple getting their freak on atop swiveling barstools, metal-folding chairs, and wooden benches. Some were standing up, copulating against the wall, their bodies twisted like contortionists as they got their freak on.

It wasn't his night, Reed angrily resolved. If he'd had a pistol he would have gladly unleashed his sinister side—the fiend that lurked within would have opened fire and, starting with that ugly little runt who called herself Flava, every hooker in the house would be dead.

••••

Someone approached from the shadows. "You dancin'?" The voice was low and lacked enthusiasm, as if she expected to be turned down.

A quick glance revealed a moon-faced, rather homely woman. The tire around her waistline spoke of too many late-night snacks and a long-expired membership at L.A. Fitness. Her appearance, coupled with a defeatist's attitude, assured Reed of getting what he wanted: a quick, cheap fuck. He nodded his head and allowed the dancer to lead him to an empty folding chair. Reed dragged the chair from the heavily populated area where it was positioned and took it to a more secluded area. "How much?" he wanted to know.

"Five dollars for a dance." The dancer quickly began to squat down into his lap. Reed caught a strong whiff of ass, which mercifully dissipated as the dancer began brushing her bare buttocks across his crotch.

Craning her neck, the dancer looked back at Reed and smiled. "My name's Unique," she offered when she felt the swollen lump that pressed urgently against her ass. "I'm giving out specials tonight—two dances for eight dollars."

He pressed his fingers into her shoulders, repositioning the woman so that she was sitting on top of his throbbing appendage. Her skin was damp—disgustingly clammy, but on nights like tonight when his sex drive was off the meter, a funky ass and sweaty skin would not deter him.

"How much to hit it?" he asked in a husky voice.

Unique stopped rotating her hips. She brushed copper-colored synthetic hair away from her face and looked over her shoulder at Reed. "You got a rubber?"

"Yeah, I got protection…how much?" Reed asked impatiently as he pulled her thong to the side.

"Um…fifty?"

"Fifty! Yo, that's too steep." He pushed her off his lap.

"Okay," she said, hastily wiggling back into position. "Thirty dollars; but I can't go no lower than that."

"Twenty," Reed insisted.

"Okay, but you gotta be quick because I'm not tryin' to break Chuck off when his nosy ass starts flickin' that damn flashlight over here," she grumbled.

Reed stuck the money in her hand. Seconds later he rolled on a condom.

"Ow," Unique complained when Reed tried to penetrate.

Reed smeared a generous amount of spit on his two middle fingers and inserted them, instantly moisturizing Unique's dry vagina. Fuck foreplay.

An adrenaline rush caused him to groan as he was overtaken by the incredible feeling of being inside wet pussy. Desiring even deeper penetration, he tightly gripped the dancer's flabby waist and pulled her closer.

Though Reed was hurting her, the dancer bit her bottom lip and bravely took the pain. Bouncing up and down with fake enthusiasm, she tried to hurry him along, hoping to get him off as quickly as possible.

While Unique pumped up and down in a seated position, Reed began to feel a familiar warm sensation followed by an increased heart rate. He was about to burst. Stealthily, he removed the condom. The music drowned out his savage cry.

Reed quickly stood up and zipped his pants. By the time Unique felt his hot cum running down her leg, Reed had vanished into the crowd.

Muttering curse words, such as "dirty," "slimy," "no-good bastard," Unique walked gap-legged into the restroom to clean herself up.

Finally satiated, Reed hopped in his car, revved his motor, and headed for home. The hell with the club meeting, he was too weary to put on the professional mask he wore around his pompous brothers.